SEEKER OF MAGIC

THE REALM OF MAGIC, BOOK 1

Susanne L. Lambdin

Seeker of Magic / Susanne L. Lambdin
ISBN-13: 978-1726348676
ISBN-10: 1726348679

Book Cover by A. R. Crebs

Dedicated to RTB, the King of Nonsense:
Your Queen of Mischief will never forget you.

Map of Caladonia

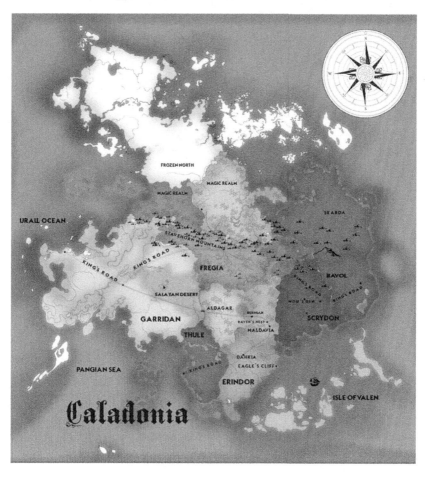

For a larger version, go to:
https://susannelambdin.wixsite.com/realm-of-magic

Chapter One

Awake of buzzards circled high above the carnage of the war-torn battlefield. From where Taliesin stood on a rocky outcrop with the sun on her shoulders, she counted more than one-thousand soldiers strewn across the twenty or so acres of cow pasture. At the base of a northern slope, a line of armored knights hung impaled on a row of stakes with their dead horses crumpled beneath them. Wild dogs and buzzards fed upon the mangled, bloated corpses, and scores of black flies worked in tight formations, their singsong buzz audible with the shift of the humid breeze.

Taliesin was not close enough to see the whites of the dead men's eyes, but she knew maggots were already hard at work. This summer in Caladonia was hotter than usual, and the stench from the field was overly ripe. A white scarf covered her nose and mouth, leaving only her green eyes visible. Her leather tunic clung to her slender body, undergarments drenched as beads of perspiration dripped from her brow and neck. She kept her long, red hair worn in a braid, but even it was damp.

A tattered light-blue pennant—caught on a capacious breeze—rolled across the field and the armored body of a knight. Somewhere close by a dog barked. She spotted a shaggy mutt with a long tail as it ran across the bloodstained grass with a severed arm held in its jaws. One of her companions threw a rock, hit the dog in the side, and it let out a yelp and vanished behind a heap of bodies.

"Two days and nights of hard rain have left the pasture ankle-deep in mud and mire," Grudge said. The tall, broad-shouldered man stood beside Taliesin with one foot placed on top of a large rock as he leaned over to gaze at the battlefield.

He kept his head shaved; his scalp glistened with sweat, and a thick brown mustache drooped from the sides of his mouth. "We'll want to head straight to the base of the northern slope when the signal is given," he said, pointing at the line of stakes where the Fregian knights hung. "That's where we'll find the best pickings. Get as many as you can, and I'll be right there to carry them. We can't have you straining your spine."

"Fine," Taliesin said. She carried three large, leather bags over her shoulder. "Let's just pretend my father didn't tell you to watch over me today, and I'll pretend you're not here. I don't need you getting underfoot, Grudge. I'm after as many valuable swords as I can find."

"Just find Duke Hrothgar's gold sword, and you'll be fine," Grudge muttered. "His body has to be somewhere; these are Fregians, and the duke was known for his love of gold swords."

Taliesin already knew that without being told by the big oaf, just like she knew a gold sword wasn't solid gold, but steel and a coating of gold. It was her job to find valuable weapons, and every time she ventured onto a battlefield, she prayed she'd find a magical blade to sell.

Long ago, she'd found *Traeden,* an enchanted longsword owned by Duke Andre Rigelus of Scrydon, said to be able to pierce through armor and dragon scales and to turn hearts to dust, but it also caused night terrors and severe hair loss. There were no more dragons, of course, and magical weapons were outlawed, but still, she dreamed of finding the weapons of legends.

Flamberge was a longsword made of red metal and enchanted by the wizard Ankharet, which burst into flames in battle, killed all it touched, and left its owner with an unquenchable thirst for blood. *Trembler,* owned by Duke Fergus Vortigern and enchanted by the sorcerer Dire Yadru, was said to cause terror to all opponents when pulled from its sheath; it also caused its owner to suffer from melancholy. There was also *Graysteel, Moonbane, Calaburn,* and *Doomsayer,* a gold sword used by Duke Hrothgar, and the very weapon she hoped to find this day.

Though the Raven Clan hadn't arrived in time to witness the battle, Taliesin imagined the shouts and loud cries of the Fregian soldiers who had followed the knights along the northern hill. Under a storm of arrows, the soldiers had run into a wall of stakes at the bottom of the hill, their retreat cut off by waiting Maldavian soldiers who had come running out of the trees and surrounded the Fregians. Stuck in thick mud, the Fregians had been slaughtered, though a few dark-blue tunics lay on the field. There were far more light-blue Fregian tunics among the dead, and on the southern side of the field a large number of bodies had been gathered into a pile and set on fire before the victors departed. The blaze had died out, leaving blackened bodies and skeletons to gaze sightlessly at the sky. Somewhere among them lay Duke Hrothgar of Fregia and his gold sword.

"When Osprey told us a battle had been fought near Burnlak, I didn't realize it would be this large," Taliesin said, glancing at Grudge. "Duke Hrothgar and Duke Peergynt have been skirmishing for ages. They've been lying here for about four days by the smell of it."

"More or less," Grudge said. "Today is a formal Gathering. I've never been to one before. All three clans are present: Raven, Wolf, and Eagle. I doubt anyone survived. But you can be sure you'll find a few valuable weapons while I collect jewelry and coins. Go for the Knights of the White Stag first; they're an elite Fregian order, the ones in white tunics. They'll have what you want unless Duke Hrothgar is here, and then you'll want his sword."

Each clan had its own job to perform. The King's Law listed what was expected of each clan. Her own clan, the Raven Clan, was considered the lowest rank and was the only one allowed to strip the bodies and take all they found. Across the field, Taliesin could see members from the Wolf Clan and Eagle Clan waiting for the signal to enter the field. By law, each clan was required to wear colored cloaks to distinguish them. The Raven Clan, wearing black cloaks with the insignia of a red raven stitched onto their left shoulder, waited behind Taliesin and Grudge, eager to collect armor, clothes, and jewelry. The Wolf Clan, in dark-gray cloaks, had the job of finding survivors among the common class that included foot soldiers, archers, and servants, along with any live animals they'd later sell to the highest bidder. Only the Eagle Clan, adorned in their gold cloaks, had the right to ransom noblemen and knights to their families or lords. They also collected important documents, from maps and battle plans to letters written to family members. If they were lucky and captured officers from the defeated army who tried to flee, the Eagles could sell them to any interested party or use them in exchange for valuable information. Their clan was always in the middle of any trouble, continuously trading information with dukes or nobles, and constantly trying to control the outcome of every skirmish or battle to their benefit.

"Get ready," Grudge said. "They're about to give the signal."

Three men from each clan walked onto the battlefield and gave their calls; the caw of a raven, the howl of a wolf, and the scream of an eagle. Not waiting for Grudge, Taliesin climbed down the rocks and began sprinting; she knew precisely where she wanted to go first, and that was the line of impaled knights.

Members of the three clans scurried onto the field, too busy in their mad search for valuable items to stop to chat. Taliesin reached the wall of stakes before anyone else and started to stuff the knights' swords into her bags, but what she really was after was the golden sword of Duke Hrothgar Volgan of Fregia. Somewhere among the fallen, she'd find his body, but she had to reach him before the Eagle Clan, or they might take his sword when they collect his body; it was always an occupational risk, and this day she meant to outsmart them.

As she walked through the battlefield, her boots made a sucking sound each time she stepped into a slick patch of mud or reddish gore. After years of scavenging, she no longer cringed at the sight of the mangled bodies; she'd been trained to concentrate only on weapons. She found six swords of quality among the dead knights; none forged by Rivalen, Gregor, or Falstaff, but still valuable. She knelt to retrieve a double-edged battle-ax with a red leather handle, a Gregor original, and spotted three men from the Eagle Clan walking along the line of stakes from the opposite direction. The men converged around a Knight of Chaos pinned beneath his dead horse. His feeble moans were carried on the breeze.

Taliesin gasped as one of the Eagle men drew his knife and sliced the knight's throat. The man stood as blood spurted like a fountain into the air. His hood fell away from his head and revealed a fair-skinned man with gray hair and a pox-marked face. The man noticed Taliesin staring, and his expression turned angry. A companion bent to cut a leather pouch off the knight's sword belt and examined the contents. With a loud curse, he emptied the pouch on the ground, spilling out a sizeable amount of coins.

"Mine, mine," a girl in a tattered red dress shouted.

Two more children in dirty tunics ran past Taliesin, eager to retrieve the coins. The three Eagles all looked toward Taliesin, turned, and headed toward the trees. She was stunned. The Eagles were required to return the bodies of knights and noblemen slain in battle to their families. The murder of a knight was unthinkable. While the children pocketed the coins, the Eagles entered the tree line, and the pouch was tossed into the tall grass.

Two golden-haired boys in rags ran toward where the pouch had been dropped. Talon and Falcon were eight-year-old twins. With blond hair and identical tunics, it was impossible to tell them apart. They were followed close behind by a tall, thin woman who wore a hooded black robe. The children who had stopped to pick up the coins took one look at Minerva, the Raven Master's wife, and scattered, shrieking loudly as they darted across the field.

"You boys come here," Minerva shouted. She pointed at the blond twins. "I have other needs. Come, come. I want these silk tunics."

The two boys returned to the old woman. Minerva turned to scowl at Taliesin, her large nose poking out from under her hood, making it quite clear that among all the children adopted by her and Osprey, she disliked Taliesin most of all.

"Girl, stop dawdling and get to work," the old crone said. "There are more swords to pick up here. Don't let Rook get them all. He had a higher count than you last month, and since he's not adopted, your father and I get a lesser share of his proceeds."

Taliesin had neither the desire nor inclination to talk to Minerva. The old woman had a soul as black as night. If she talked to Minerva, something she seldom did, it felt like she admitted the old crone was alive and not a ghoul.

"Shut up, you old magpie," Taliesin said, under her breath.

"What's that?" Minerva's voice was sharp and piercing. "Best bite your tongue, girl. I've got my eyes on you."

Taliesin walked past Minerva and went to the knight slain by the Eagle Clan. The hope that he'd been important and had carried a valuable sword propelled her feet through the carnage. From the corner of her eyes, she saw Ravens sift through the bodies. Most scurried about like beetles on a dung heap as they collected boots, velvet-lined capes, armor, rings, and necklaces off the dead. The items were placed into bags and piled into carts pulled by strong, young lads. No one bothered Taliesin. She stood beside the body of the slain knight. He'd been a Knight of Chaos. Their order wore black tunics with an emblem of a red skull on a white triangular background. The knight had fought for the Maldavians, for no Knight of the White Stag would ever fight beside such a dishonorable order. There was no reason to murder the knight unless it was personal, and she glanced around for his sword. The hilt of a silver longsword lay partially hidden under the bloated body of the horse, covered with fresh blood. Setting her bags on the ground, she squatted beside the still form and reached for the sword.

"You don't need this anymore," she said.

With fingers circled around the hilt, she gave it a hard pull. The sword moved slowly, inch by inch, until she finally pulled it free. It had no markings, but was beautiful in its simplicity, with a wide blade and a deep blood groove. The hilt was made for one-and-a-half-hands and was wrapped with red leather adorned with silver studs. A matching red leather scabbard was worn by the knight. It hadn't been ruined by the Eagles, and she liked it, so she took it. Her hand clasped the hilt of the silver sword, and she lifted it high. Her eyes locked on a tiny winged dragon that clutched the letter "M" in its talons. The trademark was etched below the crossguard on both sides of the sword.

"Mandrake," she said, trembling as a crow flapped its wings in a nearby ash tree and let out a sharp caw. She felt a vibration in the air; the name Mandrake meant something special.

John Mandrake had been her birth father. No one at Raven's Nest talked about her past, where she came from, who her birth parents were, or how she'd come to be adopted by Osprey and Minerva. She couldn't remember much of her childhood, only that she'd been the daughter of a famous swordsmith. She had learned about smiths and famous swords as a little girl, and she still remembered her father's haunting words: "Remember the name Mandrake, for I will be famous before I die."

"You must have a name," Taliesin said. "I am sure I was there when you were forged; I had to be, but I can't remember." Putting aside the resurfaced memories, she slid the sword into its scabbard and placed it into the bag with the six silver swords she'd taken off the Fregian knights.

Maybe Minerva had no use for her, but the Raven Master depended on her to find blades forged by master swordsmiths. Even at a young age, Taliesin had always been able to find valuable weapons. "I like having you with me on these hunts," Osprey often said. "You bring the clan good luck." She usually found at least one sword or ax forged by a famous smith like Falstaff or Gregor. Rivalen's swords were rare. He'd been alive five hundred years ago, though little had changed in weaponry since that day and age. Finding a Mandrake sword, however, was close to a miracle. In the last fourteen years, she'd never found one on any battlefield.

People still talked about the day she'd found the legendary sword *Traeden*. She'd known at once what she'd found and had taken it straight to the Raven Master. "*Traeden* was made centuries ago for Duke Dudley of Thule, of the noble House of Rigelus," she'd told Osprey. "Legend says the Duke's ancestor killed a hundred dragons and five thousand men with this sword. The sword was forged by Rivalen, one of eight he made for the eight dukes of the realm." An older man at the Gathering named Kloot had claimed he'd found the sword. Master Osprey had asked Lord Arundel to sort out the matter. The Eagle lord asked Taliesin and Kloot to point out the duke's body on the battlefield. Taliesin had led Lord Arundel and the Raven Master straight to the duke; she'd received credit for finding the sword and Kloot had been whipped for lying. Lord Arundel had given her three gold coins for her effort and taken the magical sword to the House of Rigelus in the dukedom of Thule. Since that day, Taliesin was the only woman in the clan allowed to own horses, carry a dagger, and have a room on the second floor of Raven's Nest; she was also the first-served at the dinner table. She imagined Osprey would be thrilled she'd found a Mandrake sword, but she did not intend to sell it or give it to anyone; she meant to keep it.

She walked towards the tree line, and in the tall grass located the red leather pouch the Eagle man had taken. Crafted in Scrydon, the 'leather capital' where Duke Fergus Vortigern ruled and the Wolf Clan called home, it matched the sword belt and scabbard worn by the Knight of Chaos. She wrapped the cut strings around her belt and made a square knot to tie it. The decision to walk along the edge of the field brought her further out than the other clans had ventured. She hoped to find the Fregian duke and the gold sword outside of the fighting area and took her time to look around. Another dead Fregian knight lay on the ground, surrounded by Maldavian foot soldiers he'd killed before finally being stabbed through the neck with a spear. A handsome sword remained clutched in the man's hand. Taliesin ran toward the blade, and in her haste, slipped on a slick patch of guts. Arms flayed as she dropped her bags and landed unceremoniously on her backside right in the middle of a pile of yellow-green viscera covered with flies.

"Heggen's Beard," Taliesin cursed, slapping flies away from her face.

Crawling on her hands and knees, she dragged her bags through the muck. The moment she reached clear ground, she glanced around to check if she'd been seen. Everyone appeared busy at their work, except Grudge, who walked towards her. She wiped her hands on her pants and turned around to pick up the bags. Sticking out of the mud was a wooden cylinder, the type used to hold scrolls; hard to find, and certainly something she wasn't supposed to pick up. Making a split-second decision, Taliesin pulled the cylinder against her stomach and quickly slipped it into the red leather pouch.

"Enjoying yourself, are we?" Grudge asked. "What did you do? Slip on horse guts and fall on your butt? Need a hand, little girl?"

"I'm taking a break," Taliesin said. "And no, I don't need your help."

Grudge's hearty laughter brought her scrambling to her feet. She placed the straps of her bags over her shoulders and turned to face the tall man who towered over her by a good eight inches, all muscle and brawn. His leather pants were tucked into tall boots and covered with filth. Beads of sweat dripped from the ends of his drooping mustache. At his smile, she saw a flash of white, even teeth; not many Ravens had all their teeth or kept them as clean as he did.

"What's the matter with you? You're sitting on a bag of coins," he said.

Grudge bent and pulled a leather purse out of the muck. With a flip of his wrist, he gave the purse a bounce in his hand and checked its weight. "Probably ten silver pieces inside," he said, "five gold and fifteen little coppers. It could mean a new set of clothes for me. Maybe even a room for the night in Padama. Come with me, and I'll give you a bubble bath."

"Not a chance, Grudge," she said. "Give me a hand so I can fetch that sword. It's a Maltese. Ever hear of Maltese? She's a swordsmith from the town of Antillean. I'd love to meet her one day and have her make me a sword."

"Never heard of her."

"That's why I pick up swords, and you cut off fingers," she replied.

Grudge slid a hand over his bald head, leaving behind five trails of dirt across his skull. "Give me your bags. I said I'd carry your load when it grew too heavy. Those bags are officially too heavy. We can't have you falling in horse guts again, now can we?" He stuffed the coin purse into the front of his leather jerkin. "Go fetch your Maltese and stick it in one of these bags. You have quite the eye for expensively-made weapons."

"I'm the best at everything," Taliesin said, annoyed. He waited while she walked to the sword, picked it up, and returned to place it inside a bag. "I also give great shoulder rubs. You'll need one after lugging those around all afternoon."

Grudge rolled his eyes. "I seriously doubt you're offering to rub my back," he said, in a sarcastic tone. "Of course, you couldn't do any better. I am a fine catch."

"And full of hot air," she said, hauling all three bags off the ground. "You asked for it, pal."

She placed the straps over Grudge's shoulder, tipping him to the side before he righted himself. Pack animal that he was, Grudge leaned down and let her adjust the straps on his shoulder. The man was strong and big enough to lift a horse on his shoulders, but he didn't know when to use a cart. For all his talk, though, Grudge could be helpful when he wanted. Today was no different. He'd said he wanted to help, and she let him carry the burden.

"It is a *little* heavy," Grudge said. He licked beads of sweat off his upper lip and walked along beside her. "Find a handsome corpse yet to admire? I've caught you staring many times into the eyes of a corpse. Who caught your eye this time? A knight with a handsome face or some young drummer boy? You know it's bad luck to gaze into the eyes of the dead."

Taliesin didn't answer, for Grudge was right. He had an uncanny ability to read her thoughts, including her secret ones. "I think it's appalling King Frederick has never formed a fourth clan to tend to the injured or sick," she said. "Field surgeons travel with the armies, and they frequently leave behind injured men. If the Wolf and Eagle Clans don't bother picking up the soldiers and nobles, they have no hope of surviving. At least our clan should be allowed to care for the injured. We have a few healers at Raven's Nest."

"I suppose you think the Royal House of Draconus is cruel and their methods inhumane," Grudge said.

"I do," she said. "But what can one woman do about changing how the royal court and the three clans operate? Fighting against rules and traditions that have existed for centuries is futile. No one else seems to care about the wounded. War is ghastly."

Taliesin wasn't that hardened, even though she'd visited a steadily increasing number of battlefields since the age of nine. Every year skirmishes and large battles were fought in Caladonia; the realm was not one of peace. While her emotional scars started to fade when she reached her twenties, it was difficult not to scream and rant and protest that what they did was gruesome.

"I've said a few prayers today," Taliesin said. "When some poor wretch catches my attention, and I see those overcast eyes in a young face, right as death sets in, I can't help it. I'm not made of iron, Grudge, and I often wake from nightmares. When you've been digging in graveyards as long as I have, you'll start saying a prayer every time a shadow crosses your path."

"I don't mind you saying prayers," he said. "But I'm not a religious man."

"How many battlefields have you and I been at together?" Taliesin asked. "I've counted three in the last eight months since you joined."

"This makes four because I'm counting the two knights we ran across last month. I told you then that praying for men who seek death is pointless. They jousted. They killed each other, and for what? Over who could cross a bridge first," he said, in a disgusted voice.

Taliesin shrugged. "Like you know anything about knighthood," she said. "You're a common thief. What do you know about honor? It wasn't just about crossing a bridge. One knight was Fregian, and one was Maldavian. Everyone knows they are sworn enemies."

"I'm not judging you," Grudge said. "Pray for whoever you want to pray for, Taliesin. It's always hot after a summer rain in Maldavia. I hate summer. I prefer the winter. Bodies rot faster in the heat." His timing for laughter wasn't appropriate but ended as quickly as it began. "Despite my best attempts to teach you to read a battlefield, this conflict wasn't merely about Fregians fighting Maldavians over a long-forgotten argument. Tell me what happened here and let's see if you've learned anything."

"Says the criminal."

"Says your teacher," he replied. "Go on. Impress me."

"The Maldavians set an ambush," she said. "Duke Peergynt's men arrived a day earlier. Finding the field muddy from the rain, they easily dug a three-foot ditch across the field and then filled it with wooden stakes before covering the entire area with straw. The Fregian cavalry arrived and, though their numbers were larger, they didn't pause to check the lay of the land and rode over the hill and right into the trap. The Maldavian archers took their time to find their targets. Time enough for Duke Hrothgar to figure out there was a trap, yet he still sent his infantry after the knights, confident they would win, but that's not what happened. While the Fregians wallowed like pigs in the mud, the Maldavian soldiers came out of the trees and surrounded them. I'd say the slaughter took less than ninety minutes, no more. Am I right or not?"

"Very good," Grudge said. "But this was only a small task force sent from Fregia. Their main army is ten-thousand strong, and I assume they marched into Padama. Duke Hrothgar was a close friend of King Frederick. Duke Peergynt has always been jealous of their friendship and made it a point to eliminate him from the game."

Taliesin wanted to ask why the Fregians had sent a task force to a cow pasture and how he knew the main army had gone on to the royal city. However, the moment she spotted a bloody flag on the ground, she held her tongue. The wind blew over a folded corner and revealed a white lion rampant on a field of blue. It was the flag of Prince Sertorius, the youngest prince of the Royal House of Draconus. The royal city of Padama was located in Maldavia, more than a hundred miles away. Duke Peergynt ruled Maldavia, but the royal city was Draconus domain, and the presence of a prince's flag meant the battle wasn't a mere domestic squabble between two great dukes. *A royal flag. A royal prince.* One of the dukes had the support of the Draconus family, and she figured it had to be Duke Peergynt, who had the privilege of protecting Padama. Taking flags wasn't against clan laws; it simply wasn't for the Ravens to pick them up, but she always took home banners and flags to hang on a wall in her room. Since she didn't have any royal flags, she stuffed it under her leather jerkin when Grudge's back was turned.

"Fregian knights fought beside the Knights of the White Stag," Grudge said. Dirt covered his nose and cheek where he'd brushed away flies. "If Duke Hrothgar was here, so was

Jasper Silverhand, who goes as does his older brother. And Jasper is a Knight of the White Stag."

"I didn't know that," Taliesin replied.

"I doubt Duke Peergynt was on the scene. He'd have sent one of his commanders. If you do your job right, you should be able to find the Volgan brothers and their swords."

"That I do know, Grudge," Taliesin said, annoyed he didn't think her smart enough to know the differences between the orders of knights. "After today, I'm done picking up weapons. I never want to see another battlefield as long as I live. I'm sick of death. Sick of warfare. And I'm sick of smelling like this."

"It's your job. What else are you good for if not finding valuable weapons?"

Taliesin let out a groan. "Excuse me," she said. "My Andorran stallion, Thalagar, is four years old now and ready to start mating. In a year, he can produce enough offspring so every Black Wing will ride one of his colts or fillies. Horse breeding is second nature to me."

"There is nothing wrong with what we do for a living, Taliesin," he said in a gruff tone. "We are in the dead business. We're scavengers. It's how we earn a living, and because we do it well, we always make a tidy profit. Unlike you, I don't care what people think of our clan. I'd rather do this than farm or tend sheep, and it's certainly a better way to make a living than knighthood."

"Like you know anything about farming, sheep herding, or knighthood," she grumbled.

"Better a grave robber than a fool, I always say."

Taliesin had never heard Grudge say such a thing. Grudge had avoided the hangman's noose and joined the Raven Clan. The King's Law provided anyone who committed a crime could avoid arrest and possible execution if they became a member of the Raven Clan, which meant the best and brightest didn't live at Raven's Nest; yet Osprey kept law and order.

Without the royal license that allowed the Raven Clan to pick the dead clean, the penalty for anyone caught looting was imprisonment or death, probably another reason townsfolk hated their clan. The Raven Clan had the right to scavenge, and no one else did. Osprey had turned a possible nightmare world into one where everyone was given a second chance. If grave robbing was how they had to make a living, and with the King's blessing, then Taliesin figured folks like Grudge had a good reason to love their lifestyle.

"This is the last time I'll ever do this job, Grudge," she said. Thirsty, she removed a flask of water from her belt. The water was from a river, tasted a bit like mud, and was warm, but it quenched her thirst. She gave Grudge the flask. "I mean it. I'm through after today. I'm going to ask to be a stable groom so I can tend to my horses. Thalagar doesn't like it when I'm gone days at a time, and since I'm not allowed to ride a horse when we're on the job, though it makes no sense at all, he has a right to be annoyed."

The big man eyed her sternly. "Your talents are greatly needed in the field," he said. "Master Osprey asked me to personally look after you because you have a special gift. I suggest you start looking for the Volgan brothers. They'll have the most expensive swords, and that's what you need to find if you ever hope of being more than what you are."

Taliesin didn't argue since Grudge was right.

* * * * *

Chapter Two

"I think Prince Sertorius fought with the Maldavians," Taliesin said.

After an hour of scouring the main area of the battle, they'd moved off the field to find shade under a nearby grove of tall birch trees. They sat on the ground eating green apples, the only food she'd eat with dirty hands.

"Why do you say that?" Grudge asked, tossing aside his apple core. A leather pouch lay on the ground, opened, and apples had fallen out. He selected one, rubbed it on his vest, and took a bite. "You know something I don't, or is this just wishful thinking? I've always wondered which of the five princes you'd like best, knowing how much you like reading about knights and princes. Figured you'd be dying to meet one in the flesh."

"That's beside the point. I spotted Prince Sertorius' banner some ways back." She had noticed it and stuffed it beneath her leather bodice, just like she'd seen the scroll and picked that up, too.

"Did you have the good sense to pick it up?" Grudge said.

"No," she said. The lie left a bad taste in her mouth. She tossed her half-eaten apple into a bush for the squirrels and ants. "Peergynt and Hrothgar are old adversaries, nothing unusual about that. They fight over every petty squabble, but I can't figure out why Sertorius would be here. King Frederick never gets involved in petty squabbles."

"Have you no sense at all, woman?" Grudge asked. "That banner could be sold to the Eagle Clan. Royal flags are valuable. If Sertorius was here, you could be sure Lord Arundel already knows it, but the royal flag is still proof. After we check the woods for the Volgan brothers, we'll make our way to the flag. I want it."

"I don't give a fig about Lord Arundel," Taliesin said, rising to her feet. "If the Eagle lord already knows Sertorius was here, he doesn't need the banner to prove it. Forget about the flag. I'm sure Minerva will have picked it up by now so she can make someone a new bed quilt out of the pieces."

Minerva made blankets from flags. It was the least objectionable of the woman's curious habits. Her collection of human skulls in her bedroom outnumbered Taliesin's flag collection four to one. As she stretched out her arms, she noticed an edge of the flag poking out of the top of her leather tunic; she tucked it inside with a finger, hoping Grudge hadn't noticed.

"I'm ready," she said. "Are you?"

"The flag is a little more important than you think, Taliesin," he said, gathering his things and standing. "Perhaps you were unaware Sertorius' older brother, Almaric, has declared war on their father. He wants the old man's throne. Fregia has always supported the king."

"Peergynt is King Frederick's cousin," Taliesin said. "Why would he side with Almaric? Honestly, Grudge, how do you know this? Gossip from a local tavern is just talk."

Grudge gave her a hard look and took a bite of his apple. He talked with his mouth full as he walked along beside her. "Without the flag, we can't prove Sertorius was here. It appears Hrothgar crossed into Peergynt's land," he said. "All Peergynt has to do is say he was merely defending Maldavia from a northern invasion. Next time, pick something up if it's important, and then tell me about it."

"I ran across a Knight of Chaos," Taliesin said, knowing this would interest him. "He was alive until an Eagle slit his throat and took his purse. He emptied the bag, didn't find what he was looking for, and dropped it. I'm wearing it now. Good leather. I also picked up the knight's silver sword, which I intend to keep."

"The Knights of Chaos are Prince Sertorius' personal order; he created them, he leads them, and, if an Eagle killed one, it means the Eagle Clan is backing King Frederick," Grudge said. "Trust me. They were doing everyone a favor by killing that knight. The Knights of Chaos are a bloodthirsty order. They eat little girls like you. Come on. I know where to find what you're looking for, so don't dawdle."

"I never dawdle," Taliesin said, irritably.

At the southern end of the battlefield, Taliesin and Grudge passed the burned bodies of the Maldavian dead, which had apparently kept anyone else from searching the area. No one had thought to look beyond the burned bodies, but Grudge knew better and made her walk the extra distance away from the cow pasture into the woods. One hand on an oak tree, he leaned against the trunk. He drank water from a flask and rested, while she walked around a mound of fifteen armored bodies. A Fregian flag, light blue with the emblem of a white bear, lay at the side of the heap. Upon the silk lay a man's arm in a sleeve of gold chainmail. She knew before Grudge spoke, she had found someone very important.

"That's Hrothgar's arm," Grudge said. "His brother will have fallen close to him. You'll recognize him by his silver hand. He lost his real hand in battle and wore the fake hand as a replacement." He frowned as he scanned the area. "The Eagle Clan must have been in a hurry to leave. Probably found something they felt the King needed to know about, but quite a few flea-backs are sniffing around. I like the Wolf Clan no more than you do."

Taliesin knelt beside the golden-clad arm, unable to see the duke's torso with so many bodies lying atop him. Grabbing a dead knight by the foot, she pulled the body off the stack and was caught off guard by the sound of a groan coming from the bottom of the pile.

"Someone is alive! Help me," she shouted.

No help was offered by Grudge as she pulled bodies off the pile. He watched her and helped himself to another apple. She hoped the green apples made him sick. The groans grew fainter, and by the time she'd dragged eight bodies off the man in gold armor, she heard nothing. Nor did she find the Fregian duke's head. One arm lay across Hrothgar's body, but the hand still gripped the hilt of a gold longsword with a thick, broad blade engraved with human skulls. The crossguard was gold, the hilt was bone — definitely human — and the pommel was circular, made of gold, and engraved with a human skull.

Had to be *Doomsayer*; it just had to be, thought Taliesin. She sank beside the duke, too exhausted to move another inch, and placed her hand on his chest. He'd tried to retreat from the field, but had been caught, and died not far from his army.

"Sorry," Taliesin said, pulling aside stiff fingers to remove the sword from the dead duke's grasp. A dark shadow swept across her path, and she shivered. 'Never step on another's man's shadow or death may follow you home,' Osprey often would say. She clutched the sword to her chest and walked to where Grudge waited beside the tree.

"Did you find *Doomsayer*?" Grudge tossed aside his apple core. "Hrothgar owned twenty gold swords. He loved gold more than anything else."

"Don't get any ideas," she said. "The sword is mine."

"Taliesin," he said with a rumble, "I'm one of the few people in the clan you can actually trust. I'm your friend. Don't be so quick to judge. I just want to have a closer look, nothing more." She placed the sword across her arm and offered the hilt. He grabbed the hilt, and she pulled her arm away. The sword point fell straight to the ground. "Damn, it's heavier than it looks," he said. "Interesting engravings. I'd say you found a magic sword, Taliesin."

"You are a little girl," Taliesin said. "It's not that heavy, so stop clowning around and give it back to me." She took the longsword from him with one hand and twirled the blade around her body, switched hands, showing off until Grudge started to clap. Smiling wide, she lifted the sword into the air. "I am Taliesin! *Doomsayer*, show me your power!" She lowered the sword. "See. Not magical. Just fancy, and that's all. I think it's Rivalen's work since it's clearly a few hundred years old. Do you want to try and swing it around?"

"I'm too tired to *swing it around*," Grudge said, annoyed. "Maybe you're stronger than you look. I won't dispute its Rivalen's work. You know your swordsmiths better than anyone else. You've found *Doomsayer*. Your father will be impressed."

Taliesin lowered the sword and looked around to make certain no one was watching. They were alone in the glade, with only chirping birds for company. "Probably just as well you didn't try to hack a tree stump. The sword has a tiny crack beneath the hilt. I don't think a magical sword would have a crack."

"It doesn't have a crack," Grudge said. "And it's too heavy for a normal sword."

"Honestly, Grudge. The sword weighs no more than a feather."

"Magical swords can be tricky. Since you found it, it apparently thinks you now own it. How else do you explain why you're able to toss it about like a stick? If it were a regular gold sword, Taliesin, it would be heavy, but not this heavy."

Taliesin gave the sword a hardy shake. "Come on, old thing. If you have any magic left, show me. I don't have all day." As she lifted the sword upwards, she felt a strange tingle in her hand, and the green apple turned in her stomach. She glanced at Grudge, alarmed as the prickling sensation spread up her arm. Her stomach gurgled, and she swallowed the bile that rose in her throat.

"I feel sick," Taliesin said. "It's like a thousand needles are stabbing into my arm and stomach. I think I may vomit."

"Your face has turned pale," Grudge said. He sounded concerned.

The sword quivered in her hand and felt cold in her grasp. Her temples throbbed as a chill spreading through her body caused her to shiver. Then, a heat wave swept over her that made her feel strong and invincible, yet also terribly melancholy and homesick. She pictured snow-capped mountains, tasted salted fish and mead—thick and sweet—and licked her lips. Her mouth opened, and words tumbled out.

"I am Jasper Silverhand, brother of Duke Hrothgar of the House of Volgan," Taliesin said, in a voice not her own. "I died for the glory of Caladonia and the royal throne. We are Loyalists and serve King and country. But we were led astray by Prince Sertorius, who promised safe passage for my lord and brother, Hrothgar, to be taken before the king to swear his allegiance. Peergynt and Sertorius were waiting for us. They intended to take *Doomsayer* and give it to Prince Almaric. Almaric returned to Caladonia a month ago with a large mercenary army. Peergynt is aiding Almaric, but Sertorius had another reason for being here, only I do not know what it was. The king must be warned. Almaric, Sertorius, and Peergynt intend to wage war against the king...he must...be warned."

Taliesin dropped to her knees, still holding the sword. The memories of Lord Jasper Silverhand entered her mind, and she saw herself on the ground, a spear sticking out from her chest, though she felt no pain. She knew where Jasper lay among the throng of bodies. Pushing herself off the ground, she staggered toward the corpses, dragging the sword behind her. Her heart pounded so hard she felt it slam against her ribs as she spotted a young man in silver armor. He was fair of face and lay next to the headless duke. She took a knee beside him.

"Jasper," Taliesin said, placing a hand on his chest. "I can hear you. Talk to me."

'Please...please tell my mother I am sorry I died,' said the dead man. The voice echoed only in her mind, yet she could hear his pain. 'Tell her I fought bravely, and I love her.'

"I will," she said. "Don't worry. Is there anything else?"

Multiple voices filled her head and asked for all manner of requests. Hundreds of dead men clamored at once, but most wanted the same thing. '*Water, water, water.*' She gazed at Jasper's ghastly face; she was certain she'd heard him moaning as she reached for her water flask. She heard Grudge say something. His voice was one of many and, for a moment, she was tempted to throw *Doomsayer* into the bushes. The sword was *magical*, there was no doubt about that, but it was dark magic, and it frightened her. As she stood, she imaged Jasper lifting a ghostly hand and beckoning her to come closer.

'Sertorius will find you and track you down,' said Jasper, though his lips never moved. 'Beware the marshes. Beware the serpent. You can trust no one, Taliesin, not even your friends. Tell no one you found *Doomsayer*, but instead go west and seek the Raven Sword...only you can stop this war. But never rely on Sertorius, for he will....'

A loud gasp came from the dead, and in unison, they said, '*Find you and betray you.*'

"Taliesin?" Grudge grabbed her shoulders and spun her around. "It's the sword, isn't it? It's *Doomsayer*. For Heggen's sake, put the sword away, I beg of you. It has a hold of you, and I fear for your sanity, woman. Do you hear me?"

"Yes," she said. "I hear you, and many others, including Jasper."

"Then release the sword and stand away. You must let *go* of the sword."

With great resolve, Taliesin stabbed *Doomsayer* into the ground and released the hilt. The voices in her head started to fade, leaving her with overwhelming sorrow. There was so much suffering and so many regrets...

"Navenna, protect me from evil," she said, touching her forehead, heart, and groin, making the sign of the goddess of enlightenment, love, and fertility. The Raven Clan prayed to Heggen, god of the Underworld, whose pet raven, Vendel, was said to eat the hearts of the slain and carry their souls to the Underworld. But Mandrake had prayed to Navenna, the eldest daughter of Stroud, the leader of the ancient gods. "I'm afraid, Grudge," she said in a weak voice. "I saw and heard things that frighten me. Please, hold me."

Grudge pulled her into his arms and held her tight. It wasn't like her to need comfort, not her style to depend on a man, but she needed to be held. Taliesin pressed her face against his chest, her eyes shut, and she felt the rhythm of his steady heart beneath her ear as his large hands splayed across her back. His body was hot. She felt his chin rest on top of her head, and he squeezed her a bit harder. The feel and smell of him grounded her, made her feel normal again, and, most of all, safe from harm.

"It's really *Doomsayer*," she said with a shudder. "I heard Jasper's voice and saw his memories as if they were my own. But why Jasper's and not Hrothgar's? It was Hrothgar's sword, and yet he said not a word to me...because he was missing his head!"

"That sword is cursed," Grudge said. "Hrothgar knew better than to use it in battle. I warned him—"

"—but I heard their voices, Grudge, crying out for help, for water, just to get word home to their loved ones. All this time I never thought about the dead, not like that, and they were so sad, so terribly sad I fear my heart may break. War is an evil thing. No one should ever have to kill another. I don't care what the reason is...it's wrong. I hope to Navenna I never see another battlefield as long as I live."

Grudge let out a growl as a sob escaped from her lips. His hug became crushing as he kissed her. The contact and force made her knees buckle. An emotion close to desire settled into every inch of her body as his tongue slid between her lips, the taste reminding her of apples mixed with sweat, and she responded. Her fingers clasped the sides of his vest as the kiss deepened, but all too soon it ended.

"Better?" Grudge asked with his hands on her elbows. She nodded, blinking several times, trying to clear her thoughts. "I warned you about magical weapons. Men like Hrothgar Volgan covet magic swords and rely on them, not only for killing but also for other reasons. Hrothgar used *Doomsayer* too often to learn the secrets of the dead. Best you know now, woman, owning a magical sword comes with a heavy price."

"You say that like I mean to find more magical swords, and I don't," Taliesin said, vehemently. "*Doomsayer* is yours, Grudge, on the condition you swear not to tell anyone what it really is. When we get home, I want you to melt it down and sell it. Jasper said no one is to know about it, so you must promise you won't tell Osprey or anyone else. No one can know I found it. Nor can you tell them what happened today."

"I swear in Heggen's name I will not tell anyone about the sword or about what happened here today," Grudge said. He patted her on the shoulder as he would a child. "Now go sit and calm yourself. One more thing must be done. I won't be long."

Grudge placed *Doomsayer* with the Maltese and Mandrake swords inside the bag she'd left on the ground and took out his knife. Going to Jasper's body, he removed the silver hand with one swipe, but Taliesin said not a word, even though it made her sick. Spotting Jasper's jeweled dagger at his side, Grudge picked it up and replaced it with his old dagger.

"I don't think Jasper the Bastard would mind. This is a Falstaff and quite valuable." Grudge slid the dagger into the sheath at his side, where it was a perfect fit, and returned to place the silver hand inside the bag with the swords. Sliding the straps over his broad shoulder, he grunted as he stood up straight. "Jasper lost his real hand in a tournament a few years ago. Did he tell you about that?"

"No, but I think his mother should have it, Grudge," Taliesin said. "And you shouldn't call Jasper a bastard, even if he was. Hrothgar didn't blame their mother or think ill of his brother. Their father hated their mother until the day he died for betraying him. Jasper did tell me there was a fifteen-year difference in him and his brother's ages. Hrothgar had no sons, and he named Jasper his heir. Both men loved their mother. She'll be heartbroken when she hears of their deaths." She fell silent. Grudge had a sympathetic look on his face.

"Jasper was a kind man," he said. "Hrothgar was his opposite in every way."

"When I held the sword, I felt things, saw things, through Jasper's eyes. *Doomsayer* isn't evil, Grudge. It showed me how much Jasper loved Hrothgar and how much his brother loved him. It showed me how everyone at Ragenvald Castle loved

Jasper. You are right. He was kind and good-natured."
Taliesin turned away. "They're not my memories, but they
feel like they are, and I want their mother to know what happened here. I don't blame you for taking Jasper's hand. It's
your job. But his mother should have it."

"That's the worst thing about the sword, Taliesin, it can
show you tender moments, but it's a trick," Grudge said.
"*Doomsayer* makes you want to know everything you
shouldn't know, to feel every emotion, *to be involved*, and
that's why it's cursed. You made me swear never to talk about
it. The same applies to you. Swear to me you won't talk about
this again or ever call upon its power. Swear it, Taliesin."

"*Deny it to the grave*," she said. "That's what we Ravens always say."

"Swear it, or I'll kiss you again."

"I swear to never talk about it again," she said. "Ever. But I
didn't mind the kiss."

"No?"

Taliesin bristled. He read too much into the compliment.
She didn't answer him, and they walked along in silence,
coming out of the trees and passing the charred remains of the
Maldavians. Out of habit, she let her gaze drop to the ground.
It was easier to look upon cremated bodies than the bodies
lying exposed on the field. Among the ashes, she spotted a
silver spear engraved from tip to shaft with sea creatures, untouched by the flames. The spear tip was broad, shaped like a
palm leaf, and edged with jagged teeth. Beautiful and deadly,
it was clearly a weapon from Erindor, a dukedom to the
south. She'd never been there. Without pausing in her stride,
she bent, agile and fast, and picked up the spear, saying,

> "*And the little black cat slipped through the door,*
> *Slipped inside and slipped right out.*
> *The little black cat went a wiggling about,*
> *Stopped at the bedroom door and wiggled no more.*
> *'May I come in?' said the little black cat,*
> *And with a meow, she slipped under the bed.*"

"Not one of Glabber's best," Grudge said with a chuckle. "I didn't only kiss you to get your mind off the dead, Taliesin. I do care about you. Very much, in fact."

Taliesin caught his gaze and watched the sunlight reflect in his honey-brown eyes. Grudge had wormed his way into her life and, as the waning sunlight shone directly on his rugged face, she pictured him in other surroundings, far from the battlefield, seated beside a fireside wearing a gentleman's doublet with his hair grown long, war dogs lying at his feet. He'd certainly found a way to end any romantic thoughts about Rook or Hawk. They'd arrived with a girl named Wren a few weeks before Grudge had shown up at Raven's Nest. That had been eight months ago. Grudge was older—a man, not a boy—and now that he'd kissed her, she no longer thought of him as a criminal on the run. Maybe it was sunstroke; her head did ache, but maybe it was more, and she impulsively reached out to take his arm.

"It's not been a pleasant day," he said. "You're tired. Why don't you head up the hill and join your father? I'll catch up with you in a few minutes. I want to go look for that flag."

A loud whinny drew their attention across the field to where a beautiful white horse trotted through the dead, its reins dragging on the ground. Several people tried in vain to catch the warhorse, but the animal was frightened, confused, and with a toss of its head, it galloped off in the direction Taliesin and Grudge had come from. Only a few seconds passed before a familiar lanky figure came walking out of the shadow of the trees, holding the reins of the horse. Hawk, his hair blowing as wild as the horse's mane, took a scarf from around his head and blindfolded the nervous horse before he continued to lead it across the border of field and trees. He'd been close enough to where Taliesin had her strange experience that she wondered if he'd been spying. In his dirty ruffled shirt, a dangling pearl earring, and a pair of cutlasses across his back, weapons used by men of the sea, Hawk reminded her of a pirate. He lifted his hand to wave, heading in their direction, handling the horse with patience and kindness.

"Ah, here comes the hero," Grudge said. "Hawk is a pretty fellow, but appearances shouldn't be your top priority." A petite, blonde girl and a young man with ebony skin, carrying bags filled with loot, came out of the trees and hurried to catch up with Hawk. "Where Hawk goes, Wren follows, and then comes Rook. I suspect both are sleeping with Wren."

"Even if they are," Taliesin said, "I don't care. I'm not interested in boys."

Taliesin glanced at the girl. Wren's hair was so blonde it looked bone white under the hot sun, and her eyes were the color of amethysts. Her skirt was torn, boots covered with dried mud, and a few twigs poked out of her hair. She and Rook held a heavy bag between them, filled with gold plate armor. Hadn't taken them long to find the Fregian duke's armor, thought Taliesin, convinced now they'd seen her speaking with the dead. When Rook smiled at her, she made up her mind to give him the Erindorian spear. Everyone at Raven's Nest fancied Rook, with his pale blue eyes, black hair worn in matted braids hung like tentacles, and skin covered in tattoos. Rook came from a place where people hunted for sharks, prowlers, blue fins, and yellowtails in small wooden boats. His leather jerkin had short sleeves, revealing tattoos of dolphins, shadow sharks, an orange spotted octopus, and a large green sea turtle on his arms.

"Do you remember the day I took the Service Oath?" Grudge said. It had been on the last Sunday of the month; it was always on the last Sunday.

"Yes, I remember," she said. "You, Hawk, Rook, and Wren stood together in your black cloaks beneath the shade of the giant oak tree, right at dawn, when the birds were singing brightly." She had smiled as they said at the same time, "*We come from nothing, say nothing. We swear to protect the Raven Clan, brothers and sisters, eggs, nest, and tree. Family first and then comes the grave.*"

The oath was binding; a lifetime commitment. Grudge, Hawk, Rook, and Wren were part of Taliesin's large extended family, something she didn't take lightly and hoped they didn't either. Perhaps one day Wren would prove her worth and finding the duke's armor was a good start.

"They better not have been spying on us," Taliesin said.

"I doubt it," he said. "Can't you see Wren is crying? This was her first Gathering, Taliesin. Show her a little compassion. She's an innocent child."

Taliesin bristled. "She's sixteen years old," she said. "I was nine when I first went out onto a field. I was an innocent. No girl sleeping with two men is that innocent, Grudge."

"Rook is a deaf-mute," Grudge said. "I seriously doubt he heard a thing, and he certainly won't talk. Wren won't either, and Hawk is very fond of you. He's a friend of mine, too. He won't say anything, or I'll break his arm."

With Taliesin in the lead, they headed away from the pasture toward the eastern escarpment, following a narrow path used by cows that had scattered during the battle. The cows were now tied behind twenty wagons. The members of their clan tossed heavy bags into the wagon beds, along with mounds of clothes and numerous weapons, massively produced and easily sold in bulk at markets. The wind had picked up as the sun started to set behind a bank of dark clouds, and Taliesin gazed up at a lone hawk circling overhead.

"It's not that I'm against making money," Hawk said. "But coming here was a bad idea, Grudge. The road home will be filled with Maldavian troops looking for Fregians who might have escaped. The Eagles left behind the bodies of the noblemen and knights. It's not like them to leave a bastard behind, as long as he has blue blood."

"I agree," Grudge said. "The Maldavians have clearly sided against King Frederick and now support Prince Almaric. I'm not sure why the Eagle Clan didn't warn the Fregians about the ambush since the Fregians are King's Men."

"The Eagle Clan? Royalists?" Hawk asked, scoffing. "That's strange. Want to hear something strange? We couldn't find Hrothgar's head. I think that crazy old crone Minerva got to it first to add to her collection."

Wren let out a sob. "Why did you bring me here, Hawk? I was happier in the kitchen," she said. Taliesin winced at the quiver of the girl's voice. She hadn't cried at the age of nine, and yet Wren went on blubbering. "It was horrible. We're nothing but grave robbers. That's how low we've sunk, Hawk. Don't ever ask me to do it again."

Taliesin glanced over her shoulder, the spear resting on it, and watched as Wren wiped tears from her cheeks. Pathetic, she thought. Rook gazed at Wren like a lovesick boy, silent adoration, but Hawk had the good sense to glare at her until she stopped crying.

"How do you know about what happened here, Grudge?" Wren said.

"Tactics are the meat and bones of winning a battle, and Sertorius is one of the best when it comes setting an ambush," Grudge replied. "The prince lured the Fregians to this particular field, doesn't matter how — a broken promise, a public insult. Any way you look at it, Hrothgar took the bait and charged without thinking. King Frederick is prudent; he deliberates for weeks, even months, with his war council. Strategy is his forte, so it's possible Sertorius was doing what his father told him to do. I doubt that though. Sertorius is a cold, calculating hunter. He is good at setting traps. Frederick and Hrothgar were good friends, and that's why I know Sertorius and Peergynt have sided with Almaric."

"You're so wise, Grudge," Wren said. "You'd have made a brilliant general."

Grudge laughed. "I simply observe more than most men. Some are good at reading animal tracks; I can read a battlefield. Rather like reading tea leaves in a cup like Minerva can, only I do it with bodies. We're coming up on the wagons. Enough talk for now."

Arriving at the carriages, Grudge walked to Osprey's to unload their bags. Hawk, Rook, and Wren went to another wagon. Keeping the spear, Taliesin headed through the crowd, trying to reach the Raven Master seated beneath the shade of a chestnut tree, surrounded by Black Wing guards. A shrill voice brought her to an immediate halt. "Did you find the Fregian duke's sword?" Taliesin's path became blocked by Minerva's tall, thin figure. The twins, Falcon and Talon, stood beside her, holding folded silken tunics.

"None of your business, you old magpie," Taliesin said. She turned around and hurried to Grudge as he hid their bags beneath a dirty horse blanket. The old crone watched them. "I wish she'd leave us alone. I hate that woman."

Grudge laughed as he unlaced the strings of his leather jerkin and opened it wide, exposing a hairy chest, wet with perspiration. He removed the jerkin and tossed it into the wagon, muscles rippling as he moved, and she took a good, long look at him. His biceps were monstrous, and his chest was broad and wide. His bald head was nicely shaped, his jaw preposterously square, and the length and size of his legs admirable. He was a fine specimen, she had to admit, and even Minerva gawked. Grudge smiled at Taliesin, dimples appearing in his cheeks. Taliesin knew she was blushing.

"I think that's the first time you've really *looked* at me," Grudge said. He leaned toward her. "I'm sure the royal flag is very happy, nestled against your breasts."

"Hush, you oaf," Taliesin said, bristling. "You saw me pick it up, did you?"

"Sweetheart, I *see* everything. I'm always watching you."

"I can't decide if that's creepy or not," she said. "We need to be on the road before nightfall, so stop grinning and go fetch my father. It's time to leave."

With a nod, Grudge walked to where Osprey was seated. They spoke briefly before Grudge helped the old man to his feet, leading him to the wagon. Taliesin climbed onto the seat, placed the spear at her feet, and held out her hand as Grudge helped Osprey into the wagon. The Raven Master took her hand as she pulled him beside her. Wrinkles appeared at the corners of Osprey's pale blue eyes. She counted seven crow's-feet, deep grooves in his skin that marked his age as seventy, making him the oldest man in the clan.

"It's been a long day, and we're tired," Osprey said, though he hadn't done more than sit on a blanket and wait for the Gathering to end. His lips quivered and pulled upwards, revealing crooked, stained teeth. "How did you fair today, my dear? Find anything worth a king's ransom?"

"A few nice things," she said. His wording seemed odd. Was he implying something or not? "I did find a silver spear that I intend to give to Rook."

"Don't get your feathers in a ruffle, my dear. I'm sure you did your best." Osprey patted her leg as she picked up the reins and the two plow horses lifted their ears, ready to leave.

"I've asked Grudge to be a Black Wing," he said, watching her intently. "He's a skilled fighter, despite what you may think of him."

"I don't think about him," Taliesin said, growling under her breath.

Osprey smiled. "I'm sure Grudge did well today. Grudge is a man of quality underneath his dirty disguise. You won't find anyone better, Taliesin. When a man builds a new nest, he uses none of the old twigs, least he makes the same mistakes that set him aground in the first place. Peel away the grim, and you may find a man worth loving."

"Whoever he once was makes no difference to me," Taliesin said, but his words had roused her curiosity. "I am happy enough to be your daughter and do my duty."

"Grudge is a Fregian, did you know? Shouldn't mention it, of course, but seeing how you take after me and love knowing everyone's business, I thought you'd want to know," Osprey said. "These were his countrymen who died here this day. Must have been hard on him. Oh well." He patted her leg again. "Perhaps in a few weeks, we'll journey east to Bavol to sell our goods at the grand bazaar in the city of Antillia. The Crystal Mosque is a lovely place. I know you'll love it there."

"We won't stop in Burnlak?" Taliesin asked. "It's only twenty miles from here." She was thinking of Grudge, his love of snow, and his dead countrymen, and somehow it seemed fitting she'd given him *Doomsayer*, after all.

"No, we're going straight home," Osprey said, not offering any explanation.

"Head out," Captain Leech shouted, a large, gray-bearded man on a tan horse. He waved his hand, signaling the wagons forward, and rode to the front of the line. Several mounted guards, along with Grudge and Hawk—riding the white horse he'd found—rode ahead. The rest of the guards remained with the wagons.

"*Be careful a scavenger does not follow you home,*" Osprey said, repeating a well-known saying among their clan. Every clan member within earshot repeated the next line with him. "*...for Death will come soon after.*"

Damn fools, Taliesin thought, tempting fate as they did.

* * * * *

Chapter Three

"**W**e'll go through the Black Mountains," Osprey said as they traveled under the stars. Leaving behind the green fields and farms, the Clan took the road toward the Gorge of Galamus, which meant three more days of difficult travel. The road narrowed to a path ascending into the mountains, requiring the men in the wagons to climb out and lead the teams.

With the rays of first light, they reached the gorge, and Grudge climbed off his horse, leading the way across the rickety bridge. Hawk followed, the white stallion blindfolded, crossing behind the Black Wings, who fanned out on the opposite side to watch the others cross. Women and children walked across the bridge. The wagons with their heavy loads came last, and despite the bridge's state of disrepair, the frayed ropes held. Descending the mountain road was even more difficult, for the path was riddled with fallen boulders which had to be moved aside before the weary travelers could continue. After three nights in the mountains, sleeping on the ground with no fires lit, the Raven Clan arrived at the main road that led into the Great Forest of Tannenberg where Raven's Nest was located.

The old trees reached into the sky like tall sentinels, and not a bird sang out as the wagons rolled through and passed a small waterfall, the carcass of an elk killed by a pack of wolves, and familiar landmarks Taliesin had memorized over the years. Bands of thieves lived at the outskirts of the forest, robbing anyone foolish enough to enter; however, the Black Wings had a nasty reputation, and Captain Leech was something of a legend among cutthroats and thieves. There'd been no incidents or any sightings of Maldavian patrols, and

Taliesin drove the team of horses, not complaining though her backside ached. Grudge, accompanied by Hawk riding his white stallion, rode off with Captain Leech and a scout, making sure their route remained safe.

"I'll be glad when we reach Raven's Nest," Osprey said, the hood of his cloak pulled over his gray head. He gnawed on a stick of beef jerky. "As soon as we're home, we'll go through the loot and make certain nothing was taken that doesn't belong to our clan. No one has given an alarm, but the hairs on the back of my neck are up, which means we're being followed. I suspect Wolfmen. But I'm sure you didn't take anything you shouldn't have. You're a smart girl, Taliesin. I can always depend on you."

She wished it were true, that she was smart and dependable, but during the night while they made camp, finally lighting fires to cook a decent meal, Grudge and Hawk rode off again with the captain and scout. Taliesin couldn't help feeling partly to blame for the clan being trailed by Wolfmen. A scent on the wind kept tickling her nose, something that smelled like wet leaves and wet dog, staying with them when they journeyed on the next morning, making her feel anxious until evening when she spotted the giant oak tree at the end of a long road.

Raven's Nest was located in a remote part of the Great Forest. The giant oak that protected Raven's Nest had been there since the Raven King ruled Caladonia a thousand years ago. The giant oak had been a sapling then, growing strong and tall over the centuries, towering above every other tree and ruling as a king of the forest. The Raven Clan had once been powerful, but as the tree aged, their clan had withered; yet the tree remained strong. Raven's Nest was built in and around the ancient tree. Over the main gate of Raven's Nest, and at every window of every room built into the tree, twigs were twisted, making frames and harbors for tiny flowers and ivy to grow. A large rectangular frame of twigs led into a fenced garden, with winding paths and wicker chairs facing a babbling stream.

Nestled high above in the tree limbs, structures built to weather seasonal storms were used as homes and for storage. Along the enormous limbs were platforms fitted with railed balconies, decorated with flowers and ivy, where flocks of doves, sparrows, hawks, and ravens dwelled together in harmony. That evening, Raven's Nest appeared dark, though; not a light was on in any of the windows, no fire in the main courtyard and guards stood at the main gate, which opened at the approach of the caravan. Around the base of the giant oak was Raven's Hall—three levels and twenty rooms painted dark green and brown, supported by broad beams, and covered by a thatched roof. The main doors, built of stout oak and engraved with the sign of the raven, were closed, appearing dark and cold as the wagons came to a halt.

Black Wings stood outside the main doors and along the wall that wrapped around the small village. Overhead, in the canopy of green leaves, men with bows and arrows watched from the platforms. The guards dismounted first and assumed defensive positions around the enclosure after handing their horses to servants who appeared from the shadows. People remained quiet as the wagons were emptied, the draft horses led to the stable for grooming and feeding, and the spoils taken to an adjoining building. No one came out of the hall to greet them, not even Hillary, the master of the kitchen, and he always came out with a glass of honeyed wine for the Raven Master. It wasn't the type of homecoming Taliesin expected. She quickly climbed out of the wagon, her mind turning to the gold and silver swords in the wagon.

"Help me, child." Osprey held out his hands as Taliesin reached up and helped him climb out of the wagon. Minerva walked past, a ghostly figure in the night, trailed by the blonde twins carrying a large bag between them. "That woman terrifies me," he said. "If I had not married Minerva fifty years ago, I would be content in my old age. Henpecked. That's what I am. Shame we didn't lose her somewhere on the road."

Both gave a burst of laughter, fading as fast as it came as they watched mothers from the journey gather at the foot of the wraparound staircase winding around the huge tree and climb to the upper rooms. No one approached Raven's Hall; two guards remained at the door. Five more guards with lit torches helped the women enter through the gate, a fire ring circling the trunk as they ascended. A second fire appeared along the circular wooden barricade that protected Raven's Nest. Soldiers appeared with torches, standing at their posts along the battlements and two towers at the front gate. Nothing more than a platform, soldiers reached the upper level by staircases. More than two hundred Black Wings protected Raven's Nest. Their brothers protecting the wagons joined them on the wall and aloft in the tree to stand guard in their perches. The greatest activity, caused by household servants attempting to carry in bags and finding resistance when the owners objected, required the attention of the Captain of the Black Wings. A tall form in a black cloak, hood raised, appeared around the front of Osprey's wagon, walking with great confidence. It surprised Taliesin but not Osprey.

"I've never seen Captain Leech walk so straight," Taliesin said. "The ride must have done him good. But he'll have trouble taking the broom from Mrs. Caldwell. The house staff never should have been asked to help...they pocket loose coins, and everyone knows it, though you always make sure they receive a fair cut."

"That's not Leech, my dear," Osprey smiled sadly. "I'm afraid Leech died on the road. Grudge said it was his heart. They've taken his body out back to bury." He patted her on the arm. "There, there, child. I know you were fond of him but keep your head high and let Captain Grudge handle things his way. Why don't you wait for Grudge on the porch? I'm sure he'll tell you what happened." A shiver went through his skinny body. It wasn't that cold, not to her, but Osprey apparently felt the chill in his brittle, old bones. "Whatever happens tonight, stay right at Grudge's side, that's what I ask."

"I'm not a child," she said, sharply. "I don't need a nurse-maid or coddling."

"Yes, yes, my dear, my thoughts exactly. Still, wait for Grudge before you go inside, just to be safe, and then find out why Hillary hasn't come out to greet us. I've a feeling this trip will be my last." Osprey's prediction of doom made Taliesin worry all the more: *Doomsayer*, Jasper and what he'd said, the strange behavior of the Eagle Clan, and Grudge's fear of a civil war. "I'd best go over and stop Mrs. Caldwell before she gives Grudge a goose egg with that broom of hers." He kissed her cheek. "Off you go, my dear."

Osprey walked off. Taliesin reached under the seat to retrieve the silver Erindorian spear and a pouch filled with wild strawberries for Hillary, but Osprey's words haunted her. 'His last trip,' he'd said, and here she'd wanted it to be her last trip as well. A spike in her intuition made her search her bags in the back of the wagon for Mandrake's silver sword in the red scabbard, which she strapped around her waist. She was ambidextrous but wore the sword on her left hip, finding the weight oddly comfortable. She lifted her bags and shouldered them as she walked across the cobblestone courtyard toward Raven's Hall.

The wind picked up, blowing the branches clear. Starlight and moonlight shone pale and silver upon the stones. Taliesin heard the name *Jasper* whispered on the breeze, a ghostly voice filling her with a sense of dread. She'd spoken to *dead* men, and now they were returning, walking corpses, and she imagined rotting hands clawing at the fence, wanting to gain entrance. Her hand fell to the hilt of her sword. A shadow appeared on the steps ahead of her, and goosebumps rose on her arms. Someone or some*thing* approached her from behind. She spun around, hoping it would be Grudge, but no one was there.

Bolting up the steps three at a time, she reached the porch and dropped her bags. One of the guards started laughing at her. She felt like driving the spear into his fat stomach; there was nothing funny about being spooked by ghostly voices

and shadows, not in her world. Her eyes scoured the courtyard as she turned, finding Grudge busy dealing with the battlefield workers and household staff, with Hawk assisting
him, while Osprey tried to calm Mrs. Caldwell before she
started swinging her broom. Nothing out of the ordinary.
Nothing scary lurked in the courtyard, but she remained
jumpy. Grudge finally left Hawk in charge of dispersing the
crowd and headed in her direction. Osprey succeeded in turning away the household staff and the head maid, Mrs. Caldwell, spun around in a huff, marching toward the door, her
big bottom swinging. By the time the rotund woman had returned to Raven's Hall, Grudge was at her side.

"Mrs. Caldwell didn't want to clean laundry tonight,"
Grudge said. "Osprey and Hawk have the situation under
control. Let's get inside." He pushed his hood away, revealing
his shiny bald head, and flashed a gold medallion at the two
guards. The Captain's Badge—passed from each commander
to the next—had a raven on one side and the moon on the
other and was proof he was the new captain. Both guards saluted Grudge by pressing their fingers tightly together and
tapping their foreheads; no explanation was needed about
Captain Leech's demise. One guard knocked three times on
the large door. It was always three times, some superstition of
Osprey's, but everything was always in threes, even invoking
Navenna's blessing: head, heart, and loins. Three knocks on
the door had nothing to do with prayers, however, and she
figured it was enough times to get people moving in the hall.

"What happened to Leech?" Taliesin said.

"I thought you knew," Grudge said, pausing when they
heard people talking behind the door growing louder. The
heavy wooden beam on the opposite side of the doors could
be heard sliding to the side, and he continued. "Leech fell off
his horse, dead when he hit the ground. Must have been his
heart. This job is for young men, not gray-beards."

"I'm sure that's why you were promoted. No gray hairs."

"Tempers are running a little high this evening," Grudge
said. "Wolfmen were spotted in a nearby glen." His gaze low-

ered, and he noticed the sword at her side. "I'm glad you're armed. You may have need of it before the night is over. Just for you, I've asked your father to allow you into the Black Wings. He's considering my request."

"I'd be the first woman in the Black Wings," she said. "Thank you."

"I said he's considering it. If you can stay out of trouble for one hour, I'll convince him it's a good idea." Grudge stepped in front of her as the doors were pulled inward by house staff, and he entered, the guards remaining at their post. She hurried after him, noting *Doomsayer* was bundled up and strapped across his back, making it easier to transport. He carried an ax, and a long dagger hung from his belt, both Falstaff weapons newly acquired. Six guards stood inside the hall, and they saluted when Grudge held up the gold medallion. They immediately came to talk to him. "I'm your new captain, lads," Grudge said, in good spirits. "Let's raise a glass to Captain Leech and bid him well on his journey to the underworld."

The atmosphere turned from grim to festive as men gathered around Grudge, patting him on the shoulder and giving him a hero's welcome. Taliesin heard someone say the fires had been kept out, not wanting anyone to see the caravan enter Raven's Nest. A plausible reason, but considering Wolfmen had followed them home, it hardly seemed time to celebrate. Taliesin dragged her gear to a table. Her eyes quickly grew accustomed to the light coming from the great fireplace. Torches on tall iron stands stationed throughout the vaulted chamber were lit by servants, casting a yellow glow. The walls were covered with tapestries and deer antlers, boars' heads, an array of impressive swords, and a shield made out of dragon scales. Women set pewter plates on four long tables placed in the center of the hall and tossed fresh straw onto the floor, stirring the hairy hounds beneath the tables. A loud commotion could be heard coming from the kitchen. She imagined Hillary scurrying about, preparing the evening's meal; no doubt he would soon appear to welcome

Taliesin home. An old man was hardly a suitable companion for someone her age, but Hillary had been her closest friend until eight months ago, and they still often spent time together, talking over hot biscuits about all manner of subjects. Until she saw Hillary and knew he was safe, she wouldn't be able to relax.

"Now let's raise a glass to Captain Grudge," one of the Black Wing guards said. Ten guards remained inside the hall, changing posts at intervals to take turns on the decks high in the tree, at the entrance to Raven's Hall, or in one of the four secret watchtowers located in the Tannenberg Forest. Grudge had a strange look on his face as the men patted him on the back, praised him for his promotion, and made a fuss that reminded Taliesin of little boys eager to please their new master. She placed the silver spear on the table beside her bags and watched Grudge and the guards drink a toast; it was interrupted by a sudden commotion at the door that caused everyone to wheel around.

"Out of my way," a man said with a deep, grating voice.

Two members of the Wolf Clan pushed aside the guards at the door and entered the hall without invitation, something that just wasn't done. Black Wings stormed into the hall to confront the two burly Wolfmen in gray cloaks, who both drew their swords. Grudge walked toward the Wolfmen, blocking Taliesin's view with his tall, broad frame, though she could see quite a few spears and swords pointed at the Wolfmen.

Creeping behind Grudge, she peered around him. Both Wolfmen looked equally dangerous. Each wore a matching steel helmet with a closed visor shaped like a wolf's muzzle. Long, gray fur cloaks attached to the steel breastplates that covered their chainmail shirts added to their fierce appearance. Plate mail covered their broad shoulders, and ornate greaves were worn from knee to ankle over tall boots. Their swords had jagged edges and needed polishing. Neither man had bathed in weeks, and their body odor was ripe. The taller Wolfman, strands of blond hair poking out from under his helmet, noticed Taliesin and pointed his sword at her. The guards glanced in her direction, and she felt Grudge's gaze upon her. She straightened as she fell in beside him.

"Our grievance is not with you, Captain," the taller Wolf-man said. He lowered his sword and removed his helmet, holding it under his arm. Long, dirty blond hair fell onto his broad shoulders. His green eyes were cold and hard. "Tell the Raven Master we've been sent by Chief Lykus and would speak with him directly. We've ridden a long way and require food and drink."

"The Raven Master has already been sent for," Grudge said. "We do not dine until he arrives, but we can offer you ale." He held his hand out, motioning for the two Wolfmen to take a seat.

"You've no right to enter Raven's Hall without invitation," Taliesin said, speaking her mind. The two gray-cloaked men glared at her. "I'm the Raven Master's favorite daughter. I've every right to ask you to show us proof Chief Lykus sent you. Otherwise, you can go outside and eat with the dogs."

Grudge took her arm and propelled her behind the line of Black Wings. He released her as she stumbled and fell onto a bench. "Keep quiet," he said in a threatening manner. "I have no doubt this has something to do with you." He returned to the Wolfmen.

A few house servants gathered at the fireplace, stacking wood and stoking the fire, their heads turned as if deliberately refusing to meet her gaze. Taliesin was appalled no one came to give her a tankard of ale, as they always did for everyone who returned from a Gathering. Several servants walked in a side door and continued setting the tables, but Hillary was not with them. The scent of roasted venison drifted into the hall from the kitchen, causing Taliesin's stomach to growl. An old man came to her table to place a tankard of ale in front of her. Taliesin took a large gulp, turned, and tried to eavesdrop on the conversation between the men. It couldn't have been that important, for at that moment the kitchen door opened, and Mrs. Caldwell came out, swaying her hips and carrying twenty mugs of ale on a tray. The men grabbed the cups, and the two Wolfmen placed their swords and helmets onto the nearest table and accepted the ale. They drained them within seconds and took others off the tray before Mrs. Caldwell could catch her breath.

"Bring us as many pitchers as you can carry, Mrs. Caldwell," Grudge said. "Our guests seem to be thirsty." The Black Wings lifted their tankards and drank as one.

"I want meat," the short, stocky Wolfman said. He had a dirty beard, mangy hair, and fleas were practically jumping off him.

Taliesin pulled her cloak tighter around her shoulders, finding both Wolfmen so crude they seemed nothing more than savages.

"Soon, soon," Grudge said, placing one foot on a bench. "Tell me, Captain Wolfgar, what brings you here? We noticed your men following us. They came all the way from the battlefield to Raven's Nest without once paying a visit to our campfires. Were you at the battlefield or did you come straight from Wolf's Den?"

Vibrant green eyes stared at Grudge. The man's face was angular, pale, and covered with dirt, along with a week's growth of blond fuzz. His nose was long with flared nostrils, and his mouth wide with thin lips. Taliesin found Wolfgar rather handsome, in a wild sort of way, and imagined the blond savage running naked through the forest in pursuit of a deer before killing it with his bare hands. Wolfgar caught her staring and smiled over the brim of his tankard, sending chills along her spine.

"You know me?" Wolfgar said, regarding Grudge. "I don't know you. Must be new around here? What happened to Leech? I never thought that old bird would die, and I tried to kill him several times in the past. Never liked him much."

"Leech died on the way here. I'm Captain Grudge. This is Taliesin, the Raven Master's daughter, and she is correct about protocol," he said firmly. "Entering another clan's hall without permission just isn't done. Do you have the proper letter of transit from your lord? If so, I'd like to see it, then I'd be glad to offer you something to eat."

Wolfgar sniffed. "This is Lieutenant Udolf," he said, wiping his nose across his arm. "And I've got such a letter. It's for the Raven Master, not the Captain of the Black Wings. I don't care for protocol, so read it if you like. But you should know captains don't need permission to enter a hall. *Any hall.* Same rule would apply if you showed up unannounced at Wolf's Den. But we'd feed you."

"Same as Wolf's Den," Udolf repeated. "But there would be meat." He took a drink of ale. "This ale is better than what we have at Wolf's Den, though; that's for certain." He didn't cover his mouth when he belched.

The Black Wings started sitting as well, legs in the aisle between the tables. Wolfgar and Grudge sat across from each other as Grudge placed his ax on the table. Taliesin slid along the bench until she was an inch from him and placed her elbow on the table, resting her head on her fist. She was so tired, she wanted to go upstairs, bathe, and then sleep. But that wasn't likely to happen anytime soon, and she suppressed a yawn behind her hand.

"As captain to captain then, answer my questions," Grudge said, not repeating what he'd asked before. He leaned forward, arms on his legs and a tankard held between his knees.

"We came straight from Wolf's Den. Udolf and me. If my men followed you here, then they've their own reason for doing so." Wolfgar reached into the neck of his chainmail shirt and removed a folded piece of parchment with an unbroken wax seal, which he handed to Grudge. "It's official business," he said. "Has to do with the Raven Master's daughter."

"Which one? Master Osprey has forty adopted daughters of all ages," Grudge said, chuckling. He looked at the letter, refrained from breaking the seal, and placed it under his belt. "I asked you which daughter you've come here to inquire about."

"That one," Wolfgar said, pointing at Taliesin. "The red-haired bitch."

"This is Taliesin, the Raven Master's favorite daughter, and I'll ask you not to refer to her as a female dog. The Raven Master will open the letter, now that I see you have one."

"Fine." Wolfgar made the one word sound like a snarl. "We'll wait for the Raven Master and hope he'll feed us. I don't mind answering a few questions now about the girl. It won't take long to find out what we want to know. I have a few tests I'd like to put to her."

Several pitchers of ale were placed on the table by Mrs. Caldwell and her staff. Udolf grabbed a pitcher, ignoring his tankard, and drank his fill. Wolfgar poured his own drink and sniffed at the large woman, sending her hurrying to the kitchen. He took a sip and looked at Taliesin, licking his lips when he lowered his mug.

"Taliesin is a member of the Black Wings," Grudge said, "and as such, you will treat her with the same respect you show me. We're not in Wolf's Den, Captain, and Taliesin has earned a place among the men."

"Then she doesn't need to be coddled," Wolfgar snarled. "I don't mind if you answer for her. Captain to captain. But you'll be honest. Agreed?"

"Agreed, but keep it civil," Grudge said.

"Chief Lykus has reason to suspect this woman is a witch," Wolfgar said, coming right to his purpose for being there. "It's no good having a witch among the clans. Magic is outlawed, and no clan can harbor one. That's King's Law and Clan Law. If she's a witch and I can prove it, Chief Lykus wants her burned at the stake. That civil enough for you, Captain Grudge?"

"You've been seriously misinformed, if that is indeed what your chief thinks," Grudge said. "Taliesin is not a witch. There are no magic users at Raven's Nest. We have an herbalist, an old crone who can read Tareen Cards, and a blacksmith who reads tea leaves. But no witches or warlocks. Why does Chief Lykus think Taliesin is a witch? What proof do you have?"

Taliesin set her tankard aside. The words were out of her mouth before she could stop herself. "If that's what your chief thinks, then he's got bats in his belfry," she shouted. No one moved. No one spoke. Grudge and Wolfgar glared at her, each for different reasons. "I'm not a witch. Anyone who says that about me had better be ready to have their teeth knocked in. That's an ugly accusation, and it's a lie, so take it back."

"What?" Grudge said and Wolfgar at the same time.

"You heard me. *Take it back.*" Taliesin finished off her ale, stood, and stepped over the bench to face Wolfgar, so angry she stomped her foot and shook her fist. "I won't have you slandering my good name or making up lies about me, Captain Wolfgar. If you won't take back what you said, then this conversation is over, and you can leave right now! Tell those dogs at our gates to return to their kennels, or I'll be the one to teach them a thing or two about manners. I don't like Wolfmen urinating on our fence."

The laughter among the men, both Raven and Wolf, was enough to send Taliesin into a fury. Her cheeks turned red. She felt her blood boiling and imagined beating Wolfgar over the head with the nearest trough of meat and skewering his smelly friend with a fork. She turned around and reached for her bags, intending to go to her room, but Grudge caught her by the arm and yanked her onto the bench.

"Not another word," Grudge said. "That's an order, Taliesin."

Udolf let out a growl and drained his tankard. "No bitch speaks out of turn at Wolf's Den." He slammed the tankard on the table. "More ale!"

"Mrs. Caldwell," Grudge called out in a loud, booming voice. "Bring more ale for our guests and send a kitchen boy to find out what's keeping Master Osprey." He crossed one leg over the other. "Let's hear why Lykus thinks Taliesin is a witch. Apart from her red hair and bad temper, I can assure you she's as normal as any other Raven girl."

"But she's not afraid of me," Wolfgar said, in a throaty voice. Taliesin lifted her chin higher; it was a compliment, at least to her, and he nodded at her, acknowledging it. "Most women are too afraid to meet my gaze. This one thinks her good looks will spare her a gruesome death. Pretty or ugly, witches are treated the same in the end. Can't have her casting spells on our clan, now can we? As I said, we've a few tests we can conduct, and if she passes, we'll leave and take our scouts with us." He set aside his tankard, untied a pouch from his belt, and placed it on the table, half-turning to open it. "You ever hunt witches, Grudge?"

"Can't say I have."

"A dash of salt will raise boils on their arms or face. They cast no reflection in mirrors and are unable to drink holy water. If she passes these tests, then we look for suspicious markings on her body like moles, blemishes, or extra teats witches use to feed their familiars."

"Familiars?" Taliesin said, unable to remain silent. She didn't know much about witches, other than they were supposed to be ugly, not pretty, have warts like Minerva, live like hermits in caves, and boiled strange things in large kettles. Nothing but stories. No one had seen a witch in decades, and none had ever been at Raven's Nest, not since magic was outlawed.

"A black cat, toads, perhaps a rat, and some witches have been known to keep spiders," Wolfgar said, going through his pouch. "The text is very specific. Here it is." He tossed a small, dirty book with a grimy cover onto the table. "I've done this before, Captain Grudge. I know what I'm looking for and how to deal with a witch. Perhaps we could examine her...."

"You'll do no such thing!" Taliesin stood up again, walked to the other table, and picked up the book, standing between the two Wolfmen to do so. Wolfgar sniffed at her; so did Udolf, and she felt like taking the book and hitting them both over their heads. Instead, she read the cover. "'How to Recognize Witches and Other Supernatural Creatures' by C. W. Pedigrew. Well, let me tell you something, Captain Wolfgar, I no more like a witch hunt than I'm sure you like wolf hunts. I can assure you I don't have any extra tits." She threw the book onto the table, spotting a nearby salt cellar, pulled it over and stuck her fingers into the middle of the white crystals. "No boils," she said, stepping away from the table and returning to sit next to Grudge. "Do you have a mirror and holy water? Might as well get this over with."

The Wolf captain held up a mirror he took from his bag. Her reflection showed messy hair and a dirty face, not how a Raven's Master daughter should look, especially when accused of being a witch. Minerva with her warts and big nose looked a hundred times better. She wasn't sure what to do, but Hillary arrived with perfect timing carrying a tray with a bowl of warm water and a cloth. Wolfgar mistook the bowl of water for milk, stood up, and took it from the tray, scowling.

"What is this?" Wolfgar asked, sounding irritated.

"It's for the lady," Hillary said. "To wash her hands and face, I thought, seeing how she doesn't lick her fingers clean like the Wolf Clan."

The water was thrown in Hillary's face. Taliesin flew off the bench at once, taking the towel off the tray to dab the water off Hillary and presenting her back to Wolfgar. Only a few men snickered. The Wolf captain returned to his seat, lifted his tankard of ale, and took a large sip. Hillary took the tray into the kitchen and sent Mrs. Caldwell out with more pitchers of ale, allowing the odor of roasted venison, wild boar, and chicken to permeate the air. Udolf was out of his seat and sniffing hard, but Wolfgar pulled him to the bench.

"What type of holy water do you have?" Grudge said. "Taliesin prays to Navenna, not Heggen like the rest of us, and if your water is blessed by a priest of Ragnal, your god, well, then you might as well have her drink from a dog bowl."

Wolfgar laughed along with the Black Wings. "All of you make sport of me," he said, holding up his tankard. "If this were the Wolf Den, you'd find our women are obedient, and servants never talk back. They each know their place. Yet, you Ravens laugh at everything, finding humor in proven tests that have sent hundreds of witches to the stake. But I too can make jests. C. W. Pedigrew sounds very much like 'pedigree,' and here my companion and I are Wolfmen. Yes, very funny, indeed." His eyes momentarily changed color, burning a bright yellow and slanting up at the corners before returning to green. Taliesin had seen it if no one else had, and she refilled her tankard, needing a drink.

"Taliesin is not a witch." Grudge was cut off before he could finish.

"Now, had I drunk the wash water, then it would be truly funny, wouldn't it?" Wolfgar punched his friend in the arm. "Udolf, you do not laugh. Come, my friend, laugh with these silly birdmen. They think the Wolf Pack is a joke. No sane man would ever think a wolf pack is a joke. Not when alone in the woods."

"Not a joke," Udolf said, repeating his captain's words with a growl.

"*Our* way is not *your* way, Captain Wolfgar," Taliesin said. "As soon as my father arrives...."

Wolfgar stood, lifting his hand in the air. He sniffed at the air in a canine manner. "The Raven Master is here. Now we'll get to the bottom of things, little miss bossy." A long pink tongue rolled across his thin lips. "If we prove you are a witch, you will burn this night."

Burned at the stake, she thought, and wished she'd gone to her room and never returned to the hall. Curiosity, impatience, and a bad temper would be the death of her yet.

* * * * *

Chapter Four

The Raven Master arrived, escorted by eight armed Black Wings. Hawk and Rook accompanied them. Osprey had put on a cloak of raven feathers that fell from his shoulders to his ankles and a silver crown with a gold raven beak in the center. The frail, old man looked impressive as he swept forward and approached the main table turned perpendicular to the rest. He sat in a handsomely-carved wooden chair, and the two Wolfmen grabbed their helmets and stepped forward to bow. Grudge stood up from the table, signaled his men to follow, and they lined up behind the Wolfmen.

"Show me Chief Lykus' letter," Osprey said in a commanding voice. "Come, come now. I am hungry, and I want this matter settled quite quickly. Captain Wolfgar, it's always a pleasure to see you. Now let's see why you've come to Raven's Nest."

Taliesin was again left alone at the table. She pulled Wolfgar's pouch over for a closer examination, half-listening to the men as she looked at the contents. There were the small skulls of a rat and a cat, a rabbit's foot, a bag of cloves, two cigars wrapped in a dirty cloth, and a small metal knife. Also, within was the mirror, a bottle of murky water with no label, a bag of salt, a handful of loose human teeth, and a human finger, female, recently cleaved off someone's hand. Not much of a kit for hunting witches, she thought, which she doubted Wolfgar and Udolf had ever done in their life; it was part of their pretense for being there. She put everything back into the pouch and picked up the little book. One whiff told her it had once been pissed on and a flea was smashed between the pages she'd opened. She found a raven feather pressed between two other pages and paused when she heard Osprey's voice.

"The signature of Chief Lykus is authentic," Osprey announced. "I would recognize his scribble anywhere. But what brings you here unwashed and unshaved, Captain Wolfgar? My clan has a reason for being dirty, but not you and your companion. I tolerate many things—pilfering, petty bickering, and sloth—but what I will not endure is rude manners in my hall."

Taliesin removed the feather, not liking it inside such a book. She put the book inside the pouch, stood, and headed toward the kitchen, taking the feather with her.

"My manners are crude at best," Wolfgar acknowledged. He stood with his shaggy head bowed. "We come as friends to the Raven Clan, and upon my master's bidding. This is official business. It concerns your daughter. My master believes she is a witch."

Taliesin felt her heart leap to her throat. Her father was quick to respond.

"My daughter is not a witch," Osprey said. "I can't believe that's why you are really here. Tell me. I am listening. What are you really after?"

"Our clan was present at the Battle of Burnlak. My men said a red-haired wench picked up many weapons of quality, including a gold sword. My master knew Duke Hrothgar would be present, and if *Doomsayer* was found, he is willing to pay for it. I've brought coin."

"Well, well, well," Osprey said, sounding pleased. Yet, he didn't turn to praise Taliesin and thereby leaving her vulnerable to Wolfgar's accusation. Instead, he defended her with aplomb. "Witchcraft no longer exists, not in the Tannenburg, and isn't needed for Taliesin to find swords of value. It is my daughter's job as a sword collector to retrieve only the best. But it's Captain Grudge who found the duke's sword. It is his sword to keep or to sell. You may ask him if he'll part with it, but as for my daughter, that subject is closed."

"I did find *Doomsayer*. It is one of Duke Hrothgar's twenty gold swords, but it isn't for sale," Grudge said. He'd removed the weapon from his back and placed it out of sight.

Taliesin's bags had been taken upstairs by Hillary. Mrs. Caldwell had sent her silver sword to her room, as well. Always looking out after her, she thought.

"There, you see," Osprey said. "Your trip has been in vain, Captain Wolfgar. I assure you my daughter, Taliesin, is not a witch. She simply has a knack for finding valuable weapons."

Wolfgar bristled. One sharp look from Grudge, and he kept his mouth closed.

"Our official business is now concluded," Osprey said, with finality. "If you care to dine with us, Captain Wolfgar, then remove your cloaks and take a seat at my table. Tonight, we celebrate!"

Showing a spontaneous zeal for knowing how to turn a volatile situation into a celebration, Osprey gave orders for music and good cheer. Several men with a lute, a tambourine, and a drum started playing, filling the great hall with lively music and merriment. Taliesin went into the kitchen to quickly wash her hands and face at a sink. Mrs. Caldwell appeared with a bundle of clothes. She helped Taliesin out of her grungy tunic, then made her strip to her undergarments, slip on a dark-green tunic that fell to the floor, and pull on a pair of soft brown boots. Taliesin grimaced as Mrs. Caldwell combed her hair, pulled it into a ponytail, spun it around into a bun, and clipped it behind her head. A dab of perfume was placed behind Taliesin's ears and on her wrists.

"I'll have a hot bath sent up for you after dinner," Mrs. Caldwell said. Taliesin was fond of the woman. She was twenty years younger than Hillary, but Taliesin knew they'd taken to sleeping together. The head maid was a widow and Hillary had never married. It was a good match, for they took care of Raven's Nest and ran an orderly kitchen and staff. The little things they did, as Mrs. Caldwell did for her now, made them near and dear to her heart.

"Thank you," Taliesin said. "You don't think I'm a witch, do you, Mrs. Caldwell?"

"Pish posh. If you're a witch, then I'm a Draconus princess." The woman chuckled heartily and turned, clapping her hands and startling her kitchen staff who were preparing to head out the door. "Don't you dare spill a drop of my stew! Our guests might be dogs, but that doesn't mean they'll be eating off the floor."

Taliesin smiled as she slipped behind a line of women in aprons carrying pitchers of ale and trays stacked with tankards. They handed these out to the workers who had come in through the doors and now sat at the four long tables. She went over and stood behind Osprey's chair. Taliesin hung back from the table, stalling, not wanting to sit and have to listen to Captain Wolfgar's accusations. The women with children had not joined them, nor were there any children in sight. Rook and Wren sat amongst the clan, and Hawk sat next to Grudge at the main table. A chair was left open for Taliesin, and she slid into it, noting both men giving her an approving look; apparently, they liked her in a dress with her hair up, a fashion she normally wouldn't have tolerated, but Mrs. Caldwell had tried so hard to make her look nice she hadn't wanted to complain.

Platters of roasted venison, boar, and chicken were placed on the tables. Bowls of hot beef stew, along with boiled quail eggs, freshly baked bread, and large slabs of butter filled the air with a delicious aroma. Large bowls of steamed clams, buttery potatoes with cloves, fresh vegetables, and baked puddings were placed out. Within seconds, Osprey's mangy war dogs wandered to his table, including his favorite, a giant red hound named Falstaff, who sat at his master's feet.

"Everyone has done well, and our clan will prosper," Osprey announced, standing to address the crowd. "Eat and drink your fill! This will be a meal to remember, my friends, I assure you." He sat to a bowl of steamed clams placed before him. "Some of our cooks come right out of the King's palace...only I didn't say that, a man's past being his own business. None of that makes any difference here in Raven's Nest, Captain Wolfgar."

Wolfgar wasn't eating, only drinking. "Of course," he said. "It is well known your clan does not speak of their past. You are given new identities when you join Raven Clan." He glanced up as a pretty girl paused to fill his tankard with ale. Taliesin wanted to club the captain when he gave the frightened girl a pat on her rump. The girl went to serve the lieutenant who chewed on a turkey leg; he was a glutton, able to eat more than any man Taliesin had ever seen.

"My daughter has changed for us," Osprey said, glancing over at her. "What a beautiful woman you are, Taliesin. Is she not lovely, Captain Wolfgar? Surely, it's her face that has attracted Chief Lykus' attention and not this silly story about witchery."

"Yes, lovely," Wolfgar said, but he didn't look at her. He finally ate.

Hillary placed a plate filled with meat and boiled potatoes before Taliesin, filled her tankard with ale, and hovered behind the table. Osprey nodded at Taliesin, and they tapped their mugs together. As he lowered his tankard, he used his sleeve to wipe away a film of foam above his upper lip.

"Here we do not judge men or women on where they were born or why they came to be here," Osprey said. "But I do admit we have excellent cooks. The best cooks have tempers, and some find themselves on the run after a particularly murderous outburst in a lord's kitchen. Don't anger Mrs. Caldwell or she's liable to cut off your ears, captain." He chuckled and took another drink of ale. "We offer sanctuary here, and a type of rebirth. It's my own version of a utopian society. Everyone here is equal, though not necessarily when it comes to the spoils of war. But I think we have the best of everything in Raven's Nest. Don't we, my dear?"

"Yes, father," Taliesin said. She stood up and held her tankard high. "To the Raven Clan!" she shouted. "To utopia!"

Everyone stood up and raised their mugs. "To the Raven Clan," voices shouted in unison. Osprey smiled at the lot of them, saving his fondest look for Taliesin, but one glance toward a dark shadow entering the room and his good humor ended. Minerva came into the hall, wearing a black velvet gown and a preposterously-large headdress made of feathers. The lute player deliberately missed a note, and the musicians chuckled, causing a ripple effect across the room as the Raven Master's wife squeezed in between her husband and Captain Wolfgar. The twins, Talon and Falcon, the only children given permission to be in the hall, stood behind her chair like obedient puppies.

"I suppose she'll toss bones over her shoulder to feed those little monsters," Hawk said, his tankard raised. He winked at Taliesin. "What is she wearing on her head? It's like a flock of blackbirds took up roosting in her hair."

Taliesin exchanged a look of amusement with Hawk, noticing Grudge was eyeing them both with disapproval. Hawk lifted his goblet to his lips, rolling his eyes towards the Wolfmen. The amount of food shoveled into their faces was astounding, and Taliesin swore they each ate enough to feed ten men. As she watched, the Wolfmen picked up speed as they ate, revealing ravenous appetites, and she heard Hawk snickering.

"Tell me, Captain Wolfgar, what is Wolf's Den like?" Minerva said, using a sickly-sweet voice that drew Taliesin's attention. The old woman looked more like a stage actress in a Glabber the Glib production than the Raven Master's wife. She batted her eyelids at the Wolfman in a flirtatious manner, for she had no eyelashes, only wrinkles of flesh. In a woman her age, it was appalling to watch.

"It's dark," Wolfgar said, his mouth full.

"What are your women like at Wolf's Den? Are they as fair as Raven girls?" Minerva placed a hand to her pale, white throat when the Wolfman glanced toward her. Gravy dripped off his chin, and he wiped it off with the palm of his hand. "And what of your wife? I am sure she is quite the beauty. Have you children, sir?"

"I have no mate, yet, nor any offspring," Wolfgar growled. He glanced toward Taliesin as if to imply he was interested.

Averting her eyes, Taliesin used her fork to stab a piece of beef and lifted it to her lips. The taste was delicious, but she hardly noticed as she watched Minerva try to cuddle up to the brutish Wolfgar. Minerva never made a fuss over anyone, and Taliesin snickered when the old magpie boldly brushed crumbs off the captain's cloak. A low growl rumbled in Wolfgar's chest. He brushed her hand away, annoyed, and continued eating.

"I heard they call Lykus the Wolf King," Minerva said, not able to take a hint. "Is your leader as intimidating as they say, Captain?"

"You talk too much." Wolfgar paused in his feeding frenzy to grab a young servant girl by the arm. She dropped her plate of potatoes, leaving it to the dogs, as he roughly yanked her to his side. "More ale!" He released the girl and smiled at Osprey. "Sir, your women are far prettier than our own and vastly more desirable." His gaze transferred to Taliesin, burning with a hunger that made her feel uneasy. "Your daughter is quite a beauty. Her hair is as red as fire, and her eyes bluer than the sky."

"I've heard it all now," Grudge said, finally speaking.

"I agree with you, sir," Osprey said, flattered by the compliments. He was oblivious to Taliesin's growing fury and seemed more interested in keeping his guests entertained than seeing to her comfort. "More ale! More of everything!"

Tankards of ale were placed before Wolfgar and Udolf. The Wolfmen had already swallowed enough ale to be slobbering drunk, but neither appeared so afflicted. Taliesin noticed the two frequently glanced around the room as if counting heads, and only broke off their assessment of her clan to stuff food into their mouths and wash it down with ale. Mrs. Caldwell was right about their guests; their manners were similar to the dogs beneath Osprey's tables. The Wolfmen ate with their mouths open, smacked their greasy lips, and licked their dirty fingers. She imagined Wolf's Den as nothing but a dark cave filled with savages, its members gathered around fire pits, gnawing at great chunks of meat, and swallowing big bites. Along with children crawling on the ground among the dogs, there would be Wolfgar and a wild-haired girl lapping up ale from the same dish. Later, they would lounge on a bed of straw together, scratching at their fleas as they mauled each other.

"They act like they never ate at a table before," she said, glancing at Grudge. He could only nod as his mouth was full. Grudge finished chewing and used a kerchief kept in his pocket to wipe his mouth and fingers.

"Now would be a good time to disappear," he said.

Taliesin didn't wait to be told twice. "Father? May I be excused?"

"Don't you approve of us, girl? Is that why you leave?" Wolfgar said, tossing a large bone onto his plate, his attention focused on Taliesin. He wiped his hands on his tunic then, finding Minerva too close, used the sleeve of her long black dress. She drew away from him, offended. He belched and picked up an ear of corn. "I asked you a question. Where I come from, when a man asks a woman a question, she is expected to answer."

"Here, in Raven's Nest, a woman does not have to answer a man's question if she does not want to," Taliesin said. At a sharp glance from Osprey, she bowed her head and remained seated.

"Gentlemen, if you are both full, we will talk business," Osprey said. "Let's see that sword, Captain Grudge. I want to show Captain Wolfgar it is only an ordinary gold sword."

Taliesin nervously tapped her foot as Grudge removed the sword he'd hidden beneath the table, removed the cloth that covered it, and lay it in front of him. A gasp went through the crowd.

Osprey gave an approving nod at Grudge. "Captain Wolfgar, as you can see, this is not a magical sword. I grant you it is beautifully forged and worth its weight in gold," he said. "As I told you, Captain Grudge found the duke's sword.

Make an offer and, if I find it high enough, I will ask my captain to sell the sword to you. My daughter is not for sale." Only a few men laughed at this, and an angry look appeared on Grudge's face.

Wolfgar stood and wiped his hand across his mouth. "In truth, I care not for the sword, Master Osprey, though I admit it is a rare find and quite beautiful," he said. "I inquired about the sword out of curiosity. Something else was taken from the battlefield that does not belong to your clan. We are here to get it back. Taliesin took an item that belongs to the Wolf Clan."

Osprey looked surprised, not offended, as he should have. "What did she take? Tell me." He looked over at Taliesin. She merely shook her head, offering no explanation.

Neither the flag nor the wooden scroll belonged to the Wolf Clan, regardless of what might be said, for their dealings were solely with flesh. Only the Eagle Clan could dispute what she'd taken, and she enjoyed watching Wolfgar's cheeks flush.

"If you are unable to tell me what you are really after, Captain Wolfgar," Osprey said, "perhaps it is time for you to return to Wolf's Den."

Wolfgar glared at his host. "Is this how you treat your guests, Master Osprey? To ask me to buy a gold sword you should give in homage to my lord strikes me as less than courteous. Chief Lykus is higher ranking than you in the Tri-Council. Our clan has always had greater prestige." He looked satisfied when the Raven Master looked offended. "As for the item your daughter stole, she knows what it is."

"Name it," Osprey said, "and if it is here, perhaps I'll give it to you."

Wolfgar stood up from the table and tapped his comrade on the arm, motioning Udolf to rise. After putting on his helmet, Wolfgar drew out a pair of black leather gauntlets he'd kept tucked into his belt. He put on each glove, taking his time. "It is best your clan does not know of what I speak," he said. "If you will not speak to me in private, then our business is finished." He flipped a stray lock of blond hair out of his eyes. His companion stood away from the table and put on his helmet, closing the visor.

Taliesin applauded their sinister performance. No one said a word. Master Osprey trembled beside her, and Grudge had covered the gold sword with his cape. Hawk stood up and pointed a table fork at Wolfgar. Taliesin might have laughed had the young man not been so serious.

"You will address our Lord as 'Master Osprey,'" Hawk said.

"I mean no disrespect," Wolfgar said, eyeing the fork. "May I speak to the girl in private, Master Osprey?" He held out a gloved hand toward Taliesin in an inviting manner. "If she has the item, we will take it and leave, to trouble you no further."

"Taliesin took nothing that belongs to the Wolf Clan," Hawk said. At Wolfgar's look of disdain he smiled, a skill he had yet to perfect. "I have the honor of being the Black Wing's second-in-command. Hawk is the name." He stabbed the fork into the table.

"I'll remember that name," Wolfgar said. He nodded at Udolf.

"A moment, sir." Osprey faced his daughter. "Taliesin, do you know what the Captain of the Wolf Clan is talking about? Did you take something that belongs to their clan?"

Taliesin felt everyone in the hall staring at her. "I took nothing that belongs to the Wolf Clan," she said, rising to her feet.

"Be more precise, dear," Osprey said. "I don't want things to turn unpleasant. There are women and children present. Be a good girl and answer him, or I must allow him to speak to you in private. I dare not risk the lives of any of our clan for any reason."

"Very well, but it's not what you're thinking." Taliesin placed her hand on Grudge's shoulder as she spoke. "I found a silver spear from Erindor, which is quite rare to find in these parts, and it is meant as a gift for Rook. I also came across two gold arrows of rare quality and workmanship, and a silver sword."

"That's not it," Wolfgar said through clenched teeth.

"If you mean to inquire about the silver hand that belonged to the duke's brother," she said, "Grudge took it off his body and brought it home. You do know who Jasper Silverhand was, Captain Wolfgar. They say a wolf bit off his hand when he was a small boy, and a skilled blacksmith fashioned him a hollow hand made of silver. I don't know what you think I took that belongs to your clan. You should be asking why the Eagle Clan left two dead noblemen on the field to rot. In the past, I've known your clan to pretend a nobleman was low-born in order to collect a finder's fee from the grieving family."

Worried looks and soft rumblings spread like wildfire across the tables. Wolfgar looked worried. The mere accusation of the nefarious activities of his own clan was all Master Osprey needed to detain both Wolfmen for further questioning.

"Is this true?" Osprey asked.

"I don't know what she's talking about," Wolfgar said.

"You carry a great and dark secret with you, Captain Wolfgar," Taliesin said, hoping to get him to admit a crime and lessen her own guilt. "I don't like secrets and have no need to keep them. As I have said before, I did not take anything that warrants such intrigue." She glanced at her father. "I will let the Wolfmen search through each and every bag I filled if that will give their lord satisfaction. I have nothing to hide."

Osprey returned to his seat. "Hillary, send a servant to my daughter's room and return with her bags," he said. "Captain Wolfgar, you may look through her belongings and confirm what you seek is not here, then you can return to Chief Lykus with our reassurance the Raven Clan remains friends to the Wolf Clan."

In a few minutes, Hillary and two young men returned with the three bags Taliesin had filled with weapons. Wolfgar returned to his seat, while Udolf walked over to search through the bags. The man found it difficult to see with his helmet on, took it off, handed it to Hillary to hold, and dug through the bags. He didn't find whatever he was looking for, snarled as he stood to his feet, and snatched his helmet from the terrified servant.

"The item is not here, Captain," Udolf said, furious.

Wolfgar pointed a gloved index finger at Taliesin's face. "You daughter has hidden the item we seek," he said, angrily. "I can smell lies like dung on the heel of my boot!"

"It's a wonder you can smell anything beyond your own armpit," snapped Taliesin.

The captain stiffened, lifted his arm, and sniffed. "There is no smell, at least none that would offend another Wolfman."

"You wanted to know my opinion of you, sir? Personally, I don't think you deserve to eat at our table, Captain Wolfgar. I let your companion examine my takings, and yet you are still unsatisfied. Nothing has been hidden. Would you prefer to search my body?" Taliesin walked to stand behind his chair and turned a full circle, aware everyone watched. "See anything you like, Captain Wolfgar, or should we go into the kitchen so you can feel with your hands what your eyes cannot see?"

"You are a bold little bitch," Wolfgar snarled. His eyes turned a curious, bright yellow. "I tell you now, if this girl does not give me what we came here for, Master Osprey, I will order the Wolf Pack to raid this hall. Members of my clan do not lie, nor do we tolerate liars. Is it your clan's desire to insult the Wolf Pack, or will you put a leash on this one and make her do your bidding? I know she lies."

"I took nothing of yours, you mangy dog," Taliesin shouted. "*You* are the liar!"

Wolfgar stood, knocking over his chair, and drew his sword. He cursed through clenched teeth, the language more animal than human. His lieutenant reached for his weapon as well. Grudge stood, holding the golden sword with both

SEEKER OF MAGIC | 71

hands, ready to fight. Rook had the silver Erindor spear in his hands, and Hawk drew his cutlasses.

"Enough!" Osprey was on his feet at once. He held his hands out before him and said in a soothing voice, "We do not want trouble here, Captain Wolfgar. You tread on thin ice; the Black Wings are not novice fighters. You will not make it out of here alive if you continue along this path. I have tried to be civil to you. I have shown you kindness and fed you both from my table. My daughter has answered your questions and allowed you to search her bags. Unless you tell me what it is you are after, leave immediately."

"I cannot say what it is," Wolfgar said. "I have my orders."

The Black Wings looked so fierce Taliesin felt certain the Wolfmen had started doubting their chances of making it out of the hall and to their horses. Osprey motioned for his men to stand down and waved at the door, signaling the unwanted guests to depart with haste.

"Very well," the Raven Master said. "Leave by the road you came here by and do not return, Captain Wolfgar. Take the rest of your Wolfmen with you. We are not cowards, sir. Nor do we run from a fight. Come back if you must and meet our cold steel; we will be waiting for you and your Wolf Pack."

"Brave words spoken by a man already sentenced to death," Wolfgar said. "We'll return and take your daughter, as well as whatever else we can carry."

"Gentlemen, it's time you left," Grudge said. He pointed toward the front doors with his dagger and smiled. With a snarl of rage, Wolfgar sheathed his sword and pushed Udolf ahead of him. They were escorted out the door by Grudge, Hawk, Rook, and all Black Wings present. Osprey sat in his chair and turned to regard his daughter.

"I am displeased with you," Osprey said, at last. "Very displeased, Taliesin."

"I swear I took nothing that belongs to the Wolf Clan," she said. "They accused me of being a witch and threatened our entire clan."

Before Taliesin said another word, Osprey grabbed her arm and pulled her into his office. He thrust her into the room, slamming the door shut behind them.

"Need I remind you that those two Wolfmen are the servants of Chief Lykus? Do you know what he's like? Have you ever met him? Well, I have, and he's not the pleasant sort. If you dislike Wolfgar, you will hate Lykus. He is more beast than man, and I mean that literally." Osprey shivered from head to toe and groaned as he placed his head in his hands. "I barely made it out of the Tri-Council the last time we met, and we'd disagreed over the smallest thing. I don't know what you took from the battlefield, Taliesin, but you should not have brought it here!"

Osprey shook his head and pulled his hands away from his face. His eyes were glimmering with unshed tears—he was frightened.

"I did take two things that belong to the Eagle Clan," Taliesin said, eager to make amends. "A flag and a scroll. I didn't think anyone saw me take them."

"The Eagle Clan?" Osprey said. "How many times must you be told, Taliesin? Do not take things that don't belong to you. We have rules for a reason. You continue to break them. I am ashamed of you, girl."

"But father..."

"Tsk, tsk, tsk. I don't want a confession," Osprey snapped. He opened the door and pushed Taliesin into the hall. Seeing his wife emerge from the shadows, he raised his voice and pointed toward the staircase. "I want you to go to your room, and there you will stay until I either come for you or send for you. Now don't dawdle! Go to bed, Taliesin!"

"Let me have her," Minerva said in a vicious tone. She held a small cutting knife, the type used to mold clay into bowls; nonetheless, it looked deadly in her hand.

"Shut up, you old magpie! This is none of your concern!" Taliesin bowed her head in embarrassment. She collected her bags, stuffed the weapons inside and ran past Hillary and the two servants as she bolted up the stairs. She didn't stop running until she reached her room.

* * * * *

Chapter Five

Taliesin entered her bedroom and tossed the bags on the floor with a loud *clank*. The interior was large, with a vaulted ceiling and an unlit stone fireplace. Her room was already prepared for her arrival. The blankets were turned over on one corner, and a yellow spring flower lay on her pillow. Candles burned, placed around the room on shelves and tables, and a vase of fresh-cut flowers was placed on a mantle. One wall was lined with the books and old manuscripts she'd collected over the years.

She liked collecting things. Besides being obsessed with swords, she had an assortment of jewel boxes and five pairs of tall leather boots. An old trunk was filled with weapons, and the banners and flags taken off the battlefields hung on a wall. Prince Sertorius' flag lay neatly folded and placed in the middle of her bed. She picked up the dark-blue flag, marked with a rampaging white lion, and hung it on the wall. A loud knock spun her around to stare at the door.

"Taliesin? It's me. Hillary."

Opening the door, Taliesin stepped aside for Hillary, holding a tray with food, and five lads carrying a large wooden bathtub and pitchers of hot water. The lads brought the tub inside and set it beside the window overlooking the courtyard. Hillary placed a basket of bread and a pitcher of ale on a table. Two large wooden chairs covered with worn maroon cushions were pushed partially under the table. The boys filled the tub with water and headed out the door. Hillary remained in the room.

"Mrs. Caldwell was quite amiss to find the Prince Sertorius' flag in your possessions," the old man said. "I had her bring the flag, along with the silver sword and the red leather pouch straight to your room. When Master Osprey ordered me to bring your bags, I knew better than to bring the pouch or the flag, since I'm sure that's precisely what those flea-biters were after. Mrs. Caldwell and I won't say a word to anyone, but I might have peeked inside the pouch."

"Wolfgar will return with the Wolf Pack," Taliesin said. She wasn't upset with Hillary. Both he and Mrs. Caldwell were more like real parents to her than they were servants. Going to the bed, she opened the pouch and removed the wooden cylinder. "This is what Wolfgar wants."

"Little goes unnoticed by Lord Arundel," Hillary said. "If the scroll were deliberately left behind, then it was either intended to be discovered by the Wolf Clan or the Raven Clan. Better you not read the contents and have a clear conscience. Find somewhere safe to hide it, Taliesin, and do not speak of it again. I'll send Mrs. Caldwell up with fresh towels. Enjoy your bath."

After Hillary left, Taliesin placed the scroll under her pillow, stripped off the gown, kicked off her boots, and slid into the bath. She rubbed a cleansing soap into her wet hair until it was frothy and then ducked under the water. She used a small wooden stick to clean the dirt from under her nails and started scrubbing with a hard brush and bar of soap. Mrs. Caldwell tapped on the door and came in, waiting silently until Taliesin finished bathing, and held a towel out for her. Taliesin reluctantly stepped out of the tub, dripping on the rug, and the stout woman wrapped the towel around her body.

"That old squirrel only brought you a loaf of bread for your supper," Mrs. Caldwell said. "I brought you a bowl of my stew. Eat it while it's hot. You are getting too skinny. And no reading tonight, Taliesin. You have dark circles under your eyes and look a fright."

Taliesin waited until the door closed before drying off. She dropped the towel onto the floor and stood in front of a silver shield hung on a wall and gazed at her reflection. Her jaw was square, not pointed, and her cheekbones were too high. Her face was tan, as well as her hands, but the rest of her was white. Where she wanted curves, she was bony, and where she wanted to be soft, she had hard muscles. She slid on a soft wool tunic with long, tapering sleeves. The green shade was the same as her eyes, and the tunic fell to the floor.

She sat at the table and used the bread to dip into the stew. When she'd had her fill, she retrieved the wooden container and pulled off the cork to peer inside. She caught a whiff of cologne as she removed the rolled parchment and gazed at the blue wax seal, imprinted with a coiled snake.

"Royal," she said. "Looks like Almaric's emblem. Cologne smells expensive."

Unable to resist, she slid her thumbnail under the edge of the wax seal. Taliesin managed to loosen the seal without breaking it and paused, hearing a loud commotion in the hallway. She placed the scroll back inside the cylinder and looked around the room for a safe place to hide it. Outside her door, she heard raised voices, scuffling, and lots of banging about, as if someone were having his skull slammed against the wall. Taliesin ran to a suit of armor standing in the corner of the room and placed the cylinder inside the helmet, turning as the door crashed open.

Hawk tumbled into her room with a Wolfman clasping the young man by the throat. Taliesin grabbed a sword off the wall and stabbed the intruder in the thigh. The Wolfman released Hawk with a howl of pain, clutched his leg, and fell to the floor, bleeding profusely from the wound. Hawk staggered backward, gasping and rubbing his bruised throat. Checking to make sure no one else was coming down the hall, Taliesin slammed the door shut, threw the bolt, and stood over the Wolfman.

"How many men did Wolfgar bring?" Taliesin asked, pointing her sword at his chest.

Hawk poured a glass of ale and took a drink. "I'm not sure. Maybe fifty or more. Grudge killed three at the door of Raven's Hall. The Black Wings took care of the rest. This one got past Grudge and headed straight to your room. He fights dirty. He tried to bite me. Fortunately, his teeth didn't break the skin."

The Wolfman gazed up from the floor. His hands pressed over the hole in his leg. Blood seeped through his fingers. Taliesin threw her damp bath towel at the Wolfman. The injured man pressed it against his injury. She again pointed the sword at the man.

"We need to secure your room," Hawk said. He walked to each window, closed the shutters, and latched them. "Maybe we should just kill him. The only good wolf is a dead one."

"I think we should question him," she replied. "First, tie him up. I don't want him to try to bite me. He's covered with lice, or didn't you notice?"

Hawk found a coil of rope in a chest. He did as she requested with speed and skill. When he finished, Hawk took a step back and slipped on the pool of blood. He righted himself and grimaced when the man snickered. Taliesin tapped the tip of her sword against the man's shoulder, getting his attention. His dark eyes widened, and she caught the faintest glow of a yellow flash in the pupils.

"What does your clan want with me?" Taliesin said. "Your captain called me a witch. Why would he say that? Tell me what I want to know, and I might let you live."

"I'd rather die," the Wolfman snarled.

A loud knock brought Hawk to the door. He unbolted and opened it wide. Grudge came stomping into the room, carrying the bloody gold sword in one hand and a severed arm in the other. At a stern look from Taliesin, Grudge dropped the arm onto the floor, but it did not lay there for long. Falstaff, Osprey's favorite war dog, had trotted in behind the large man. The beast was as large as a small pony, with thick, red fur and a studded leather collar. The dog eyed the severed arm, snatched it off the floor, and dashed out of the room. More dogs waited in the hallway, but at the red dog's growl, they raced along the hall, barking loudly.

"Falstaff should enjoy that," Grudge said, kicking the door closed. Without warning, he broke into a fake eastern accent.

"I will not lie, great lord, nor stir my soup with a bone. I'll eat all that you give me and the bone, too." Not missing a beat, he added, *"'Ha, ha,' said the Knave, when at last he saw the Queen faint upon seeing the King's best bitch gnawing at his royal bone."*

"That's from Glabber the Glib's play, 'The Black Mergus,'" Taliesin said. "Ever notice how Glabber's plays never end well for the villain? Every villain finds his end, whether it's a hangman's noose, poison, a pit of wild dogs, or the point of a sword. Guess how your story ends, Wolfman?"

"Have your laugh," he replied. "My captain will return for me."

"This one is a villain. Be sure of that," Hawk said. His dagger appeared in his hand and flashed silver in the candlelight.

Grudge sat on a chair. "I didn't expect your captain to return so soon," he said. "But I was still ready for him. Now, what could he possibly want from the Raven Master's daughter? See anything in this room that belongs to the Wolf Clan?"

"Just the girl," the Wolfman growled.

Taliesin placed her sword aside and took Hawk's dagger from him. She knelt beside the prisoner and pressed the blade to his throat. "I make no idle threats, sir. You will talk, or I'll take something from you." The tip of the blade slid along the man's neck, leaving a trail of red, not deep enough to kill him, but enough to leave a thin scar.

The Wolfman snarled and jerked forward, trying to bite her. Hawk let out a warning cry and grabbed the man by the shoulders, pulling him back before he could sink his teeth into her hand. Taliesin stood and patted the prisoner on the head as she would a dog before she stuck the tip of the dagger into the opening of his ear.

"Go on," Hawk said. "Teach him manners, Taliesin."

"Imagine, if you will," she said in a honey-smooth voice, "how it would feel to have a dagger rammed through your ear and into your brain. A simple flick of my wrist is all it would take to mix your brains about like pudding."

The Wolfman laughed. "I'm not afraid of any Raven," he said.

"Maybe not them, but you should fear me. I've gelded stallions before, sir." Taliesin watched the tiny yellow flame appear once again in his pupils as he writhed about like a caged beast. "It's easy as slicing off a piece of cheese."

The Wolfman spat at her. He missed his mark and instead hit Hawk's leg. A furious Hawk kicked the man twice in his injured leg. The prisoner winced and let out a deep growl.

"That settles it," Taliesin said. "I will have blood before I hear the truth."

Damning the consequences, she released her dark side. With no guilt or remorse, she cut off his ear along with a handful of hair and tossed it to the ground. The Wolfman bit his lip to keep from screaming. Hawk looked shocked, but Grudge wore a look of approval on his rugged face. Taliesin watched the blood seep along the side of the prisoner's head.

"I didn't know you had it in you, Taliesin," Grudge said.

She glared at the large man. "Shut up! He has another ear."

"Well, you best hurry," Hawk offered as motivation. "I'm sure your father is on his way here. You're his top priority, Taliesin. You and this prisoner."

"Will you both please be quiet?" Taliesin said. "I want this dog to talk. If I must cut off the other ear, sir, then so I shall, for the truth, I will have this night. What does Wolfgar think I stole from the battlefield? I took nothing that belongs to the Wolf Clan, though I admit I did pick up a flag. Is that what you want? Prince Sertorius' flag?"

Hawk gasped. "You have a royal flag?"

Grudge nodded. "Chief Lykus and Prince Sertorius have joined forces," he said. "The flag proves the prince was at the battle."

"I told you both to be quiet. I meant it!" Taliesin's attention returned to the Wolfman. By the way he was twisting his eyebrows about and making the strangest expressions, she felt her chances to get him to confess had increased. She lowered the dagger to his groin.

"Talk, Wolfman. I grow impatient," Taliesin said. "Did you come for the flag?"

"I...I...would rather be gelded than tell you the truth," the man croaked.

"By Heggen's white beard, man, she means to do it!" Hawk shouted. "Just tell her what she wants to know before you lose your manhood."

Hawk swallowed a lump in his throat as Grudge glared at him, for he'd only caused Taliesin to press on the dagger. The Wolfman yelped and squirmed.

"I have given my oath," the Wolfman said, panting hard. "I will break it not. Do what you must, but I won't be called a traitor."

"By all the Gods!" Grudge snarled. "Move aside, woman. I'll do it," He knelt beside her and took the dagger from her. "This is going to hurt, lad. Last chance. It's clearly not the flag or gold sword you're after, so what is it? What does Lykus deem so valuable?"

The point of the knife pressed downward, and the prisoner screamed and fought against the ropes, trying to break free. As Grudge stood, the Wolfman stuck out his tongue and bit hard, severing it in half. Blood burst from the Wolfman's mouth, frothy and thick. Grudge made no move to help, holding Hawk away when he stepped forward. Taliesin watched in horror as the Wolfman choked on his own blood, and with a last twist, grew still.

"That's a first," Hawk said, turning a bright shade of green. "I've seen a wolf bite off its own leg to get free from a trap. Never seen one bite off its own tongue to keep from talking. All he had to do was tell us what we wanted, and he'd still be alive."

"Oh, I think he'll talk now." Taliesin went over and picked the golden sword off the floor. Both men stared at her, one in disbelief and one in anger. "Come on," she said. "Don't you want to know what the Wolf Clan is really after?"

Hawk nodded. "I very much want to see you use the sword again."

"So, you did see Taliesin when she found *Doomsayer*," Grudge said. "Then you know using the sword comes with a price. The last time she used it, she was overcome with grief and the memories of Jasper Silverhand. I doubt this scoundrel had pleasant thoughts."

"I don't care," Hawk said. "Let's get to the bottom of this."

Taliesin glanced at the dead man lying on the floor of her room. "We need the name of the real mastermind behind this conspiracy," she said. "Who sent you here, Wolfman, and what were you after?"

"Give that sword a hard shake," Grudge said. "It worked the last time."

She held the hilt in both hands, closed her eyes, and gave it a hard shake. Coldness slid up her fingers and arms, and she opened her mouth and said, "*Sertorius.*" Her eyelids fluttered against her cheeks. "*The prince hired our clan to retrieve the sword. We came here to acquire Doomsayer, the Raven Master's daughter, and a royal scroll. A scroll left behind by the Eagle Clan. A scroll the prince wants more than anything else.*"

Taliesin fell silent as an image appeared in her mind. The Wolfman, from the shadow of the trees, had watched her find the golden sword. He'd seen her kneeling beside Jasper Silverhand and heard what she'd said, confirming the clan's belief she was a witch. The image changed, and she saw the Wolfman standing in Wolf's Den beside a skinny woman holding a babe in her arms. His wife and child. But when he looked at the child, it was a black pup wrapped in swaddling rags. Then his thoughts grew dim.

Taliesin gasped and opened her eyes. Grudge came over, caught her by the elbow, and helped her sit in a chair. He took the sword from her and placed it on the table.

"I have blood on my feet," Taliesin said, still dazed. Her feet and the edge of her gown were covered with blood. She pushed Grudge away and went to the tub, stepped inside, and watched the water turn red. She picked up the bar of soap and washed her hands clean of lice and the odor of the Wolfman and scrubbed until Grudge came and took the soap from her. He washed his hands as she stepped out of the tub and collapsed onto the ground.

"It's all right," Grudge said. "I'll get rid of the body. Don't think about it." He grabbed a blanket off the bed and wrapped it around her shoulders.

"But the baby. It wasn't a baby at all. It was a wolf pup."

"What baby?" Hawk gave them both a curious look. "What is she talking about?"

Grudge frowned. "The sword gives its owner visions," he said. "Taliesin must have seen this man at Wolf's Den, and he apparently had a child. A child that was a wolf, not human."

"Maybe she shouldn't have called on *Doomsayer's* powers," Hawk said. "Talking to the dead is something no one should be able to do. It's unnatural. You've turned pale, Taliesin. I think we should take the sword away from Raven's Nest. We could hide it at the gorge."

Grudge shook his head. "It's too late for that," he said. "The wheels are already in motion. The Wolf Clan has sided with the rebel princes. They'll return for the sword and Taliesin. But what is this scroll he mentioned? What is he talking about, Taliesin?"

Taliesin glanced at the suit of armor where she'd hidden the scroll. Sertorius knew she had the scroll as well. Had he dropped it by mistake? She imagined a list of the conspirators who wanted the king dead and Almaric on the throne. Such an item was too dangerous to possess. Sertorius, the Wolf Chief, and, most likely, Duke Regis Peergynt of Maldavia knew she had taken it. Peergynt was a tyrant and had the right to order the Raven Clan off his lands or to take them prisoners.

"I found a scroll on the battlefield," she said. "It's in a traveling container. I haven't read it yet, but I think it carried Prince Almaric's seal. It may be a list of traitors. I'm not sure. I was about to read it when Hawk burst into my room."

"When I told you to pick up important items, I never imagined you'd find a death list. Where is it? Do you have it here?" Grudge asked, looking around the room.

Taliesin nodded and pointed at the suit of armor. "It's right inside," she said, noting how Grudge scowled, while Hawk turned pale.

"Great," Hawk said, with a loud groan. "We're all going to die."

* * * * *

Chapter Six

Morning found Taliesin in bed, buried under the furs. She heard a servant tapping at the door but ignored the knock, wanting to stay in bed and sleep until noon. The knocking grew louder, and, with a groan, she kicked off the furs and grabbed a robe. Sliding into it, she tiptoed across the wooden floor as the door handle started to jiggle. She wiped the sleep from her eyes and glanced over her shoulder as she tied a knot in the sash of her robe. The tub had been removed, along with the Wolfman's body, but the blood remained on the carpet.

"Who is it?" Taliesin asked. She flipped her hair away from her face, expecting to hear a servant's voice and was surprised to hear Hawk say, 'good morning.' She opened the door and stepped aside. Hawk was dressed for the day, looked rather chipper, and wore his cutlasses strapped to his back. His ruffled shirt was clean and neatly tucked into pants stuffed into knee-high boots. The scent of lavender hung in the air, not the type of odor she was used to smelling on a man. "What?" she said. "No hot green tea and biscuits?"

"I'm not here with your breakfast," Hawk said in a dour tone. "The Eagle Clan has been spotted on the road. Word must have reached Lord Arundel that you found *Doomsayer*. Unless this is about the scroll. Did you look to see what it says, yet?"

"No," she said. "We agreed not to last night. It's still hidden away."

Taliesin moved aside with a yawn. Hawk entered and shut the door behind him. She noticed Hawk staring and felt awkward in only a robe. While she hurried to her wardrobe to find something to wear, Hawk walked to the window, opened the shutters, let in the morning sunlight, and looked at the courtyard.

"Don't look," Taliesin said. She slid out of the robe, put on her undergarments, and selected a long green gown to wear. It was a lovely silk dress, easy to put on, and flattering. Hawk kept his back turned as she put on leather slippers and combed out her hair. "Just because they are here, doesn't mean this is about me."

"This is bad. Very, very bad," Hawk mumbled. He turned and gave her a sour look. "Why else would the Eagle Clan send an envoy here? Lord Arundel surely knows why the Wolf Clan came here. You attract trouble like flies on dung."

Taliesin went about making her bed instead of waiting for a servant. Having Hawk in her room made her nervous, and knowing an Eagle envoy was approaching made it all the worse.

"No matter how careful you think you are," he said, "it's never enough. Someone is always watching, and that's why we don't take what's not ours to keep." He smoothed out the ruffles on his shirt. "Well? What are you waiting for? Let's read the scroll."

"Not before I've had a cup of tea," Taliesin said. She groaned when someone else knocked on her door. She stomped to the door, hoping it was a servant with her breakfast. She opened it and found Grudge, clean and tidy in a Black Wings tunic, standing outside. "I don't suppose you saw Hillary in the hallway? I'm a grouch until I have my tea."

"Forget about breakfast," Grudge said. "We have much to talk about before the Eagle Clan arrives." His hand on his sword, he entered the room and shut the door behind him. Noticing her frown, he let out a soft chuckle. "I'm sure Hillary will be here soon enough. You run that man ragged with all your orders. A hot bath in the middle of the night, indeed."

Taliesin took a sniff at Grudge. He'd bathed. He didn't smell like lavender, but he did smell a great deal better. He'd shaved off his whiskers. Seeing his bare jaw came as a shock and not without a second glance, just to be sure he actually was handsome when scrubbed. He grinned at her, and she looked away.

"I've already decided to lie about what happened," she said. "I'll bury the scroll and be done with it. As for the flag, I have so many, I'm sure no one will care I have another."

Hawk caught Grudge's eyes. "She didn't read the scroll. Don't worry."

"We agreed not to," Grudge said, sitting on a large, ornate trunk. "But to be safe, I think I should take the scroll. I'll decide what's to be done with it. You two should be left out of this affair. Neither of you is any good at lying, nor keeping secrets. Give it here, Taliesin."

"Why would I give it to you?" Taliesin asked. "Because you're the new Black Wing captain? Forget it. I'm responsible for the scroll, and I'll decide what to do with it."

"Ten Wolfmen were tossed into a fire pit and are still smoldering, and more will be coming to Raven's Nest." Grudge held out his hand. "You wanted to be a Black Wing. I just gave you an order, Taliesin."

She gave a hard shake of her head. "I don't have to follow your orders," she said. "You told me last night Osprey had to consider whether or not I could be a Black Wing. I never should have told either of you about the damn scroll. Now get out and let me finish dressing. I want to look presentable for the Eagle envoy."

"I'm trying to help you, and all you can do is act offended. I actually care," Grudge said, throwing his hands in the air. "I don't have time to argue this morning. Osprey has sent the women and children up the tree and ordered the stairs destroyed. Captain Wolfgar will return, and there isn't much time to prepare for a major assault." He walked to the door and glanced at her. "Do the right thing for once. If you won't give it to me, then burn the scroll." He glanced at the young man standing at the window. "Hawk, come with me. We have work to do."

Hawk hurried to Taliesin as Grudge opened the door. "Don't worry," he said. "We won't let the Wolfmen or the Eagle envoys harm you. Grudge is just being, well, Grudge." He gave a rare smile. "Never trap a raven in its own nest, that's what I always say. Fighting on our home turf has its advantages."

As soon as Grudge and Hawk left, Taliesin went to check on the scroll. It was where she'd left it, inside the helmet. But Grudge and Hawk knew it was there, so she took it out, placed it inside an armored leg, and stuffed a scarf on top. With one last look around the room, she went into the hallway, shut the door, and headed to the main hall.

A flurry of activity was going on. Servants were laying fresh linens over the tables and placing the best silver plates and chalices atop them. Hillary spotted Taliesin from the kitchen door and waved her to the Raven Master's table. The moment she took a seat, a servant with a tray came out the door. A pot of hot green tea, a plate of warm biscuits, and jars of honey and fresh-churned butter were set before her. Hillary poured tea into a cup for her. He'd shaved and wore a bright yellow tunic over which hung a fresh apron. His white hair was tied into a sparse braid, and a smile appeared on his face as Mrs. Caldwell's voice was heard in the kitchen.

"Good morning, my dear," Hillary said. "Sleep well?"

Nodding, Taliesin buttered a biscuit and stuffed it into her mouth. He handed her a napkin and brushed crumbs off the table. "You've gone out of your way to decorate the hall," she said. "Wreathes of summer flowers and fresh straw on the floor. Must be someone important. Who is it this time? Orell or his brother?"

"Secretary Glabbrio, the son of your favorite playwright," Hillary said. "He's not been to Raven's Nest in ten years, but you've met him. A ponderous old fool who suffers from gout due to his gluttonous appetite. Black Wings scouts spotted his caravan entering the forest. They are but a mile down the road. I suspect Glabbrio was at the Gathering and stayed a few days in Burnlak before coming here. Eagle legionnaires travel with him, so you can be sure they know about the Wolf Clan's visit."

"Glabbrio, son of Glabber the Glib," she said, in a melancholy voice. "The man is nothing like his father. He hasn't a shred of wit or charm."

"Do you need any assistance? Anything that needs to be...removed from Raven's Nest?"

"Just keep Minerva out of my room," Taliesin said. The old man nodded. "And see if you can learn from the envoy's servants if they returned for the bodies of Hrothgar and Jasper. I'll feel less inclined to think ill of Secretary Glabbrio if he did."

Hillary bowed his head. "Of course," he said. "You know me. I like to snoop."

Voices at the main doors caught their attention. The doors lay open, letting in sunshine and a warm summer breeze. Master Osprey and ten Black Wings entered the hall and walked toward her. She took several quick sips of tea, feeling nervous as Hillary scuttled between the aisles, chattering away to the guards. Osprey wore a moss-green robe and a long gold necklace with a ruby medallion. Clasping his hands together, Osprey stood in front of the table in front of Taliesin and stared at the biscuits and jar of honey. She slathered a biscuit with honey and offered it to him, frowning when he snatched it away in a frantic manner.

"Is all well, father?" Taliesin asked.

"Not in the least. I see I must use my instincts, along with my natural born skills of perception to root out the mushrooms growing in this manure," Osprey said, in a tone that reflected loosely-controlled fear. "Twenty Wolfmen...that's how many we killed and burned last night. Captain Grudge has tightened security. Wolfgar won't return while the Eagle envoy is here, and Glabbrio will be eager to know everything that happened."

"If this is about Captain Wolfgar's allegations..." she sputtered, unable to finish.

"The Eagle envoy will be here any minute," Osprey said, raising his voice as he eyed the plate of biscuits, "and here you are stuffing your belly. Hillary didn't mean for you to eat all of them, you greedy hen." He crammed the biscuit into his mouth, crumbs falling on his robe and onto the floor. Falstaff appeared at the edge of the table, and his shaggy head dipped as he lapped up the crumbs. "I'm a nervous wreck," he whispered to Taliesin, speaking with his mouth full. "A complete and utter wreck."

Aware the guards were staring at her suspiciously, Taliesin calmly wiped her hands on a napkin, one of a few kept in the kitchen specifically for her, and offered it to her father. He shook his head and reached for another biscuit.

"Please, let me speak with Glabbrio," Taliesin said, "and I'm sure I can sort this all out, father."

"Not one word shall pass from your lips," he said, crooning softly. "I am sure Captain Grudge and the Black Wings can handle what may arise from this visit." He gazed toward the staircase and motioned the guards to go up to the second level. Three obeyed, swords drawn, moving up the stairs with urgency. "I have questioned Minerva and the others thoroughly and know what I'm looking for, but I wish to do so in silence. Now hush, child, and follow me."

Part shaman, part bloodhound, Osprey took his time to absorb the energies in Taliesin's chamber as soon as they entered. The guards spread out to search her belongings. Taliesin stood by the door, arms crossed, furious with the manner in which the Black Wings tossed about her belongings, upset furniture, and turned her mattress. A large trunk was pulled out from beneath the bed, the lock broken, and the lid opened to reveal fine dresses made for a rich noblewoman. Each was lifted out and tossed into a corner. Despite her protests, the guards treated her wardrobe in the same manner, throwing cloaks, boots, and tunics onto the floor.

Osprey only took a few minutes of waving his arms and turning in a full circle before he pointed at the wall where the banners of each noble house and the royal family hung. The guards approached the flags; however, not one was touched. They turned to Osprey for instructions. A gnarled finger pointed at the flag of Prince Sertorius hanging among the others, yet the guards made no move to remove it.

"There is the culprit," announced Osprey. "Fetch it, girl! And be quick about it. Time is against us, and I must decide what to do with you. Quick, girl!"

Taliesin hurried to her collection of flags and removed the royal banner of Prince Sertorius, wondering whether it had been Grudge or Hawk who'd betrayed her confidence. Holding the flag over her arm, Taliesin walked to her father under the disapproving looks from the guards. She offered the prince's flag to Osprey. He merely slid his hand over the embroidered white lion, making a clucking sound as he flicked his tongue against the roof of his mouth and shook his head in disbelief.

"I am sorry, father," Taliesin said, embarrassed. "It was wrong to take the flag. I have no excuse. To me it was but one more flag to add to my collection." She said not a word about the scroll, not did Osprey. Her initial anger with Grudge and Hawk faded. Neither had betrayed her trust or Osprey would already have the scroll in his hand.

"Alas, you took the banner of the most dangerous prince ever born into the Royal House of Draconus. It was careless of Prince Sertorius to leave this behind, but you see, my dear, it was he who paid Captain Wolfgar and the Wolf Clan to come here last night. I do not blame Chief Lykus for refusing to be bribed with the gold sword, but the problem is someone witnessed you picking up the flag. I'm sure that's why Glabbrio is here."

"Sertorius doesn't want anyone to know he was the one who killed Duke Hrothgar," Taliesin said. "Giving the flag to the Eagle envoy will not change this fact. The King must be told Duke Peergynt and Prince Sertorius have sided with Prince Almaric. If you took the flag to King Frederick and explained...."

A red flush appeared on Osprey's wrinkled face. "Me? Go to the King?" He trembled from head to toe. "It cannot be done. The Raven Clan has never been involved in court politics, nor will we do so now by exposing Prince Sertorius' crime. I will give the flag to Glabbrio and let him sort out this ugly business."

Grudge appeared in the doorway. Sweat lay thick upon his brow, and he appeared as if he'd been running, for his breathing was labored. "The envoy has arrived," he said. "Hillary is serving the Eagles a large breakfast, but the envoy is eager to speak with you, Master Osprey. Is everything in order here?" He met Taliesin's gaze. "Are you all right?"

Taliesin nodded.

"If that's your sly way to inquire whether or not I intend to give this flag to Glabbrio," Osprey said, "then the answer is 'yes.' Why? Don't you think it's a good idea, Captain?"

"I think you should deny it to the grave," Grudge said. "Our problems with the Wolf Clan have little to do with this flag. I suggest you hang the flag on the wall and don't mention it. I'm certain the envoy is here about the golden sword. I can hear the elephant coming up the stairs. Quickly. Hang it up!"

Osprey grabbed the flag out of Taliesin's hands upon hearing the sound of approaching heavy footsteps. A beefy hand took it out of Osprey's clutches, and Grudge gave it to Taliesin. At his nod, she hung the flag on the wall and turned around as two golden-cloaked Eagles appeared in the doorway. The footsteps grew louder, heavier, and the Eagle guards stepped aside, forming a line with the Black Wings behind the Raven Master. Osprey stepped forward with Grudge at his side. Taliesin remained near the flags, watching a large, obese man waddle toward them. Two men followed the envoy, Hawk and Hillary, their heads barely visible behind his large body.

"Greetings, Master Osprey!" The envoy wore an ivy-green cloak over a long yellow robe and dark green shoes. Eagle feathers were hemmed into his cape, and a feather stuck out of his wide-brimmed hat. He wore gold rings on his stout fingers and rouge applied to his chubby cheeks. His girth required him to squeeze through the doorframe, and with a hand over his heart, he bowed his head.

"Secretary Glabbrio! I was about to join you for breakfast," explained Osprey. "There was no need for you to come all the way up here. Not in your exhausted condition." He bowed his head and motioned toward the door. "Shall we adjourn to the hall and take refreshment, my Lord? I have yet to take my breakfast, and I hear Hillary has set out a large meal."

"There is always trouble in the hen coop when young chicks disobey the long-standing rules and regulations of their clan," the envoy said. His piggish eyes turned on Taliesin. Great beads of sweat rolled from his forehead and throat like marbles. "Rules are made for a reason, girl. They bring order into a chaotic world. In the world we live in, we need rules lest we become the ones preyed upon." His stomach rolled as he bellowed. "And I will have order!"

With one swipe of his arm, the Eagle Clan envoy moved forward, brushing aside Osprey and Grudge in order to reach a table. He peered at the books stacked haphazardly on the desk, and knocked everything to the floor with his hand, including a crystal decanter and small matching glasses that shattered when they hit the floor. His arrogance and flagrant disregard of her father's courteous offer for breakfast made no introduction necessary. Taliesin had seen the corpulent, greasy-chinned fat man in a nearby town a year ago, at a play performed by a traveling troupe of actors. It seemed a cruel twist of fate the envoy was the son of Glabber the Glib. Secretary Glabbrio had never written a poem in his life. Nor did he have any appreciation for the theater or his father's masterful plays. Despite her low opinion of him, Glabbrio was a powerful man and carried not only rolls of fat, but the absolute authority to carry out any punishment he deemed necessary on behalf of Lord Arundel. If Glabbrio wanted her punished, there was nothing the Raven Master could do but obey.

"Come here, girl," Glabbrio said, lifting his hand.

Taliesin knew what was expected of her and went to the envoy, sinking before him to kiss the signet ring. The stench on his hand came from a sweet-smelling perfume that was overbearing on purpose. Beneath the perfume came an odor from his body, stronger than horse manure, and twice as acrid as pig dung. Her eyes started watering, and she stood up, suppressing her anger as the odious man leered at her. Out of the corner of her eye, she spotted Grudge shaking his head, cautioning her to remain silent.

"What a beauty this one is, Osprey. I realize now why Chief Lykus has made such a fuss over her." Glabbrio licked his puffy, pink lips. "You've kept her hidden from me for too long. I generally like girls a bit younger, as you well know. This one is how old? In her twenties?"

"I am twenty-six," Taliesin said, unable to hold her tongue.

"And still not married?" Glabbrio asked. He reached out and pinched her chin between his sausage-thick fingers. "You have spirit. I like that. Alas, your skin has already begun to wrinkle from age and from the sun." His hand fluttered to his side. He eyed Osprey. "I already know Captain Wolfgar was here, so don't pretend otherwise, Master Osprey. The Wolf Clan has sided with Prince Almaric and Prince Sertorius. We are at war, sir, and it's time to pick sides."

"Is that why you are here?" Osprey asked. "What interest do you have in my daughter?"

"The same as Lykus," Glabbrio said, as he glanced at Taliesin. "I hear you have a knack for finding rare weapons, girl. Swords of quality bring a high price. You can make a fortune in the market, especially if you found a magical sword. I would see it."

Taliesin didn't respond.

"If you're after the duke's sword," Hawk blurted, "it's over there in the corner!" He ran to where the sword was hidden, threw the cloak aside, and grasped the hilt. He was unable to lift it and fell against the wall, breathing hard. "Damn. That's heavy. How did you manage to kill a Wolfman with this, Grudge?"

"Brute strength," Grudge muttered, casting a murderous look at his friend.

Taliesin, equally angry, glared as Glabbrio waddled over to inspect the weapon. A thick finger slid across the golden blade as he made a purring sound in the back of his throat. "This is lovely, simply lovely," he said. "Did the girl say if this was *Doomsayer*, Master Osprey?"

"I'm right here," Taliesin said. "And it's not *Doomsayer*."

Grudge walked over and grabbed Taliesin by the arm. She tried to shake him off, but he refused to release her. Osprey let out a weak giggle and walked to stand beside the envoy. He was as thin as Glabbrio was fat, making them an odd pair. The two Eagles moved away from the Black Wings and gazed at the sword.

"It was my captain who actually found Duke Hrothgar's sword, my lord," Osprey said. "Answer the Secretary. Is this *Doomsayer* or not?"

"It's one of twenty gold swords owned by Duke Hrothgar," Grudge said, speaking with authority. He released Taliesin and joined Osprey and Glabbrio. Using one hand, he lifted the sword, acting as if it were a normal sword, though Taliesin knew by his wince doing so gave him discomfort. "Duke Hrothgar used this gold sword in battle. If it were magical, he would have defeated Duke Peergynt. As you can see, Secretary Glabbrio, it is unmarked by its maker, and it has a serious flaw." He placed the sword across his left arm, lifting it for the Secretary to scrutinize, and pointed at an imaginary flaw below the hilt. "Do you see the crack? One more blow and it would have broken in half."

"I...I think I see it," Glabbrio said, straining to see the imaginary flaw. "I think I see it. The crack is very small. But yes, now I see it. Good man. I'd never have noticed it. Of course, this is not *Doomsayer*."

Grudge nodded. "It's damaged but still valuable. Gold is gold. If you are agreeable, my Lord, I suggest we melt it down. I will give you half the gold and keep the rest to sell at a market."

Taliesin suppressed her laughter behind her hand. Grudge had nerve.

"Just who are you to make such an offer?" Glabbrio pressed his hands over his belly, indignant and unforgiving. "I do not know this man, do I, Master Osprey? What is his name?"

"This is Captain Grudge, so named on account of his nasty disposition," replied Osprey. He put on a faint smile. "Forgive my captain for his lack of couth, Secretary Glabbrio. Of course, you may take the sword with you to Eagle's Cliff, as a gift for Lord Arundel. You will be compensated, Captain. Now, shall we all adjourn to the hall to take refreshments?"

Grudge walked to the Black Wings. After whispering in Hawk's ear, he sent the young man out with the rest of the guards and remained outside the doorway. The Secretary gave Grudge a disapproving look and addressed Osprey with a sniff.

"It is a handsome offer and would please Lord Arundel," Glabbrio said. "The sword is pure gold?"

"I believe so," Osprey said. "Please tell Lord Arundel this gift is a token of my esteem. You will also leave with a wagon filled with other fine weapons taken from the battlefield, as a tribute to Lord Arundel. I will give you the Fregian Duke's armor, and a noble stallion found wandering the field. Please, give the armor and horse to Lord Arundel and ask him to accept our humblest apology for having caused any trouble."

"Come then," Glabbrio said. "Let's find a more suitable place to discuss business."

* * * * *

Chapter Seven

Osprey led the way to the main hall. Two guards stood at the doors as servants tossed fresh straw onto the ground. A contingent of twenty Eagle legionnaires sat at one of the long tables, eating their fill, as a fire crackled in the large fireplace. Hillary and his kitchen staff aimed to impress and had gone out of their way to set out a feast for the Eagles. A large roasted boar was placed on the main table beside bowls of steaming, buttery potatoes, peas, and carrots, with baskets of fresh brown bread and pitchers of ale. Several war hounds, Falstaff among them, wandered around the tables looking for scraps. The Black Wings and two Eagle guards sat at a table. Hawk and Rook joined them, but Grudge remained beside Taliesin. Osprey caught Glabbrio by his sleeve and pointed toward his office door. The Eagle envoy huffed and puffed, greatly annoyed to be denied a large meal, but waddled after the thin Raven Master.

"We're not having breakfast?" Taliesin asked. "But I'm hungry."

Grudge held her elbow and guided her toward the Raven Master's office. A number of Black Wings and servants were watching them. She didn't imagine they'd ever seen Grudge looking so clean and sharp. He held her in a possessive manner that raised a few eyebrows, she noted, and Hillary and Mrs. Caldwell watched from the doorway of the kitchen like two conspirators.

"Act like a lady," Grudge said, tersely. "Don't speak unless you're spoken to, woman. You've placed your father in a difficult position. Glabbrio has heard you are a witch, so be on your best behavior."

The office Osprey used for business and clan meetings was a large chamber with a vaulted ceiling supported by immense timbers where birds built nests. Wrens, thrushes, and blue jays flew in and out by means of an open window that overlooked the main courtyard. On a cushioned bench beneath the window, a large yellow cat lay curled in a ball, one green eye open to watch the birds. The birds seemed to know to keep to the fresh hay spread on the floor because no droppings could be found on any of the stacks of maps, shelves of books, or tapestries on the wall.

"I talk to the birds," Osprey said as if an explanation was required, "and they repay me for the shelter I provide by not making a mess."

"Indeed," scoffed Glabbrio. The envoy stepped around a large goose which honked loudly and chased after six runaway brown and white goslings. "Are we not to have breakfast, Master Osprey? I do so love roasted boar and boiled potatoes. The seat which is currently occupied by your cat would do me nicely."

Osprey walked behind a large desk and stood in front of a painting of Tantalon Castle, centered between two ornate gold candlesticks hanging on the wall. Osprey reached up to the candlestick on the left and turned it sideways. A hidden door in the wall moved inward, revealing a heavy wooden crate with a gate and a railing.

"This is what I call 'the Ascender,'" Osprey said. Demonstrating with his hands, he formed a square with his fingers and, starting low, swiftly lifted his arms. "Most people call it 'the Birdcage,' but it's a little invention of mine that allows us to travel up, to the upper branches, for that is the aviary where we house the women and children. It's also where my private council room is located, and I intend to treat you to a bird's-eye view of the world." He held out his hand. "Please, enter without fear, my friend. We will have our breakfast at the top. Hillary has cooked your favorite. Wild boar."

Glabbrio licked his lips. "I do so love wild boar," he said. "Very well, Master Osprey, to the top we go, in your little birdcage."

An enormous pulley reeved with heavy chains was attached to the top of the crate. A strong breeze came from the square-shaped opening that had taken years to carve, running the entire height of the giant oak around which Raven's Nest was built. Taliesin had ridden the Ascender many times, though the normal route to the upper branches was the winding staircase built around the trunk of the giant tree, now partially removed after the Wolf Clan attack. Intrigued, Secretary Glabbrio eagerly entered the crate and held onto the railing as Osprey, Grudge, and Taliesin followed.

"Do the honors, Captain Grudge," Osprey ordered as soon as he closed the gate.

Grudge pressed a wooden lever, and the large crate gave a hard shake and groaned as it rose at a steady rate until it came to a jarring halt. During the few minutes in which they ascended one hundred feet, the envoy had turned pale, and the knuckles of his hands holding the railing appeared bright red. Osprey opened the gate and walked onto a large roofed platform attached to a massive branch. Two other railed platforms, leading to a network of buildings built among the leaves, forked out to either side. Guardhouses could be seen at the ends of several branches where the Black Wings had a bird's eye view of the area below.

"I assure you, Glabbrio, it's quite safe," Osprey said. He took the envoy by the arm and guided him along a walkway and into a room with a spectacular view of the distant mountains.

Cushioned chairs were placed around a wicker table set with a decanter of red wine, glasses, a plate filled with several varieties of cheese, a bowl of cracked walnuts, and a tray of salted crackers. A male servant stood in the corner, ready to serve. The chatter of women and children could be heard, along with the music from a lute, fading in and out as the breeze rustled through the leaves. Osprey pointed to a large chair for Glabbrio and waited until the envoy was comfortable before he took a seat across from him.

"You have many guards stationed up here," Glabbrio said, sounding impressed. He nodded as he took a glass of wine from the servant. "But you and I are realists, Osprey. There are not enough Black Wings to defend Raven's Nest against the Wolf Pack. We encountered quite a few on the road, but none were bold enough to approach my caravan."

"They came for the sword," Osprey said, "and for Taliesin."

"Lykus' desire to obtain magical weapons is known to Lord Arundel, and that is why he sent me here for *Doomsayer*." Glabbrio smiled petulantly. "But as your Captain said, it's only a gold sword. As for Taliesin, I am aware the Wolf Clan believes she is a witch, for those rumors have been around as long as she has lived with you. Of course, Lord Arundel does not believe these wild rumors. Still, we must be cautious, Osprey, and that is why I have come to ask you to accompany me to Eagle's Cliff."

Osprey leaned forward. "Then it is true," he said. "The clans are picking sides in this civil war. Why now, Glabbrio? The dukes have always warred against one another, and the princes frequently rebel against the king. Are Almaric's chances of winning that strong?"

"Indeed," Glabbrio said. He paused to place crackers on his plate and selected three slices of different-flavored cheese, smacking loudly as he ate and talked at the same time. "We find ourselves in a serious situation, old friend. While Lord Arundel is reluctant to involve you in affairs of the state, this time it cannot be avoided. Your clan resides in Maldavia, and the royal city will soon be under siege by Duke Peergynt's and Prince Almaric's army, which means it is too dangerous for you to remain here. Lord Arundel thinks it best if you, your wife, and your children came to Eagle's Cliff to remain for the duration of the war. We have been advised the Wolf Pack intends to destroy Raven's Nest and your entire clan. Peergynt wants you out, and the Wolf Pack will get the job done."

"Thank you for the generous offer. Of course, we'll come with you," Osprey said. "But I would like to know why your clan left behind the bodies of Duke Hrothgar and Lord Jasper Silverhand. Leaving their bodies has roused many questions, and I cannot help but wonder if this is merely a ruse to mislead the Wolfmen into thinking Lord Arundel favors Prince Almaric and his younger brother."

Taliesin felt her pride in Osprey grow. Osprey had rooted out the mushrooms of intrigue with his first attempt; the question clearly ruffled Glabbrio's composure.

"Troubling news that reached me while I was in Burnlak prevented me from attending the Gathering," Glabbrio said. "A local farmer was hired to collect the noblemen's bodies and return them to Fregia, while I have spent the last few days trying to locate Lord Arundel's son."

He took a sip of wine, aware he held a captive audience. "Master Xander intended to go to the Gathering and rode ahead. However, when he failed to meet me in Burnlak, I immediately started inquiring, and now I suspect he is a prisoner of the Wolf Clan. Lord Arundel is too busy helping gather a royal army and has asked the Raven Clan for assistance."

"What can we do for Lord Arundel?" Osprey asked, looking rather pleased with the turn of events.

"My Lord has asked that you send the Black Wings to Wolf's Den in search of the boy. It will be dangerous, but quite necessary. In exchange, Lord Arundel offers sanctuary for you and your family."

Taliesin's mouth fell open. Grudge shook his head at her, and she remained silent.

"This is a great deal to ask, Glabbrio," Osprey said. "Lord Arundel honors me by asking the Black Wings to rescue his son. Rest assured, the Black Wings will find his son and the Raven Clan will gladly support King Frederick. Of course, my entire clan must be given sanctuary, not just a select few, for this will mean open war with the Wolf Clan."

The secretary eyed Osprey as he licked each finger. He selected a date and popped it into his mouth with a belch. "A pity you did not find *Doomsayer*," he said. "I realize magic is outlawed by royal decree; however, if we hope to defeat Almaric and Peergynt, such a magic sword would be an invaluable asset. The King's enemies are growing in number. Though the king does not approve of magic, Lord Arundel is desperate to see him remain on the throne. Of course, since your daughter has a knack for finding valuable weapons, it's only logical the Wolf Clan believes she is a witch. Chief Lykus is as anxious to find magical weapons as is Lord Arundel, but we cannot allow that to happen."

Another date was selected by the fat envoy. Taliesin noticed Glabbrio chewed sparingly and practically swallowed the fruit whole. She was tempted to tell Osprey and the envoy the truth about *Doomsayer*, but Grudge had his eyes on her, and as if he could read her thoughts, gave a shake of his head. The royal flag was no longer important, which was a relief, but Taliesin had a feeling Glabbrio's men at the Gathering had been looking for the scroll. Master Xander could have arrived at the onset of the battle with that goal in mind, but the Wolfmen had abducted him before he could acquire it. Grudge certainly wasn't mentioning it, and she likewise remained silent.

"No, we cannot," Osprey said. "Captain Grudge, you will handpick a rescue team and leave at once. If Master Xander was captured, he might still be in route. There is a very good chance you will find him on the road and be able to join us in Erindor."

"I'll leave as soon as I see you packed and on the road." Grudge didn't sound pleased. "Of course, men will have to remain behind to give the impression Raven's Nest has not been entirely abandoned. You'll have to travel light, Master Osprey. All the spoils of war will have to be left behind, along with the barn animals. This war will not be over in a few days or weeks. It could last a year or more, and it's doubtful Raven's Nest will survive the duration."

"I will not leave behind one goose or gold coin," Osprey said, unnerved. "But I do agree a few men should remain behind and keep the torches lit."

"I realize the imposition placed upon your clan," Glabbrio said, holding up his sticky hands. "My allegiance is to Lord Arundel, but my affection for you, Master Osprey, is long abiding. We have been friends all our lives. If you want to take your goose, Osprey, then take him, and your dogs and goats and sheep." He wiped his fingers across the front of his robes. "It will not be a pleasant journey, in any case. The Wolf Pack will be on our heels the entire way."

A raven fluttering its large wings appeared from out of nowhere and, without pausing, grabbed the nut from Osprey's fingers and flew off. Three more ravens appeared on the railing in front of Taliesin and, remaining silent, eyed the bowl of nuts, which Osprey set upon the ground. The black birds hopped onto the floor and rushed toward the food, pushing each other out of the way to be the first to reach the prize. Glabbrio ignored them and continued eating cheese and crackers.

"I don't like the idea of leaving Raven's Nest," Taliesin said. "A whole year? How will our clan make a living if we're hiding at Eagle's Cliff?"

"Oh, you're not coming with us," replied Glabbrio. "Our duty is to the King, first, and it is imperative I bring Master Osprey to Eagle's Cliff. Your clan will be instrumental in helping us collect weapons from the battlefields, as always, but *you* are wanted by the Wolf Clan. Do not think me a heartless man; I like it no more than any of you, but if we are to reach Eagle's Cliff unmolested, then a decoy is necessary."

"A *decoy*? I'm to be a *decoy*?" Taliesin was horrified. "Am I to stay here then, or am I to leave with Captain Grudge?"

"Someone has to be a decoy, my dear," Glabbrio said. "War has not been openly declared; not yet, but time is of the essence. Your father and I must reach Eagle's Cliff. What greater sacrifice could you make to protect your clan than remaining here?"

"She can't stay here," Osprey said. "The Wolfmen will burn Raven's Nest if they think she is hiding here. Am I to send her off into the wilderness alone? You've already requested my Captain seek Lord Arundel's boy at the very place that harbors our enemy. I cannot send Taliesin into the unknown. There must be another way."

"Then what is it?" Glabbrio said, annoyed. "Tell me. I'm open to reason."

Osprey shook his head. "I don't know," he said. "We could send guards in every direction, carrying one of her garments, and lead the Wolf Clan on a wild goose chase. Taliesin must go into hiding. She will need a guard. Perhaps young Rook should go with her; he is a clever boy and can take her somewhere safe to hide until this blows over."

"A sound plan," Glabbrio said. "Make your campfires large tonight to give the impression Raven's Nest is still occupied and the girl still here. But do not send her into hiding, Master Osprey. Taliesin should keep on the move, so the Wolf Pack gives chase."

Grudge rose from his seat, his brown eyes shimmering with anger. "It won't take Wolfgar long to figure out the four guards are decoys, and he'll be on Taliesin's tail in no time," he said. "Better she comes with me than end up dead."

"Absolutely not!" Glabbrio slammed his hands onto the table. "Find Master Xander! That's your job! Taking this witch-girl along will only complicate things. Let her ride with the old farmer hired to take the two dead Fregian lords home. Stroud knows, no one will smell her among the dead."

Taliesin thought of the day she'd found *Traeden*, winning Lord Arundel's favor and securing her position as a woman of property among the Raven Clan. After so many years collecting weapons, her life suddenly had no value to the Eagle Clan. Feeling sick to her stomach, Taliesin stood, walked to the railing, and gazed at the tiny figures below in the courtyard, busy packing wagons. The man serving wine had apparently told the clan they were going to Erindor. On the other side of Raven's Nest, outside the wall, she spotted black smoke from the funeral pyre for the dead Wolfmen. There were no vultures in the sky as if they knew to avoid Raven's Nest, and no birds sang in the trees. Apart from the four pet ravens Osprey fed, no birds were roosting in the branches. It was an ill omen.

Osprey clasped his hands together and leaned forward. "Do we know where Prince Sertorius has gone? Is it safe for us to be on the road? Going to the royal city of Padama seems like the logical place for us; the journey is only sixty miles and, once there, we will be protected by the King's army."

"Peergynt's castle stands between Padama and us," Grudge replied. He filled his wine glass and grumbled as he took large sips.

"From what I understand of the princes," Glabbrio said, not missing a beat, "each is vying for his father's throne, and each has his own supporters among the noblemen. The Eagle Clan may curry favor with the princes, and we may ransom this lord and that duke, but Lord Arundel, as well as every member of the Eagle clan, loves our king. All would give our lives to support him, but we do not condone the methods of any of the princes. Almaric sold his brother Galinn to the northern tribes, leaving Dinadan, Konall, and Sertorius nipping at their father's heels. From what I hear, Galinn is a slave of Lord Talas Kull. As for Prince Sertorius, he disappeared a day ago, but we believe he is headed toward Garridan to solicit the help of Duke Richelieu on behalf of Almaric. Our spies are looking for him, fear not."

"Taliesin," Osprey said, turning. "Tell Minerva to start packing for the journey to Erindor. Captain Grudge, you will arrange for Taliesin's departure. I will see you both before the clan departs."

"As you will," Grudge said.

With nothing further to say, Osprey dismissed them with a wave of his hand. Taliesin was far too angry and upset to speak any pleasantries and left with Grudge. Osprey said he'd see her off, but something told her she'd never see him again. She entered the Ascender and let Grudge close the gate. As the crate descended, she allowed an impulse to override her usual calm, and, throwing her arms around Grudge's hard body, she pressed her face against his back.

"I can't believe this is happening," Taliesin said. "Glabbrio might as well put me in a sack and hand me over to the Wolf Clan. Rook won't leave Raven's Nest without Wren, and she won't part from Hawk. The only person I can rely on is you. Please, let me come with you, Grudge. I won't survive on my own."

Grudge snorted. "That pompous ass wants the scroll, just like Wolfgar, but didn't have the balls to admit it," he said. "I'm sure that is what the Eagles were looking for on the battlefield. We should be going south with the clan. King Frederick will rely on Lord Arundel and the Duke of Erindor to gather an army and defend Padama. The last thing I want to do is go after Arundel's wayward son."

Taliesin felt Grudge's hands caress her arms. He turned to embrace her, and in the next second, he was kissing her. His lips were firm, and his tongue tasted of wine as it entwined with hers. A shiver went through her body as she clung to his shoulders, kissing him passionately. For a moment she wondered if he'd stop their descent, but he did not. When they reached the ground, he drew away, leaving her holding onto the railing for support, and opened the gate.

"Is that it?" Taliesin questioned as they walked out of the crate. "You go on this mission and leave me to fend for myself?"

Grudge walked with her to the door. "I have no intention of going to Scrydon after Master Xander," he said. "But I must select a new commander for the Black Wings and see that the clan is ready to leave before night falls. Hawk is coming with us."

"Thank you," Taliesin said. "I knew I could depend on you."

"I like this change in your attitude," he replied, laughing. "I'll select four guards to act as decoys. Hillary can provide them with a piece of your clothing. Go find Rook and tell him what's happened. As soon as it's dark, I'll come for you."

Taliesin watched the tall man open the door. He marched across the hall and bellowed at the few guards seated at the table with the Eagle legionnaires to join him outside. She headed straight to the kitchen, told Mrs. Caldwell to find Hillary, then grabbed a bag of green apples before going out the back door. Circling Raven's Nest, Taliesin went through the garden, taking a quiet stone path to reach the stables, where four grooms were putting bridles and saddles on the horses. The Ravens had 20 wagons pulled by horses and a number of smaller carts pulled by mules. Minerva had been notified they were leaving and had made certain everyone in the village loaded their meager belongings into the wagons.

Rook was inside the stable grooming Hawk's white stallion with a soft brush. Wren sat on a bale of hay repairing a broken bridle, and she looked up as Taliesin entered. The grooms returned and walked straight to where Taliesin's eight horses were stabled. Wren softly whistled and stood, putting aside the bridle.

"It's about time you showed up," Wren said, sounding irritated. "I told Crane and his buddies Thalagar belongs to you, but they're planning on stealing him. Isn't that right, Crane? Isn't that what you just told me?"

Taliesin hurried to Thalagar's stall and placed the sack of apples over a hook as the black stallion snorted and walked toward her. "Is this true, Crane?" she asked, turning to face the grooms. "You know Thalagar is mine. So are the horses in these four paddocks. You're not taking them. They belong to me!"

"I'm not walking to Erindor," Crane said. He was fifteen years old and large for his age. His hair was the color of straw, and his nose had been broken from brawling. Crane was a notorious bully, and he clenched ham-sized fists as his three friends stood behind him. They were gawky boys with pimples and dirty faces. Crane, Toad, Buzzard, and Drake were sons of Black Wing guards, and like most boys their age, acted as if they were entitled to take whatever they wanted. Taliesin wasn't about to let them take her property, and she glared at their ringleader.

"If I were going to Eagle's Cliff, I might let you borrow a horse, but I'm going elsewhere. Rook, Wren, Hawk, and Grudge are coming with me, and we'll need horses," Taliesin said. The four boys weren't as tall as she was, but they were heavier and meaner. Her rank didn't impress them; they only saw a woman standing in their way. "Buzzard, don't you dare open that latch. I'm warning you. These horses belong to me, and I'm not parting with a single one."

Drake reached for a nearby rake. Lanky brown hair fell into his gaunt face as he spun around and lifted the item like a sword. "The Raven Mistress is getting too big for her britches," he said in a threatening manner.

"Needs to be taken down a peg," Crane agreed. He cracked his knuckles. "Boys?"

Wren and Rook walked over as Thalagar snorted and pawed the ground in his paddock. A blush appeared on Crane's face as Rook motioned for him to stand aside. Crane nodded at his companions. Drake swung the rake at Taliesin as Toad, a fat boy with red curls, lifted a riding crop he'd been hiding behind his back. Toad went for Wren while Buzzard and Crane ran toward Rook. Taliesin ducked under the rake, punched Drake in the stomach, and knocked him to the ground.

With an angry cry, Rook threw the brush at Crane's head, knocking him backward in a daze, and then caught Toad before he reached Wren. Buzzard came to Toad's aid, and the two boys scuffled with their larger adversary. Rook knocked Buzzard into a pile of dung, where he held a hand over his broken nose. Toad received a right hook to the jaw and fell to the ground. Sniffling, Toad jumped to his feet and ran for the door. Rook picked up the rake and shook it in the air. A mad scramble ensued as the other three boys, chased by Rook, dashed out after Toad. Wren and Taliesin stood together and watched the door, laughing, until Rook returned.

"Thank you," Taliesin said, out of breath. "I suppose you heard what I said about us not going to Eagle's Cliff with the clan." The girl nodded. "The Wolfmen have made it impossible for me to go with the clan. I have to go into hiding and Osprey wants Rook to accompany me, but I know he won't leave without you or Hawk. Grudge said he'd come with us. Will you go with us, Wren?"

"Go where? If the Wolfmen are hunting you, I'd rather go to Eagle's Cliff. You best give Thalagar an apple. He's upset. I'll ask Rook what he wants to do."

Turning to Thalagar, Taliesin gave a whistle, and he trotted to her. She took an apple out of the bag and held it out to the big black stallion. He sniffed her hand, nostrils flaring as he breathed in her scent, and took the fruit. Thalagar was every bit as impressive as the white horse Rook was grooming, though considerably smaller. Thalagar was an Andorran, from the desert of Garridan, known for speed and endurance, while the white horse was a Morgenstern. Taliesin also owned a Morgenstern, a horse for a knight, and intended to let Grudge ride it. She glanced at Rook and saw he was watching her.

"I'm not sure where we'll go," Taliesin said. "Grudge and Hawk will come up with a plan. You will come with me, won't you, Rook?"

Wren used sign language to speak with Rook, and at his nod let out a heavy sigh. "Rook will follow Osprey's order and come with you," Wren said. "I guess that means I have to go, too. But I'm picking the horse I will ride."

Taliesin smiled as the girl walked to the horses. Wren favored a white mare with a black patch on her nose and black forelocks and gave the horse an apple. Rook put aside his currycomb and walked to Taliesin. He moved his hands, speaking to her in sign, but she didn't understand, for she'd never learned the language of the deaf and mute. When she shook her head, he gave an exasperated sigh and turned toward Wren.

"Rook wants to thank you for the silver spear," Wren said. "He believes it's our duty to keep the Raven Master's favorite daughter safe from harm." The girl's tone sounded less than sincere. "He also thinks you should give four horses to Crane.

Hawk will keep the white stallion, and we can use a mule to carry our gear."

"Rook said all that?" Taliesin laughed. Her intent was misconstrued, and Wren took immediate offense.

"If you desire to understand the art of sign language," Wren said, "then take the time to learn, Raven Mistress."

"That is not my title," Taliesin said, disliking the girl's impertinence. "Tell Rook I appreciate his help. Please ask him to give Crane the four brown horses. I'd appreciate you both staying here until the clan heads out; I don't want anyone else to try to steal my horses. We'll leave when it's dark. Take only a change of clothes and a few necessities. I'll provide weapons and money because I know you don't have any."

Wren nodded. "Please ask Hillary to pack us a few of those raisin scones." She sounded meek when she wanted something, Taliesin noted. "They are my favorites...."

Making a mental list of supplies, Taliesin took the same path through the garden and entered the kitchen to find the house staff busy packing for their long journey. Mrs. Caldwell came over, and Taliesin procured enough food for fifteen days; the typical amount carried by the Black Wings. She also secured a bag of raisin scones for Wren. Taliesin hugged Mrs. Caldwell, moved by the older woman's tears.

"Take care, Mrs. Caldwell. I shall miss you."

"And I you, dear child." The woman turned to wipe away a tear.

Taliesin said her farewells to the house staff and went in search of Hillary. The kitchen master stood outside the hall doors with six lads and handed out rations to the families leaving Raven's Nest. When Hillary saw her, he came over, tears in his eyes, and hugged her.

"I gave four of your best dresses to the riders," Hillary said, sniffing. "Things didn't turn out quite as I imagined. I'm sorry you won't be going with us, Taliesin. You've grown into a fine young woman. I'm very proud of you." He set her down. "I still remember the day you first came to Raven's Nest, a frightened little thing hiding in Osprey's wagon. The only way I could convince you to come inside was to bribe you with a sugared pastry. Back then you had scabs on your knees, freckles on your nose, and a nasty habit of biting people when you didn't get your way."

"And I remember how you spoiled me," Taliesin said. "I'm surprised my teeth didn't rot out of my head with the treats you gave me. You and Captain Leech were my best friends. He taught me to ride and how to fight with a sword, but you were the one who tucked me in at night and told me bedtime stories." She wiped a tear off his cheek. "My favorite stories were about the Red Bandit of Scrydon and the Assassins Guild. I used to daydream about the Red Bandit, and how he snuck into Tantalon Castle through a secret tunnel to steal the King's crown, and his many adventures trying to avoid being caught by the guild."

Hillary laughed. "Tried and succeeded, for I am still alive, my dear."

"*You*? *You are the Red Bandit*?" Taliesin started laughing when the old man nodded and tried to imagine Hillary as a younger man climbing over castle walls, running across rooftops, and fighting off assassins. Mrs. Caldwell certainly found him a romantic figure, and despite the wrinkles and sagging gut, she still saw a twinkle in his eyes. "It's no wonder I was never able to fool you when I raided the kitchen pantry for a few treats. You always knew it was me the next morning."

"Sugar on your pillow attracted ants, my dear," Hillary said. "I'm thicker than I used to be, and I've lost the red mask, but not the memories." His expression turned dour as he placed his gnarled hand upon her shoulder. "Minerva has been up in your room all afternoon, helping herself to whatever she wants. I tried to stop her, but that dagger of hers is deadly; I barely made it out with my guts intact." He gave her a wink. "But she didn't find that certain something you hid in the suit of armor, which I know nothing about of course. It's still there."

"I'm going to miss you most of all, Hillary. I wish I were coming with you. But I'll never forget the tales of the Red

Bandit or your sugary treats." Taliesin kissed the old man on the cheek. "You never told me what happened to the King's crown? What did you do with it?"

Hillary chuckled. "Sold it for less than it was worth, but Frederick had another made," he said. "Now go up to your room and pack your things. I'll make sure you have enough green apples to take with you; I know how much Thalagar loves them." He turned away and started passing out bundles of food, but he seemed happier in his task. Taliesin no longer would ever think of him the same—Hillary would always be the Red Bandit, the notorious thief who became a Raven cook to avoid a blade in his back.

* * * * *

Chapter Eight

The Black Wings and Eagle legionnaires were already on the road. The envoy's carriage and a line of wagons formed a procession through the main gate. The children were loaded into wagons, and the women walked behind. The older boys, assisted by Falstaff, herded sheep, pigs, and cattle behind the wagons. Crane and his three companions, each with a girl, rode the four brown horses. Mrs. Caldwell sat with Hillary on the seat of a wagon and drove the team. A loud squawk from Osprey's pet goose made Taliesin smile as she spotted the bird seated in a wagon Minerva was driving. The twins, Falcon and Talon, were seated beside several girls the goose kept biting. Osprey never came to say farewell, and Taliesin had avoided Minerva, but upon seeing the old crone leaving Raven's Nest, she had felt a lump form in her throat.

Taliesin watched from a window as an officer in a black cloak and winged helmet stood up on his horse. The last to leave, Quail, a veteran Black Wing, gave a fierce cry, put his heels to his horse, and galloped out of the gate. The guards ran forward to close the gate, and she turned away from the window.

"May we come in?"

Grudge stood at the open door to her bedroom, wearing a long black cape and carrying a single bag over his shoulder. Hawk pushed his way into the room from behind Grudge. He glanced at her bed where she'd laid out the best weapons she'd collected over a lifetime and walked over to select what he wanted. The rising moonlight coming through the window reflected in his dark eyes.

Hawk picked up a dagger. "Mind if I take this?"

"Take whatever you want." Taliesin turned to Grudge. "Quail is a good man. I'm glad he'll look after the Clan in your absence. What did you tell my father?"

"I told Osprey I was taking Hawk and two more men with me to Wolf's Den. Ten men volunteered to remain and defend Raven's Nest. The horses are already saddled, and the mule is packed. Rook and Wren are gathering more supplies. Are you ready to leave?"

"Just about," she said. "Where are we going?"

"We'll be traveling north," he said. "I have friends in Fregia who will provide shelter. The moon will be high tonight. As long as we keep to the trees and off the road, we should be able to slip past the Wolf Pack."

"But isn't that where Prince Sertorius is headed? Will it be safe?" Taliesin fastened on her Mandrake sword and put on her black cloak, fastening the brooch before picking up her saddlebags. One more bag lay on the floor.

"Safe enough," Grudge said.

Hawk helped himself to a quiver of javelins. A frown hung heavy upon his handsome face. "I know Wren doesn't appear to be able to throw one," he said, "but she has a good aim. I taught her myself."

"Take whatever you think Rook and Wren will need." Taliesin went to her desk and pointed at five leather pouches. "Each of you gets a bag of coins and gems," she said. "Hopefully, we won't become separated on the road, but we should be prepared for anything. I packed Sertorius' flag just in case we're stopped and need to show it to get by Peergynt's men."

Handing three bags to Hawk, she gave another to Grudge and tucked one for herself into a pocket of her leather jacket. The scroll sat inside a leather pouch hanging on her sword belt. She picked her bedroll off the bed and returned to stand by the bag on the floor, turning to look around the room, trying to think of what else was needed.

"I don't suppose Osprey came to see you off," Hawk said. She shook her head. "You know he is fond of you, Taliesin, but he's also superstitious. Saying farewell would be too permanent for him." He grabbed a longbow and a quiver of yellow-feathered arrows; he had what he wanted and went to stand by the door. His cutlasses were on either hip, and he wore a long cloak that touched the floor.

"Hold up," Grudge said, with a rumble. He gazed at the weapons on the bed. "You have a very nice selection here, Taliesin." He selected a double-edged battle-ax with a handle covered in leather and silver studs, a hunting knife in an ornate sheath, and a smaller, short-handled knife that could be used for shaving a beard or slicing a Wolfman's throat. "I've always admired the weapons made by Marcus Gregor," he said. "Shame you have to leave so many of his weapons behind."

Taliesin pointed at small throwing ax with a handle covered in red leather that lay on the bed. "If you like Gregor, then you should have this, too," she said. "It belonged to a Knight of the Blue Star. I'm sorry to leave the rest. I thought about packing a few to sell, in case we need more money, but we'd be weighted down."

"We have enough, Taliesin," Grudge said, sliding the weapons into his bag. "I know you don't want to leave, but trust me, this is for the best. You've packed too much. What you have in your saddlebags will have to do. Leave that bag on the floor."

"It contains rations and raisin scones for Wren. I can't leave it behind."

Grudge picked up the bag and walked to the door. The finality of their departure formed a large lump in Taliesin's throat. Tears started to stream down her face as the two men headed along the hallway, and she turned her head aside, trying to hold back a sob, but it managed to slip out. She trudged behind them, leaving her door open and the candles burning.

"I've spent so much time wishing I could see the world," she said, her voice quavering. "Now that I'm able to do so, I don't want to leave. If I hadn't stolen those items from the battlefield, if I'd admitted the theft, then this might not have happened."

"For the love of Heggen," Grudge said. His loud voice echoed through the hallway. "There's no reason to cry. Cut it out." When she sobbed harder, he cleared his throat. "Hawk, say something to make her stop. I can't abide tears."

"Like what?" Hawk replied, glancing over his shoulder. "I feel the same way she does. Raven's Nest is my home."

"I don't know," Grudge said. "Just make her stop."

Hawk let Grudge pass him and waited for Taliesin. They walked along the hallway side-by-side; every door was open as if the occupants would return home soon. He nudged her with his elbow. The corners of his mouth lifted, and two dimples appeared in his cheeks. Taliesin noticed a thin scar in the shape of a crescent moon on his right cheek. He hadn't shaved, and the hair growth along his jaw reminded her of a fuzzy young chick. She stopped crying and wiped the tears away with the back of her hand.

"A few weeks ago, I met an old man on the road," Hawk said. "He told me about a magical place located in the Salayan Desert called the Cave of the Snake God. There, he said, lays the Raven Sword, hidden away all these centuries. I know you've always wanted to go in search of *Ringerike*; you've talked about it for ages, and I've just been waiting for the right moment to tell you about it. Now is that time."

Taliesin felt her heart skip a beat; she'd dreamed of finding *Ringerike*. Mandrake had told her the legend of King Korax. The first and only king of the Raven Clan, he had been defeated in battle by the treacherous Tarquin Draconus, a northern barbarian from Skarda. As Korax lay dying, Tarquin took up *Ringerike* and was pronounced king of Caladonia. His rule was short and ended with his premature death, and the magical sword vanished from history.

"I cannot deny the thought of finding *Ringerike* hasn't crossed my mind countless times," Taliesin said. "But who was this man, Hawk? How can you trust him? Did he give you a map?"

"He drew one for me; not a very good one, and I know it's a hard journey, but *Ringerike* is said to be the most powerful magical sword ever forged. When we find *Ringerike*, we can give it to Lord Arundel and restore our clan's honor," Hawk said. "We find that sword and all our fortunes will change overnight." Grudge kept walking, not saying a word about Hawk's plan, but Taliesin was excited.

Shadows moved along the corridor, creeping in and out of the doorways and followed them down the stairs into Raven's Hall. It was deathly quiet in the large chamber. The long tables were cluttered with dirty plates and platters of uneaten food. Expensive tapestries had been taken off the walls, and the large fireplace held only smoldering embers. The kitchen door lay open, and a few rats scurried across the floor and vanished inside. Hawk handed Taliesin a glass of wine and took one for himself. Grudge turned and joined them. All three raised their glasses, tapped them together, then drank the contents in one gulp. The large man slammed his glass onto the table.

"Many have gone in search of the Raven Sword," Grudge said. "None returned. We're going to Fregia, not Garridan, and that's the end of it."

"But they weren't as clever as the three of us." Hawk's mood had changed, and he appeared almost giddy as they walked toward the main doors that lay wide open. "Magic is exactly what we need if we're going to help defeat the Wolf Clan and put Prince Sertorius and his older brother in the grave," he said. "We're Royalists, aren't we? We've sided with King Frederick, right? So, let's find the one magical sword that can defeat the King's enemies."

"*Doomsayer* won't help the King," Grudge said. "Nor will magic save his throne."

"*Ringerike* can," Hawk said. "My map is a poor one, I admit, but you've been to the desert before. I know you can get us there, Grudge. Look, Taliesin has stopped crying. She wants to go. Make us both happy and say 'yes.'"

With a loud growl, Grudge marched out the door. Taliesin hurried to catch up and stopped him on the porch. Five horses and a mule were tied to posts in the courtyard. Hawk walked around the two of them and headed toward the horses, but he had an odd look on his face. There were no guards in sight. The torches were lit around the wall, but it was dark on the platforms high in the ancient oak. A light wind blew past, and the scent of flowers remained thick in the air. Taliesin gazed up at the sky. The moon sat high, and the stars sparkled like diamonds in the dark sky.

"I made *Doomsayer* speak," Taliesin said. "Maybe I do have a little magic in me. I believe I can awaken the powers in *Ringerike*. It's the one sword I've always wanted, Grudge. The one prize that's always been out of reach. What's the harm in going to Garridan? I know the prince is headed in that direction, but we can be careful and stay off the main roads."

"It's not a good idea," Grudge replied. "The risk is too great."

"Of course, you'd say that," she said. "You're afraid!"

Annoyed with Grudge, Taliesin headed to Thalagar, placed the saddlebags over the stallion's rump, and tied them to the saddle. When she was a child, Mandrake had often told her the story of King Korax to help her fall asleep. "*Ringerike* is the greatest of magical swords because it was the first one made by the gods themselves," he had told her. "It is made of silver, with a gold hilt, and dragons on the crossguard. It is said to be so beautiful that, once unsheathed, people are held transfixed."

Grudge looked at her. He stood beside the big bay, Kordive, and tossed the bag of food over the horse's rump. Rook and Wren had yet to appear. Hawk was loading his weapons onto the white stallion, but she knew he was listening and counting on her to convince Grudge the quest was a worthy one.

"I know all about the Raven Sword," Grudge said, his tone sour. "You asked me to protect you, Taliesin, and that's what I intend on doing. We go north where I have friends."

"Please, Grudge," she said. "It means the world to me. I'm the one who has placed our clan in danger. If I can do this and find *Ringerike*, I can make amends for everything."

"I agree," Hawk said, coming to stand beside Grudge. "Imagine what Taliesin could do with *Ringerike* in her hands. Better still; imagine the money we will make selling it to the Eagle Clan, and how much prestige Master Osprey will receive. The clan can return home, and Osprey will probably be made a lord."

"I have been to the Salayan Desert," Grudge said. "It's a dangerous place. If the nomads don't kill us, the sandworms will."

Hawk jiggled the bag of coins fastened to his sword belt. "Hear that?" he said. "That's the sound I live to hear. It means money. Trust me. Someone will pay a high price for a sword that cuts through steel, cannot be broken, and enables its owner to fly. For all we know, it can do many more things. Why don't I find Rook and Wren, and we can take a vote?" Before anyone could say anything to the contrary, he ran to Raven's Hall.

"Magic is nothing to trifle with, Taliesin," Grudge said. "A sword that talks to the dead is one thing. *Ringerike* is a king maker and a king killer." He climbed onto the Morgenstern stallion. Kordive snorted and flipped his black tail as Grudge hung the double-edged ax from the saddle horn. "We're in the dead business. It's not for us to go in search of magical weapons. Nothing you can say will change my mind."

"I'll sleep with you if you agree to take us there," she said.

Grudge glared at her. As her words sunk in, his expression changed. "Well, that changes things," he said. "Does it mean that much to you?" She nodded with enthusiasm. "I won't hold you to this bargain, but if you want to go after *Ringerike,* I'll take you there. Just remember this was your idea. Not mine."

Taliesin untied the reins from the post and climbed into the saddle, thrilled they were going after *Ringerike* to restore the Raven Clan's former glory. Thalagar gave a snort, and she patted his neck. Hawk led Rook and Wren from Raven's Hall. They wore black cloaks with the emblem of the Raven Clan removed from the left shoulder and carried one bag each.

Wren went to the little white mare, and Rook climbed onto a piebald gelding and fastened the silver Erindor spear to his saddle. He looked over at Taliesin and smiled.

"We're going after *Ringerike*," Taliesin said.

Hawk laughed as he climbed into the saddle. The group rode across the courtyard and through a back gate. A guard appeared and shut it behind them. Taliesin refused to look around or say farewell, but as the tall trees closed around them, she had the feeling she'd never see home again.

* * * * *

Chapter Nine

A morning fog lay thick on the forest floor. Since she was the most acquainted with the landmarks, Taliesin led the group through the Tannenberg Forest, marking them in turn as she passed — tall spruces with curious white needles, an oak so twisted and gnarled it appeared like a crippled giant in the fog, an ancient temple covered by moss with only the spiral visible. A grove of ash with golden leaves meant they were ten miles from where the forest ended and opened into thick grasslands on the western border of Maldavia. They'd covered thirty miles during the night, stopping only twice as they picked their way through the trees. Avoiding deadfalls and gorges, Taliesin listened for the trickling of water in Downy Creek. The moment she heard the stream, she held up her arm and turned to see her friends coming up behind her, the fog lapping at the legs of their horses.

"We're stopping," Taliesin said, keeping her voice low. "Take a break."

She slid out of the saddle and led Thalagar to the stream. The horse dipped his head to drink, stomping his front hoof against the soft muddy ground. Wren, wrapped in her cloak, appeared at Taliesin's side and pointed toward the bushes, in desperate need of relieving herself.

"I can't go by myself," Wren said. "Come with me."

Rook came over and took the reins of their horses, and the two women walked a short distance and paused behind a tree to urinate. Neither said a word as they lowered their pants and squatted, fog covering them as they did their business. Overhead, a woodpecker knocked its beak against a tree limb. A warm stream trickled between Taliesin's feet and created a steady rivulet in the dirt. She noticed a green beetle caught in the swirl of piss and watched it wash away before glancing at the girl to her side.

"Hawk likes you," Wren said, eyeing Taliesin shyly. "Ever since we were little, I've always been able to tell when he's keeping a secret. I think my brother has liked you since the first day we arrived at Raven's Nest. But you're with Grudge, aren't you?"

"Huh?" Taliesin said, grabbing a leaf to wipe dry. She pulled up her pants and fastened her sword belt around her waist. "Hawk is your brother? I thought you were sleeping with those two boys."

Wren gasped. "You made me piss on my boot," she said, angrily. She finished her business and jerked up her pants without wiping. "Is that what everyone thinks? That I am sleeping with Rook and Hawk? I'm only sixteen years old. I haven't even done that...yet. How could you think that about me?"

"You can't blame people for getting the wrong idea, Wren. The three of you are always together. No one knew Hawk was your crib brother; you don't look a thing alike. Not even Osprey suspects you are kin, and he knows practically everything about everybody."

"Hawk is my half-brother," Wren said, defensively. She pulled the hood of her cloak over her head. "He takes after our father, but we have the same eyes. I cannot believe no one noticed. Rook and Hawk are blood brothers. Rook's not my lover. He's like a brother to me."

Taliesin tried not to laugh when Wren gave her a hateful look. "Don't be mad at me," she said. "It's not my fault everyone imagined you three were humping like bunnies at night. You did share a room." She headed around the tree and turned when she noticed Wren didn't follow. "Anyway, I do happen to like Grudge."

"You're mean, that's what you are." Wren came around the tree, fog swirling about her legs, and looked extremely upset. "Hawk has only had nice things to say about you. Rook idolizes you, and to think I seriously thought your gift to Rook was out of friendship, and here you've been laughing at us the whole time." She wiped a tear from her pale cheek. "I'm going to tell Hawk what you said. I'm sure he won't care a fig about you when I tell him."

"You can go suck eggs, for all I care," Taliesin said.

The girl stomped off, returning to the group. Wren didn't get far before she let out a piercing scream. Taliesin ran toward the sound, sword drawn, and glanced at Wren who pointed at the fog. Kneeling, Taliesin waved the vapor aside and spotted a long, black snake wiggling across the forest floor. Unable to contain her annoyance, Taliesin severed the snake's head and held it for Wren to see. It seemed a waste; the snake was simply doing what snakes do and not hurting anyone, but its death put Wren at ease.

"I stepped on it," Wren said, biting her bottom lip. "It has a black tail. It's venomous."

"For Navenna's sake." Taliesin rolled her eyes as she lifted the still-wiggling body higher. "That is a Blacktail Crawler, Wren. If it had a red spot on the end of its tail, then it would be a Red Tip, and yes, those are venomous. This one doesn't have a spot. It eats only mice, so calm down." She tossed the snake aside. "You really are a little lamb lost in the woods. It's no wonder Hawk and Rook have to keep their eyes on you. You're helpless."

Wren's cheeks turned bright pink. "I wish we'd gone to Eagle's Cliff and left you behind," she said, her voice growing louder. "We're only here because of you. You're the one who picked up that magical sword and talked to the dead. Maybe I don't know much about snakes, but I'm not the one who led our clan to ruin. That's on you, Raven Mistress." She bowed her head, rammed Taliesin out of the way, and marched to her horse.

"You nasty, little blue jay," Taliesin said. "If you feel that way, then why don't you and your shadows return to Raven's Nest?"

"Keep quiet," Grudge said. He ran over, carrying his battle-ax. "All this squawking will rouse the Wolfmen. What's this about?"

Taliesin shook her head, wanting to punch Wren as she started to cry as loudly as a baby. The girl scurried to Hawk and threw her arms around his neck. Wren carried on as if she'd been beaten. "I didn't do a damn thing to her," Taliesin said. "She blames me for the situation we're in. If she can't hack it, then bundle her up and send her home."

"I suggest you try harder to get along with her. If we're going to the Cave of the Snake God, we'll need Hawk's and Rook's help." Grudge walked beside Taliesin to the stream. The fog began to dissipate. She knelt and dipped her hands into the water. "I think it's time we looked at the scroll of yours. I want to see what you found."

Taliesin splashed water on her face and stood. "We have about thirty miles to go before we reach the grasslands," she said. "There's an inn where we can stay the night. We can look at the scroll then, and not before." She gave a nod in the direction they'd come. "The Wolfmen have been on our tail since we left Raven's Nest. We'd best get moving."

The forest grew still, and Taliesin placed her hand on the hilt of her sword. Grudge turned around, eyes narrowed, and peered into the fog that curled around the tree trunks. A strong odor of wet dog hung in the air. Somewhere in the forest, an owl hooted three times.

"Three times," Taliesin said. "It's a warning."

Grudge nodded. "Wolfmen scouts," he grumbled.

"Should we run or fight?" Taliesin asked. Her heart beat rapidly in her chest. She couldn't see anything in the dense fog, but she believed him.

"You've never fought a Wolfman before. Best let me handle it." Grudge glanced at their friends. "Get out of here. I'll join you soon enough."

Hurrying to her horse, Taliesin gave a soft whistle as she climbed into the saddle. Hawk, Wren, and Rook hastened to mount their horses and followed Taliesin. Kordive, left tied to a low tree branch, let out an angry neigh and stamped his hoof as they rode past. Taliesin clicked her tongue against the roof of her mouth, and Thalagar quickened his pace. As they cantered along the narrow path, she spotted a familiar tall birch tree with the initials of Black Wings carved in the trunk. Captain Leech's initials were right above her own, but he'd been the one to do that, not her. A soft growl caught her attention, and Taliesin glanced to her right to see dark forms running through the trees, but they weren't men in gray cloaks; five black wolves gave pursuit. She let out a whistle and bent low, branches passing over her head as Thalagar, sensing the danger, started to gallop.

Ahead, Taliesin saw something large and white dash out of the trees. A white stag appeared on the path, led the way through the trees, and then swerved to the right. The wolves snarled as they took after it.

"We need to get out of the woods," Hawk shouted behind her. "Keep going!"

Thalagar gave an angry snort and pulled hard to the right, fighting the reins as Taliesin's companions continued along the path. Her horse refused to obey her commands, and running with his head bowed, took after the wolves. Unable to control the stubborn horse, Taliesin was forced to hold on tight as Thalagar caught the last wolf in the pack. With a toss of his head, the horse knocked the beast off its feet, trampled it, and continued, eager to reach the next. The stag was nowhere to be seen, and, at the cries of pain from the wounded wolf, the pack separated, circling to the left and to the right.

"Enough of this," Taliesin shouted, but the horse refused to heed. She pulled on the reins as they reached a small clearing, but before she could draw her sword, a rush of large, furry bodies charged from every direction, snarling and growling.

Thalagar reared, flailing his front legs and sending Taliesin tumbling out of the saddle. As she scrambled to her knees, Thalagar swung around and stomped on a wolf, crushing it beneath his hooves. With a mouthful of dirt and blood, Taliesin rolled aside to avoid being trampled by Thalagar as he flattened another into a bloody pulp. A loud snort from the horse warned Taliesin of danger as a large wolf leaped through the air. The horse reacted swiftly, kicked out with its hind legs, and caught the wolf in the head. The beast flew through the air and slammed into a tree, breaking its spine. Taliesin climbed to her feet, wincing from bruised ribs, and drew her silver sword as the pack circled her and her horse.

Sucking air through her open mouth, she swung the silver sword as two wolves rushed her. Thalagar intervened and charged one wolf, while Taliesin struck, slicing into the side of the other. She heard a man-like cry as the wolf crashed to the ground at her feet. The remaining wolves regrouped and slinked into the trees and out of sight as Thalagar trotted to Taliesin, his reins dragging on the ground. She felt a stab of pain in her side as she reached for the saddle horn, intending to mount before the wolves attacked again.

"Hold still, boy. Let's see if I can mount."

Thalagar's tail whipped about and hit her face, knocking her aside. The horse spun around, pawed at the ground, and snorted. A loping figure in gray came around a large pine tree, followed by four Wolfmen dressed in pelts carrying tree trunks for weapons. Two wolves slunk behind them, panting hard and glaring at Taliesin with yellow eyes. As she pointed her sword at the Wolfmen, she saw the flattened wolf had turned into a naked man. Thalagar had trampled the creature flat, but its body was reshaping, healing, and he groaned as he rose to his knees.

"Demons!" Taliesin shouted. "Stay back! Death is all I have for you!"

There was no time to worry about Thalagar as she prepared to fight the closest man. He had a wicked scar across his cheek and carried the antlers of an elk. The antlers were sharp as daggers, and he raised his weapon high as he rushed her. Lifting her sword over her head, Taliesin used both hands to swing it in a wide arc and felt the blade sink into his shoulder. The man stumbled, his arm missing, and fell to the forest floor. The Wolfmen started snarling, and the two wolves responded with growls. Thalagar ran past the front of the group, and the two wolves took after him, leaving Taliesin to deal with the four Wolfmen. Their injured companion stood to the side, one hand to the stump of his arm, and searched for his weapon.

Taliesin swung her sword at a tall man wielding a tree limb. The man moved too close, and his chest split open. He dropped his weapon and sank to his knees. Before he could stand, she struck off his head and stepped around a log as the Wolfmen separated to surround her. One came around each side of the fallen tree, and the third started to climb over it. The fourth man, now recovered from being trampled, picked up a tree limb. She charged him, screaming as she attacked. Her sword arced through the air and missed as the Wolfman danced out of the way. His body seemed to shimmer, and the limb dropped as he transformed into something mixed between a man and a wolf.

Rising on its hind legs, the Wolfman towered over Taliesin, muzzle dripping saliva as it howled with rage. Taliesin kept her sword raised high, aware its three companions were also in the midst of morphing into things out of a nightmare; things that snarled and snapped with elongated muzzles, stood like men, but had the heads of monsters and showed no fear of her swinging sword.

"Navenna, help me," Taliesin cried out.

As the creatures advanced with claws raised, her prayer was answered as a large ax flew out of nowhere and slammed into a beast's head. Grudge, holding a sword, ran from the trees and attacked the Wolfmen from behind. All four turned on the captain.

Taliesin heard a growl and watched in horror as the Wolfman reattached its arm and then its head to its body. A decision had to be made and quickly; help Grudge or kill the reassembled monster? She rushed the freakish beast and pierced it through the heart. As she lifted her sword, the Wolfman toppled over, stone cold dead. She spun to face another wolf-thing lumbering behind her with gleaming yellow eyes. Its claws slashed through the air, barely missing her face as she plunged the sword into its stomach and sliced upwards, cleaving through the rib cage with ease, leaving its head dangling on exposed tendons. She hacked again and took off the head. As the body dropped, she stabbed it through the heart; it was the only way to be sure of killing the damn things.

Turning, she saw Thalagar returning with the two wolves on his heels. The horse ran toward her, turned when he reached her side, and kicked out with its hooves. A wolf, caught in the head, flew backward, while its companion raced toward Taliesin. She swung her sword side to side as the furry body leaped toward her. It received a slice across its abdomen and dropped to the ground. She stabbed it through the heart and turned as the wolf Thalagar had kicked jumped to its feet, sniffed the air, and glared at her with glowing eyes. Taliesin stepped in front of her horse and held her ground, horrified, as the wolf rose onto its hind legs, growing taller and more hideous by the second. Like the other Wolfmen, it turned into something between a wolf and man, and she heard it laughing. A scream rose in her throat as she raised her sword with both hands and charged the creature, too frightened to think, caught by an impulse to kill or be killed.

The sword sank into flesh and bones with no effort, as if the sword had magic, *real* magic. But the horror of what she had struck overwhelmed all other thoughts.

"What *are* you?" Taliesin shouted.

"I...am...*Wolfen!*"

The wounded beast dropped to its knees, its human voice still ringing in her ears. It howled, and voices in the fog joined in. It came rushing toward her on his hind legs, foam dripping from his opened jaws. Reason fled her mind, and she reacted on raw instinct and fear. With one mighty swing, she lopped off its furry head and then stabbed it through the heart. Blood splattered everywhere. Red on the trees. Red on the leaves. She hacked the beast into pieces, unaware of anything around her. Her sole desire was to cut the creature into pieces to make sure it *stayed* dead.

"Stop it, Taliesin! It's dead," Grudge shouted.

Taliesin let out a growl of her own as the sword was knocked out of her hand and flew through the air. For a moment, she glared at Grudge, barely aware he was human, or that he held an ax used to knock aside her blade. She took a step toward her sword and Grudge stepped in front of her, shaking his head.

"We've killed them all," he said. "Calm down! We're unharmed. You, our horses, and me. I'm not the enemy, Taliesin. It's me. Grudge! Your friend."

Her blind rage faded, leaving her exhausted, and she collapsed into a heap, sobs ripping through her body as she lifted blood-soaked hands into the air. A scream ripped out of her throat, and she sagged forward. The smell of death was thick in her nostrils. She trembled from head to toe. When she grew silent, the forest grew still, and she heard a loud snort. It was Thalagar. A whinny came from Kordive as he trotted to the black stallion. The horses were soaked with blood, and their saddles showed visible claw marks, but neither was injured. She drew in ragged breaths as Grudge calmly walked over to grab Kordive's reins. He also managed to grab Thalagar's reins and led the horses to her.

"Get on your feet and climb into the saddle," Grudge ordered in a firm voice. "We killed ten scouts, but more will follow. Many more. Now that you know what we are dealing with, Taliesin, it's still not too late to change your mind about going after *Ringerike*. I'm sure Prince Sertorius and Captain Wolfgar are each going after the sword. When we catch up with your friends, be sensible and convince them to come with me to Fregia."

Taliesin stood up, walked to her sword, picked it up, and wiped the bloody blade on the grass. She sheathed it away and returned to her horse. Thalagar nudged against her body with his head and stomped his foot.

"He fought. Thalagar fought for me. I never saw a horse do that before. I've never seen men turn into wolves. None of it was natural, Grudge." Taliesin grabbed the saddle horn as Grudge held her horse. "I've never killed a man before. This was my first battle."

"You did well, Taliesin," Grudge said, his voice gentle. "So did Thalagar. He must come from a line of warhorses. I saw him fight for you. Only a warhorse will fight like that, and it comes from good breeding. Now come on. Get in the saddle. We must hurry."

"You? Kordive?"

"We both fought, but neither is injured. That's wolf blood. Now hurry, woman."

Grudge grabbed her by the waist and helped her climb into the saddle. She let out a cry and held her hands to her side. He jerked her hands away and checked for wounds, but when he found none, he retrieved his battle-ax and remained standing beside his horse.

"Ride on and catch the others. I'll meet you later at the Black Rock Inn. I must burn the bodies." Grudge flashed a wide, toothy smile. "Take a bath. You could use one. Just don't start drinking ale until I get there; I want to give the first toast. Later, I intend to do things to you that you've only dreamed about."

"Sure, whatever. Sounds like a plan," Taliesin said, not aware of what he'd said until she'd ridden out of the forest. But by then, too many miles had been covered to change her mind.

* * * * *

Chapter Ten

The sign of the Black Rock hung outside the door of the modest inn, the light through the windows shining goldenly as the sun set behind the mountains. Made of stone, with a second level, it lay nestled on a plain of tall grass that stretched for miles to the west. No horses were tied to the posts outside, and no music or noise came from inside the inn, leaving Taliesin with the feeling few ever stopped. She slid out of the saddle and led Thalagar to a rickety, old stable, finding a stable boy inside who gave her a suspicious look.

"There's a good lad," Taliesin said, holding out a coin. "My horse is to be treated with kindness, fresh water, a bucket of grain, and rubbed with a cloth. Check his hooves, too. I don't want him coming up lame."

The boy took the coin, his eyes widening as he saw it was gold, and with the customary quick bite between crooked teeth, he placed it in a pocket of his tunic. He took the reins to the big black horse. "This one is Andorran," he said, "They're desert horses known for their speed. I think they're the finest horses of any breed." He scratched behind his ear and smiled at her. His hair was bright red, and his nose hosted a score of freckles. "No one has ever paid this much. He must be special."

"Oh, he is," Taliesin said. On her way out of the stable, she noticed the crusted blood covering her hands and leather jacket. She'd lost her cloak somewhere in the forest. Stopping at a water trough to wash up, the task of removing her jacket proved painful. It fell to the ground, but even bending to reach for the item made her ribs ache, so she left it there and headed toward the inn.

"A moment, miss. You forget your bags." The red-haired boy came running over, carrying her saddlebags across his shoulder. "I already brought in the bags on the mule and placed them inside. You're Raven Clan, aren't you? Scavengers. We don't get your kind here."

"That a problem?" Taliesin placed her hand on the hilt of her sword, and the boy's cheeks turned bright red. He gulped and quickly shook his head. "Clean that jacket, and it's yours. It's wolf blood. Wash it well, boy. In return, I'd appreciate your carrying my gear inside."

A trail of dust followed the boy's heels as he rushed toward the jacket and picked it up. His skinny legs knocked together as he hefted the saddlebags onto his shoulder and came to open the door for her.

"My dad said he knows Master Osprey. He said I'm not to talk to you, but you seem nice. I'll brush your horse and make him a bed of straw."

"Come inside, boy," called out a voice as the boy led Taliesin inside the inn. The voice belonged to a large man with a wide girth given him by a robust appetite and rosy cheeks from consuming too much ale. He was in his forties, with a pleasant enough face situated on a short neck, and eagerly waved his son to the bar. "Another Raven?" the man asked.

"That's right." Taliesin offered a smile and scanned the interior. A cheery fire burned brightly in a large fireplace off to the side, with plenty of tables and chairs wiped clean, and a long bar placed against the far wall. Shelves behind the bar contained an odd assortment of glasses and jars and bottles of booze. The innkeeper wiped a glass. "Are my friends here?" she asked. He pointed to a table in a corner where she saw Rook and Hawk eating their dinner. Wren wasn't with them but couldn't be far away. Taliesin caught a glance of her appearance in a mirror hanging behind the bar and shuddered at the blood in her hair. Waving at her friends, she approached the innkeeper. "I need a bath, sir. Is it extra?"

"The boy says you paid with gold," the innkeeper said. "Got a washroom you can use. There's a hot spring beneath us, so the water is fresh, comes from the ground. Your friends didn't complain. As I told my boy, I know you're from the Raven Clan, so I know you can pay. Osprey is a friend of mine. Make yourselves at home."

The innkeeper needed a bath, himself. His apron barely fit over his stomach, and he wore his sleeves rolled to his elbows. He pointed to a door. A woman, presumably the boy's mother, descended the stairs and waved at Taliesin. "We have rooms for you," she said, pushing back a wisp of black hair under her white cap. "Go on in, lady, and clean up. Water is hot as it gets." She grimaced as Taliesin walked by, the scent of wolf and blood distinct among the odors of baked bread, ale, and the age-old wooden interior. Most likely, they hadn't seen too many Raven Clan members in their inn, much less a woman carrying a sword while soaked in blood and bits of fur, though Taliesin wanted to know how the innkeeper knew Osprey. The story was likely to be interesting.

Inside the small room, she found a large copper tub filled with murky water bubbling from a hole in the ground. The fresh spring produced hot water and gave off an odor of moss and dirt. There was a small window with a cracked pane of glass and a lit lantern on a small table. She shut the door, sat on a stool painted bright blue, crossed one leg over the other, and removed a dagger from a sheath on the side of her boot. She repeated the process with her other leg, and then pulled off both boots. The wooden cylinder rolled across the floor and stopped at the side of the tub. She picked it up, trying not to think about the pain in her side, and set it aside. She stripped out of her filthy clothes, left them on the floor, and stepped into the tub. The water was hot, a welcome surprise. A bar of soap with no scent rested in a bowl beside a folded washrag on a shelf. She grabbed both, sank to her chin, and then went under, coming up to find a layer of reddish scum covering the surface of the water.

Taliesin heard a rap at the door and sank into the water as the door opened and the innkeeper's wife came inside the bathing room. The woman bent over to retrieve Taliesin's dirty clothes and reached for her boots, wrinkling her nose in disgust.

"I'll clean your things and return them to you, mistress," the woman said. "Bathing salts can be found on the shelf. You best use them if you want to get rid of the smell of wolf. We don't get many guests, but now and then Wolfmen do come here. Nothing smells worse than one of their kind; I knew the moment you entered what happened." She turned around and went out the door.

When Taliesin finished bathing, she dressed in a soft wool tunic the color of a robin's egg, gray slacks that hung wide at the ankle, and a pair of socks instead of her second pair of boots, then she tied her long hair into a ponytail with a leather band. She felt better, no longer stunk, and was ready for a tankard of ale and a hot meal. She winced in pain as she grabbed the scroll, her sword belt, and the saddlebags and went out the door to see Wren, Rook, and Hawk waiting at a table. She joined them and placed her gear on a bench. Wren sat next to Rook and, as she took a seat, Taliesin noticed the girl held his hand under the table.

Hawk wore an anxious look on his face. He slid a pint of ale in a wooden tankard toward Taliesin and glanced toward the door to the inn. "Where is Grudge?" he asked.

"Behind me," Taliesin said. She lifted the tankard to her parched lips and finished it in two big gulps. The taste was just right and took the edge of her grumbling stomach.

"Moon is up," Hawk said, nursing a tankard. "He better get here soon, or we may have to go look for him." He took a sip and foam covered his upper lip. "I heard the boy tell his father your saddle had deep scratches, and you *were* covered with dried blood. You didn't murder Grudge, did you?"

She grinned. "No, but we did see a little action."

"When I realized you weren't following, I wanted to return and help, but I didn't know what type of trouble I'd be riding into. Wren can get very scared in the woods. I have to think about her, you know. She is my sister."

Rook made hand signs, which Wren translated. "Rook says he's sorry we didn't come back for you and hopes you aren't too bruised." She gave Taliesin a sharp look. "You were limping when you came in. Are you injured?"

"Thalagar threw me, but I'm fine," Taliesin said. "Grudge and I killed ten Wolfmen scouts. He stayed behind to burn the bodies. It was probably a good thing you didn't return. Trust me. It wasn't pleasant."

The innkeeper's wife came to the table carrying a large bowl of delicious-smelling stew. Under her arm, she held a fresh-baked loaf of bread Taliesin hoped wouldn't taste of body odor. To the surprise of all, Wren took the bowl from the woman and set it before Taliesin. Waiting for Wren to spit into the thick, meaty dish, Taliesin stared at the pale hand that offered her a spoon.

"Thanks," Taliesin said. She grabbed the spoon and dipped it into the stew, eating a mouthful. Wren smiled at her. It didn't make her feel very confident about the bowl's contents.

Rook started moving his hands, and again Wren translated. "Rook says the Wolfmen have been following us the entire time," she said, in a matter-of-fact voice. "I knew this would happen, of course. I had a dream about the Battle of Burnlak before it happened, and later dreamed the five of us were on the run, pursued by Captain Wolfgar."

"I didn't know you were *gifted*," Taliesin said. "Minerva would have never let you out of her sight if she'd known; she always wants to know her future. Boils and bad breath, that's basically all she can look forward to." She finished the stew in several mouthfuls and pushed the bowl aside. "So, let's hear about one of these dreams. Impress me."

"The future is not set in stone and can change, so things don't always turn out the same in real life, but they do come to pass in one form or another," the girl said, using a finger to place a strand of hair behind her ear.

"Explain," Taliesin said.

"I dreamed about the white stag we saw in the woods. My mother always said seeing a white stag was a symbol of good fortune," Wren said. "And it helped distract the Wolfmen. I've dreamed about them, too. The Wolf Clan is cursed." She paused, apparently working up the courage to confess what she knew. "They are shape-shifters. I never thought Osprey or the others would believe me if I told them, so I didn't. Few humans the Wolf Clan takes off the field are ever sold into slavery; they sacrifice the humans and eat them afterward."

"That's because they're not men," Taliesin said. "They are *Wolfen*. I saw what I saw. I saw them turn into wolves. They can also turn into something between a man and beast...something *monstrous*." She tore off a section of bread and dipped it into the remaining liquid at the bottom of her bowl.

"My mother told me about men who turn into wolves at will," Wren said. "She said the disease spreads through a bite or a scratch. Once infected, a person can shape-shift at will, though normally they prefer to change when the moon is high above, which is when they hold their rituals. She said these creatures can control their animal nature, are clever, and have kept their secret for centuries, killing or turning anyone who learns the truth."

"Why didn't you tell Osprey about this?" Taliesin asked. "The whole time you've been at Raven's Nest you kept this information to yourself. I think that's irresponsible." She glanced at Hawk. "My father should have been told before he set out for Eagle's Nest. The Wolf Pack will follow, just as they are following us. I left Grudge to deal with those dead things, but if he's bitten..." she shuddered, "it's just too awful to think about."

"It's nonsense," Hawk said. "Legends about men turning into wolves have always been told to children to keep them from wandering off into the woods alone. There was a lot of talk about the Wolfmen at Raven's Nest. Osprey said the Wolf Clan are werewolves; mindless creatures that kill without thought and spread their infection the same way described by Wren. But what he didn't tell me was how to kill one of them. If there is a secret, let's hear it."

Taliesin slid her hands across the table in an outward motion. "By cutting them into tiny, little pieces with a silver sword. That's the only way to keep them from reassembling or re-growing missing body parts. You also have to salt the ground after you kill them. Fire works just as well, and that's why Grudge burned the bodies of the Wolfmen. It wasn't just to get rid of evidence."

"I don't understand why you don't believe me, Hawk," his sister said. "I was right about being captured by pirates, and I was right about being rescued by Rook, and I'm right about the *Wolfen.*"

"If I'm such a bad brother, then maybe you should have gone with Master Osprey," Hawk said, but he immediately changed his attitude. "Did you dream about the Raven Clan, too? You know something. Will Osprey and the clan reach Eagle's Cliff? Tell us if you know."

Taliesin felt sorry for Wren. Hawk had a strong influence over his sister, more so than Rook, and she pictured the girl as a bird trapped in a cage.

"I have only dreamed about Wolfgar," Wren said, sounding embarrassed.

"Horse manure." Hawk downed his ale. "You dreamed the guy has fangs, and now you all think he's a werewolf. I don't know what you think you saw, Taliesin, but until I see one change in front of me, I can't believe any of this."

Rook made a gesture at Hawk that caused the young man to look greatly offended. He reached out and placed his hand on Wren's shoulder. Wiping tears from her eyes, Wren gazed at the mute with undisguised love. Taliesin was touched by the return look Rook gave the girl and, when he placed his hand over hers on top of the table, in plain sight, she wondered if the door to Wren's birdcage had finally opened.

"Rook thinks you are foolish," Wren said, angrily. "The people of the Isle of Valen avoid the mainland and keep to the sea because of their fear of werewolves."

"Werewolves can't swim?" Hawk laughed without humor. "Look, I know the Wolf Pack is intimidating, but these guys are not supernatural creatures. I killed a Wolfman at Raven's Nest with my steel cutlass. The one in your room chewed off his tongue and choked on his own blood. He died right in front of both of us."

The innkeeper was listening. Taliesin gave him a stern look. The man grabbed a glass and wiped it with a dirty rag, but she knew he was paying attention. Giving Hawk a fully-detailed picture of what happened no longer seemed prudent, not unless she wanted wild rumors to get out...and that was the last thing she wanted. Rook, however, had plenty to say and moved his hands in front of him, his gestures eloquent but frantic.

"There are many supernatural creatures in the world people claim do not exist," Wren said, translating for Rook. "Things that swim in the oceans or live in the mountains, hiding away from the world. Werewolves used to come out only at the full moon, but Rook says they are evolving, like many creatures that now walk on land instead of swimming in the ocean."

Reaching behind her, Taliesin picked up the red leather scabbard, pulled out the silver sword, and placed it on the table. The hilt was plain, lacking Mandrake's usual engravings, and had not even a pommel stone. Rook handed her a cloth, and she cleaned the blade, rubbing it to remove all traces of blood.

"This sword was used by a Knight of Chaos. I found it on a battlefield, but I know it's a Mandrake; I recognize his work. When I used it on the Wolfmen, I was able to slice right through them like a piece of cheese, and they stayed dead afterward. Call me crazy, but I believe this sword has magical properties I somehow summoned. Wolfgar called me a witch, and well, maybe that's what I am."

"I don't know why you worship Mandrake," Hawk said, watching her. "How do you know he forged this particular sword? I see no marking, and I never heard Mandrake forged magical swords. He was born fifty years ago, Taliesin, long after magic was outlawed, which means your sword isn't magical. You were just frightened at being caught off-guard, and you killed a few men, that's all there is to it."

"Mandrake always marked his swords with his personal emblem," Taliesin said, turning the sword over and pointing out the small icon. "Each has a small winged dragon holding an 'M' etched where the blade meets the crossguard. Finding one is very rare, and I found one, so don't argue with me. I know my business, Hawk. And I know this sword is silver and killed those things dead."

"Fine. Whatever you want to think. But I bet you don't know Mandrake was commissioned to make five swords for the sons of King Frederick." Hawk brushed a lock of black hair from his eyes and laughed when she looked surprised. "Five silver swords for Almaric, Dinadan, Galinn, Konall, and Sertorius. Pity your sword isn't engraved with one of the prince's names. I suspect Mandrake was killed before he finished the job, but that still doesn't mean your sword is magical. Nor does it have a name. The sword is not that special."

"It is to me," Taliesin said, defensively. Hawk could be stubborn as well as stupid at times. Silver swords were valuable, regardless of the swordsmith, and the weapon had worth. "And I bet you didn't know magic swords are named to represent their powers, like *Doomsayer*, and it was certainly magical. You saw what happened when I picked it up." She set aside the rag and slid the sword into the scabbard. "That's why I'm now going to call this sword *Wolf Killer*, for it has a thirst for *Wolfen* blood."

"Whatever. I think you're all drunk," Hawk said, rising to his feet. "I'm going to see if Grudge has arrived yet."

Taliesin watched Hawk walk across the room. She hadn't noticed a hooded man in the corner of the inn, drinking ale, but she did when Hawk opened the door. The man's hands were wrinkled and speckled with age spots. He looked harmless. An old yellow dog sat beneath the table, looking no more aggressive than its owner. The innkeeper's wife went over and set a boiled chicken in front of the customer, cut it into small bites, and then started to feed him with her own hands.

Taliesin looked again and realized the old man's hands were crippled with age and unable to hold a knife and fork. Small bits were given to his dog as well.

Taliesin remembered what Hawk had told her, about the old man who had drawn the map to where the sword was. She couldn't shake the feeling the old man sitting in the corner was the same one Hawk had met. Unsure, she made a point to remember to ask Hawk later.

"Why do you favor Mandrake over any other sword-smith?" Wren asked.

"Because John Mandrake was my birth father," Taliesin said. Rook and Wren looked surprised. "On the night my father was murdered, Master Osprey appeared and took me away. I don't remember much about my childhood, but I remember we lived in the shadow of Tantalon Castle. My father stayed up late at night, hammering away at his anvil, and taught me how to recognize the quality of each swordsmith. He told me in the days of magic, sorcerers were hired to place spells on swords, and that wasn't that long ago. Hawk can think what he likes, but I do know what I'm talking about because Mandrake is my true father."

Hawk returned. "Did I hear right? You? Mandrake's daughter?" He laughed until he turned bright red and tears welled in his eyes. "You're nobody. We're all nobody. Next Rook will be telling me he's the son of an island lord and will one day inherit a vast fortune and a throne of his own. I might as well say I'm a pirate prince and Wren is a pirate princess."

"I don't care what you believe, Hawk. I am John Mandrake's true daughter. That's why I can identify swords so easily, that's why I have a knack for finding only the best ones on any battlefield, that's why Osprey took me in, and that's why you asked me to come with you to find *Ringerike*."

Hawk sat. "I'm sorry," he said. "I believe you. About everything. I can't help being the way I am. You might as well know Wren and I come from a small fishing town in Erindor. Our father had an apothecary shop. My mother died when I was born, and our father remarried a healer. Wren knows the name of every herb and the uses for them." He touched the dangling pearl hanging from his earlobe. "We were only with the pirates for a few months before we managed to escape one night when we came into port. We swam to shore and hid in a cave, and that's where we met Rook."

"Rook is from the Isle of Valen," Wren said. She made it sound like it was the dreamiest place in the world. "His father was an important man, and they did live in a palace. I'm not sure why he decided to leave; he never said, but thanks to Rook we made it to Raven's Nest."

"A very touching story," replied a deep, growling voice. Everyone looked to the entrance as the tall, imposing figure of Grudge came in through the door. He appeared unharmed, a bit worse for wear, and he'd apparently washed off most of the muck outside in the horse trough, for he was still damp about the ears.

"Grudge!" Taliesin went to kiss him. "You had us worried. Are you all right?"

"Yes, I'm fine," Grudge said throatily. He took off his cloak, tossed it over a chair, and sat at the end of the table. "You started drinking without me. Well, there's still time for me to make a toast." Rook pushed a tankard of ale toward him. "Innkeeper, bring me whatever was in these bowls — smells like beef stew. Bring me a big bowl."

The innkeeper sent his wife over with a pitcher of ale and a bowl of stew. The old man and his dog were no longer in the corner; Taliesin wondered where they'd gone, but she soon forgot about them. Grudge eyed the food, picked up a spoon, dug in, and ate quickly. He dipped chunks of bread into the bowl and consumed his meal in seconds, then he reached for his tankard, downing it just as fast.

"I suppose none of you noticed the silver talismans hanging outside the inn," Grudge said. "Wards off werewolves. That was a narrow escape. Tonight, I intend to get drunk and sleep very soundly." He refilled his tankard.

"You were not harmed?" Wren inquired.

Grudge gave her a comforting smile. "No, my little Wren, I was not harmed," he said. "But I think it's time we took a look at that scroll, Taliesin. Let's see what the Wolf Clan is so eager to obtain. Put it right on the table, and everyone gather around."

Turning, Taliesin reached into her pack, pulled out the wooden cylinder, and faced the table as she unscrewed the cap. She pulled out a rolled parchment, which she laid on the table and spread open. It lay flat without curling up, which Taliesin found quite strange. Hawk leaned forward, trying to reach for the parchment, but Grudge came around to stand behind Taliesin and knocked his hand away.

"It's just an old piece of parchment," Hawk said, disappointed. "Why would Wolfmen want a blank piece of parchment? This makes no sense at all."

"Hush," Taliesin said. She leaned over and peered at the parchment as a tiny line appeared. More lines appeared, making a pattern. "Interesting. It's a map. A fully-detailed map of the realm." She leaned aside, letting the others get closer looks. "Do you see how the lines are moving? It's as if the map is deliberately changing land formations. I can't imagine why, but I can tell you this map has dark magic—I can almost smell it. Can't you?"

"It's a Deceiver's Map. That's why it's playing tricks," Grudge said. He was excited. He pointed out the dukedom of Aldagar, which was now visible. "Not many were made, and they are very rare. Only those trained in magic or natural-born witches can read them. I happen to have been trained to read magic scrolls. This is us, right here, smack dab in the middle of the plains of Aldagar. See these little red stars that seem to appear at random positions on the map? I bet each represents something of importance, waiting to be found."

"I wonder who was carrying this at the Battle of Burnlak," Taliesin said. "The Eagle Clan knows Wolfgar is working for Prince Sertorius, and the prince is headed north. But is he? I suspect both Sertorius and Wolfgar are after *Ringerike*. If they are, then you can bet the Eagle Clan is as well, and that's why everyone came to Raven's Nest looking for it. They just wouldn't admit what it was because they were afraid I'd go after the sword."

"That means they are all looking for you now," Wren said.

"Yeah, that's right," Hawk replied. "Everyone must believe you really are a witch, Taliesin, and they certainly believe you have the Deceiver's Map. It certainly is better than what I was given; at least I think it is because I still can't see a damn thing."

"It's better." Taliesin smiled. She remembered the old man who had been sitting in the corner moments before. "There was a man here earlier, an old man, but he vanished when Grudge came in. Did you get a look at him, Hawk? Was he the same man who drew you the map?"

Grudge, Hawk, Rook, and Wren looked at the corner. The old man and his dog were gone, but his dirty plate and tankard remained on the table. Hawk walked to the table, sniffed around, and returned. "Nothing," he said. "I thought maybe there would be a clue or something, but it must be your overactive imagination, Taliesin." She glared at him but said nothing more on the subject.

"King Morgus rounded up the witches and sorcerers two hundred years ago," Grudge said. "All known magical weapons were collected and destroyed or disenchanted if they belonged to a noble family. It is widely believed there was no more magic left in Caladonia. The only ones left practicing magic are phony soothsayers and gypsies, and even then, they have to stay one step ahead of the hangman's noose. Magic is outlawed, and this map is a dangerous item to have." He lifted his tankard. "But I'm glad we didn't burn it. I can read it well enough, but I can't control it. I don't have any magic. You do, Taliesin. You must."

Wren looked offended. "I'm a soothsayer," she said. "I have visions."

Grudge laughed and set his drink on the table. "Can't say I've met a soothsayer before, but you must take after your mother. Magic is usually handed down on the maternal side;

your skills will be helpful, as well." She smiled at him. He pointed to a star that appeared on the left of the map. "See this, Taliesin? I'll venture a guess this star indicates the exact location of where we are headed. It's in the middle of the Salayan Desert and could be where we'll find *Ringerike*. We'll have to pass through Aldagar to get there, although I'm not sure if Duke Volund has sided with the king."

"We are still going," Taliesin said. "I want *Ringerike*."

Grudge's dark eyes found Taliesin's in the firelight. "You realize if Sertorius gets his hands on that sword, no one can stop him from claiming the throne. He'll be invincible."

"I thought Sertorius supported his brother Almaric," Taliesin said. "Or is that not true either?"

Grudge shrugged. "Can't say for certain."

"The trick is not to get caught," Hawk said, sitting on the bench. "I'd say that's reason enough for a toast. Let's drink to good fortune." He grabbed his tankard. "Well? Lift your mugs, my friends!"

Everyone tapped their tankards and drank. It tasted so good to Taliesin that she finished it off and refilled it to the top. She was both excited and frightened. That combination along with her luck at finding the very map they needed made her indeed feel magical.

"Let's not get too carried away here," Grudge said, always the downer. "Deceiver's Maps were made with dark magic. I've read my fair share of books on the subject. Books on magic are just as hard to find. But I read something about these types of maps, and I know they can't be trusted. You have to be able to control magic to use it accurately. It will take some practice, Taliesin. I think you have a better chance than Wren. Her magic is different from yours."

"So, the map will lie to us?" Wren asked. Grudge nodded. "That's not good."

"My finding this map is not a coincidence," Taliesin said. "Someone planned for me to find it." She put her hand on the map, and the images vanished. "No more games, Grudge. Who were you before you joined the Raven Clan? You know too much to be a mere thief. Are you a spy working for the king?"

"You're very demanding," he said. "What do I get out of it?"

"I told you before what you get in return," she said, hoping Grudge wanted her enough to tell the truth. "Everyone else has revealed their past this night. It's your turn. Who are you, Grudge? Why did you leave Fregia to come here? I know that's where you come from, but I don't know what you did there. Farm boys don't learn magic, and sheepherders can't handle a sword the way you do. You must have been a sword-for-hire. Is that it?"

"That's right," Grudge said, hunching over his ale. "I'm really a man of many trades, but what I want is to grow old, fat, and rich, and die with grandchildren seated at my feet."

"Rich and fat," Hawk sighed. "I've always dreamed of being rich." He placed a finger against the side of his nose. "Maybe we'll find *Trembler*. That sword was made for Landau the White, a master sorcerer who would fly into the rooms of the prettiest women and seduce them at night. I'd like to find that one. Wealthy and well-loved, oh yes, that's for me."

"Landau drowned, by the way," Taliesin said, unimpressed with Hawk's knowledge of magical folklore. "He took the sword with him to the bottom of the sea. Flying isn't all it's cracked up to be. For someone who didn't believe in werewolves an hour ago, you certainly are gobbling this up. Grudge, you still haven't told me anything I didn't already know about you. Guess you'll be sleeping alone tonight." She rolled the map up, grabbed her sword and saddlebags, and stood. "I'm calling it a night, folks. You should do the same."

Heading to the bar, Taliesin glanced at the innkeeper as he stepped forward. "You can have any room upstairs, ma'am," the man said. "Just don't pick the one at the end of the hall. Old Viktor has that room, and his dog has fleas. Any other room will do just fine."

"Who is Viktor?" Taliesin asked. "You know him well?"

"Just a peddler," the innkeeper said. "He comes through now and then. He's not a werewolf. Heard you talking. Wolfmen aren't allowed here. Don't like them."

Climbing the staircase, Taliesin noticed cobwebs in the corners and dust on the old paintings hanging at odd angles, showing the innkeeper's wife to be a lazy maid. She picked the third door on the left and opened it, revealing a modest room with a large, puffy bed and one window with closed shutters. She set the candle on a small table and tossed her gear onto a dusty, red-velvet chair. She placed the map into the pouch on her sword belt, kicked off her shoes, and sat on the bed. Someone had recently laid out clean sheets, and the top blanket smelled like soap. As soon as she'd removed her clothes and gotten herself situated beneath the blankets, the door opened, and Grudge stuck his head in.

"What do you want?" she said.

"You made a deal with me, woman," Grudge said, entering the room. He dropped his gear to the ground, his weapons clanking, and kicked the door shut with his heel. "I was born in Ruthenia, a mountain village in the far west corner of Fregia. The people from my village are hunters. I learned at a young age how to hunt and how to fight. One day I was out pursuing a boar, and I met a knight on the road who convinced me to come with him. He knew a little about magic and was good enough in tournaments that I learned my trade as his squire. We traveled from place to place; he jousted, and I groomed his horse. After he died, I made my living as a sword for hire."

"Not a knight?"

"No, a sword for hire," he replied.

Grudge stood at the foot of the bed, kicked off his boots, and unfastened his sword belt. He laid his sword beside the two axes sticking out of his large bag and pulled off his socks while she watched, not saying a word.

"But how I came to be in service to the king, now that is an interesting story. You see, I was fighting for coin in the town of Gregge when I saw King Frederick and his wife, Queen

Henrietta, among the spectators. They'd stopped for the night and saw me win a particularly bloody contest."

"How fortunate for you," Taliesin said.

"Not fortunate at all," he said, coming to sit on the edge of the bed, "for I fought under the guise of the knight whom I'd served, a crime in this realm, and when it was discovered I was but a squire, the king ordered my immediate arrest. Being rather fond of my head, I escaped and went into hiding. Fortunately, Master Osprey took me in and gave me a name and his protection on the condition I do him one favor."

He pulled his jacket off, then his undershirt, damp with sweat. His back was hairier than she'd expected, and she pulled the blanket to her chin.

"Shall I tell you what that favor was?"

"Go on, you hairy wolf," she said, catching her breath as he yanked his belt free.

Grudge's brown eyes fastened on hers as he started to unfasten his pants. "On the night John Mandrake was slain," he said, in a husky voice, "Osprey arrived in Padama to find the swordsmith's only daughter and returned with her to Raven's Nest. A girl with superior knowledge of swordsmiths and legendary weapons, and an uncanny ability to identify those weapons on the battlefield. A beautiful girl with flaming hair and eyes the color of moss. Osprey adopted this girl and ordered the Captain of the Black Wings to keep her from harm. 'Rosamond' was the name of Mandrake's daughter; your real name, Taliesin. Osprey asked that I protect you, and that is what I have done since I joined the Raven Clan."

His pants fell to the floor, rendering Taliesin speechless and unable to ask questions that needed to be asked. Every inch of his body was muscular; a warrior's physique, and like a warrior, he had a number of scars. His arms were dark brown but the rest of his body, due to lack of exposure to the sun, looked pale in comparison. He was a hairy beast; dark hair covered his body, thick and black, though he didn't have the slightest fuzz on his flanks or buttocks.

Taliesin sat up, excited, and let the blanket fall away. His eyes narrowed, and his breathing quickened, until he was almost panting, as was she. "You swear you are telling me the truth," she said, barely holding on to any sense of reason. She wanted him but refused to swallow his lies. "I want the truth, Grudge, or you can find somewhere else to sleep tonight."

"Oh, I swear it." Grudge climbed onto the bed. "You can go anywhere you want, do anything you want, and I shall defend you with my last breath."

"Whatever I want..." she repeated after him, unable to look away.

There was no rest for her during the night, for afterward, in her dreams, she saw Grudge, in the woods, transform into a glorious white stag. He bowed his head to her three times before bolting. She awoke, expecting to be cold and shivering, and found Grudge spooning her with his muscular arms wrapped tightly around her. Snuggling against his body, she realized she'd never felt safer. She'd awoken him. At the touch of his lips against her shoulder, she shivered, remembering how he'd touched her, and felt her desire return with a vengeance. She rolled over, and his lips brushed across hers.

"'Roland' is my true name," he said, kissing her.

* * * * *

Chapter Eleven

Morning sunlight streamed through the window and warmed Taliesin's face. With a yawn, she reached out for Grudge. No, not Grudge, she remembered; his name was Roland. Her fingers reached into empty space. Sitting up in alarm, she gazed around the room, worry replacing her yearning. Throwing aside the covers, she climbed out of bed. Roland was not in the room, and his gear was gone. The fear he might have left her behind sent her scurrying. She pulled a clean pair of riding leathers from her saddlebags, although her cleaned clothes were folded and placed on a table, presumably by the innkeeper's wife. Her boots had been polished and placed at the door. Once dressed, she belted on her sword, fastened on the spare black cloak she'd brought, packed the rest of her gear, and used a twig to clean her teeth. Gazing around the room one last time, she tossed the twig aside, grabbed her gear, and bolted out of the door, slamming into Hawk.

"Watch out," Hawk said, nearly dropping a bag he carried over his shoulder.

"Sorry," she said. "I didn't see you."

A frown appeared on his face. "I guess you didn't get much sleep last night," he said, his tone angry. "My room was right next to yours. Ask me how I slept?"

"Excuse me?" Taliesin gave him a hard look. "I don't recall promising you anything, Hawk, other than helping you find *Ringerike*. I've made my choice. Accept it."

Wren's laughter spun Taliesin around. Rook and Wren came out of a room, holding hands, and grew silent as Hawk hurried off. With a kiss to Wren's cheek, Rook dashed after Hawk, leaving the two girls to walk together.

"Your brother is angry with me," Taliesin said.

"With me, as well," Wren replied. A wave of red crept up her neck and spread across her cheeks. "I'm sure he thinks you set a bad example. Rook and I...well...we spent the night together. It was wonderful. I was scared at first, but he was gentle. It was his first time, too."

"Then I'm happy for both of us."

Wren laughed and placed her hand on Taliesin's arm. "I never should have said I didn't like you. It's not true. I do." The morning was full of surprises. "Minerva didn't like me, so I took out my frustration on you. That wasn't fair. When Rook and I are ready, we'll wed." She lowered her hand. "I am tired of my brother telling me what to do. You've inspired me to become a healer, like my mother, and one day Rook and I will have an apothecary shop."

"I can't say I'm ready to get married. Perhaps one day," Taliesin said. As they descended the stairs, the big yellow dog ran past them, barking loudly. She turned around, expecting to see Viktor, but he was nowhere to be seen.

After eating a quick breakfast served by the innkeeper's wife, Taliesin placed a gold coin on the table and followed Wren outside. The innkeeper and his son were in the yard, tossing grain to the chickens as the yellow dog ran barking around them. The horses were saddled, the gear packed on the mule, and the men already mounted and waiting.

Peeking from behind a layer of dark clouds, the bright yellow sun fought a losing battle against a storm front moving in from the east. The far horizon was swathed in dark purple and gray, with huge rain-filled clouds moving at a steady pace, bringing shadows across the grasslands. A flock of chirping sparrows flew overhead, moving away from the clouds. Taliesin tied on her saddlebag as Wren loaded her bag onto the mule and hurried to her horse. Taliesin climbed into the saddle, glanced toward the red-haired boy, and waved. He waved back.

"Good morning," Roland said, riding up to Taliesin. "We ride due west, toward the Hills of Riddick. Hopefully, we can take shelter in the Ruins of Pelekus before nightfall." He gazed at the clouds. "I doubt we'll reach the ruins before it rains, but that's the least of our worries."

"We can handle a few Wolfmen," Taliesin said, grinning.

"I hope to stay ahead of them," Roland replied. "Move out!"

Wasting no time, Roland kicked Kordive in the flanks, and the horse broke into a gallop. Standing twenty hands tall, the Morgenstern was the preferred breed ridden by knights of the realm. Thalagar could have easily out-raced the big tan horse; Andorrans came from the finest bloodline of racing horses. The others ridden by Taliesin's companions were a sturdy, sure-footed breed called Brennens, used mainly for herding cattle and not built for speed or endurance like Thalagar and Kordive. The Brennens were soon lagging behind as the two powerful horses pulled ahead. It was to be a race then, thought Taliesin, catching Roland's grin.

The two horses ran another five miles before Thalagar drew several yards ahead of the larger horse. Laughing and feeling quite satisfied, Taliesin reined in her horse, stroked his black neck slick with sweat, and glanced back at Roland. A few droplets of water fell onto her hands and face, and Thalagar snorted as a light rain started to fall. Chuckling, Roland reined in beside her, wiped a hand across his bald head, and leaned to the side of his saddle to catch her hand. With a yank, he pulled her closer for a quick kiss. When he drew back, his smile was bright, and his honey-brown eyes danced.

"I think you enjoy life on the run," Roland said, laughing.

Taliesin scratched Thalagar behind his ear. "This is the first time I've ever felt like I'm free to do what I want," she said. "Is it so wrong to be happy?"

"Not at all," he said. "I'd like to think I have something to do with your good mood."

Both turned to watch their friends galloping toward them. Taliesin saw black smoke rising in the sky behind the riders. It was coming from the Black Rock Inn. No one said a word, but Taliesin had the terrible feeling the innkeeper and his family were dead. Roland set the pace again, keeping the horses at a brisk pace, and hours passed along the road toward the hills, with only a few breaks to rest the horses.

When the rain ended, the sky turned from dark gray to purple, and tall grass turned into rocky landscape. Only then did Taliesin allow herself a moment to think about the boy and his parents, and what might have happened to them. Pushing the grim thoughts aside, she studied the enormous white boulders sticking out of the ground and noticed their size grew the farther west they rode. Pine trees and bramble bushes with yellow flowers grew around the huge stones. She spotted a covey of quail moving through the thick bushes, searching for berries, and lost sight of them when it started to rain again. The birds took cover, and she wished they could do the same as the temperature dipped, causing her to shiver beneath her hooded, wool cloak.

"It's not much further to the ruins," Roland said, breaking the silence. "Make certain you can get to your weapons if needed. We're in Ghajaran territory. If we run into the gypsies, let me do the talking. Shan Octavio is their leader. Let's hope we find him in a good mood, and he may let us pass through without requiring a tribute."

"How can you be sure the Shan will let us pass?" Hawk asked. "We've heard all sorts of stories about gypsies." He eyed his sister. "They are very fond of fair-haired girls."

"I don't," Roland said, "but we have no other choice. We need shelter for the night. When we reach the pass, stay in tight formation and don't dawdle."

As darkness fell, Taliesin spotted the ruins of Pelekus on the highest hill, surrounded by rocks and a thicket of gnarled pine trees. The once-great castle had only a tower that remained intact. Soaked to the skin, cold, and hungry, they rode through the remains of a stone gate and into a courtyard overgrown with tall weeds. Green moss grew on the rocks and covered the north side of the tower. Trees grew between the large blocks of stones lying on the ground, and a few wren nests were built at the top of the tower. The wooden door was still attached, but the tower looked abandoned and in sad disrepair.

"Wait here," Roland said. "I'll make sure it's safe to go inside."

Dismounting, Roland dropped the reins and drew his double-edged battle-ax. Kordive bowed his head and nibbled at the moss as his master broke through the door's rotted wood with a swift kick and ducked inside to investigate. Taliesin grew concerned when Roland didn't soon reappear. The moment she slid off Thalagar, he appeared in the doorway and waved.

"Bring the horses inside," he shouted. "There's plenty of room!"

Taliesin grabbed Kordive's reins and brought both horses inside, followed by her younger friends and their mounts. Roland had lit a small candle in a broken clay dish that provided enough light to reveal a chamber sizeable enough to hold a large number of horses. Rook and Hawk set up a tether line while Taliesin and Wren unsaddled the horses. By the time the two women had removed the supplies from the back of the mule, Rook had feedbags ready to slide over the horses' heads. Hawk barricaded the door after crudely patching the damage caused by Roland's entry.

"I found more candles," Roland said. "Get these lit, Rook, and spread them around. I'll get a fire going. Looks like the fireplace has recently been used." He handed several candles to Rook. "Probably sheepherders, by the look of it. I haven't checked the upper level yet. Taliesin, finish up and let's go see if anything is hiding up there."

She smiled, for it seemed like a ruse to get her alone.

The faint light from the candles illuminated the lower level of the tower as Roland used a stack of wood to get a fire going. Taliesin noticed a small table and several wooden chairs. A vase of freshly-cut yellow flowers was placed on the table, and she hardly thought sheepherders responsible. Pots and pans lined a mantel above the fireplace. The wooden beams of the ceiling showed no signs of cobwebs, and the floor was clear. Someone had even filled the gaps in the stone walls with bits of cloth held in place by small stones.

"It's cozy enough," Wren said as she gave the mare a green apple. "Merryweather is quite content. She's a fine mare and sure-footed. I wonder who has been here before us."

"You heard Roland," Hawk said. "Sheepherders."

"I don't think so," his sister replied.

Taliesin shook out her wet cloak and hung it to dry. Wren walked to a tall set of shelves made of pine and painted a bright green. Taliesin joined her. There were jars and bottles labeled 'A' through 'Z' on all twelve shelves. The glassware came in different shapes, colors, and sizes, and each had a belt of cloth with the name of the contents written in black ink. In several slender crystal bottles were liquids that radiated a pink, yellow, or blue light. There were carved figures of dragons, unicorns, and birds. Taliesin was able to identify a collection of gems, from bloodstones, coral, and quartz crystal to hematite on the top shelf. Inside an orange bowl were sprigs of holly, jewelweed, and elderberry cuttings with the tiny berries still clinging to the branches. Wren found a human skull, a dead rat, and a frog floating in a glass jar filled with yellow liquid. Both women watched Rook as he picked up torches of the type frequently used by fire-breathers performing in traveling circuses.

"Whoever collected this menagerie is eccentric," Taliesin said.

"Someone lives here," Wren said. "Smells like bacon. Burned bacon. It must have been cooked earlier today."

Hawk sat at the table and wiped his face dry with a kerchief kept tucked up his sleeve. "I smell sheep dung," he said, grumpily. "Has to be a sheepherder."

"Butterbur extract, valerian root, wolfbane, sage, master wart, snakeweed, and lizard eyes," Wren said, setting jars on the shelves. "There's mustard seed, parsley, and thyme, which you use for cooking, but snakeweed is a poison. Who would put a poisonous weed beside black pepper? They look the same, and you could easily make a mistake if you're not careful."

"The jars are marked," Taliesin said. "Whoever lives here may be a healer."

"I feel like a kid again in my parent's apothecary shop," Wren said, grinning as she looked over her shoulder. "In fact, that's what this is. Have a headache, fine; I'll fix you a cup of peppermint tea…" she paused, processing what she knew to what was displayed on the shelves, "otherwise you could exhume a relative's body, preferably an old woman, remove any roots growing in the skull, bury it at midnight, and eliminate pain for any living female relative. That's what angel's breath is for. Anyone who knows about potions can tell you sometimes it's about the ritual, not the contents you mix and use."

"Be careful, Wren." Taliesin watched the girl place a twig of holly behind her ear. "You shouldn't go about touching everything you see. And stay away from the pickled pig's feet. I saw a jar of them on the fourth row. I'd rather eat a bowl of worms than one of those horrid little pink hooves. They're ghastly."

Wren laughed. "You're so funny, Taliesin. How bad can baby pig feet taste?" She took the very jar Taliesin was referring to and unscrewed the lid. One sniff and she wrinkled her nose, grimaced, and set the jar aside. "Oh, that is horrible."

"I warned you," Taliesin said. She walked to Roland who waited at the foot of the stairs. "Shall we go on up?"

"It's too quiet. Sometimes silence is a sure giveaway you are not alone." Roland picked up his ax. "Stay close behind me. Hawk, you're in charge here. If you see anything moving outside, let us know. We won't be long."

Roland ascended the stairs. He held a long finger to his lips and took each step slowly and steadily. The stairs creaked with each step they took. The wood was solid, not rotted, and not a step was missing. A draft coming down the stairs smelled of lavender incense, parchment, mildew, and pipe smoke. When they reached a closed door at the top of the stairs, Roland opened it as Taliesin placed her hand on the hilt of her sword. A single candle lit the room. She pressed against Roland's back as they entered a tidy bedroom, complete with a bed topped by a red velvet coverlet that appeared ragged, not dusty, a small writing table, and an open wardrobe that contained a pink robe and fuzzy yellow slippers.

"Still think it's a sheepherder?" Taliesin asked.

"No," Roland grumbled. He walked to the table. The chair was pushed aside, and there was no sign of dust on the floor.

Taliesin joined him. A bottle of ink and a quill lay beside a piece of fresh parchment. Someone had drawn a large raven on the parchment. Placing his finger on the parchment, Roland smeared the drawing; the ink was still wet.

"The artist is very talented," Taliesin said. "It's a raven."

"That's odd," Roland said. "I'll look under the bed. Check out the wardrobe. Let's find out if it's a woman or a man who lives here."

Taliesin and Roland froze at the sound of a loud sneeze.

A second sneeze brought Taliesin hurrying to the far corner of the room. Empty space greeted her eyes, but as she stared harder, she noticed a shape starting to materialize. She gasped as a short, skinny, old man with white hair that fell past his shoulders appeared. The man, dressed in a ragged blue robe that stopped at his bony knees, apparently didn't realize he was visible, for he ignored Taliesin and gazed at a large, yellow cat that reminded her of the dog at the inn. It was the same color and just as brazen, for the cat jumped from the top of the wardrobe into the man's arms.

"Is your name Viktor?" Taliesin asked.

The old man gave a shriek of alarm. "Oh dear! You can see me." The cat jumped to the ground and went to Roland and curled around his boots, purring loudly. "Ginger, you traitor. Come here this minute. You haven't been formally introduced yet, you strumpet."

"I think we found the artist," Roland said, bending to lift the cat into his arms. The animal purred as he scratched it behind the ears. "Is this the man you saw at the Black Rock Inn?"

Taliesin moved aside as the old man brushed past her. "Maybe I am. Maybe I'm not." The curious fellow gazed at Taliesin. His eyes were gold, reminding her of the eyes of an eagle, and his voice was cheery. "I'm so embarrassed. I've been using so much magic of late my invisibility spell faded too quickly. I must be getting rusty. The cat is Ginger. I already said that, didn't I? Well, Ginger normally doesn't take on so fast to strangers. What's your name, big man?"

"I'm Roland, and this is..."

"I know...it's a female," the funny, little man said. He wiggled his bushy eyebrows. "Brought her here to catch a pinch and tickle, didn't you, big man. I can't say I blame you. I like redheads, too."

"I don't suppose you also draw maps?" Taliesin asked. "Been near Raven's Nest recently? I only ask because an old man turned up a few weeks ago, gave my friend, Hawk, a poorly-drawn map, and told him a story about a magical sword in the Salayan Desert. That wouldn't have been you, would it?"

"Maybe, just maybe. I'm Zarnoc. And who are you?"

"I'm Taliesin of the Raven Clan. We aren't alone. We came with friends."

Taliesin wasn't quite sure what to make of the little man. He certainly wasn't an artist, and 'rusty' was not a word she would have used to describe his magical abilities. She had never met a magic user before, but all signs pointed to that. He owned a yellow cat, had jars full of lizards' eyes and potions, and had, suspiciously, drawn a raven. It didn't seem like a coincidence at all. Roland seemed quite taken with the cat and continued to pet the purring feline.

"Are you and your friends staying the night?" Zarnoc brushed a hand over the front of his robe, and it grew in length and turned yellow, like the cat. "I really have nothing to offer for dinner, but you're welcome to stay. It's going to rain all night."

"If you don't mind, yes, we'd like to stay the night here." Taliesin expected a response. He merely blinked at her. "We brought our horses inside. There are five of us, or rather eleven, if you include the horses and the mule."

"Leaving animals outside in the rain would be rude," Zarnoc said. "But it may get a bit messy by morning. The bed isn't large enough for all of us, but you can use it, Taliesin. Send Roland downstairs, and I'll show you something really magical."

"Um, no, but thank you," Taliesin said. She grabbed Roland by the arm. The cat let out a loud hiss and jumped to the floor. "Aren't you going to say anything? What's wrong with you?"

"All he wants is food," Roland said. "We brought food, old man, but it isn't that grand. You'll have to make do with cheese and bread." His grumpy mood caught Taliesin by surprise. The cat continued to curl around his ankles. She watched, amazed as his surliness vanished, replaced by a big, toothy smile. "We brought ham. We have pears, too, and apples. A good dinner will be our payment for staying the night in your home. I'm sure we have something for Ginger, as well."

"That would be nice," the old man said.

"Have you cast a spell on Roland?" Taliesin asked, annoyed. "It has to do with your cat, doesn't it? She's been rubbing herself all over him. Tell Ginger to stop it at once. I can't have Roland giving you everything we've brought with us. Don't try to put a spell on me because I won't like it. I have a little magic myself, so I don't think your magic will work on me."

"No?" Zarnoc smiled.

His teeth were perfectly even, sparkling white, and reminded Taliesin of tiny teeth set in the mouth of a doll. She found it impossible not to like him. Had to be a magic spell. His toenails needed trimming, and he smelled slightly of cat piss, but she didn't mind.

"I am Zarnoc the Great," he said, a hand to his chest. "I am the last wizard in the realm. Technically, I'm the only wizard, which is why I'm the greatest. But what does that matter, dear lady? Stay the night. Stay the week. And welcome! Welcome to my humble home!"

The old man walked over and shook Roland's hand, pumping it theatrically. He reminded her of one of Osprey's friends, Blunt, an elderly man who preferred the company of cats and lived in a shack at the back of Raven's Nest.

"Thank you," Taliesin said. Zarnoc turned toward her and extended his hand. She took it, finding his skin to be warm and soft. The old wizard kissed her hand. "That isn't necessary. I'm not a noblewoman."

"Oh, yes, it is," Zarnoc said. He giggled when Ginger jumped into Roland's arms.

The big man held the cat close and kissed her head. While it was novel to see Roland petting any animal, it was more astounding to see how much the cat liked him. The animal was purring loudly and seemed quite content with her new friend.

"Ginger should be ashamed of herself for acting so brazen," Zarnoc said.

"I'm sure she is a fine cat," Taliesin said, thinking the old gent was a bit senile. "Roland, is that you purring? Stop it and put the cat down." She glanced at the doorway at the same time as the old man. Voices below could be heard in idle conversation.

"There is nothing to fear from us, old man," Roland said. "We're really quite nice, once you get to know us. Come downstairs and say hello to everyone. None of us have ever met a wizard before; I'm sure they will all be delighted to meet you."

Taliesin walked to Roland and let the cat sniff her hand. Given permission by a loud purr, she began to pet the animal. Her hand brushed against Roland's, and she caught her breath as she met his dark-brown eyes. The cat grew silent, then hissed. Taliesin jerked her hand away and stepped aside.

"I don't think Ginger likes me."

Zarnoc took the cat from Roland's arms. "Ginger only likes men," he said. "I hope you have an interesting story to tell me.

I love stories about families on the run, fleeing from the persecution of some awful baron or knight, or about wives running away from their cruel husbands, or questing knights." He paused. "Yes, I get all sorts coming through here on their way to somewhere else."

Zarnoc turned around and around, searching for something. The cat jumped out of his arms and streaked down the stairs. He went to the table to collect a long ivory pipe with the bowl shaped like a sea turtle, and a bag of smoking weed. "I don't like people from Garridan," he said. "It's not that nice of a place, so the people aren't so nice. Its sand, scorpions, and nomads. I hope you're not going there."

"Like you don't know already," she said. "I have no doubt you are the one who arranged for us to come here, so don't pretend otherwise. What I don't know is how you knew about me, or why you have any interest in the Raven Sword? Just admit it and then come downstairs and explain to my friends what is really going on."

"Do you have any cheese?" Zarnoc headed toward the stairs. "I love cheese."

"Guess that makes him a wizard." Roland winked at Taliesin.

Hurried on by Roland and Taliesin, Zarnoc descended the stairs two at a time. He behaved in a sprightly manner as if underneath his wrinkled skin were young bones full of energy and zest. His chattering voice could be heard, along with a friendly greeting from the Ravens. Roland nudged Taliesin and nodded at the bed. She shook her head, mortified at the thought, and headed to the stairs. He caught her arm and pulled her against his chest.

"Do you think we can trust the hermit?" Roland said. "I mean, if you seriously think he's the one who put Hawk up to this, then it's obvious he has an ulterior motive, and the last thing we need to do is become too fond of him. Wizards are notorious for getting people to do what they want, and it has more to do with personal charm than mere magic. The question we should be asking is why he wants you to find *Ring-erike*."

"Why not just ask him to come along with us? Besides, I like him; but I like you much better." Taliesin slid her arms around his neck and kissed him. "Not everyone has an ulterior motive. Some people can be obvious about what they want in life. This place reeks of urine, and I don't mean the cat. I very much doubt the sheets on that bed are clean." She glanced at a small square window filled in with a pillow. Water dripped around the corners of the pillow, pooling into a bucket on the floor. "I don't imagine that's only water in the bucket."

"If that's supposed to be romantic," Roland said, "it most certainly is not." Despite his comment, Roland held her close and kissed her passionately. Something brushed past their legs, and they separated, glancing at the cat as it slid past them holding a small hunk of cheese between its teeth. An outraged Zarnoc gave a shout; apparently, Ginger had stolen his snack.

"This is probably his wife," Taliesin said. The cat went to Roland and dropped the piece of cheese between his boots. "I think that's for you, darling."

Roland grabbed her hand. "Come on, woman. Let's join the others. I'm hungry."

"Food before love," she laughed. "You'll never change, you big oaf."

* * * * *

Chapter Twelve

The warm glow of the fire was contagious, spreading a feeling of goodwill amongst the Raven Clan. Outside the tower, the wind howled, and the rain pounded against the old wood shutters that covered the narrow windows. Crates and planks of worm-ridden wood were stacked in front of the door, providing an adequate barricade against the storm.

Taliesin sat next to Roland on a rickety bench beside the cheery fire. Hawk perched on a crate on the opposite side of the table, a glum look on his handsome face, while Wren and Rook set the table for dinner. A white cloth was placed over the table, and Wren placed the flower vase in the center of the table. Provisions set out included a large portion of ham, cheese, bread, sliced pears, and apples. An odd assortment of chipped teacups was used to drink wine.

"I think we should take another look at that map," Roland said. "Maybe the old wizard can read it, Taliesin."

"What if he really is the old man Hawk met on the road?" Taliesin rested her chipped blue cup on her knee. Her back felt warm. She'd removed her leather tunic, and her undershirt had a funny smell, similar to the odor of a smelly old shoe. Roland didn't seem to mind and didn't smell any better. "Hawk? Is he or is he not the man you met on the road?"

"I can't be sure," Hawk said. "He's shorter than I remember. The man I met had a deeper voice, and his beard was gray and groomed." He opened his own map and laid it on the table. "Funny thing is, this map leads us right to Pelekus. It's a straight line from here to the cave, and no towns are listed, just bad drawings of small towers and castles along the way. Each one is marked with an 'X' that I figure means we are meant to avoid them."

"He seems harmless enough, Roland," Taliesin said.

"So, we're not to call you Grudge anymore, but Roland, is it?" Hawk finished his cup of wine and refilled it to the brim. "That's an upper-class name if I ever heard one. How high and mighty you've become after sleeping with the Raven Mistress. Don't you want to know my real name, Taliesin? Do I get a turn if I tell you my birth name?"

"Are you drunk?" Taliesin asked, angrily. "Nobody gets a *turn* on me, *Eugene*."

"Don't call me that," Hawk said. "I hate that name. I was stupid to think I had a chance. Of course, you'd prefer a Roland to a Eugene."

"Honestly, Hawk, you're acting like a jealous little boy," Taliesin said.

The yellow cat returned and circled around Rook's legs until he stopped slicing the ham and picked her up. Ginger purred as he rubbed the top of her head. Taliesin glanced over at Zarnoc, who was kneeling beside her horse holding a bucket beneath as Thalagar pissed with great force.

"What is that crazy wizard doing?" Taliesin said.

Hawk tapped his skull. "The old fella isn't right in the head. Said he's an astronomer and the only way to keep his instruments safe from bugs is to soak them in urine. Clearly, he doesn't know anything about rust, let alone hygiene."

Wren went to Zarnoc and made him wash his hands before sitting at the table. There was only one chair left. She glanced at her brother, and he drained his cup before standing.

"Fine. I'll go stand watch," Hawk said. "I know when I'm not wanted."

The young man grabbed a hunk of bread, removed his sword harness from the back of the chair, and went to the door. There was a hole in the center, and he peered out at the rain, chewing on the hard crust. Rook took several slices of ham and joined him. The Erindor spear rested against the wall beside the door, along with Wren's javelins. The wizard helped himself to a cup of wine, making yummy sounds as he drank. Roland cut into the cheese with a knife and handed a piece tor Zarnoc. With a cry of glee, Zarnoc stuffed the cheese into his mouth and eyed the cat curled under his feet.

"If you want to keep your instruments clean," Roland said, pointing at a rusty telescope leaning against the wall, "you should wipe them every day with a soft cloth."

"If I don't soak them in urine," Zarnoc said, with his mouth full, "the beetles will eat them. They won't eat metal that has started to rust." Cheese caught between his teeth, he pointed at their bags on the floor. "Mind you keep your weapons off the floor tonight, or you'll have nothing but the leather wrapped around the hilts come morning."

Wren sat next to Zarnoc and hid a yawn behind her hand. She'd put on a wool tunic to keep out the chill. The wizard patted her on the head as he would a child, leaving a tiny piece of cheese behind where her blonde hair parted. "Are there truly beetles that eat metal?" Wren asked. "Do they eat anything else?"

"No, but they are a nuisance and caused this fortress to fall long ago," Zarnoc said. "One night beetles arrived and ate the guards' weapons, so in the morning they were defenseless against Dire Yadru, a powerful sorcerer, who arrived with an army of mercenaries. Dire Yadru had summoned the beetles to eat the weapons and then laid siege to the castle, tearing it down, stone by stone. The sorcerer left no one alive, but he didn't keep Pelekus for long; King Magnus heard what happened and had Dire Yadru tied to a stake and burned alive. The beetles are still here."

"My mother often talked about a wizard called Karnok the Magnificent," Wren said. "He knew about magical herbs and potions like she did. Karnok made a love potion for a client but drank it by mistake and fell in love with a goat."

"That is true," Zarnoc said, giggling. "Have you heard of Prudilla of Eagon, my pretty little starling? Prudilla had long fingers she'd wave in front of her enemies, and when they watched her fingers moving, they turned to stone."

"That worked," Wren said, "until one day, when a lad named Doran used a silver shield to reflect the witch's fingers. She looked, as she was meant to, and turned to stone. Then Doran saved Princess Hermenia, and they lived happily ever after." She refilled Zarnoc's cup of wine. "Who else do you know about? Tell me more."

"Let me see now," Zarnoc said. He took a sip of wine, wiggling as the tasty liquid trickled down his throat. "There was Ankharet the Wise. Grangwayna of the Lake. The White Witch Ismeina. The Ruby Sisters, Jesmond and Iseuda, and Ysemay the Beguiling. Her eyes were like emeralds, and her lips were ruby red. When she'd dance before the lords, they were hypnotized and compelled to do her bidding." His smile was one of melancholy. "She was bewitching, but I got over it."

Taliesin glanced at Roland. "Zarnoc couldn't possibly have been alive a thousand years ago. Ysemay lived in the court of King Korax, the Raven King."

Roland, thoroughly amused, winked at her and made himself a sandwich.

"I always liked Frithswith," Wren said. "I hope I'm saying the name right. He was a royal sorcerer. They say every morning he created a rainbow for the king to enjoy, and every night he made the moonrise full and bright just for the queen. Frithswith cast out demons and dragons from the realm with a wave of his wand. He knew every magic spell and could make every potion. The king and queen relied upon him completely."

"Especially the queen," Taliesin said, recalling the story. "Glabbrio the Glib wrote 'Frithswith the Fresh,' a rather good play, but it ends sadly. When the king learned of the queen's affair with the sorcerer, he cut off Frithswith's hands and threw them both into the dungeon to die of starvation."

Zarnoc turned his attention to the ham. He ate with his fingers, ignoring the knife and fork set out for him. Wren laughed and refilled his cup with wine.

"Master Zarnoc," Roland said. "How long have you lived here?"

"A very long time, but I come and go as I please."

"Have you been to Maldavia recently? Hawk met an old man on the road who gave him the map that sits before you," Roland said. "I noticed the ink is the same as you used to draw the raven we found in your room. Taliesin saw an old man and his dog at the Black Rock Inn. Was that you and Ginger?"

"Yes, yes," Zarnoc said, nodding. "There has been an increase of interest in magical weapons of late, and everyone knows Taliesin has a knack for finding swords. You do prefer being called by that name, don't you?"

"Yes, I do. Thank you for asking."

"Not at all, my dear. As I was saying, I simply thought it time Taliesin found *Ringerike*. If you intend to find the Cave of Chu'Alagu, you should take the route through the Volgate, but it's a terrible place filled with marshes, swamp gas, and quicksand, and you will need a guide if you hope to reach the other side."

"You been that way?" Roland asked. "I suppose you want to be our guide."

"Not recently, nor willingly," Zarnoc said. "The Volgate is not half as treacherous as the Salayan Desert. No water or living creature can be found for miles around, and then there are the Djaran nomads. If you thought the gypsies were bad, the Djarans are far worse. Have you met any gypsies before, Roland?"

Taliesin wondered why Roland didn't answer and assumed his reluctance was due to unpleasant memories. Through the years, the Ghajaran gypsies had visited Raven's Nest to trade, but that had stopped a year ago. She'd never met Shan Octavio, their leader, though Osprey had thought well of the man and spoke highly of him.

"Do gypsies visit you here?" Taliesin asked. "My father traded with them every spring. He exchanged a Gregor sword

I found for an Andorran colt, and that's how I came to own Thalagar."

"Sometimes they visit," replied Zarnoc. "I am on good terms with them."

Zarnoc finished his meal and filled his ivory pipe with smoking weed. He raised his index finger and produced a small flame at the end. He lit the pipe, puffed away happily, and, as the weed started to snap and crackle, spouted smoke out of the corner of his pursed lips. The cloud turned into the shape of a rabbit and quickly darted off, fading away. Wren laughed, and Zarnoc let out a gruff chuckle that didn't remotely sound like his own voice, but he caught her watching, and it turned into a giggle.

"I don't trust this guy," Roland said, turning to whisper into Taliesin's ear. She slid her arm around his shoulders and brushed her nose against his cheek. He turned his head, and they shared a deep kiss before she pulled aside, smiling widely.

"Be nice," Taliesin said. The wizard was making animals out of smoke rings for Wren, but the girl was tired and sagged in her chair. "I want him to feel comfortable with us. Having him as a guide is exactly what we need, but I want to proceed with caution."

"A direct approach is best," Roland said. He turned to the wizard. "Zarnoc, if you were near Raven's Nest, why didn't you make contact with Taliesin there? Why all the secrecy, and why the interest in the Raven Sword? I want the truth, old man."

"We all want the truth," Zarnoc said. He puffed on his pipe and gazed at Roland with curious, amber eyes. "There had been a great deal of activity at Raven's Nest, and I decided it was safer to approach Hawk. I'm well aware the Wolf and Eagle Clans are anxious to collect all the magical weapons they can find. We can't have that, now can we?"

Roland shook his head.

"I'm a witch," Taliesin said, unable to stay quiet a moment longer. "Captain Wolfgar of the Wolf Clan arrived at our home a few nights ago and demanded Master Osprey allow him to interrogate me. But what he was really after was a scroll I'd found on the battlefield outside of Burnlak. The Eagle Clan was looking for it as well. It's a map."

"That is interesting. You see, a fine lord arrived the other day and asked me how to reach the Cave of the Snake God," Zarnoc said. "I have a reputation as a wise hermit in these parts, and many people come here to ask for my advice or help. 'Just passing through,' he said. Wanted to know if I could tell him about *Ringerike* or take him to its hiding place."

"What was this man's name?" Roland asked. "Was it Prince Sertorius?"

Hawk walked over and stood behind the sorcerer, while Rook remained on guard duty at the door. He'd heard everything and didn't look happy. Roland stood, his hand on his sword, both doing everything she'd hoped to avoid. Bullying the wizard wasn't the way to get answers, and Taliesin feared for Zarnoc's safety. Wren, however, folded her arms on the table and rested her head, eyes closing as she gave a little shudder.

"What did you do to my sister?" Hawk said. "Did you put a spell on her, old man?"

"Dreaming can be a paradox," Zarnoc said. "Is it real what she dreams, or is it only a dream? Does she dream of the ghosts who live here? Perhaps Paris and Matilda, the former bailiff and head maid. Oh, the White Lady and Hangman linger here, too, although they usually appear for a chat right before sunset." He gazed at Wren and puffed on his pipe. "I knew the child was gifted the moment I laid eyes on her. Like Taliesin, Wren is a natural-born witch, while I had to study for years to acquire my magic skills. Dreams and visions are similar, but there is a difference. You dream when you are asleep, and you have visions when fully awake. Wren isn't sleeping. She is awake, I assure you, so please don't shout, Eugene."

"Don't call me that," Hawk said. "And Wren is fine. She does this all the time. Just tell us if Sertorius is here? Is he going to return? Is the Wolf Clan coming here to meet him?"

Zarnoc's eyes narrowed, reminding Taliesin of his cat. "He was a rich man," the wizard said. "Wore a very handsome pair of tall black boots. I sent him to the Volgate. I very much doubt he will find his way out once he enters. Not without a guide."

"Old man, if this is a trap, you'll be the first to die," Roland said. He drew his dagger as Hawk grabbed Zarnoc by the shoulders. The knife was pressed against Zarnoc's throat, but the old man remained calm.

"Yes, it was Prince Sertorius. And no, he is not returning." Zarnoc looked at Taliesin and placed his pipe into his mouth to puff. "I know Osprey, know him well, and he always treated me with kindness. Shall I not be treated with the same respect?"

"Let him go," Taliesin said. "Roland! Hawk! Both of you release Zarnoc and stop acting like brigands. I want to hear what he has to say, and he can hardly talk freely with a knife at his throat. Let him go before someone gets hurt."

Roland lowered the knife and stepped aside, but Hawk jerked the wizard from his seat and shook him like a rag doll. Zarnoc dropped his pipe but somehow managed to catch it before it hit the ground. From the bowl of the pipe came a cloud of white smoke that turned into a large ghostly hand. The hand slapped Hawk with great force and sent him flying backward across the room. Hawk groaned as he sat up, dazed and visibly in pain. The ghostly hand vanished. Rook hurried over, assisted Hawk to his feet, helped him to the table, sat him on a crate, and then knelt beside Wren.

"Just calm down," Taliesin said, rising to grab Roland by the arm. She pointed at the chair. "Sit and shut up. Hawk, no more outbursts. Zarnoc, no more magic. We're not used to magic, and it's rather nerve rattling."

Zarnoc blinked. "Ever?"

"Just for now," she said. "Please, sir. Answer our questions. I don't want anyone else to be hurt, and it feels like we should be friends, so tell us what we need to know, Zarnoc."

"Very well," he replied. "When your father, John Mandrake, died, I'm the one who had sent for Master Osprey and told him to rescue the child before the king could get his hands on her. Even then, I knew you were gifted, Taliesin. So did the king. But Osprey arrived in time and whisked you away to his home. I've come to visit you, from time to time, traveling with the Ghajaran or as a peddler, but I've kept my eye on you."

"You knew my real father?" Taliesin was stunned by the news.

"I'm more than one hundred years old, child. I know many people, and John Mandrake was one of them. Sometimes I'd stop by, and he'd feed me dinner, and in return, I'd say a spell or two over his forged swords. I'm surprised you don't remember me. The silver sword you carry, the one you call *Wolf Killer*, is a sword I enchanted. It was meant for Prince Sertorius. Strange it should find its way to you, for two nights ago he arrived with his Knights of Chaos and a handful of royal guardsmen. I'd say there were at least sixty men in his company. They are traveling to Garridan. Let's hope they never arrive."

"Wait, what?" Taliesin said. "You enchanted *Wolf Killer*? What is the enchantment? What does it do?"

"It does this and that and will cause you to do the other thing," the wizard replied.

The information was far more than she'd expected. Knowing *Wolf Killer* had been enchanted by Zarnoc was important but knowing it had been meant for Sertorius troubled her. It didn't seem like a coincidence, and she hated to think her life was prearranged, but that was how she was starting to feel. Everyone else knew about her past, about Mandrake, and about her ability to find valuable weapons, and here she'd immersed herself in a race to find the Raven Sword. Even that seemed prearranged, and she longed to speak to Osprey, wanting to know what he knew about her past, but that wasn't going to happen any time soon.

"Now is not the time to talk about John Mandrake," Zarnoc said in a kind voice. "But I knew him, and I know Osprey. I consider both my friends. The last thing I would ever do is cause you any harm. Throughout your life, I have been your protector, and I am still doing that job, as is Roland. When Prince Sertorius came here and asked if I had a spare Zoltaire map, I pretended to be quite mad."

"That's not a far reach," Hawk muttered.

The wizard ignored the comment. "Zoltaire was an evil sorcerer," he replied, "but he did one good thing in his life; he created the Deceiver's Maps. Maps that will lead the user to every magical weapon in the world. I only know of three that exist, and one happens to be inside your pouch, Mistress Taliesin. Why don't you show it to me now? I think I've proven to be trustworthy."

"You are clever," Taliesin said. "I found it at the Battle of Burnlak, and it's caused nothing but hardship and grief for my clan." She removed the map from the pouch and placed it on the table. The texture felt like smooth leather, different from before when it had appeared as parchment. "The lines keep moving when I try to read it. Roland could see the lines, but Hawk couldn't."

Hawk let out a snort. "Can you read it or not, old man?"

"Of course, I can read a magical map. I'm a wizard! Zoltaire was a sorcerer. It's not quite the same thing, Eugene," Zarnoc said, taking delight in needling the young man. "For all his flash and style, Zoltaire enjoyed using his magic to make people suffer. I am quite the opposite; in fact, I go out of my way to help *most* people." He cleared his throat. "It was quite careless of someone to drop this map on the battlefield. Either the map was dropped by someone stupid, or it was deliberately placed there for the daughter of John Mandrake to find."

Ginger jumped onto the table, landing so lightly it went unnoticed by Wren, though the cat landed close to her head. The yellow cat glanced at the map, took a sniff, and commenced licking her front paw.

"Zoltaire maps never look the same," Zarnoc said. "These maps have a mind of their own. It can reveal itself as paper, leather, or even a board, whatever you desire. Sertorius wouldn't be able to read the map, even if he had it. Nor can his silly priests or Knights of Chaos. Nor can Wolfmen and Eagle legionnaires. Only a real magic user can read a Deceiver's Map and not be misled or tricked. It's no wonder Roland couldn't control it, or Eugene saw nothing at all."

"I told you not to use that name," Hawk said, but he sounded less angry, overcome by sudden sleepiness. He placed his head on the table like his sister, and his snores were proof he was soon asleep. Rook, seated on the floor next to Wren, rested his head on her leg and was also soon fast asleep.

"Is that necessary?" Taliesin said. "I asked you not to use magic, Zarnoc."

"Yes, well, I need peace and quiet," he said, "and Eugene is very annoying."

The wizard gave the map his full attention, tracing a finger along the lines as they appeared, shifted, and then held still. Taliesin and Roland came around the table, stood behind Zarnoc, and gazed at the map. Five red stars appeared along their route through Aldagar and into Garridan.

"Magical weapon," Zarnoc said. He pointed at a larger red star far to the west that appeared along with the words 'Cave of Chu'Alagu.' "This is where we need to go. It'll shift again on you, Roland, but Taliesin will be able to control the map, in time. Now put the map away; I've seen all I need to. Perhaps you'll let me ride the little mule. We really don't need all the equipment you brought; I'm perfectly able to provide what we need. You two may use my bed. You'll find clean sheets in the wardrobe."

Taliesin folded the map and placed it inside the pouch. As she and Roland started for the stairs, Zarnoc sprang out of his chair. His arm grew distressingly long as he reached out to grasp Roland's Black Wing medallion. The necklace vanished, and the old man held the medallion to his narrowed eyes.

"This is the very medallion I gave to Osprey to keep him safe," Zarnoc said. "I had no idea the old goat would let his captains wear it all these years. But then, sometimes keeping something in plain sight is the best way to keep it safe."

Taliesin and Roland exchanged a quick glance. The wizard tapped the medallion, and the raven faded, replaced by a coiled snake, but the moon on the opposite side remained.

"It's obvious you placed some kind of spell on this badge to hide the snake. I don't think I like illusions," Taliesin said. "I never asked Osprey about it. I just figured it was a lucky talisman. Is it magical?"

"To be precise, my dear, it is a key. A key needed to open the door to the temple inside the cave, and when you have an item like this in your possession, it's always best to rely on an illusion to hide what it really is." Zarnoc handed the gold medallion to Taliesin. "You should keep this on you, not with Roland. If you are not in a rush to bed the maiden, Roland, then both of you sit, and let's have some more wine."

Roland tossed several more logs onto the fire and sat in front of it. He produced a flask of wine and quickly filled the three cups that appeared in front of them.

"Many centuries ago," Zarnoc said, his cup in hand, "a cult built the temple, and there they prayed to their snake god, Chu'Alagu. Chu'Alagu had been a god, but he angered Stroud, the leader of all gods, who turned him into a giant snake. The cult worshiped the snake and offered him human sacrifices. Back then, the Salayan Desert was a jungle where plants and animals flourished, but as the weather changed it turned to desert, and the cult and their god were forgotten. So was *Ringerike*, which King Tarquin's son placed inside of the temple, along with the body of King Korax. Now, about Korax..."

A small cry came from Wren. Rook rapped his knuckles on the table to get their attention. Rook held her as the girl started to groan and thrash. Hawk lifted his head and sat up. Taliesin was surprised the sleep spell hadn't lasted longer; apparently, it wasn't one of Zarnoc's more powerful spells.

Her curiosity gave way to concern for the girl, for Wren remained in restless slumber.

"What's wrong with her?" Hawk asked. "Why doesn't she wake up?"

"I told you, boy, she's not asleep," the old wizard said. "She's having a *waking dream*." He went to Wren and placed his hand on her hair. "You hold her heart and trust, young man," he said to Rook. "Without you, Rook, I doubt she'd have lived this long. Eugene doesn't understand the magic that runs through her veins, but you do, and so does Taliesin. It is for you to protect her at all costs, Rook. She loves you."

Rook nodded and hugged the girl tightly.

"What's this?" Hawk questioned, sounding angry. "Rook can neither hear, nor speak, yet he just nodded. He understood you, and he wasn't reading your lips."

"You're as obtuse as you are stupid," Zarnoc said. "Rook isn't a deaf-mute. He has his own secrets. Some things that happen to children are best not mentioned. It's easier to forget if you pretend you cannot talk or hear. Just as it was easier for Roland to pretend he was nothing but a criminal when he's actually the King's man, though a good man. As for you, Eugene, that's a story for another day."

Rook pounded the table again, his dark eyes shimmering with worry.

"A cup of Lumeister mint tea will do the trick," Zarnoc said, "and she'll be right as rain." He went to an old chest covered with hay. With a wide stroke of his arm, he swept the hay aside and opened the lid, revealing a very clean and tidy array of bottled potions and jars of herbs. He picked up a box and opened it to reveal a bowl containing tea leaves the color of lavender. "Ah, this is what I want," he said. He set the bowl on the table, reached into the sleeve of his dirty robe, and produced a cup. He set the cup beside the bowl and then pointed his finger. Hot water appeared inside the cup, along with purple leaves that swirled with a wave of his hand as steam rose, and he gave a nod to Rook. "Have her drink the tea while it's hot," he said. "It's my own remedy. It will help with the headache she'll have after the vision passes. Always does."

Rook lifted Wren's head, and her eyes opened. She took the cup from him and sipped on it, shuddering as the hot tea flowed down her throat. Taliesin's attention returned to Roland, a man of many secrets; so many her head was spinning, and she felt like drinking her own cup of tea to clear her confusion. *A King's man*. What did that mean? Zarnoc turned on Hawk, a stern look on his face as if he were a father about to scold a disobedient child.

"A selfish man such as you never noticed this girl suffers from terrible headaches as a result of her gift of sight," Zarnoc said. "You have the empathy of a vulture. But Rook knows Wren suffers when she dreams. He knows far more than you, Master Hawk, and I know a great deal more. If you ever lay hands upon me again, I'll tell them every secret you've ever had, and we'll see then what your friends think about you."

"What you said earlier," Taliesin interjected, "about Roland...is this true?"

Zarnoc nodded and pointed at the tall man. "This is Sir Roland of the Fregian Order of the White Stag. Fortunately, I see everything quite clearly. No one can fool me with their disguises. More important, Taliesin, you should ask why King Frederick sent Roland to Raven's Nest, for I assure you, it was not only to win your trust."

"Why would you keep the truth from me?" Taliesin asked. She felt her temper rise when Roland refused to meet her gaze. "Those were Knights of the White Stag who died at Burnlak field. Duke Hrothgar's knights. When I held *Doomsayer*, Jasper talked only about himself, but he should have told me who you really were. He was obviously protecting you, even in death."

"You're mad at a dead man?" Hawk said. "All of us have secrets, Taliesin, this little shit of a wizard most of all, but you're not angry at him. Roland has not done anything the rest of us haven't. We've all come to the Raven Clan to hide from our past. What does it matter if he's a knight as long as he helps us find *Ringerike*?"

Taliesin waved him off. "Because Roland wants the sword for his precious King," she said, too angry to cry or shout. Too disappointed to feel much of anything other than terribly abused. "All this time, I thought Grudge was a criminal; granted, a criminal with good manners, but a man wanted by the law. I should have known a man with a fancy name like Roland was more than a thief. A King's man, indeed."

"I did not lie to you, Taliesin. In truth, I did kill a knight at the very tourney King Frederick first saw me compete in," Roland said, "and I did fight in the guise of another, not that it matters, but I did not exactly lie. I simply avoided telling you everything." She snorted. "The king learned of you after reports came in about Duke Andre Rigelus' sword, *Traeden*, being found by the Raven Clan. Even Lord Arundel suspected you were Mandrake's daughter. His clan has kept an eye on you for years. It's because Lord Arundel suggested to King Frederick you be brought to the palace that I was sent to Raven's Nest to find you; only when I arrived, I didn't count on falling..."

"Spare me your emotions, Sir Roland," Taliesin snapped. Her green eyes glinted with the hardness of stone. "What you did, what you do, is in the name of the king. But not my king, Sir Roland. Frederick Draconus' ancestors killed the Raven King, stole our kingdom, and outlawed magic. His son, Prince Sertorius, has sent the Wolf Clan to hunt me. For all I know, the great lord you serve gave the order to murder my real father. There's the door. Why don't you leave, *Grudge*?"

"Don't tell me what to do," Roland growled.

Zarnoc clapped his hands three times. His dirty robe turned into a long, flowing robe of dark purple, embroidered with silver stars, gold suns, and tiny red stars, and a conical wizard's hat appeared on his head. His outfit was precisely what everyone imagined a wizards might be: ostentatious, flashy, and slightly ridiculous. "It's the hat, isn't it? Too much, right?" With a snort, the embroidery vanished, the sleeves shrank until they ended at his wrist, and his hat diminished to the size of a hunter's cap. Scruffy and well-worn boots appeared on his feet. "Much better," he said, taking a seat. "Now you may continue, children."

"I have nothing more to say." Taliesin walked over and sat on the stairs. She'd been made a fool, let her guard down, and trusted him, but he'd never touch her again. Never. If he'd been what he'd said, a criminal, a sworn Raven, they might have had a life together. But as things were now, she'd lost far more than a lover; she'd lost a lovely dream.

Roland stood at the fire, his back to Taliesin. Hawk stood beside him. Wren stirred and Rook helped her to her feet.

"How are you feeling, my dear?" Zarnoc asked. "Feeling better?"

"I want Taliesin," Wren said, in a soft voice. The girl turned and held out her hand. Unsure why she was selected to offer comfort, Taliesin came over, but Wren collapsed as she grasped for Taliesin's hand. Taliesin caught and lifted the girl, pushing Rook aside, and looked for a comfortable place to lay Wren; her first thought was the bed upstairs.

"Bring her here," Zarnoc said.

The wizard rose from his chair, moving faster than a normal man, and created a cot out of thin air that Taliesin placed the girl on. The wizard snapped his fingers, and a plush pink blanket appeared over Wren, which he tucked around her.

"What did you see, Wren?" Taliesin asked. A horrible feeling had settled in the pit of her stomach. She took hold of the girl's hand. "It's all right. You can tell us."

"Our clan was captured by Wolfmen on the King's highway." Wren squeezed Taliesin's hand as tears slide down her cheeks. "Master Osprey, Minerva, and Glabbrio were seated in the carriage, looking out the windows as the wolf pack surrounded them. Quail and the Black Wings fought them. The Eagles did not for they show loyalty to no one. Those who were not killed by the wolf pack were chained and dragged behind the wagons. Captain Wolfgar has taken them to see Master Lykus. They are to be given a choice; be turned into werewolves or be devoured by the Wolf Clan." A visible tremble went through her body, and she gasped. "I fear they will all be slain, Taliesin. But why didn't the Eagles help them? Had they fought beside the Black Wing, they could have defeated Wolfgar's men."

"I don't know," Taliesin said. "Perhaps Roland knows." She gazed at the knight, seeing him as a stranger, not as her lover, but when he turned, he wore a look of guilt that broke her heart. He'd known it would happen. He'd known and said nothing.

"Wolfgar isn't going to Wolf's Den," Wren said. "He's taken a few of his men, and he's headed here with orders to kill Prince Sertorius, to kill us, and to kill anyone who searches for *Ringerike*. Chief Lykus wants the Raven Sword; he now has *Doomsayer*, but I cannot say whether he supports Prince Almaric. Everything went dark, so dark, and so cold."

"If they are coming here, then we need Sir Roland and the protection he offers," Hawk said. "With so many against us, we dare not go against the king. Come. We should pack and leave at once."

"Cross the Volgate at night?" Roland shook his head. "Even with Zarnoc as our guide, it will be too dangerous. We should leave in the morning."

"Zarnoc? You will come with us?" Wren asked. "Now is not the time for us to quarrel or separate. Our family has grown smaller. Everyone here is needed. I have seen what will happen if Taliesin does not find *Ringerike*. It will be far worse than Burnlak. War will spread far and wide if the Raven Clan does not prevail."

"Family, you say? I am to be part of your family?" Zarnoc sounded delighted. "No more living off rabbits and snakes and bugs and birds. Ginger is a fine huntress, but a man does miss cheese, and that I can't make out of thin air. Not the good stuff. Do not fret, little Wren. Of course, I shall come with you. And so shall Sir Roland. If Taliesin is going to find *Ringerike*, she will need all of our help."

A loud wolf howl filled the air, and everyone turned toward the door. Ginger hissed, jumped to the floor, and hid inside an overturned basket.

"Wolfmen," Taliesin said, drawing the silver sword. "They're here."

* * * * *

Chapter Thirteen

With the passing of the storm, vicious snarls and inhuman laughter echoed inside the tower of Pelekus. The volume was deafening, making it impossible to tell how many Wolfmen were outside the door.

Taliesin held *Wolf Killer* in her right hand and listened as the horrific cacophony intensified. Zarnoc and Wren were gathering arrows and placing them on the small table. Roland, Hawk, and Rook wore their Black Wings heavy leather coats and black capes. They had gathered every piece of furniture in the lower level and barricaded the door.

The only way in or out of the tower was through the main entry, which also meant there was no escape, except for running up the flight of stairs to the next level; even then, there was no place to hide. Taliesin and the three Raven men took defensive positions behind the barricade, but she wondered if werewolves could defy gravity and climb the walls of the tower, or if they could gain entry through the narrow windows. Hawk held both cutlasses, but a longbow and a quiver of silver-tipped arrows were within reach. Rook stood with his silver spear, and Roland held his double-edged ax and a dagger.

"I hope you have something up your sleeve," Hawk said. Zarnoc paced in front of the fire, holding onto a long staff. "Can't you summon beetles to eat them? Or open a hole in the ground that will swallow them whole?

"Stop badgering me. I'll think of something," Zarnoc said. He went to the table and stared at the yellow cat. "Time for you to grow up, Ginger. There is work to be done."

The cat jumped off the table and circled around his legs, making a perfect figure 8 as Zarnoc lifted the staff. But it was his sneeze that caused Ginger to grow as large as a lion, her color a bright yellow that matched the light coming from the end of the staff.

"What are you going to do?" Taliesin asked. "What *can* you do, Zarnoc?"

"Something amazing," he replied. "Here it comes."

A whirlwind came from the staff, growing in size and speed as the magical current of energy circled around the tower, all the way to the roof. The horses remained calm, something Taliesin found extraordinary under the circumstances, and continued to munch on the grass growing from the dirt floor, not minding the spectacular show of light. Nor were they disturbed by the audible howls and snarls that filled the stone tower or the fiery barricade that now lined the inner walls.

Taliesin went to check on the horses but bounced back as if she'd slammed into an invisible barrier. She reached out a hand and felt the electricity in the air, confirming her suspicion Zarnoc had indeed raised a magical barrier to protect the horses and mule.

"Come on, old man. Do the same for us!" Hawk shouted.

With a wave of his hands, Zarnoc stood with a delighted look on his wrinkled face that disappeared the moment the whirlwind vanished with a *pop, snap,* and *crack.* The tower wall also vanished, leaving only a line in the dirt where it had once stood, and the horses bolted into the dark. Their whinnies of terror were drowned out by the snarls of the wolves that trailed after them.

Hawk looked horrified. "Was this part of your plan?" he groaned. "You've left us all standing out in the open, you stupid, old gobbler!"

Yellow eyes glared at Taliesin and her friends. She lifted her sword in both hands. Wren turned the table over and knelt behind it, holding a javelin with more beside her. The men remained behind the barricade but were exposed on all sides. With a shriek, Zarnoc turned and pulled his robe over his head, revealing skinny legs and dirty feet. Ginger remained in tiger form and stood before him, jaws opened wide and roared at the Wolfmen. Dark, hairy shapes leaped over the remains of the outer walls and appeared on top of big stone slabs as the enemy surrounded the Ravens, wizard, and big tiger. The giant wolves paced, maintaining their distance as Taliesin and her companions lifted their weapons, ready to fight the moment the Wolfmen's leader gave the signal to attack.

"Now would be the time to surrender," a familiar deep voice said.

Out of the darkness stepped a man in full armor, a black cape, and a silver helmet shaped in the likeness of a wolf. Captain Wolfgar wore a longsword and carried a large double-edged ax on his back. Gauntlets with silver spikes covered his hands to mid-arm, and barbs protruded from the tips of his leather boots. As he lifted his hand, the wolves grew silent and sat on their haunches, eyes focused on the alpha male. Lifting his visor, he revealed a sharp face, glowing eyes, and long, blond hair tied behind his head.

"Captain Grudge, you have led us on a fine and merry chase. I knew you'd come to the ruins," Wolfgar said, drawing his sword. "In fact, I was counting on it."

"We have no intention of surrendering," Roland said, anger in his voice. "How did you find the Black Rock Inn?"

"It's how I left it that's more interesting."

"Shall we settle this like men?" Roland asked. "What do you say, Captain Wolfgar? Just you and me. A fight to the death. Winner takes all."

Wolfgar laughed. "But we aren't men, Captain Grudge." His eyes shimmered bright yellow. "But I will give you a chance to live. Come with us, Taliesin. We know you have the Deceiver's Map. You shall lead us to the Cave of the Snake God, and we shall recover the Raven Sword. My master has need of it. Come with us, and your friends don't have to die."

"Don't trust him," Roland said, turning toward her. "He has no intention of letting any of us leave here. If you go with him, I doubt you reach the cave as a human; he'll turn you."

"I've no intention of going anywhere with him," Taliesin said. "Nor with you."

"We are waiting, Captain Grudge." Wolfgar pointed at the former tower. "I've already seen what that old wizard can do. He's made it easy for us. Someone should have told you Zarnoc the Great lost his ability to use magic a long time ago. Otherwise, we would have taken him prisoner days ago." He pointed his sword at Rook. "I like this one's look. What is your name, boy? Step forward and we will make you our brother."

"Rook isn't interested in your offer," Roland said.

"Let him speak for himself. Well, boy?" Wolfgar smiled widely. "It takes only a few seconds to be turned. I'll even let you eat the little blonde girl, or at least take the first bite."

Rook picked up his silver spear and shook his head, but he said not a word.

"We know what your clan did to Master Osprey," Taliesin shouted. "The only thing you'll get from us is vengeance. My sword is silver, Captain Wolfgar, and it has magic. I've already killed ten of your scouts. Come no closer, or I'll do to you what I did to them."

"Is that your final answer?" Wolfgar asked.

"You heard her," Roland growled. "No deal, flesh eater!"

Wolfgar signaled the Wolfmen to rise. The wolves stood in unison. More emerged from the dark and joined their brothers, removing their armor and dropping their weapons to the ground. Each changed in appearance, becoming half-man and half-wolf. They stood seven feet tall on their hind legs, monsters of the night. A gut-wrenching howl came out of Wolfgar's mouth, and he dropped his sword. His armor fell away, and he tore off his helmet as his tall body morphed into a *Wolfen*. Drool dripped from his fangs, and his fingernails turned into claws. At his signal, the creatures circled the former tower and rushed the Raven Clan from all sides.

Taliesin, Roland, and Rook swung their weapons, Hawk shot his bow, and Wren threw a javelin that connected with a large body. The big tiger pounced on a wolf, tackled it, and bit into its head.

"Back I say," Zarnoc shouted as he waved a rabbit's foot.

A strong gust of wind sent the Wolfmen tumbling away from the Ravens and tiger and scattered bodies across the yard. An enormous wall of yellow flames that rose fifty feet into the night sky appeared around the small group. Ginger paced, roaring like mad as the Wolfmen clawed at the flames and tried to break through. Several caught fire and let out piercing screams as they ignited into fireballs and, unable to regenerate, were reduced to blackened lumps in seconds. More wolves charged the firewall from the backside. Taliesin and Roland turned and watched the predators fail at their attempt. The flame wall held, and despite all the snarls and growls, the Wolfmen were unable to break through.

"Taliesin, duck," the wizard cried.

A ball of blue flame sailed over Taliesin's head, passing through the firewall, and slammed into a group of *Wolfen*. An explosion sent the monsters flying through the air, engulfed in blue flames, and with a loud *poof*, they turned into lumps of gray ash and crumbled to the ground. Two other creatures morphed into naked men, grabbed spears off the ground, and hurled them at Taliesin. The spears hit the flame wall and fell to the ground. Zarnoc let out a shout of delight and lobbed another fireball at Wolfgar, scattering the creatures.

"Well done, Sir Wizard," Roland said. "How long can you keep it up?"

"At his age?" Hawk said with a snort. "Not that long."

Rook, his cape billowing behind him like wings as he drew back his arm, prepared to hurl his spear at Wolfgar. He threw the spear, and it slid through the flames, but a creature jumped in front of Wolfgar and dropped to the ground, taking the deathblow meant for its commander. Rook picked up the bow and shot arrows; he was the only one doing anything besides Zarnoc and his fireballs. Hawk ran to his sister and grabbed one of her silver-tipped javelins. Finding his target, he threw the javelin and struck a creature in the stomach.

Wren stood and threw as well, hitting a monster as it galloped around the flames; it doubled over in pain. Hawk continued to throw silver javelins until he ran out and yanked his cutlasses out of the ground from where he'd stuck them.

"I'm out of projectiles. They'll have to get up close and personal for my blades to have any effect," Hawk muttered as he glanced at the knight.

"We still have arrows with silver tips," Roland shouted, "but we've only one bow!"

Rook turned and pointed at the ground with the bow, but when no one understood, he made a quick motion with his hand. Wren let out a shout. "Rook says look to your feet, they are coming," she said. "I'm not sure what that means."

The ground quaked beneath Taliesin's feet, and she saw a shiny green beetle with enormous claws emerge from the ground. It went for the tip of her boot, and she stomped it into mulch. "It's the Scourge of Dire Yadru!" she shouted.

Hundreds of thousands of beetles came from the ground on either side of the firewall and converged on humans and *Wolfen* alike in a moving carpet of green. A loud chittering was heard over the roaring fire and the snarls and growls of the wolf pack. The beetles attacked the weapons in each of the Raven's hands along with the Wolfmen's weapons that lay on the ground. Anything made of metal was devoured, from the buckles on their belts to the daggers still tucked inside their boots and all the Wolfmen's armor.

With a loud cry, Hawk threw up his arms and tossed off the hungry green beetles. He waved his weapons in the air and tried to throw off more bugs as they scurried along his body in a rush to get to the metal. Roland's dagger and ax vanished. His companions suffered similar affliction, including Rook's bow and Wren's javelin, as well as the metal on their armor. Only Taliesin's silver sword withstood the attack. She stomped on clusters of bugs and pinned several slower crawlers to the ground with the tip of her blade. Beetles ran the length of the silver sword and sent out a silent message that caused the bugs to drop to the ground in clumps and scuttle into a massive mound. With nothing left to devour, the bugs dug into the soil, leaving the agitated wolves milling about in a frenzy.

Roland rubbed his hands and looked for a weapon of any kind. "Frankly, a silver butter knife would do." He glanced at Taliesin, and a sad smile appeared on his rugged face. "It's up to you, woman. You are our last line of defense."

The wall of flame continued to burn brightly, but Taliesin could hear Zarnoc muttering, which seemed less than a good sign. Roland gathered a pile of rocks and ordered Hawk, Wren, and Rook to do the same. The wolf-beasts ran around the circular firewall on their hind legs and eyed the Ravens, snarling and snapping. It wouldn't be long now, thought Taliesin, risking a glance at the wizard. Zarnoc stood behind Taliesin and muttered in a strange language. His white eyebrows knitted together, and his nose wiggled. Ginger prowled around the area, snarling.

"How long can your magic last?" Taliesin asked. "There must be fifty wolves; I can't kill them all."

Zarnoc shrugged. "Long enough for help to arrive, my dear," he said. "I told you I had gypsy friends, didn't I?" He shook a finger at the furry bodies in front of the flames. "When Shan Octavio arrives, you'll be sorry you came!"

"Gypsies?" Roland hurled a rock through the firewall and hit a Wolfen in the forehead, knocking him to his knees. "How can you be so sure they'll come?"

"Tsk," Zarnoc said. "Must I tell you all my trade secrets? The firewall is more than fifty feet high and can be seen for miles around. We might even get Prince Sertorius to help us. How can I know everything? Just be ready to fight as I am a bit tired."

"What's wrong, Roland? Don't you like gypsies?" Taliesin said, mildly impressed with his good aim. She wasn't ready to forgive him quite yet, though.

"Alvarado Octavio's son and I had a run-in a few years ago. I don't care to renew the relationship." Roland sounded none too pleased. He threw more rocks at the wolves. Rook,

Hawk, and Wren also pelted the Wolfmen who had reverted back to their naked human forms but missed most of their targets.

Taliesin watched a *Wolfen* piss on the fire. The liquid sizzled and sputtered in the orange swirling mass. She could tell by the shape of his eyes it was Wolfgar and wondered what he might have looked like as a wolf instead of a monster that walked on its hind legs. He faded into the background and joined the pack which morphed into giant wolves. One wolf stood out with blond fur and lifted its head to howl. This had had to be Wolfgar, she thought. A chorus of howls signaled another attack. The pack charged forward and rushed the flames at the same time. The Ravens hurled rocks through the flames, but only Roland's struck, hitting the blond wolf in the head. Wolfgar rolled to the ground and ran off into the dark, yelping like mad and trailed by a score of its kin.

War cries, along with the thunder of galloping horses, rose in the distance. A shower of silver arrows fell beyond the flame wall in front of Taliesin and her friends and struck the retreating wolves. She watched the injured wolves scream in pain as they crumpled to the ground and turned into men, not to stir or rise again. The gypsies arrived in number and chased the pack into the night.

The Ghajars were mounted on swift horses and shot arrows from short bows with speed and accuracy; the gleam of silver was unmistakable. Taliesin watched a score of wolves fall to the ground. She never considered she stood in harm's way until a large shape appeared at her side; one wolf had managed to jump the diminishing firewall. Roland yanked her out of the way and used a rock to crush the creature's skull. Taliesin knew it would only regenerate and stabbed it through the heart.

"Thank you," Roland said, wiping his bloody hands on his cloak.

"You owe me, Knight of the White Stag," Taliesin replied.

Zarnoc dropped his hands, and the magic wall of flames vanished as he sagged to the ground. "I'm too old for this," he gasped.

Taliesin hurried to the wizard and pulled him to his feet. Rook retrieved his silver spear, Wren at his side, and joined them. Hawk and Roland stood together and watched the gypsies as they jumped off their horses, went to each Wolfmen, and cut off its head with a silver dagger or sword.

Hawk elbowed Roland. "Price on your head very high, my brother?"

"Too high for you to reach," Roland said.

Leaving Zarnoc with Rook and Wren, Taliesin sheathed her sword and went to Roland. She slid her arm through his, catching him by surprise. As he met her gaze, she felt her anger melt away, replaced by an aching desire to forgive him.

"Pull your hood over your head, you big oaf," Taliesin said, but she did it for him, tugging the edges of the hood tight around his face. "It'll be safer if we call you 'Grudge.' Keep your head down and don't talk to anyone. As far as the gypsies are concerned, you are a Raven, and we protect our own." His fingers slid along her jaw, and she gave him a quick kiss before turning to face the approaching gypsies.

Shouting and whistling, the Ghajar rode around Taliesin's group in two circles that moved in opposite directions. They were dressed in short-cropped jackets, baggy black pants tucked into riding boots, and colorful sashes tied about their waists. Their extravagant beards were braided with silver beads, and each looked more spectacular than the next. Every man was armed with a bow and arrows, javelins, and scimitars made from silver. They generated so much excitement and ferocity with their shouting and piercing stares that they seemed the perfect natural enemy of the wolves. The Ghajar had been around forever and moved from place to place, never staying in one location for long—shunned by society. They used trees as ancient as the great oak of Raven's Nest to build their wagons.

Taliesin stood protectively in front of her friends as they were forced closer together when the riders closed in around them. She had no reason to be afraid of them; after all, they'd come to their rescue, but she sorely wanted to find Thalagar and searched the darkness in vain for a sign of their horses

The riders finally came to a halt, slid out of saddles, and commenced dragging the Wolfmen's bodies into a large pile to burn. An older man with a white-flecked beard who wore bright red caught her attention. He reined in his large, dapple-gray horse and dismounted. Taliesin counted the crow's feet at the sides of his lustrous brown eyes as he approached Zarnoc; six deep grooves told her he was around sixty years old. His shoulders were broad, and he looked strong. His bright red coat fell mid-thigh and had shiny silver buttons. Under his coat was a red vest with silver threading; beneath that, he wore a ruffled white shirt that reminded her of one of Hawk's shirts. His slacks were black and tucked into knee-high leather boots. A silver scimitar hung on his right side in a jeweled scabbard; Erindorian, she thought. On his left hip hung three different-sized silver daggers, each decorated with jewels. He wore a necklace made of wolf fangs.

It was obvious this man was the leader Shan Octavio, and though she'd never met him, his powerful presence was hard to ignore. The Shan was intimidating, standing several inches above Roland, but handsome, and for a moment as he held her gaze, she imagined dancing around a fire for his pleasure. She'd heard plenty of stories from the gypsies who visited Raven's Nest and knew the Shan loved his people. They in return were devoted to him, especially the females. Osprey had told her the Shan had eight wives and more children than Osprey had adopted; it was an impressive tally.

With a deep, throaty laugh, Shan Octavio pulled the wizard into his strong embrace. "Fortune smiles upon you this night," Octavio said. His voice was rich and warm, with a thick, guttural accent.

"Shan Octavio Alvarado," Zarnoc said, bowing his head. "You truly are my lucky star."

"You must be blessed by the gods, old friend. We are camped three miles east. When we saw your fire in the sky, we knew you were in danger and rode straight for Pelekus. Seems I've finally repaid my debt." He placed a large hand on his chest, indicating a prior injury. "If it were not for your wisdom and magical arts, I would not be alive." He glanced at Taliesin, causing her to blush. "These are Ravens," he said. "Friends of yours?"

"Yes, yes," Zarnoc said. "I sent for them."

As Zarnoc started to lead the Shan toward Taliesin, a young man rode up. He held a lead line attached to the reins of Thalagar, the mule, and the other Raven horses. The five horses and the mule looked unharmed, which seemed a miracle.

Octavio gestured for the young man to come forward. "My youngest, Nash, has found your friends' horses," he said. "You know the law, Zarnoc. What we find, we keep."

"You dote on Nash too much, Octavio," Zarnoc said, disapproving. "He is spoiled."

Spoiled or not, Taliesin wasn't about to let some gypsy boy keep her horses. She felt Roland's hand grip her arm to hold her still as if he knew she was about to tell the Shan exactly what she thought of their 'gypsy law.' The horses belonged to her, and she wasn't about to let anyone claim them; Thalagar was not a spoil of war. Her slight movement drew the Shan's attention; he'd seen her reaction and leaned over to whisper into Zarnoc's ear. A look of delight appeared on the old wizard's face as she heard Roland say, "Keep silent. These men do not like outspoken women."

"Then we are doomed," Hawk said, sounding almost gleeful.

Nash jumped out of his saddle, still holding the lead line. He wore a light-blue headscarf, from which blond curls stuck out, and a colorful vest covered with silver beads. His arrogant attitude set Taliesin's nerves on edge. At Thalagar's nervous whinny, she jerked away from Roland and hurried to her stallion.

The riders did not make it easy for her to get through and blocked her path as if playing a game, refusing to let her near the horses. Nash turned, his cheeks flushing as Thalagar slipped his bridle and, with a toss of his head, dashed straight for Taliesin. The gypsies moved out of the way and allowed the black stallion to come to her. Voices whispered as she pressed her forehead to Thalagar's and placed her hands upon his narrow head.

"That's my brave boy," Taliesin said, planting a kiss on his nose. "I know you protected the others. You were right to lead them away and not fight."

Taliesin noticed Nash storming toward her, smacking a riding whip against his thigh. Another gypsy held the lead line of the horses as the youth stalked around Thalagar. The horse snorted and kicked out a hoof that connected with Nash's kneecap.

The boy let out a cry of pain. "You'll pay for that, you damn beast!"

Taliesin stepped forward as Nash drew back his arm, about to strike. "No, you don't!" she shouted. Acting on impulse, she gave Nash a hard push that sent him tumbling to the ground. "Nobody hurts my horse, you *damn beast!*"

Nash tossed the whip aside, drew a curved knife, and jumped to his feet as Taliesin reached for her sword. Thalagar interceded again and unexpectedly smacked the young man in the face with his long black tail. The gypsies laughed as Nash let out a yelp of pain, rubbed his eyes, and pointed the knife at Taliesin. The Shan interceded and stood between his son and Taliesin. The dagger was lowered, and Nash stepped aside, head bowed, and Taliesin dropped her hand from the sword hilt.

"Clearly this stallion belongs to her," Octavio said. "These folks are from the Raven Clan. We do not take from a fellow thief, Nash. You know the law. Let the woman have the horses and see the bodies are burned."

"This woman has shamed me," Nash said. "I would have my revenge, father."

Shan Octavio let out a furious snarl and moved so fast Taliesin never saw him remove the dagger from the boy's hand. The disarmed boy spun, regarded Taliesin with an expression of anger and hate, and then ran off. The Shan looked her over in admiration.

"Who is this woman who brought shame to my youngest?"

Zarnoc stepped forward. "This is the Raven Master's favorite daughter, Taliesin. She is as deadly as she is beautiful. Taliesin, this is Shan Octavio."

The gypsy king's eyes were hypnotic and held her gaze as she reached to shake his hand. His grip was strong, and she thought he held on longer than necessary. He turned her hand over, contemplated the lines on her palm, and again met her gaze.

"A pleasure to meet you, Raven Mistress," Shan Octavio said. "Your father and I have known each other for many years. I've been meaning to pay him a visit since he never seems to get out and travel anymore. What brings you and your friends this far north?"

"Raven business," she said, removing her hand.

Octavio laughed. "The woman is strong of spirit, Zarnoc," he said. "She has no fear. I take it she is the leader of this small group?" The wizard nodded. Octavio looked away and shouted at his men, ordering them to burn the bodies and to salt the earth. The gypsies did as he commanded. After stacking wood under and around the headless Wolfmen, the men threw a smelly liquid on the bodies. When lit, it ignited quickly, and fire soon covered the corpses.

"Do you know why we salt the earth and burn the bodies?" Octavio asked.

Taliesin nodded. "So buzzards won't eat their flesh and spread the disease," she said.

"A disease?" The Shan's expression was thoughtful. "The Wolf Clan is a cursed clan and our enemy. We consider the Raven Clan friends of the Ghajar," he said. "If that were not the case, we would have let the Wolfmen pick your bones clean, Taliesin of the Ravens."

"These are good people, Octavio," Zarnoc said. "I've asked them to join me on a great adventure. As Taliesin said, it's Raven business, but I shall be their guide."

"It's not like you to take orders from a woman. Nor is it like you to join such a circle of friends. The Raven Clan are scavengers, like us, so I assume you seek something of great value."

"We seek the Raven Sword," Taliesin said. She found no reason to keep the fact secret but was aware Roland had stiffened beside her. "The Wolfmen you killed wanted to prevent us from doing so. Their captain will come back for us, and he'll bring more men."

"Not men," Octavio said. "They are *Wolfen*. Cursed wretches that have no right to breathe the same air we do or to live among us as normal men. We hunt them whenever we have the chance."

For a moment, Taliesin caught the gypsy king ogling her breasts, but then realized he was staring at her silver sword; he had never seen a woman carrying such a weapon, more than likely. Octavio reached out and touched the silver hilt. Alarmed, her hand closed around his, holding it firmly against the hilt. She'd meant to throw his hand off, but she detected no malice or deceit in the Shan. His fingers were roughened by sun and wind, but his skin was warm; the rings on his fingers felt cool by comparison. Carefully, she peeled his fingers from the hilt and released his hand.

"Thank you for your help, Shan Octavio," she said, lifting her head high.

"My help does not come for free. If not the sword, then what will you give to repay your debt to me?" The Shan glanced at Roland, who hid his face beneath the hood. "You are taken by this one?" He eyed Roland, trying to see under the hood. "What is his name?"

"That is Grudge. I'm Hawk. This is my sister, Wren, and my blood brother, Rook." The young man looked embarrassed when the Shan gave him a stern look. He'd clearly spoken out of turn, and the introduction was not his to make.

"I am my own woman," Taliesin said. The Shan eyed her breasts, his meaning clear. "You suffered a recent injury Zarnoc healed with his magic. He is our friend and, in helping him, you helped us. I think your debt to him includes us, and no payment is required. Or, am I wrong?"

"Not at all," Octavio said, grinning. "Oh, I like her, Zarnoc. I like her a lot."

Thalagar snorted and came to sniff the gypsy leader's leg. A large hand slid down the horse's neck. Taliesin was surprised when her horse whinnied and nudged the Shan with his head, something he only did with her. Her opinion of the Shan wavered as Octavio patted the stallion on the head and ruffled the black mane. However, she wasn't about to sleep with him to repay a debt she considered paid. The Shan and his men didn't think much of women, and knowing they considered females beneath them didn't sit well with her.

"You and your friends are welcome to stay in our camp tonight," the Shan said. "We will have dinner and dancing and get to know each other."

"That is gracious of you, Shan Octavio," Taliesin said. "We accept your offer."

Octavio looked pleased. He pointed toward the north. "Then ride with us to my camp where you and your friends may rest for the night," he said. "You will find the Ghajar are most hospitable to people we consider our friends." He threw his arms in the air and turned toward his men. "*Drom va!* We take to the road!"

His dapple-gray horse was led over by one of his men, and the Shan mounted the large animal in one smooth leap. With a whistle, he whipped the reins across the side of the horse and set off into the dark, laughing loudly. His men rode after him, leaving the Ravens and Zarnoc standing beside their horses.

"You don't seriously mean to go with them?" Roland asked. He walked to Taliesin and Zarnoc, leading Kordive. "I think it best we go on without them."

Taliesin sensed Roland was jealous of the Shan's attraction to her, as well as being nervous about going to the gypsies' camp. "I've accepted the Shan's offer," she said. "We need to rest, and we need their protection." She didn't know what they were getting into at the Shan's camp, but she did know what waited in the dark. "Wolfgar is still out there, and so is Sertorius. We're unarmed and out-matched, Grudge. We need the gypsies' help if we're to get through the Volgate. Of course, you can leave if you are uncomfortable with my decision."

"I'm sworn to protect you, Raven Mistress," Roland said. "I'm going with you."

Climbing into the saddle, Taliesin found Zarnoc wiggled right behind her. He slid his arms around her, tighter than necessary, she thought. She felt the cat moving between them and wasn't startled when it hissed. She was relieved when the wizard loosened his grip and Ginger settled down. As soon as she confirmed everyone was mounted, she gave a parting look at the burning bodies and nudged her horse, heading in the direction taken by the Ghajar.

* * * * *

Chapter Fourteen

The Ghajar camp was set among a cluster of white birch trees beside a stream. Campfires blazed among more than forty wagons, painted bright red, blue, or yellow. Taliesin noticed the wagons had three shapes: cottage-shaped, bow-topped, and spindle-sided. Women and girls sat around the inner fires and cooked dinner as the boys ran out to meet the Shan and the returning riders. A large campfire surrounded by wagons was circled with cut logs to provide seats and tables set with food.

Taliesin and Wren were mobbed the moment they arrived. She felt a hand tugging on her pant leg and looked down at a young boy with buckteeth eyeing her. Dismounting, she allowed the boy to take Thalagar's reins. He also took the reins to Kordive as Roland walked to her. Both horses were taken to a yellow wagon, and the boy quickly provided a bucket of water and a mound of hay for them. Another boy, with hair as long as Wren's, took the other three horses and led them to a red wagon, while the mule was taken to a bright blue wagon. Zarnoc walked beside Shan Octavio and waved the Ravens over, heading toward the main campfire for dinner.

"They seem friendly," Taliesin said, keeping close to Roland. "Are you worried?"

"Don't let their smiles fool you," Roland grumbled. "If Zarnoc were not a friend of the Shan, I assure you, our reception would be much different." His hand slid under her elbow, guiding her through the press of bodies; everyone seemed to want to meet the Ravens. "If the Shan asks again if you are claimed, tell him you are mine, or you will end up in his bed this night. Most of these women have already been there, and many of these children are his, Taliesin. I suggest you try to resist speaking your mind freely with these people."

A young man in a red vest came over and bowed his head to Taliesin. He pointed at the campfire and escorted the Ravens to where they were expected to sit. Taliesin removed her cloak as she and her friends joined the men. Roland kept his hood over his head and tried to remain hidden, but as the second largest man present, after the Shan, it was impossible not to be noticed. Men turned to watch as she and Roland were led to Shan Octavio, seated on a large overstuffed chair. Zarnoc, smoking his pipe, sat beside him on a smaller chair, with Ginger curled on his lap. Hawk, Rook, and Wren sat on large pillows to the right of Zarnoc and gratefully accepted glasses of wine. Hawk chatted with a tall man with gray eyes and a long, braided beard, who Taliesin had seen slice a Wolfman in half with his scimitar.

As she and Roland approached the Shan, the young man in the red vest pointed at the pillows at the foot of the large chair. Taliesin sat at the feet of the Shan and Roland sat beside Hawk, directly in front of Zarnoc. The moment she was seated, Taliesin felt the tip of the Shan's boot brush across her backside. She scooted forward and heard his deep laughter.

"You know what this is?" Hawk asked. He picked up a flask. "This is *baju*. With a name like that, you know this must be a strong brew. Drink up, Grudge. Don't look so dour, we are among friends. There's going to be dancing, too."

Wren sat between Hawk and Rook, and her long, blonde hair had drawn a number of people who wanted to touch it. Among them was a beautiful gypsy girl with long, curly, black hair and dark eyes. She knelt behind Wren and leaned over her shoulder to talk to her, fingers sliding through the girl's blonde hair.

"That's the Shan's daughter," Hawk said. "Her name is Jaelle."

"You're certainly winning friends fast," Taliesin said, laughing. She watched Roland drink from Hawk's flask and lick his lips. "Maybe you should have joined the Ghajar and not the Raven Clan, Hawk. Some girls are staring at you. I don't think you'll sleep alone tonight."

Hawk turned to look where she pointed. "I think I may have died and gone to Mt. Helos," he said. "How am I ever going to choose just one?"

"Why pick?" Roland asked. "Ghajaran guests are allowed to sleep with whoever they want and with as many as they can handle. It is a man's paradise, I'll grant you that."

Many gypsies were trying to trade with Rook and Wren for their warm, wool cloaks. Wren handed her cloak to Jaelle in exchange for her short red jacket with yellow trim and big silver buttons. The gypsy girl soon had Wren on her feet, pulled her away from the fire, and they vanished in the crowd. As Rook started to rise to follow, Hawk pulled him to the pillow.

"She'll be fine, brother," Hawk said. "Stop worrying and drink."

Hawk took the flask from Roland. It had a silver mouthpiece shaped like a swan's neck and beak. After he drank, he handed it to Rook, who was surrounded by children eager to touch his long braids. A girl started weaving silver beads into his dreadlocks. Rook smiled, delighted, and let the children maul him. Hawk was busy flirting with the young women standing off to the side, pointing at him and giggling as they batted their painted eyelashes. One stepped forward and tied a purple scarf around his head, giving him the appearance of a pirate with his dangling pearl earring. He pulled the girl into his arms while another woman hugged him from behind.

"I hope they bring us a plate of food," Taliesin said. "I'm starving." She leaned against Roland and rested her arm on his leg. The tip of the Shan's boot kept nudging her in the butt as if she didn't know he was seated right behind her.

"Drink up, brother," Hawk said. He tossed the flask to Roland again and laughed as the two girls started fighting over him. Somehow, he managed to pull the second girl onto his lap and traded kisses with each one, ending their quarrel.

Roland drank from the flask and offered it to Taliesin, but she shook her head, wanting water, not wine. She was thirsty, certainly; wine would only make her drunk, especially on an empty stomach. Everyone around the campfire seemed intent on getting drunk. Zarnoc dropped a flask into her lap that felt cool and damp. Taking off the cap, she sniffed, detected water, and with a grateful nod at the wizard, drank her fill.

"Just water?" Roland asked. "I have no intention of remaining sober. Tonight, I am Grudge again, and anything goes."

"Good. Because I'm still mad at Roland, but not at Grudge," Taliesin said, softly. She didn't care if it made any sense or not. A smile spread across her face as he leaned close and kissed her cheek. She quickly turned her head, and his lips brushed across hers.

Music started; a hypnotic rhythm played on lutes, a violin, and several drums. A number of shapely young women walked to the fireside and started dancing, using scarves, which they lifted and lowered as they wiggled their hips. The tip of the Shan's boot touched her backside again, and Taliesin wondered how long it would take before she was forced to turn around to set him straight. She turned to see a girl with long brown hair and dark eyes wriggling against Roland. The girl pulled back Roland's hood and revealed his bald head and whiskered jaw. She tied a peacock-blue scarf around his head.

Roland grinned. "Thank you," he said. "My ears were starting to get cold."

The girl pulled a red-and-yellow checkered scarf from between her large breasts, and Taliesin groaned as the girl tied the scarf around her head. The girl laughed and threw herself into Roland's arms, kissing him, and rather rudely pushed Taliesin aside. Trying not to react with anger or jealousy, Taliesin reached to adjust the scarf. Something was inside it, and she pulled out a Tareen fortune-telling card. One side of the card was solid black, but on the other side was the figure of a skeleton holding a sword in one bony hand and a torch in the other. Minerva owned the same deck of Tareen Cards and had often told fortunes at Raven's Nest when everything was quiet and still. Taliesin had never asked for a reading, but she

knew enough about the cards to know the skeleton represented 'death.' She wanted to ask the girl why she'd given it to
her, but Roland had pushed her aside. The gypsy girl stole the
cloak off his back and slipped away into the crowd.

"Not much of a fair trade," Roland said, drinking more of
the *baju*. He reached for Taliesin's hand and nodded as Hawk
and the two gypsy girls drifted away from the fire. Rook was
right behind them, taking the crowd of children.

Another girl came to Zarnoc and presented him with a fine
pair of silver slippers to replace his worn boots. The wizard
giggled with delight and wiggled his feet before him. "Oh,
these are comfortable," he said, lighting his pipe.

Flasks, along with long pipes of feather leaf, were passed
around the circle of gypsies seated on pillows around the
campfire, and platters of food were laid out on colorful blankets at everyone's feet. When a pipe reached Taliesin, she
smelled it, wrinkled her nose, and passed it to Roland. Whatever it was, she wanted no part of it; smoking wasn't something she liked to do. She watched Roland take a large puff,
cough hard, and then hand it to the wizard.

Feeling a tap on her shoulder, Taliesin turned. Shan Octavio held out a flask to her. "It's *baju*," he said. "Drink and
make merry, Raven Mistress. Everyone drinks *baju* at my
camp. It's a tradition. Even Ravens have traditions, yes? I
would consider it an insult if you refused." He smiled, his
eyes never leaving her face as she drank from the flask.

"Oh, this is so sweet," Taliesin said, not liking it at all.

Whatever *baju* was made from, it had a sickly-sweet taste
that reminded her of honey mead and blackberries. She wiped
her hand across her mouth and handed the flask to Roland;
not that he needed more alcohol. Another tap caused her to
look at the Shan once again. The Shan wasn't going to give her
a moment's peace; that much was certain. Another flask was
handed to her, and taking a cautious sip, she found it to be
wine. Not bad at all, she thought. Roland took the flask from
her and drank what he wanted.

"Will you dance for me, Taliesin?" The Shan pointed at the dancers. "It is a tradition female guests dance for the host?"

"Me?" she said, horrified. "Dance? No, no, no. Dancing isn't for Ravens."

With a roar of laughter, Octavio crossed one leg over the other, and a pretty girl with long, curly, black hair sat on his lap. Another girl, with her black hair pulled into a braid on top of her head, pulled the Shan's beard and nibbled on his ear. Taliesin turned and slid her arm through Roland's, pulling him close. He drank from the flask containing the sickly-sweet *baju*, having put aside the wine.

"You are beautiful," Roland said. Already drunk, he gave her a goofy grin. "I'd very much like to see you dance." He took another drink, and the reddish baju dribbled off his chin. She wiped it off, and he grabbed her hand and licked her fingers clean.

"Tastes like blackberries," Taliesin said. "I don't like it, but you seem to like it too much. Slow down, Grudge. You'll make yourself sick."

"I like *baju*," the knight said. He took a swig, and then another.

"If you're going to get drunk," Taliesin said, "then eat something." She'd been given a plate of food—lamb and rice—and tried to feed it to him. He grunted and refused to eat, so she ate a few mouthfuls. "You're missing out. It's tasty."

"I'm not hungry...for food." Leering, Roland reached for her breast. She swatted his hand away. "I know you have feelings for me," he said. "Admit it, or I'll return to Fregia."

Taliesin was overcome with an urge to tell him the absolute truth. "I love you," she said, kissing him. "All I can think about is making love to you."

Roland grabbed her plate and started eating. Taliesin turned to talk to Zarnoc, who was curled in his chair and puffing on his pipe. Tossing aside the plate, Roland stood, yanked Zarnoc out of his chair, and sat in it, leaving the wizard to find a new place beside Taliesin. A young woman sat in Roland's lap and his arms wrapped around her as she covered his face with kisses. So much for his wanting to know what she really felt, thought Taliesin. It was too easy to tell him how she felt; she knew it had something to do with the *baju* and vowed not to drink another sip.

Zarnoc found the Tareen Card she'd cast aside and held it up. "Where did you get this?"

"I found it under my scarf. Someone clearly wants me to get the hint."

"It doesn't only mean death, but also rebirth and change." Zarnoc placed the card in the sleeve of his robe. "Tareen cards have two messages, one good, one bad, but this particular card means you will be given a choice in the future that will forever affect your life. What it is, I cannot say. I may be the last of the Lorians, but just because my people were fairy folk doesn't mean I know everything."

Taliesin had heard of Lorians. The fairy folk had vanished hundreds of years ago, but people still talked about them when a rainbow was seen or when the fires sparked and seemed to reflect images within the flames. Zarnoc dropped his pipe. She picked it before it burned a hole in the pillow and heard a loud hiss. Ginger was cowering beneath the chair Roland sat in, hissing at her. Placing the pipe between her teeth, she grabbed a small-fringed pillow and placed it behind Roland's boots, blocking the cat so it couldn't try to scratch her. Before she knew what she was doing, she'd taken a toke from the pipe and found the weed tasted of honey.

Careful not to burn Zarnoc's beard, she placed the pipe into his mouth, removed the flask of *baju* that had started leaking onto his robe, and handed it to a girl who had fallen off the Shan's lap and landed on her butt. The girl took the flask and crawled back onto Shan Octavio's lap. As he caressed the girl's breast, she felt the toe of his boot tap her buttocks.

"Where did you meet the Shan?" Taliesin asked.

"Octavio found me living at the tower when he was a boy," Zarnoc said, puffing on his pipe. "He was even more fearsome when he was eight years old and eager to make a name for himself. I was tired of running from the king's guard; always hiding, always in fear for my life, and he took pity on me and gave me his protection. A boy of eight, just imagine." He blew a smoke ring into the air. "Not long after we met, I learned an illness had spread through the wagons, and many had died. I was still powerful back then, so I brewed a magical cure and earned their respect."

"Your visit was long overdue, Great Zarnoc." Octavio's deep voice was as low as the playing drums. "Taliesin, come sit on my knee. Your companion has found another, and I would have you enjoy yourself this night."

The Shan turned when she didn't obey and talked to the tall man with the long beard and gray eyes who had killed the Wolfman with one swipe. The man gave Octavio a lit pipe made of clay painted bright blue. The Shan puffed on it, eyes closed, and smoke rolled out of his nostrils. He opened his eyes and blew out the rest of the smoke from the corner of his lips. Taliesin shook her head when he offered her the pipe. He gave the pipe to Roland, who stopped kissing the girl, made sure Taliesin was watching, and took the pipe. The Shan grabbed Taliesin by the arms, and before she could resist, jerked her onto his lap.

A cheer came from the men. Taliesin found a pair of strong arms wrapped around her waist. Aware Roland watched, she leaned against the Shan's chest and let him hold the pipe to her lips, took a deep draw, and exhaled a puff of smoke.

"We are to leave before another full moon," he said, his mood serious. "Dark times are upon us, Taliesin. There is much unrest in the realm. Trade and bartering are no longer profitable. It's dangerous everywhere we go. I dare not let you venture west. Not when the Wolf Pack is hunting you."

"I am worried," Taliesin said, finding she couldn't lie to the Shan. "Master Osprey and my clan have been captured by the Wolf Clan. I fear I will never see them again. But we are not only hunted by the Wolfmen. Prince Sertorius visited Zarnoc a few days ago; he's looking for me as well. Our only hope is to slip through the Volgate unseen and find the Raven sword before him or the Wolf Pack. I'm the only one who can find it. I have to go."

The Shan nodded. "I understand," he said. "But I cannot allow you to go with so few people. I will select my best men and send them with you."

"I don't want to involve you or your tribe."

"Many allegiances have been made and broken in these last few weeks," Octavio said, his lips against her ear. "I was told by a reliable source the dukedoms of Fregia, Thule, Erindor, and Bavol have sided with King Frederick. However, the lords of Aldagar and Scrydon have pledged to help Almaric. Garridan has yet to choose sides. I believe Prince Sertorius is headed to Garridan to convince Duke Richelieu de Boron to help the king, but whether that is true or not remains to be seen."

"Sertorius supports his father? I was certain he has sided with Almaric," Taliesin said. "I know for a fact Sertorius and Duke Peergynt attacked and killed the Volgan lords who were bringing a magical sword called *Doomsayer* to the king. Magic may be outlawed, but everyone seems to be scrambling to find magical weapons. Now *Doomsayer*, along with my entire clan, is in the hands of the Wolf Clan. I fear the worst, my lord."

Octavio slid his fingers along her arm. "As do I," he said. "I cannot be certain of Sertorius' intentions unless I capture him and bring him here. Under torture, perhaps, he would talk. As for Lykus, that one is dangerous, as all wolves. One Draconus is no better than any other, but Almaric sees himself as the Wolf King, and that makes him my enemy."

"If Almaric is crowned, the Wolf Clan will rise in power, too," Taliesin said. "That means Lykus could be the next chancellor. Or Arundel, because he certainly won't sit and let Lykus claim all the glory when that's what he wants. I say neither the Wolf nor Eagle Clans should be rewarded for their misdeeds and cruelty but driven away or imprisoned."

"What can you do about it? Hmm?"

"Kill Lykus and Arundel, for starters."

The Shan's hand slid across her shoulder and neck, until he cupped her chin, and turned her head to whisper in her ear.

"Many eyes are watching us, my dear girl," he said, nibbling at her ear. "It's known to me Lykus and Arundel have spies in my camp; fear not, for I have spies watching them as well — one must always know what his enemy is doing. And so, one must be careful what is said in public. Besides, holding you on my lap and nuzzling your ear is quite cozy, don't you think?"

Taliesin gave a little sigh. She knew she should extradite herself from the Shan's lap. His hands were roaming, making her shiver, and she had the feeling she might dance beneath the sheets in the privacy of his wagon. Octavio suddenly leaned back, allowing her to sit straighter, and as if on cue, both casually glanced at Roland.

"Who is the ruffian you travel with, Taliesin? The one you call Grudge? That is not his real name; no Raven uses their true name. He's hearty stock. All that meat packed on his bones and skin so pale it easily burns in the sun comes from living in the north. Most Fregians are fishermen or spend the winter cutting blocks of ice to sell on the market. Fregians are no better than Skardans. Men of the north are all barbarians."

"Grudge isn't so bad," Taliesin said.

"How long has he been a Raven?"

A lie was on her lips, ready to be spoken, but the wizard turned and ruined everything; he was honest.

"Oh, that's Sir Roland of the Order of the White Stag," Zarnoc said. "Roland took the Service Oath eight months ago and travels with the Ravens as Taliesin's protector. He's a King's man but is trustworthy and honorable."

Octavio released Taliesin's arm. She slid off his lap and returned to her seat on the pillows at his feet, aware the Shan regarded Roland with more than simple curiosity. The gypsy girl climbed off the knight's lap, a frightened look on her face.

"I seem to have lost my hostess," Roland said, with a belch. "There is room on my lap, Taliesin. Join me, woman."

"Perhaps the lady prefers me," Octavio said. "If you have no claim to her, Sir Roland, then Taliesin is free to pick whoever she wants."

Taliesin felt her temper soar. "I have no intention of bedding either of you. This isn't some pissing contest where the winner gets the girl." She felt her heart racing as sweat beads broke out on her brow, signs the *baju* and weed had taken hold of her.

"I have eight wives," Octavio said. "If Taliesin were my wife, I would have no need of the others and would send them away. Are you a married man, Sir Roland?"

"No," Roland said. "I need only a warm, naked girl to take off the chill and drive away all thoughts of snarling wolves."

Taliesin turned away, not liking the turn of the conversation as the two conceited louts started naming the women they'd slept with. The Shan had Roland beat. She glanced at the wizard, who had removed the pillow blocking the underside of Roland's chair and was trying to coax the cat out. Ginger let out a hiss and struck. Zarnoc replaced the pillow and held a finger to a scratch across his face.

"Ginger has not forgiven me for turning her into a dog," Zarnoc said. "A tiger she doesn't mind, but cats do not like being turned into canines."

Turning to gaze at the dancers, Taliesin listened to Roland, Octavio, and Zarnoc discussing their sex lives, and when she heard Zarnoc say 'five hundred' she wondered how an old man had slept with so many women; he had to be older than he let on, unless he'd been very active in his youth. When the men's laughter faded away, she felt the Shan's boot tip prod her backside again. She spun around, about to say something nasty, but held her tongue when she noticed his dark eyes had hardened; his anger was directed at Roland. She was amazed the Fregian knight and the wizard were oblivious to the change in their host's attitude.

"I have heard the name 'Sir Roland' before," the Shan said, his tone cold and hard. "Your face looks familiar, but you pale northerners all look the same to me. However, I am sure one of my sons remembers meeting you." He scanned the crowd and stood up. "Tamal! Come here! I would speak to you, son!"

"The Shan's eldest," Zarnoc whispered.

A young man with small, dark eyes, a crooked nose, and curly black hair sat on Taliesin's far left. Hearing his name, Tamal stood and walked toward the Shan's chair. His jacket was pale green, and peacock feathers were stitched into the sleeves. Taliesin tensed as Tamal approached his father, who pointed out Roland. The young man immediately drew a curved dagger, launched himself at the knight, and knocked him out of his chair, all the while shouting like a maniac. The music stopped, and the dancers fled from the fireside as Roland and Tamal rolled across the ground toward the roaring fire. Roland was drunk and in no condition to defend himself, and Tamal managed to straddle him and pressed the knife against the knight's throat.

Taliesin was on her knees, her hand on her sword. She felt a large hand fall onto her shoulder as the Shan held her back.

"You will pay for shaming me, Fregian," Tamal shouted. "With your death, I shall earn the respect of my tribe and my honor."

Taliesin reacted without thinking, knocked away Octavio's hand, and ran toward the two men. She grabbed Tamal's arm and pulled the knife away from Roland. The gypsy swung his held arm and knocked her off her feet. The men started to laugh and cheer as Taliesin threw her arms around Tamal's thick body and yanked him away from Roland. Tamal jerked free and struck her across the face. She hit back and flattened his nose with one punch. In an instant, she yanked the knife out of his hand and held it to his genitals. The young man froze, breathing hard, and she watched a lump slide down his throat.

Roland was on his feet, staggering slightly, and had a hand to his throat. He'd been cut, though only slightly, and blood appeared between his fingers. He tore the scarf off his head and bound it around his neck.

"If you want your eldest son to rule after you, Shan Octavio, then you'd best explain why he was going to kill Sir Roland," Taliesin shouted.

"Taliesin," Roland said, mortified. "Let the boy go. This is a matter between men."

"They drugged us with *baju* and weed, Roland. They made us feel at home, and then tried to kill you," she replied, looking toward the Shan. She pressed the tip against Tamal's crotch, and he whimpered. "Shall it be Nash or Tamal who takes your place one day, great Shan? Why not let a daughter rule instead? A woman can produce more heirs, but a gelded man can do nothing but live on his carnal memories."

Men stood with weapons drawn, but the Shan waved his hands, silencing his warriors, and stepped away from his large chair.

"Daughter of the Raven Master," the Shan said, "I ask you hear me out before you turn my son into a eunuch. Men, lower your weapons. We, Ghajar, value honesty above all else. Put away the knife, Taliesin, and we will hear both men speak. The truth should be known before you take justice into your own hands."

Taliesin removed the dagger and Tamal scrambled away from her. Quickly standing, she threw the knife into the fire, placed her hand on the hilt of her sword, and stood beside Roland. She knew Roland was horrified by her behavior, as much as the Shan, but she cared not. Her gaze remained on Octavio as he approached, aware everyone was staring, but she felt wild and dangerous, heedless to the danger she'd placed herself in. For a second, she pictured every single Ghajar lying on the ground, dead, and buzzards circling overhead. Where her rage came from, she did not know, but she heard Ginger purring, the sound loud in her ears, as the yellow cat jumped onto the Shan's chair and commenced licking between its legs. It struck her as humorous, and she started to laugh. The tension in the air immediately dissipated, and the Shan and his men laughed with her.

"Well done, Ginger," Zarnoc said. He stood beside the chair, holding his staff, his pipe in his mouth. "Allow the Raven Mistress to sit, Shan Octavio, before she faints. You have plied her with too much *baju* and valley weed. I warned you she was not to be trifled with."

Taliesin felt her head spinning as she walked toward the chair. As she approached the Shan, two large hands settled onto her shoulders, and he suddenly pulled her into his arms. His kiss was sudden, hard, demanding. She responded, aware the men laughed even harder, but with effort, pushed him aside, aware he was breathing as hard as she was.

"I am bewitched," Octavio said, raising a hand to his lips. "Her kiss burns."

"She's a witch," the men said.

Roland stared at Taliesin, shaken out of his drunkenness, a look of jealousy and anger hanging upon his rugged face. The tall man with gray eyes she'd admired for his fighting skills stood between Roland and Tamal. Zarnoc motioned Taliesin to come forward and picked up Ginger. Taliesin sat in the large chair, and the cat was placed in her lap. This time the cat did not hiss and seemed content to curl up and purr. The Shan walked over and stood on her left side, while Zarnoc puffed on his pipe and leaned against the right side of the chair.

Everything stilled around Taliesin. Not a man moved. The wind stopped blowing, and the fire ceased both crackling and flickering. Taliesin caught her breath and placed her hand on the Shan's arm. He didn't move or look at her. Roland stared at her but did not stir. She turned to Zarnoc and found him grinning.

"All will be well, Raven Mistress," Zarnoc said. "The Shan will allow you to hold court. This has never been done before. No woman has ever ruled over the gypsies, but you will do so now. They believe you are a witch, and so you are. Take control of the situation. The man with gray eyes is Charon, the Shan's second-in-command. Tamal is brother to Jaelle, the girl who whisked away Wren, and they are the children of his first wife. Use this knowledge to your advantage. Demand to know what the problem is and resolve this matter before there is more bloodshed. Your heart will know which man speaks the truth."

Before she could question Zarnoc and find out what had happened in the past, the wizard blew a smoke ring into the air, and all at once, everything returned to normal. The men whispered. The Shan shifted his weight and placed his hands on his hips. Roland held his head higher and looked proud and arrogant, while Tamal stewed and glowered.

"Charon," Taliesin said, speaking firmly, "bring Sir Roland and Tamal forward. I am the Raven Mistress, your honored guest, and blood has been drawn. Since my man has been injured, it is my right to preside over this matter. I demand to know what happened."

"Tamal claims he was wronged by Sir Roland in the past," Octavio said.

"The accused shall speak first," Taliesin said, loudly. "It is our way. The Raven way."

She cleared her throat. "Sir Roland will speak first and tell his story, and then Tamal will respond. I will know which one speaks the truth, and what punishment is required if deemed necessary."

Octavio nodded. "Raven blood has been drawn. It is the Raven's Mistress's right to make such a demand, and we will respect her decision," he said in a loud and commanding voice. No one argued or offered any negative comments, obeying their lord.

"I am Sir Roland Brisbane of the Knights of the White Stag." Roland offered a courtly bow and stood tall as a low murmur of voices could be heard among the gypsies. "It was in Fregia, three years ago, outside a tavern, that I came upon Tamal in the process of raping a local farmer's daughter. My order requires its knights to uphold the law, and no rapist is to go unpunished. I had the right to take this man's life, but the girl's father asked for leniency, so I gave him the thrashing he deserved and let him go."

"He's lying," Tamal snarled. "That isn't what happened. I want revenge. Is it not the law, Father? I have been wronged by this man, and yet you allow this woman to sit in your chair and act as my judge."

"You will show the Raven Mistress your respect," Octavio said. "Do not shame me further by speaking in this manner, Tamal."

Taliesin thought of Osprey, and what he would have done. The accused always spoke first and then the accuser. Tamal stared at the ground, while Roland met her gaze; a clear indication of who lied and who spoke the truth.

"Roland has taken the Service Oath and is a Raven," she said, in a firm voice that surprised even her. The cat purred loudly. "At Raven's Nest, a man found guilty of rape would be gelded. Shan Octavio, tell me what the Ghajar does to a man found guilty of rape."

"Such a man would be whipped and branded for his crime," Octavio said.

A shout in the crowd disrupted the quiet. The men made a path for a blond-haired figure that stumbled forward, drunk, angry, and holding a knife. It was Nash. Charon blocked Nash's path, grabbed the drunken boy by the arm, and jerked him aside. The men started to laugh, but it ended when the Shan waved them silent.

"You will tell the truth, Tamal," Shan Octavio said. "Give him *baju*."

Four armed men approached Tamal. The young man's arms were held by two, keeping him from struggling, another held his head, and the fourth picked up a flask and poured *baju* into his mouth. Tamal sputtered as he gulped large mouthfuls of the sickly-sweet liquor. Released after he'd consumed the majority of the contents in the flask, Tamal sank to his knees and puked the red liquid onto the ground.

"Now, my son," Octavio said. "Tell the Raven Mistress what happened. Three years ago, you returned home with a story that has never set right with me. Does Sir Roland speak the truth? Did you rape the girl?"

The young man nodded. "Yes, I did, father."

"Yet, you claimed Sir Roland raped her, and it was you who tried to stop him." Octavio drew a dagger and stepped forward. "You know the penalty for lying, son."

"Let him speak, Shan Octavio," Taliesin said. "Tell us what happened, Tamal. I will decide your fate and not your father. Look at me and tell me what happened."

"The farm girl flirted with me. She wanted me," Tamal said. "When I went to kiss her, she pushed me away and called me an *animal*, so I took what she had offered and then denied to me. Sir Roland came upon us, and we fought. When I returned home, I told everyone the knight had raped the girl, and I had tried to defend her, but I lied." He lowered his head. "The Knight of the White Stag had every right to kill me, but he let me go. I am ashamed at what I have done." He looked to Shan Octavio. "Please, forgive me, father."

Octavio's eyes glittered angrily. He turned to Taliesin. "The Raven Mistress will decide your fate, not me," he said, putting away his dagger. "She's heard both stories. Now, let her decide what will be done with you. Will it be life or death?"

An audible gasp went through the crowd.

The cat ran to Roland, circled his legs, and hissed at Tamal, who cringed from where he sat on the ground. Roland looked grim, while Tamal held hope in his small, beady eyes. Taliesin knew what the Shan and the Raven Master would have done to Tamal for raping a girl and then accusing another falsely. But she was not a man and did not believe an act of violence was the right punishment. Standing, Taliesin held her head high and gave her verdict.

"From this day forth, Tamal shall be Sir Roland's squire. In order to regain his honor, Tamal shall do whatever Sir Roland tells him to do. But hear this," Taliesin commanded, gazing at both men. "I am the Raven Mistress, and as such, my word is law. While you are in my company, if you so choose to follow me into the Salayan Desert, both of you will obey my orders without question. If you agree, then swear your loyalty to me."

Tamal met her gaze. "I swear to be faithful to you, Mistress Taliesin," he said, but the words came hard. He turned toward Roland, hand over his heart, and sounded no more sincere than he looked. "And I shall do my best to serve as your squire, Sir Roland."

"Now swear your loyalty to me, Sir Roland," Taliesin said. "I know you are a King's man, but while on this quest, you shall belong to me and no other."

The knight bowed. "I swear to serve the Raven Mistress faithfully," he said. "For better or worse, our fate is now in your hands."

* * * * *

Chapter Fifteen

Taliesin and Roland walked through the gypsy camp behind a barefoot boy in ragged pants. A carpet of grass lay beneath their feet, and the branches of ash and birch trees provided a canopy to block the shine of the moon. The Ghajar were settling in for the night. Women bathed their children in large tubs of water, youth dressed for bed watched from the steps of their colorful painted wagons, and a few dogs scampered out of the way as Taliesin and Roland walked. This night was different, calm, peaceful, and when Roland took her by the hand, Taliesin didn't pull away. His callouses were comforting, making her think of how gentle he could be when he touched her.

"What you did back there," Roland said, "for me, for Tamal, I thank you. I have never seen a woman show so much bravery or dispense justice with such fairness. The grand master of my order, Banik Dzobian, and King Frederick would have ordered Tamal killed. Having a gypsy as a squire should prove to be interesting. Clever of you to make us both swear our allegiance to you, for you know I am a man of my word."

"Now that you have, it means you must do whatever I want, Sir Roland," Taliesin said in a playful voice.

"Stop undressing me with your eyes, Raven Mistress. People are watching. When we are inside the wagon," Roland said, "you may order me to do anything you want. What does Shan Octavio say all the time? It will be *my pleasure.*"

A group of young women was seated on a blanket, pillows scattered around them, outside the door of a blue wagon painted with yellow and orange constellations. An old woman wearing a purple scarf around her head dealt out Tareen Cards for several girls. Female laughter could be heard from inside the wagon, and Taliesin heard Wren's silly giggle. The door opened, and a dark head popped out. Jaelle glanced in their direction and came outside in a long gold skirt cut high on both sides and a fluffy blue blouse; she barely noticed the women seated on the blanket as she swept toward Taliesin and Roland. Spinning, Jaelle revealed tan legs and knee-high sandals with black straps crisscrossed over her muscular calves. A thick mane of black hair fell down her back and brushed across her hips as she came to Roland. Her lips were full and painted a dark maroon. Her eyes were the color of honey, and as she spun around, she gazed lustfully at Roland and grabbed his arms.

"Let me read your fortune, big man," the girl said. "Come, come. I promise Jaelle is always accurate. Maybe the pretty lady wants her future read as well? For a small price, Jaelle will tell you everything." She slid her arms along his body and wrapped them behind his neck.

"I have other plans tonight," Roland said, "but I appreciate the offer."

"Jaelle, leave them alone," an old woman said as she cast a stern eye in the girl's direction. "Go inside and tend to your guest. You are being rude, child." She laid a card for one of the women sitting in front of her who responded with a loud gasp, clutched the girl beside her, and trembled with fear

"I've not met a knight before," Jaelle said. She kept Roland's arm and pulled him toward the wagon. "My father says knights are chivalrous, but I would know what type of man my brother will serve. I would come on this quest as well. Let me prove how helpful I can be, great knight. Bring your Raven Mistress as well. I do not mind."

"It's Taliesin's decision," Roland said. "You ever have a threesome before, Taliesin?"

"No, and don't tell me you have, since I already heard how many girls you, Octavio, and Zarnoc have slept with, and I'm rather disgusted."

Jaelle tossed her long black hair, reached behind Roland, and held up a green apple as if he'd been hiding it behind his back all along. Her teeth flashed a brilliant white in the moon-light as she bit the apple, let the juice drip from her chin, and placed the fruit between her ample breasts. "Take a bite," she said, in a seductive voice. "It is juicy. You will like it, Sir Knight. Bite whatever you desire."

"That's quite an offer," Roland said, laughing.

The gypsy girl glanced at Taliesin, as did Roland, but he wasn't asking permission; his expression was one of a man in trouble. Jaelle quickly removed the apple, stuck it between her teeth and bit hard, while she slid her hands across Roland's chest and wiggled her backside. Her nimble fingers unfas-tened his heavy coat and pushed it open, and then she started untying the laces to his shirt. Taliesin wasn't about to share her lover, and the moment the leather was pushed aside, ex-posing his hairy, muscular chest, she pushed the gypsy aside and stood between her and Roland. The apple dropped out of Jaelle's mouth and fell to the ground as she came to Taliesin and rubbed her large breasts against the angry red head's arm.

"Your man is big and strong," Jaelle said. "Between us, we could ride him into oblivion."

Taliesin wondered if the man called Grudge might have agreed to take the girl to their wagon back at Raven's Nest. Jaelle offered a coquettish blink of her long black eyelashes as she again tried to grab Roland, but he caught her arm.

"I think you should return to your wagon, young lady. The Raven Mistress has need of my attention tonight, and she does not play well with others."

"Not before I read your palm," Jaelle said. She removed his hand from her arm, turned it over, and spread her fingers across his palm. "You have a long life for a knight, relatively good health, but I see your love line interwoven with several others. You are fickle, my lord. You have more than one love."

This time Roland chuckled. "I assure you that is not the case," he said. "I do not believe in divination or a woman's intuition to predict my future." He drew his hand away. "You flirt with danger, little girl."

A smile appeared on Taliesin's face at his response. She took Roland by his arm, stood close to him, and looked directly into the gypsy's eyes. "The big man said 'no,' and I don't share, so go inside, Jaelle, and leave us alone."

Jaelle grabbed Roland's other arm. "Whatever she can do, I can do much better. We gypsy girls know how to please a man," she said. "I will be good to you, Sir Roland. Very good. Let the Raven Mistress bed my father. I know he wants her."

"You really don't listen," Taliesin said, her temper boiling. "Let go of him. I won't tell you again, silly girl."

"Let the knight make up his own mind," Jaelle said.

Roland brushed Jaelle aside and pulled Taliesin into his arms. He nuzzled her ear. "I can't help it if gypsy girls find me irresistible," he growled. "She is right about her father. You responded with passion. That was quite a kiss."

"Shut up, oaf!" Taliesin pulled on his arm and dragged him away from the girl who released him, spun around laughing, and returned to her wagon. "All these gypsies think about is fornicating. No Raven girl would ever throw herself at a man like that. I certainly never have, and don't make any cute remarks because I'm going to make you pay for making me jealous. You'll start at my neck and kiss all the way down my body."

* * *

An hour later Taliesin lay in Roland's arms. He was asleep, his head on a pillow, and his large body pressed against her back, generating so much heat that sweat beaded along her forehead and upper lip. From their berth on a large, soft mattress at the back of the wagon, she watched the shadows created by a bright lantern move across the walls, dancing; like figures around a campfire. Bright curtains at the windows on either side of the cottage-shaped wagon fluttered as a cool breeze swept across their bodies.

The interior was modest, with simple charm. Rugs covered the floor, three chairs were shoved beneath a wooden table painted with designs, and a row of cooking utensils and crockery hung from the ceiling. Their gear was stacked beside the table. Overhead, multicolored skirts, ruffled blouses, and brightly colored scarves hung on a line, and three tambourines with red and blue streamers were nailed to the rounded wall above the table.

"This could be our new home," Taliesin said, softly. Her feet brushed against his, and she snuggled closer. A shiver ran through her body. "I didn't mean to wake you."

"You think too loudly," he said, after a moment's pause. "Shall I make love to you again, or do you want to talk, Raven Mistress?"

Taliesin turned in his arms, tossed a leg over his hip, and slid her hand along his hairy chest. "Roland is complicated," she said. "I understood Grudge. I made you swear an oath to me tonight, but I can't help but wonder if you really belong to the king or to me."

"I'd never make love to the king," he chuckled. "And if I told you every dark, little secret or every heroic deed, my story would be told, and you'd lose interest. You don't like simple. I could see you marrying the Shan. He and his men treated you like a queen tonight, though I tried my best to do the same."

"I only want you," Taliesin said.

Turning her head, she saw a dark shadow crouched behind her and felt the fingers glide upwards to grip her throat. Her hands grabbed a pair of warm fingers crushing her windpipe, and she flung her body to the side, bringing along a smaller form to crash onto the floor. She heard shouting as they rolled across the floor, her assailant still strangling her, knocked into the table, and upset a bowl of green apples.

"You shamed my brother," an angry female voice shouted. "Now you shall pay for it!"

As the fingers dug into her throat, Taliesin's head was banged against the floor. Stars burst inside her skull and obliterated the view of the figure straddling her. She balled her hand into a fist, and using all her strength, struck upwards and connected with a pointed chin. A cry of pain came as Jaelle fell to the floor. Taliesin was on her in an instant, grabbed a fist full of hair, and slapped the girl across the cheek.

"Don't hurt her," Wren said. "This is Jaelle, the Shan's daughter!" She pulled Taliesin away and knelt beside Jaelle. Wren had cut her hair short and dyed it black. Her violet eyes were outlined in black cosmetics, and she was dressed as a gypsy.

"Why did you bring her here, Wren? Didn't you know what she intended to do?" Taliesin asked. She stood naked and tall, glaring at the other two girls. Wren shook her head. "Get her out of here, then, and we'll forget this business."

A flash of silver and Taliesin saw the knife in Jaelle's hand. The girl jumped to her feet and ran toward Taliesin with the dagger held high, only to be flung away by Roland's arm as he knocked her aside. With a loud *smack*, Jaelle slammed into a wall and dropped the knife. Wren, with fear oozing from her every pore, kicked the dagger across the room and stepped away from Jaelle.

"Jaelle, stop it!" Wren cried. "What will your father say?"

"My concern is only for my brother, Tamal," the gypsy girl said. "He has been shamed, and I would win back his honor by killing the Raven Mistress."

Roland grabbed his pants, stepped into them, and buttoned them quickly. "Ravens do not take murder lightly; you know this, Wren," he said. "Even if you were unaware this girl had murder on her mind, Jaelle's attack on Taliesin is just as much your fault as it is hers. Where is Rook anyway? Why isn't he watching over you?"

"In a wagon, sleeping," Wren said, wiping away a tear. "But I swear I didn't know what Jaelle was planning to do. She dyed my hair and then wanted me to show you my new costume. I had no idea she was going to try and kill you, Raven Mistress."

Taliesin picked up the discarded dagger, grabbed her black cloak, and slipped it around her shoulders. Somewhere outside a dog barked, but Taliesin had eyes only for Jaelle. Roland sat in a chair, breathing heavily and still shaken. Wren helped Jaelle to the bed and sat next to her.

"You're a fool, Wren," Taliesin said. "And so are you, Jaelle. I was wrong to think the Ghajar were like the Raven Clan. All we have in common is a fondness for gold. I should have let Tamal die at the hands of his own father. Perhaps I should take *you* to the Shan and tell him what you have done. I do not think he would be lenient; you have tried to kill his guest."

Wren hung her hands. "The Shan will kill her. You can't do that, Taliesin. Please don't tell him—Jaelle is sorry for what she's done."

"I am not," Jaelle said, spitting out the words. "My brother has been shamed. I must avenge him. It is the only way to clear his name."

"We Ravens do not forget. You take a life, your life is forfeit," Taliesin said. "Be thankful you did not kill me, or you would be dead as well. Roland would have seen to that."

"The Ghajar do not forget either," Jaelle said. Her nose was bleeding; she wiped the blood off her face with her skirt. "Tamal is not some servant you can order about. He will be the next Shan, yet he now serves this knight as a lowly squire. It is shameful."

"Does Tamal know you came here?" Roland asked with a growl.

Jaelle's honey-colored eyes filled with bright tears. "No," she said, bitterly. "This was my idea. I wanted only to redeem Tamal's honor, which you have taken from him." She pushed Wren aside and rose from the bed. "So now what? Will you tell my father?"

"And see him beat you?" Taliesin arched an eyebrow. "I don't think I'll tell your father, Jaelle. I am the Raven Mistress with only four clan members, and I must see our ranks swell. Also, I think you would learn more about the error of your ways if I made you a member. Therefore, your penance for trying to take my life will be to protect it with your own."

"You want her to take the Service Oath?" Wren asked, shocked at the generous offer.

"Why would you want me to join your clan after I tried to kill you?" Jaelle asked.

"Because I value the spirit of strong women," Taliesin said. "You are nothing more than a servant here, Jaelle. Your father allowed me to decide your brother's fate. I'm not a knight, so I can't have a squire, but as the Raven Mistress, I am entitled to having servants." She glanced at Roland and enjoyed seeing the confusion on his rugged face. "If she takes the Service Oath, she will be mine to command. If she fails to serve me faithfully, I have the right to take her life. Do you think I can make a Raven out of some would-be-murderess?"

"Your decision," Roland said. "But I wouldn't trust her."

Jaelle stared at her with the same hope Taliesin had seen in Tamal's eyes.

"I am not your enemy, Jaelle, but I could be your friend," Taliesin said. She knew she was taking a big risk, but it felt like the right decision. "Will you take the Service Oath? Will you serve me faithfully? Can I trust you, or should I turn you over to your father?"

Jaelle came forward and took Taliesin's offered hand. "I do not know the words of the Service Oath," she said, "but I swear on my father's life and on my brother's life that I will faithfully serve the Raven Mistress. Take me on your quest, and I shall help my brother regain his honor as I regain my own. If you will have me, then I would be your friend."

"Then is it settled," Taliesin said. "Welcome to the Raven Clan, Jaelle." The gypsy girl threw her arms around Taliesin and kissed her on the mouth. She didn't know if it was a tradition with the Ghajar or not. She heard Roland chuckling and drew away, unsure how to react.

"We are now sisters," Jaelle said, strangely excited. "I will tell my father I have joined your clan. He will have to let me come with you now."

Roland's big body seemed to fill the entire space in the wagon as he took two strides toward the women. He had a sour look on his handsome face.

"What's wrong? You don't approve?" Taliesin asked as she started to dress.

"Of course, I don't approve. I need warriors, not little girls." Roland reached for a bottle of wine. "But I'm not in command. You are. And I'm sure you'll do whatever you want, Taliesin." He snorted as he lifted the bottle to his lips. "*Women.*"

* * *

At the break of dawn, Taliesin, Wren, and Jaelle had saddled their horses while the Ghajar women prepared breakfast for the men around the campfires. After their fill of raisin scones and sliced pears, washed down with strong coffee, they were ready to leave. Taliesin, in gypsy garb, red hair dyed black as a raven's wing and dabbed with enough gypsy perfume the sharp-nosed Wolfmen wouldn't be able to identify her, blended into the crowd. Hawk and Rook were saddling their own horses, and the mule was loaded with provisions.

"Roland is with the Shan," Hawk called out and pointed at the Shan's bright red wagon.

With a nod, Taliesin headed to the wagon and heard loud voices coming from inside. The Shan's sons, Tamal and Nash, stood outside the wagon with four other young men. Nash stepped forward to block her path, mistaking Taliesin for a gypsy.

"What are you doing here?" Nash asked. "Get back to work."

"Stand aside, boy. I'm the Raven Mistress," Taliesin said. She revealed the hilt of her silver sword from beneath the folds of a dark purple cloak. "Your father is expecting me."

"Women are not allowed to attend war councils," Nash said aggressively. "You are not our equal, Raven scum, and you need to be taught your place in life."

Tamal put his hand on Nash's chest and pushed him away. Red blotches appeared on the younger brother's cheeks, and the pair scuffled before one of the guards stepped between them.

"You're a fool, Tamal," Nash said. "I take no orders from any woman."

Walking around the men, Taliesin again found her path blocked by Nash. The young man grabbed her arm, and she brought her knee up and connected with his groin. Nash dropped to his knees, his hands held between his legs, and groaned. Tamal and the guards started to laugh, showing no compassion for the boy, and Taliesin ascended the stairs. She opened the door and entered the large wagon. Roland, also dressed as a gypsy, sat across from the Shan and Zarnoc at a table with clawed feet. Zarnoc, painted like a gypsy, fed his yellow cat small pieces of raw meat. The wizard smiled. The cat purred loudly.

"Sorry I'm late," Taliesin said. "What did I miss?"

Octavio rose from his chair and bowed as she sat next to Roland. His long, graying hair was loose and hung freely across his broad shoulders. He wore an open white shirt that revealed his hairy chest. "We're discussing the route you will take," he said. "My scouts report the prince has been penned by the Wolf Pack inside the Volgate. Tamal has selected four men to accompany you through the marshes. I have already provided silver weapons for your companions, Taliesin, but you will need more than silver and Zarnoc's magic if you hope to reach your destination." He pointed at a large silver ax on the table that looked familiar. "This is *Moonbane*. It was made for the sole purpose of killing Wolfmen. With your permission, I would like to give it to Sir Roland."

Taliesin caught her breath. "I thought *Moonbane* was destroyed long ago," she said. "It was forged by Rivalen. This is a very generous gift, Shan Octavio. I can think of no better man than Sir Roland to use such a weapon. See if it responds to you, Roland."

The Shan smiled as Roland reached for the ax. At his touch, it started to vibrate. He pulled his hand away, and the ax grew still. Zarnoc kissed Ginger on the head and placed her on Octavio's pillows. The cat kneaded away until satisfied the pillow was soft enough before she curled into a ball and tucked her nose into her side. The wizard returned to the table and eyed the ax with a gleam in his eye.

"Yes, yes," the wizard said. "*Moonbane* is precisely what we need. Well done, Octavio. I had forgotten you owned this ax. It will be quite handy."

"I cannot accept such a powerful weapon, Shan Octavio," Roland said. "An ordinary silver ax will do."

"The Wolf Pack and the Ghajar have been at war since long before you were born," the Shan said. "*Moonbane* has served me well through the years, and I have no doubt it will save your life many times over, Sir Roland. You have more need of it than I do; I have all the weapons I need." He pointed at a row of silver spears and swords that hung on the wall. "All are fine weapons," he said, "but none as fine as *Moonbane*."

Roland let his fingers run across the ax's handle, and *Moonbane* vibrated, eager for his touch. He closed his hand around the handle and lifted the ax from the table. "I can feel its energy running up my arm. Had I used this the other day against Wolfgar's men, Taliesin need not have cut them into tiny pieces. But I am a simple knight. This should go to Tamal, not me."

Octavio thoughtfully stroked his triangular-shaped beard. "Tamal is not worthy of a magical weapon," he said. "Not until you teach him the meaning of honor, humility, and wisdom, Sir Roland. I know of your heroism at the Battle of Dunhill and at the siege of Clairmore Castle. Zarnoc has also told me that Master Osprey gave you the task of protecting the Raven Mistress. *Moonbane* will ensure you are able to do that, Sir Roland. Take it, and I will rest easier knowing I have done what I can for the Raven Clan."

"If you insist, my lord," Roland said, "then I will gladly accept the ax."

"Good. It is settled, then," the Shan said. "The horses are saddled, and provisions have been provided for your journey. Tamal knows a way through the Volgate. He will make sure you do not encounter Prince Sertorius or the Wolf Pack. The sun is up. Come, and I will see you off."

Octavio stood and walked to the door, keeping his head bent to avoid knocking into the pans hanging from the ceiling. He caught Nash eavesdropping as he opened the door, and the young man staggered down the steps at his father's angry look. Nash scurried away as though a pot of scalding water had been thrown at him. Roland followed the Shan outside, but Taliesin hesitated when she heard a loud, piteous meow, and turned to see the cat lift her head from the pillow. The old wizard stroked the cat's head and wiped his hand under his nose when he sniffled.

"You must stay here, Ginger," Zarnoc said. "I will fare better knowing you are safe with Octavio. Keep him company and catch rats. I will return before you know it, sweet girl."

A horrible sound came from of the yellow cat. Razor-sharp claws struck and left a deep scratch across the back of Zarnoc's hand, and the cat jumped off the bed, passed between Taliesin's legs, and ran out the door.

"Really! This is outrageous behavior, Ginger!" Zarnoc exclaimed. He ran after the cat and caught her on the steps of the wagon, and the gypsies and Ravens grinned as he chastised her. "Do you really want to be a meal for a wolf or a giant scorpion? Or do you think I am unable to manage without you? I dare say I was casting spells long before I picked you out of a litter of thirteen, so mind your manners and be nice to Octavio while I am away."

A hearty guffaw came from the Shan as he took the cat from the wizard. Ginger purred when he scratched behind her ears.

"I will take good care of her, Zarnoc," Octavio said. "We are already good friends!"

"Just remember when you pet the cat, I can feel it as well," Zarnoc said, with a shiver. "We are connected soul-to-soul, that cat and I. If Ginger should happen to bear you a litter of kittens while I'm abroad, you may take them all, but leave me the runt. Runts make the best familiars. Most sorcerers go for a sleek black cat with eyes of green. Rank amateurs."

"How do mice taste, Zarnoc?" Taliesin asked, laughing as she walked past him.

"Not so good," replied the wizard.

Heading to Thalagar, Taliesin saw that Rook, Hawk, and Wren, all dressed as gypsies, were already in the saddle and ready to depart. The four men she'd seen guarding the Shan's wagon were with Tamal and Jaelle and had silver weapons tied to their saddles. All four had a similar appearance, and Taliesin assumed they were brothers.

Tamal's and Jaelle's horses were of exceptional breeding and liveried handsomely with black leather saddles and bridles adorned with silver studs. By the time Taliesin had made certain the cinch was tight on Thalagar's saddle and climbed into in, the gypsies had mounted and ridden to the red wagon to bid the Shan farewell. Octavio set Ginger on the ground and spoke to his children as Hawk rode beside Taliesin, a blue scarf tied around his head and his pearl earring dangling beneath its edge. He'd exchanged his cutlasses for two silver scimitars strapped across his back, and a new bow with a quiver of black-tipped arrows hung from the saddle horn.

"Who is that girl?" Hawk asked. "I tried to talk to her, but she ignored me."

"The Shan's eldest daughter, Jaelle," Taliesin said. "Octavio is sending four guards with us as well. I don't know their names, but I suggest you stop ogling Jaelle. Her brother is possessive, and she has a murderous temper."

"She's beautiful," he replied. "I think I might be in love."

Taliesin wasn't surprised Hawk was already smitten; Jaelle was exceptionally lovely. Her long, wavy black hair was tied in a long braid, and she wore a bright red cape with a silver clasp in the shape of a dragon with spread wings. Silver earrings hung from her ears and rings adorned every finger. Her lips were colored red, her eyes were outlined with black kohl, and a light shade of blue powder was upon her eyelids. Finding Hawk's scrutiny more annoying than flattering, Jaelle turned her roan gelding around to wave at the Shan, gave Hawk a hard look, and rode to her brother and the four men chosen to escort them.

Tamal was mounted on a long-legged bay that snorted and tossed his black mane as he struck the ground with his front leg, displaying a similar temperament to its owner. Tamal touched his hand to his heart as he looked at his father. The Shan returned the gesture.

Taliesin patted Thalagar on the neck as he snorted and tossed his head. "How are you, boy?" she asked. The stallion wore a bright blue blanket and a new black leather saddle with silver studs and tassels. The bridle was similarly adorned. The saddle was unused and the leather hard and unyielding. Nothing was harder on the buttocks than breaking in a new saddle.

Octavio walked over, and Taliesin felt her stomach lurch as the older man brushed his hand against her leg. A soft squeeze from his large hand set her heart pounding; he certainly had a way with women. His eyes danced as he met her gaze.

"I am sorry I have no gift for you," the Shan said. "John Mandrake was one of the finest swordsmiths in the realm. The silver sword of his you carry will serve you well, Taliesin. I recognized it immediately. Mandrake was a friend of the gypsies, and we shared many adventures together. When we meet again, I will gladly tell you all about your father."

"I'd like that very much," Taliesin said. "I promise I'll bring Jaelle back to you, safe and sound. Her pledge to serve me isn't binding without saying the Service Oath, so she is not obliged to remain a Raven. And Tamal is in good hands. Roland will make certain that no harm befalls him." She noticed Nash glaring at her from beside a wagon. Tamal's safety was paramount; the last thing she wanted was to see Nash become the next Shan.

"The Volgate is a deadly place for even the most seasoned traveler," the Shan said. "Tamal is an excellent scout, and Sirocco and his brothers are all good men. You should be able to cross the Volgate within two days. Rest for only a short while, and without making a fire. Keep to the path and never allow your horse or party to drink from the marsh waters, for it is poisonous. Once you are on the other side, Sirocco Nova and his brothers will rejoin our caravan, unless Tamal deems they should remain with you as an escort. I will leave the decision in my son's hands."

Taliesin stared at the horizon. The sky was blue as a robin's egg and not a cloud was in sight. She'd never been so far from home before. Her face must have revealed her concern, for the Shan squeezed her calf again.

"A *Sha'tar* should not fear the unknown," Octavio said in a warm voice. "I knew the moment I laid eyes on you that you were a natural-born witch. You are a strong woman, Taliesin, and magic is strong with you. There is no reason for me to fear for my children's safety while in your company; the gods will favor and protect you, Raven Mistress."

The Shan tapped his hand to his forehead, turned, and returned to his wagon. Taliesin had heard the term used before but knew as little about *Sha'tars* as she did about witches and all other magic users. *Sha'tars* were spoken of in legends and stories. Glabber the Glib had written about a *Sha'tar* in a poem she couldn't quite remember, though it hadn't ended well. Most of his poems were tragic, and perhaps that was why she was so drawn to his work. Although she wanted to ask the Shan how he knew so much about her when she knew so little, herself, his son stood in the stirrups and waved his hand.

"*Taveachi*," Tamal shouted.

Striking his horse across the flanks, the young man rode past his father, the Nova brothers, and Jaelle, and he took the lead ahead of the Ravens. The entire camp materialized around their wagons, and, as they rode out of camp, Taliesin heard cheers and shouts, but she kept her eyes on the far horizon.

* * * * *

Chapter Sixteen

Under a clear, blue sky, the small group headed north, leaving Maldavia and entering the dukedom of Fregia. Large cavalcades of troops, carrying Scrydon and Thule banners and pulling siege equipment behind elephants, were seen coming from the east, presumably heading to the royal city of Padama. Taliesin was relieved when their guides turned northwest, leaving the enemy troops behind, and headed through hills covered with tall, green grass that brushed the bellies of their horses and slid across the riders' legs. Small black birds with red spots on their wings rested on the tips of the tall grass and chirped in a cheery singsong as they rode past. A lone hawk flew overhead—a good omen in Taliesin's opinion—and a fragrant floral scent that reminded her of the garden at Raven's Nest hung in the air.

The Ghajar were disciplined riders and only rested for short periods to water the horses and attend to personal needs. Food was eaten while riding—strips of dried venison, a handful of raisins, and apples washed down with water from a flask. When the sun passed its zenith, the terrain changed from tall grass into a high-desert plain, and the ground turned to a hard layer of crust that broke into flaky chips beneath the horses' hooves and cracked under their heavy weight, leaving behind large, jagged seams.

Roland caught up to Taliesin and rode beside her. "About a mile back was a road that leads to Ragenvald Castle, home of my order," he said. "We've been following the tracks of Prince Sertorius and his troops. They passed this way a day ago. It's not too late to turn back and go south around the Volgate."

"Backtracking through Maldavia into Aldagar will put us in harm's way," Taliesin said. It seemed a little late to have doubts about the path they'd chosen. Roland was no coward, and his concern seemed generated solely for her benefit, ever the protector. "Those troops we saw must be heading to Padama. I wouldn't dare retrace our steps into enemy territory. The Deceiver's Map clearly shows two days are shaved off our journey by going through the Volgate. I know it's more dangerous, but Jaelle assured me if we stay on course, we'll avoid the town of Tunberg and will reach the bridge across the Minoc River far ahead of Sertorius and the Wolf Pack. From there, Roland, it's a straight shot to the caves."

"That's if your map is telling the truth," Roland said. He wore a red scarf tied around his head, and his beard had grown thicker. In his gypsy garments, he looked relatively cooler than when wearing the heavier Black Wing hauberk; he'd rolled up the chainmail shirt and tied it across Kordive's back.

"You've got that look on your face. Why didn't you say something at the gypsy camp? I've never been this way before, so I'm relying on you and Tamal to get us to the Cave of the Snake God more than I'm relying on the map."

His brown eyes narrowed. "There's a thousand miles between us and the cave. A few days of backtracking would have been safer than going through the Volgate," he grumbled, "but I'm not leading this expedition; you are. See that fog bank ahead? That's the Volgate, Taliesin. Best pray no clouds are blocking the moon tonight, or we won't be able to see a thing in this fog, and one misstep on the path means death."

"When you offered to make me a Black Wing, I'm sure the last thing you expected was for me to lead a mission," she replied. "Be supportive. That's what I need from you, Roland, especially since there's no going back. I mean, it's not like I haven't seen fog before."

"Not fog like this. It clings to your skin and stings your eyes. Best pull your scarf up. The last thing you want is to breathe too much swamp gas and pass out." Roland led by example, as always, and tied the scarf from his head around his face, leaving only his eyes visible.

Taliesin did the same and noticed everyone else was also doing so, even Zarnoc. If Tamal and the guards thought it a bad idea to venture into the Volgate, she wished they'd said something earlier. Squawking about poisonous swamp gas and low visibility in the encroaching fog only made her nervous, and she wanted to appear as confident and calm as possible. The gypsies kept turning to glance at her and the Ravens as if the gypsies expected them to bolt as they neared the enormous fog bank. Being a *Sha'tar*, if she really was one, didn't seem at all important, not when she didn't instinctively know what she was getting into. She couldn't see into the future like Wren with her visions, nor did she have Jaelle's foresight of reading Tareen Cards.

The sun was setting as they neared the fog bank. Taliesin felt moisture in the air that dampened the saddle and her clothes. There was an odd smell in the air, like rotten eggs, and the hard ground softened beneath the horses' hooves. Large mud pits appeared, surrounded by wisps of fog, ringed by tall reeds, and home to long-legged cranes with slender, blue beaks and fat green bullfrogs with ridges that covered their backs. The riders rode in single file with Tamal in the lead, followed by Sirocco, Jaelle, Hawk, and then Taliesin. Roland remained directly behind her, then Zarnoc, Rook, and the other Nova brothers in the rear.

The moment they entered the fog bank, Taliesin found it difficult to see Hawk's white stallion ahead of her and felt her heart start to race. Thalagar lifted his head, showing signs of uneasiness, and she patted the stallion's neck as she glanced to the side. The fog parted beneath the horse's legs and revealed the path, and on either side, thick yellow mud surrounded small pools of stagnant black water. Tufts of reddish grass and spindly black reeds grew beside the rank water. Ankle-deep in the yellow mud, the horses made slow progress, as if the Volgate were designed to keep anyone who entered from leaving.

Tamal's whistle caught her attention, and she glanced over, unable to see him but able to hear his voice carried on the foul breeze. "Stay on the path! Watch the horse in front of you and keep up," he shouted.

Taliesin did the opposite and glanced over her shoulder.

"I'm still here," Roland said. "Try looking at Thunder's tail instead of me, woman."

Taliesin refrained from saying something rude in response to his deep chuckle and concentrated on Hawk's horse, which he'd named Thunder. The gypsies had braided each horse's tail with strips of material that glowed in the fog. Thunder was a handful and pranced nervously as a loud screech from a vulture brought Taliesin's gaze upwards. Out of habit, she lifted her gaze to the moon, able to make out the silhouettes of five vultures, which could only mean one thing; something lay dead on the path ahead.

Seeing vultures wasn't a bad omen, it was a reality check; where dead things lay, the thing that killed them was nearby as well. She knew, though, Osprey would have considered it negative, like most members of her clan. The Raven Clan was a superstitious lot. A crow seen at dusk meant bad luck and hearing a robin sing at the break of dawn meant a baby had been born. A wren always meant good luck, and a lone, frantic starling meant a lover was pining, but ravens…ravens had several different meanings. A raven at dawn foretold of bloodshed later that day, but at night it meant a calm evening ahead. To see a murder of crows acting calmly meant a funeral was in progress but seeing them agitated meant someone had just been killed or died a violent death.

But vultures had only one meaning, and as messengers of death, she wondered if they'd soon find the corpses of Prince Sertorius and his men on the path ahead.

A shout from Roland made Taliesin look at the ground. The fog parted for a brief moment, allowing her a glimpse of dead men partially hidden among the reeds and beneath the surface at the water's edge. Most of the corpses wore silver armor, and she was certain a Maldavian flag floated on top of the stagnant water before it sank.

"This battle was recent," Roland said, his voice a deep rumble. "The Wolf Pack caught up with Prince Sertorius. Keep your hand on your sword, Taliesin. Those fanged devils could be anywhere. They'll be able to see the glow of the horses' tails, the same as us, but we'll hear their howls before they attack. Arrogant bastards."

A large bubble rose to the surface of a pool on her right and popped. Taliesin tucked her chin to her chest, able to smell the noxious odor despite the scarf worn over her nose and mouth. Gas bubbles popped in the pools on either side of the winding path; they created a yellowish cloud she rode into, which caused her to gag. Thalagar snorted, annoyed as well, and she heard Zarnoc mutter a cadence of unintelligible words. The fog swirled away from Thalagar's chest and converged around her head, causing her to cough deeply, and she sagged forward in the saddle.

In that instant, an image appeared of a dark-haired boy in a golden cloak standing in the shadows of Tantalon Castle, throwing rocks into the murky green moat. The boy's black hair fell past his skinny shoulders, and his teeth appeared even and white as he turned and smiled. He wore a gold circlet on his brow and held a blue ribbon. Memories returned in a sudden rush, and she felt a lump form in her throat. It didn't seem possible, not after so many years, yet she recognized Prince Sertorius Draconus, fifth son of King Frederick; he'd been her dearest childhood friend. He gazed at her with eyes a shade of dark blue that appeared almost black, and she heard the prince laugh as he ran through the rose garden holding her blue hair ribbon.

'You can't catch me, stick legs,' he shouted. 'Stick Legs Rosie; try to catch me!'

Roland had said her birth name was 'Rosamond,' but she remembered 'Rosie' was a nickname used only by John Mandrake and the prince. All sorts of images flooded her mind —

Sertorius and her, in autumn, running through piles of leaves in the courtyard pretending imaginary creatures chased them; in spring, picking flowers to make a wreath for Queen Henrietta who died that same year; in winter, reading stories in the grand hall while snow fell outside the castle windows; in summer, watching tournaments in the royal gallery, eating chocolates, and shouting at their favorite knights. Sertorius and his guards had visited her father's swordsmith shop to watch John Mandrake forge a sword for the king.

John Mandrake stood forth in her memory, as clear as if he'd stepped out of the fog and onto the path—a tall, red-haired man with a leather apron covering his barrel-shaped chest. Not one strand of hair grew on his face or on his muscular arms, all burned away by the fires of his forge. He held the king's sword with the tip buried in the smoldering, hot embers until the metal turned a deep, molten red. After he drew the sword from the coals and laid it flat across the anvil, he picked up an iron hammer and pounded smooth the rough edges.

Clang, clang, clang.

The sound echoed in Taliesin's ears, and she swooned in the saddle, only righting herself when she heard Zarnoc's voice. "I have a vile taste in my mouth," the wizard said. "That blasted cat has eaten something most foul."

Taliesin pictured Ginger gagging on a fur ball and leaving a present for the Shan on his pillow. Her mind turned a page, she pictured a white lion on a blue flag and again thought of Sertorius as a boy, holding a stem of lavender he presented to her as though it had great significance. She leaned forward to smell the lavender, unaware she leaned over the side of her saddle until the reins dropped from her hands, and she tumbled, creating a large splash as she plunged into the dark, murky water.

The water dragged her down with a cold bite. Taliesin unfastened her sword belt and pulled off her cloak and scarf, but she continued to sink to the bottom of the pool. As her feet touched the muddy bottom, she felt a strange sensation, her stomach lurched, her head spun, and she blacked out.

* * *

Warm lips pressed against her own as air was forced into her lungs. A young man bent over Taliesin, alternating between pushing on her chest and breathing air into her lungs. With a hard cough, water gurgled out of her mouth, and she felt the man turn her onto her side before she blacked out.

When she came around, it was night. Taliesin wasn't sure how long she'd been unconscious, but she was aware she lay close to a campfire, able to feel the heat through a woolen cloak she'd been wrapped in that scratched her skin. She lifted her hand, touched her arm, and felt bare flesh; someone had removed her clothes. A wiggle of her toes confirmed her boots were removed, too. She heard men's voices in the dark. From the corner of her eye, she saw a group of armored men gathered around a second fireside, muttering softly. A heightened sense of tension hung in the air. She recognized Duke Peergynt's soldiers by their dark-blue cloaks with the insignia of a red dragon, while the men with a white lion on their cloaks belonged to Prince Sertorius. There were Knights of Chaos in silver mail and black tunics with red skulls, and a few Royal Guards, King's men—perhaps deserters—in gold cloaks. The soldiers, positioned around the camp and facing the wall of fog that reflected the glow of the campfires, wore helmets with brims and padded hauberks, and they held spears.

"Is all in order, Sir Barstow?" a man asked at the fireside. A slight inflection in his voice, a mixture of arrogance and petulance, meant he was a nobleman. "Every third man stands guard. Breaks every two hours. We must be ready when they come at us again."

Taliesin watched the nobleman cross his bare hands behind his back; a gold ring sparkled on his index finger, and he kicked embers at the side of the campfire. She remembered Shan Octavio had cautioned her against building fires at night. The nobleman was aware they were in danger, yet she counted five blazing fires. His black tunic and silver chainmail were expensive—so were his leather boots—but he wasn't Duke Peergynt. Her heart raced as the man turned and offered a view of his aquiline profile. He was handsome, pale, and clean-shaven. She knew at once this was Prince Sertorius Draconus. The knight called Barstow also wore a black tunic but boasted a thick red beard and held a helmet under his arm.

"Ever since I was a boy, I have heard disturbing reports about the Volgate, for few who enter ever leave this cursed place. Had our situation not been so desperate, Sir Barstow, I would never have agreed to ride through these marshes," the prince said in a velveteen voice. "We lost twenty men last night. I fear we will lose many more this night."

"This place reeks of death, Your Grace," Sir Barstow said. "The wizard deliberately sent us this way. If I ever make it to the ruins of Pelekus, he's a dead man."

The fire crackled and popped. A loud wolf howl pierced the night.

Taliesin pulled the cloak to her nose and pretended she slept as several soldiers passed in front of her. Sir Barstow excused himself, went to speak with the men in hushed tones, and glanced in her direction before returning to the fireside.

"Sir Morgrave has lined the ground with the last of the salt and wolf's bane," the red-bearded knight said. "The priests are saying prayers. Stroud willing, we will not be attacked this night, but I wouldn't count on it, Your Grace. The men are uneasy."

"Prayers won't keep away the Wolf Pack," the prince said, his tone thick with sarcasm. "Chief Lykus, traitor that he is, has a mad dog for a captain. Wolfgar's relentless in his pursuit. My father suggested we hire Lord Arundel's legionnaires, but my pride got the better of me, and I refused the offer."

"Let them come, Your Grace," Sir Barstow said. "Silver and fire are all we need to kill these beasts. We're ready for them this time."

A loud sigh came from Sertorius. "Distract me, Barstow. Talk about something else," he said. "Tell me something I don't know. Impress me. You are a well-traveled man, and you fought in many campaigns for my father, yet you never talk about Fregia. Is it because you were not chosen to be a Knight of the White Stag? Your bitterness against your compatriots was obvious at the Battle of Burnlak. You do not admit it; however, I know you are the one who beheaded Hrothgar Volgan. What did you do with his head?"

"That was Sir Morgrave, Your Grace," the red-haired knight said. "I killed the bastard's brother, but it was hardly a contest since he had but one hand. If I showed any resentment toward the Knights of the White Stag or my fellow countrymen, I hope it showed in the numbers I left dead on the field."

"I was fond of Hrothgar and Jasper," Sertorius said. "Killing them brings me no pleasure, and hearing you brag makes me ill at ease. On foot, Jasper would have skewered you; don't pretend otherwise. What I wouldn't give for a warm fireside, a cup of mead, and a pretty girl to remind me life can be beautiful."

Taliesin was moved by Sertorius' velvet voice. If she reminded him of happier times, would his recollection of their friendship be welcome news? His voice had changed since she'd last heard it, but the Maldavian accent was always music to her ears—each syllable pronounced slowly as if every word was important. The people from the eastern dukedoms had a nasal pitch to their voices, and the rapid speech of southern Erindor came with the clicking of their tongues on the roofs of their mouths, strange yet fascinating. Sir Barstow was Fregian, like Roland, and he had a guttural way of speaking, more like growls than words, especially when agitated. People who came from Adalgar had a charming drawl, but she could have listened to Sertorius all night.

The prince had the type of voice one wanted to hear on stage, giving a recitation or some powerful speech, like from Van Cliff's 'Pale Monarch,' a play about a prince who'd married a stable girl. The opening lines of Act I, Scene 8, were '*Oh give me a lady of quality and I shall search the stars for a crown of diamonds to lay upon her head, worthy of a queen,*' always brought her to tears. She had seen Van Cliff's play performed several times by good actors, as well as several times by pathetic clowns who had insisted they were 'master thespians.'

Taliesin realized she must have sighed, for Sir Barstow turned toward her, peering intently, and then turned away. In the distance, she heard a wolf howling, and the large, red-bearded knight placed his hand on his sword.

"I'm no good at small talk, Your Grace," Barstow said. "But I do know a little about swordsmiths. Who is the best? Falstaff or Gregor? You're the educated man. One sword looks like another to me; all I require is a sharp edge. Well?"

Prince Sertorius laughed. "I have used swords forged by both smiths, old friend," he said, his mood lighter despite the eerie howls. "Both swords were nearly weightless, yet well-balanced, sharp, and proved deadly in battle, but if I had to choose, then I would pick Falstaff. Most would say Gregor was the finest swordsmith, but I find his hilts a bit too ornate. Plain is better. Falstaff was best."

"Gregor was before either of our lifetimes, so he doesn't count, Your Grace," Barstow said, with a rumble. "I asked Sir Morgrave the same question. He claims the best swordsmith was Mandrake, but I didn't mention him because I know your father hated the man."

"Sir Sacramore had a Mandrake sword," Sertorius said, "but lost it when he fell at Burnlak. As for my father, I don't care what he thinks. You said pick between Falstaff and Gregor. Of course, John Mandrake was the best. My father liked his work; it was the man's personal life he didn't approve of." He held his hands out before the fire. "Sacramore claimed his sword was one of five Mandrake had been making for my brothers and me, but on the night Mandrake was slain, someone crept in and stole all of his weapons. I asked Sacramore to give me the Mandrake sword, and he refused—he actually refused *me*."

Barstow took a step back, his helmet tucked under his arm, rubbing his belly with his free hand. "Sacramore was a conceited lout, Your Grace," he said. "The duke killed him with *Doomsayer*, a sword I wish we'd been able to acquire. I told you it was *Doomsayer*, but you listened to Morgrave, who told you it was one of twenty gold swords."

"You can't be sure, braggart," Sertorius replied, tersely. "Hrothgar's main army was but five miles away, and had we stopped to look for *Doomsayer*, we might very well have joined the Volgan's in death. Why are you backing up? Is my conversation that boring?"

"Your Grace," Barstow said, turning to gaze at Taliesin, "I believe the gypsy girl is awake. She's been listening to us. It's time we found out what she's doing here."

At the knight's approach, Taliesin held the cloak to her chin as she sat up. Her hair spilled around her shoulders in a shower of golden-red curls that fell to her slender waist. Lifting a hand to her ears, she found the hooped earrings missing, along with her gypsy disguise. She frantically looked for her belongings and saw her clothing drying on a rope pulled across a second fire. Her attention returned to the red-bearded knight as he glanced at the prince.

"Not a gypsy," Barstow said. "Her hair is redder than mine. Maybe a Fregian spy."

The prince walked to where Taliesin lay beside the small fire. His features appeared chiseled from stone, all sharp edges, and his mouth was pulled into a thin, straight line. A muscle twitched in Sertorius' right cheek as he leaned over for a better look. Taliesin noted his ornate belt with a large silver buckle in the shape of a lion. A silver knife and a silver sword hung on the belt; he'd come prepared to fight Wolfmen.

"Perhaps she's a wolf girl," Barstow said. "Shall I skin her, Your Grace?"

Alarmed, Taliesin spoke. "I'm not from the Wolf Clan. Nor am I a Fregian spy."

A suspicious expression that should have frightened her appeared on the prince's handsome face, but she took greater fear in the fact she was naked and in the company of a great number of armed men.

"Then what does that make you, my red-haired beauty?" the prince asked.

"I am lost, that is what I am." Taliesin sounded pathetic, and to emphasize a mask of female vulnerability she clutched the cloak to her chin and felt a chill slide along her spine as Sertorius crouched beside her. She caught her breath as his cobalt-blue eyes locked with hers and he reached out to lift a long red curl off her shoulder.

"You need not be afraid of me, girl," Sertorius said. "I won't hurt you. Perhaps you did not know if you fall into one of these pools, you never end up at the same place you started. If you weren't lost before, you certainly are now." A smile played at the corner of his mouth. She couldn't help thinking of the boy she'd known and smiled back without hesitation. He lowered his hand and let out a soft chuckle. "Do you know who I am, girl?"

The correct response was to deny any knowledge of his identity. Taliesin shook her head and batted her eyelashes. There was safety in pretense. No matter what the prince intended to do with her, Taliesin did not intend to tell him who she really was.

"No? Allow me to introduce myself then. I am Prince Sertorius Draconus," he said with great pride. "I have never seen a gypsy girl with bright red hair that she didn't dye. You come from Octavio's camp. Is that correct?"

Nodding in response, she kept her gaze lowered as she'd seen Ghajar women do in the presence of Shan Octavio. He didn't remember her from the past. Why would a prince remember a swordsmith's daughter, she wondered, feeling strangely disappointed.

"How did you come to the Volgate? Were you following us?" Sertorius paused, watched her reaction, and lifted an eyebrow in inquiry. The shape and color reminded her of a furled raven wing. "You are a pretty thing. Were the Wolfmen chasing you, girl?"

Her tongue darted out to moisten her lips. "I...I don't know," she said, giving a shudder. "I can't remember. I was drowning, and now I am here. Am I dead?"

"If you were dead, would we be talking?" With a laugh, the prince jerked his royal head toward the red-bearded knight. "Do you hear that, Barstow? Our little gypsy thinks she is dead. I normally don't have that effect on women." He locked his gaze upon her. "Tell me your name? Surely you remember your name, girl."

Taliesin shook her head. Damn the man. He was toying with her, she knew that much, trying to weaken her with his good looks and fancy accent like he did with all women, high and low born alike. He was a seducer of women; she knew the type. She merely shook her head and bit on her bottom lip.

"What shall we do with a girl with no memory, Sir Barstow?" The prince placed his hand on the top of the cloak she held to her chin with clenched fists. "You can't be a mermaid this far from the ocean. Perhaps you're a witch. Was it you who summoned me to be in this exact place, at this exact time, to save you from death? No? Perhaps you are a demon, though I must admit, I saw no mark or blemish on your flesh when I removed your clothes."

"Shall I fetch her clothes, Your Grace?" the knight asked.

"Don't interrupt," Sertorius said. "Can't you see I'm talking to this poor girl who has lost her memory?" He stood without breaking eye contact with her. "A red-haired gypsy girl. The Shan must be heartsick about losing a beauty like this one."

"She's come out of poisoned waters," Sir Barstow said. "If she drank any, Your Grace, it may be why she can't remember. Probably a sheepherder's daughter who got lost. If you don't want her, I wouldn't mind a turn. It's been a while since I've had a pretty woman."

Taliesin felt her temper rising and spreading like wildfire throughout every inch of her body. A retort was swallowed before she launched herself into a scolding. She liked neither man, nor did she like the fact no one intended to provide clothing for her and said the first lie that entered her thoughts.

"I am Shan Octavio's fifth wife, Jaelle, and he will send men to look for me when I do not return to camp," she said. "Give me my clothes and let me go, Your Grace."

"Ah, the Shan's wife!" Sertorius laughed. "The mystery is solved, Sir Barstow."

"Keep your voice lowered," Taliesin said. "You heard the wolf howl. One howl means more will follow. You and your men are surrounded. You should have come to Shan Octavio and asked for his help."

"Now this is fun," the prince said. "Your hair is red as the flames, and your temper matches." His smile widened. "I haven't lost my touch after all."

Taliesin remembered his vanity. Sertorius had not changed in that regard; even as a boy, he'd demanded the attention of adults and children alike.

"Anyone can plainly see you're not a gypsy," the prince said. "I don't believe you are Shan Octavio's fifth wife or even sixth wife. No gypsy ever gets lost in the Volgate. I do believe you are sincerely afraid of the Wolf Pack. Everyone fears the Wolfmen. So, how did you do it? How did you avoid being caught by them, girl? Do you know a secret path through this place? Help us, and I shall reward you. You may have your clothes and a horse if you will agree to take us out of this cursed place."

"My pleasure," Taliesin said. She stood up, wrapping the cloak around herself, and noted how quickly Sertorius stepped away from her. One-step forward and she caught a whiff of his cologne. The idiot really went out of his way to make himself an easy target for the Wolfmen.

"Not tonight," he said. "I don't trust you. You're too eager to leave."

"Yes, well, Wolfmen are on the prowl. May I at least get dressed, Your Grace?"

With a nod, the prince sent Barstow to retrieve her clothes. The two soldiers drying her garments turned to hand them to the large knight, but with a chuckle, Barstow tossed them into the fire and gave his prince an amused look. All that remained of her disguise was a pair of gypsy boots set aside on the ground. Barstow grabbed the boots and handed them to the prince, who personally handed them to Taliesin. She slid the boots on, keeping the cloak wrapped around her slender body, and wished she still had her sword and the pouch with the precious map and key that now lay at the bottom of the pool.

"I am sorry Sir Barstow has butterfingers," Sertorius said. "My men will find you something to wear. Surely a page has something that will fit." He paused, lifted his head to sniff the air, and let out a shout. "Sir Barstow, wake the men! I smell wolf in the air. They've closed in around us while we've been talking to this girl."

The prince strode to the far side of the campfire to address a large group of archers, leaving Taliesin alone. She needed a way to escape from her precarious situation. The dry patch of land that served as the main camp was large and bulged out on each side, like an egg. Two paths at either end led into the marshes, but the camp was vulnerable on all sides. Torches were set in the ground and lit the encampment. At the sudden, loud howl of a wolf, Taliesin gazed into the fog and saw a pair of yellow eyes staring at her.

A shout went up from the far side of the campfire as the giant wolves moved in from all sides, barely visible in the fog. The ring of archers set the tips of their arrows alight and fired off a volley. Flaming arrows shot into the air with a brilliant, crackling glow, pierced several furry targets with silver, and set the brush on fire. Across the water, she saw numerous dark, furry bodies moving through the burning reeds. Another barrage of arrows scattered the pack and sent them yelping and howling away from the pool.

'The way is clear,' a voice said in her mind. 'Dive, girl. Dive into the water.'

Without thinking twice about what she was doing, Taliesin let the cloak fall to her feet, ran to the pool, and dove into the murky, cold depths.

* * * * *

Chapter Seventeen

Spitting out a mouthful of sludge, Taliesin gripped a handful of coarse reeds and dragged her body out of the murky pool. Chilled to the bone, she remained hidden within the reeds with her toes and fingers buried in the mud. She'd lost her gypsy boots. Whatever magic enabled her to travel from one pool to another had to be *dark*. Every inch of her felt grimy, and the deep cuts from the coarse reeds stung. She heard Prince Sertorius and his men a hundred yards away, fighting the Wolfmen. Their frantic shouts and the snarls of the creatures filled the night with dread. From the reeds, she watched flaming arrows arc through the air, yellow orbs in the fog, but she could see little else.

She couldn't stay there and watch. She needed to find her friends.

Light from the full moon filtered through the fog and lit her way as she crawled through the reeds, found dry ground, and, while remaining on all fours, headed away from the battle. She crawled until her hands and knees hurt and yellow mud covered her from head to toe, but only when the cries of men and the wolf howls had faded away did she stand and run. The fog parted and formed a border along the path that led her, unsure of the direction, through a serpentine maze that wrapped around dark, gurgling pools and putrid reeds where the croaks of bullfrogs rang out. Sporadically she heard a howl somewhere in the dense fog but never broke stride. A strange tingling that started in her feet made it feel like she never touched the muddy path, and as the sensation settled over her entire body, she felt her mind rise out of her body and found herself gazing at the path from high above. A naked woman with long, red hair ran beneath her, and though

247

she knew it was, in fact, her, she witnessed it as through the eyes of a bird. Weightless and untiring, Taliesin guided her body through the marshlands. The distance traveled and her own exertion no longer mattered as she repeatedly recited, "*Light as a feather, fast as a raven.*"

Unsure as to how many miles she'd covered, she grew excited as the fog ended and she entered a field that stretched toward tall pine trees. As soon as she neared the trees, the strange sensation ended, and she was back in her body running hard across the solid ground. Flying beside her was a large raven that kept pace until she entered the forest; then, with a loud squawk, it flew up and sat upon a branch.

Taliesin sank to the ground as the miles she had run caught up to her, and feeling exhausted and sick to her stomach, she vomited. With the toxic waters out of her system, she collapsed to the ground, laid on pine needles, and gazed at the patches of starlight that appeared through the branches. The pain in her muscles and stomach slowly subsided, and as her temperature lowered, she felt the chill in the air and wrapped her arms around herself.

Faint voices could be heard on the breeze. She recognized Roland's deep voice, got up, and sat with her back to a tree. Looking in every direction, she saw no sign of the Fregian knight, yet heard his ghostly voice repeating a prior conversation from days before.

"What do you know of the Cave of Chu'Alagu, Zarnoc?" Roland asked. "It's said to be in Garridan, far beyond the Volgate, far to the west."

There was a long pause. The wind calmed, and she heard the faint tinkle of bells — gypsy bells — and a horse snorted.

"A long journey it is," Zarnoc said. "Marshes and deserts, quicksand, and sandstorms. There is no water or living creature to be found for miles around. Many enter the Salayan Desert, but few ever return."

The disembodied voices faded away on the breeze, replaced by far-away laughter that sounded like Prince Sertorius; but that too ended, leaving her feeling alone and afraid.

Standing, Taliesin held onto the tree for support and gazed at the moon hanging in the sky, flanked by two gray clouds that shifted in the upper atmosphere and morphed into the bodies of giant, winged creatures. She fought her fear and waited for the voices to return, for footsteps to approach, or for the familiar whinnies of a horse. No one appeared, and the raven that had guided her seemed to have abandoned her. She waited until her heartbeat steadied and then headed west through the forest, her arms wrapped around her body; each footstep took her further away from the Volgate.

A loud squawk brought her eyes searching through the trees, and there, on a low limb, she spotted the raven. Its black eyes stared at her with intelligence. The bird tilted its head and squawked again.

"Hello there," Taliesin said. "Did Zarnoc send you to help me?"

The bird landed on her upraised arm. Taliesin slid a finger across the raven's head and marveled at the silkiness of its feathers. A ripple went through the bird's body, and her fear vanished, replaced by heartfelt relief. With a soft squawk, the raven burrowed his silky head into the palm of her hand and affectionately rubbed against her.

"That's a good boy," Taliesin said. "You're a very smart bird. Do you know where my friends are? I'm a little lost, I must admit."

The raven hopped off her arm and landed on the ground. Before her startled eyes, the raven turned into Zarnoc, dressed in a black robe. In a bird-like manner, he gave a hard shake of his shoulders and cawed softly from the back of his throat. Taliesin threw her arms around the wizard and hugged him tightly, until he started to wiggle. She stepped away, acutely aware he was staring at her breasts in the moonlight and raised her hands to cover her bosom. Typical male, she thought.

"You old coot," she said. "Did you bring anything for me to wear? I'm freezing."

"What? Not a thank you?" grumbled Zarnoc. "I went to a lot of trouble finding you, young lady." He smoothed his rumbled cloak. "Turning into a raven isn't that easy. You try flapping your arms for twenty leagues and see how you feel afterward."

"That's not possible. I couldn't run that far."

"Excuse me?" Zarnoc said, a bit snidely. "It's called magic. I *am* a wizard."

He snapped his fingers and Taliesin was instantly dressed head to toe in her familiar old leather pants, bodice, jacket, and boots. She ran her hands across her body, across the flat of her stomach to her hips, and felt the sword belt fastened around her waist. *Wolf Killer* hung at her side. She checked for the pouch next and confirmed it too was on her belt; inside she felt the map and round medallion.

"You are amazing, Zarnoc. Thank you," Taliesin said, kissing him on top of his scraggly head. "I feared I'd lost everything. I am in your debt."

"Not at all," he said. "I was the only one who could find you. Retrieving your sword was easy. Getting you out of the Volgate took a bit of doing; I haven't turned myself into a raven in quite a few years." Zarnoc scratched at his ear. "Most people who fall into the marshes die. Only those with magic can transport from pool to pool as you did."

Taliesin followed Zarnoc through the trees. "The marsh gases restored my memories, and that's why I fell out of the saddle," she said. He handed her a flask of water, which she thirstily drank from. "Prince Sertorius pulled me out of the pool. He's not the boy I remember, nor did he recognize me."

"The marsh gas can have a strange effect on people," Zarnoc said. "You don't need to tell me what was said, because I heard everything. I'm the one who told you to dive into the pool when the Wolfmen attacked. He's not dead, in case you were wondering; he even managed to drive off Wolfgar and the Wolf Pack."

Although not sure how she felt about Sertorius, she was relieved he was still alive, and her thoughts turned toward her friends. "Where are Roland and the others?" she asked.

"A few miles behind us. Roland wanted to stay and find you, but I thought it best I handle things," Zarnoc said. "Thanks to Tamal's skill as a scout, they managed to find a short cut through the marshes and avoided the Wolfmen. We are lucky to have that boy with us. He'll prove himself useful before all is said and done." The old wizard smiled. "Is he as handsome and charming as you remember?" He wondered, referring to Sertorius.

"I was eight years old when I last saw him," she said. "Yes, he's handsome. Very handsome. But nice? I can't be sure. I don't trust him. Do you think Roland and Sertorius are working together to find *Ringerike*?"

"I don't know yet, and that is precisely why you will say nothing about this to anyone," Zarnoc said. "You are in love with Roland, that much I do know, and the prince can charm anyone to his way of thinking. He believes you led the Wolfmen to his camp, and I suspect he'll try to kill you the next time you meet, while Roland only wants to protect you."

"I never said I was in love with Roland."

"You don't have to," the wizard said. "But I should think it best not to mention you ran into Prince Sertorius."

"Why not?"

"Things the prince said do not sit right with me," Zarnoc said. "Sertorius claims to be loyal to his father and friend to Hrothgar and Jasper; yet he killed them. He came to me asking about *Ringerike*, yet left *Doomsayer* on the battlefield. I don't know where Roland fits into this puzzle, but until I do, I think it best not to tell him what happened."

They came out of the trees onto an old road and glanced around. The wizard went to a log and sat. Taliesin joined him and drained the water flask, only to find it refilled. She didn't ask Zarnoc about the water flask; it was obvious he was using magic, but the water tasted the same, and she drank more.

And then it dawned on her. Everything they'd gone through was unnecessary. She seethed.

"I don't get it," Taliesin said.

"What is that?" Zarnoc asked.

"Why can't you just air bridge us to the cave?" Taliesin asked, her eyes ablaze. "Your powers are incredible, yet you allow us to ride straight into danger at every opportunity. I don't understand your logic. *Why are we going through all of this if we don't have to?*"

Zarnoc made a motion with his hand, and everything around them froze. "Observe my dear," he said, "I can stop time, as you can see. It is one of the many things I *can* do. What I *can't* do, though, is give you experience; the only way you can get that is to earn it yourself. Knowledge is a precious gift, but experience is even more valuable. Knowledge freely given is worthless; it has no meaning without the context of the struggle for attainment."

He turned away from her, and she could barely hear his voice as he continued, "I have seen too much violence in my lifetime…far too much…and I am not interested in making it easy for others to choose the path of violence." His arm moved — *was he wiping away a tear?* — before he turned back to Taliesin. "Wielding *Ringerike* would give you great power…but are you prepared for that? It is only through the struggle to become a leader that you achieve the experience needed to rule with wisdom and vision. *That* is the purpose of this quest, and why *you* must do things yourself, even if I provide aid from time to time."

"I understand and will try to respect your wishes. But I do find it odd a powerful wizard shows restraint. You did not need to live in those ruins like an old hermit. At any point, you could have created a palace and filled it with servants, riches, and whatever you desire. Why didn't you?"

"For the simple fact I am not the only wizard who escaped King Magnus' war against magic. There are others, Taliesin, and they watch me with keen interest. I dare not use my magic to interfere with this civil war. Nor can I stop the bloodshed. If I lifted a finger to change events, or to even undo what has already been done, things would be far worse. Trust me and leave it alone. Now is not the time to discuss these things, for even now, our enemies listen on the wind and watch us. We must proceed, my dear, by putting one foot in front of the other. That means slowly and carefully."

"Carefully..." Taliesin muttered, her thoughts drifting to another topic she had wanted to discuss with the wizard. "It seems ages ago that I lived in Padama. Our little house was on the main street, right in the shadow of the palace. My father often went to court and was hired to make swords for important noblemen as well as the king. The knight, Sir Barstow, said the king didn't like my father. Sertorius made it sound personal. Did the king have something to do with my father's death?"

"The shock of your father's death is the reason you forgot your childhood," Zarnoc said. "I asked Osprey to look after you in the hopes this day would never come. Are you sure you really want to know the truth, Taliesin? It will open a door you may not want to enter."

"I'm not Rook," she said. "I don't want to hide from my past. Someone murdered my father, and I believe it was the king. Please, Zarnoc. If you know what happened, then tell me."

Zarnoc produced his pipe from the folds of his robe and filled it with tobacco. A green apple appeared on his lap, and he offered it to Taliesin. As she ate the apple, a tiny flame appeared at the end of his finger, and he lit the pipe, drawing on it long and hard; the smoke came out his ears.

"To understand why your father was killed, you must first understand why some men covet magic and why some men fear it," Zarnoc said. "Magic is a combination of the powers of the earth, water, sky, and air. Magic is neither evil nor good; it can either cause harm or be beneficial, but that depends on the heart of its owner and how they apply their magical skills."

"Wolf Killer has magic," she said. "I know it does. Yet, my father forged this sword for one of the princes. Was my father using magic, Zarnoc?"

The wizard blew smoke into the air. "Let me talk," he said. "I'm explaining why some fear those who have the ability to manipulate magic and why two hundred years ago King Magnus Draconus decided it must be outlawed to protect his realm from magical warfare. During the Magic Wars, King Magnus killed, exiled, or imprisoned all of the magic users he could find, and all things magical were either destroyed or disenchanted. Many magical weapons survived the Magic Wars, though, but only the Deceiver's Map can locate them. A few magical weapons are still owned by noblemen, like *Doomsayer,* which remained in the House of Volgan. The interesting thing is that this sword was disenchanted, that is until you found it. It's the same with *Wolf Killer.* You see, all things made of magic want to serve their true master, be it for evil or good, and magic weapons that lay dormant for long periods require a powerful wizard or a clever witch to reactivate them."

Zarnoc paused, looked at the length of the road in each direction, gave a sigh of disappointment that their friends had yet to appear, and continued.

"A magical weapon can be given to anyone, but that still doesn't mean the new owner can control the weapon. One weak of heart couldn't control a weapon like *Doomsayer,* but you had no problem calling upon the sword's dormant powers, and *Wolf Killer* responded to you as well. I suspect *Ringerike* will also respond to your touch. *Ringerike* is the most powerful magical sword ever made, and it is the oldest, forged by the Lorians long ago. But *Ringerike* and other magical weapons are only as strong as their owners."

"So how is my father involved in all of this? Octavio called me a *Sha'tar,*" she said. "I believe that is a term for natural-born witches, like Wren, but I thought they were rare."

"Wren's magic comes from the maternal line of her family. Only witches are born with the magic they inherit from their mothers. Every sorcerer and wizard must learn their trade from years of study, years of practice. But to be a *Sha'tar*, the magic must come from the paternal side." Zarnoc removed the pipe from his lips. "John Mandrake was a warlock, which he inherited from his paternal side, and that is very rare. That is why Mandrake was the best at crafting weapons. Falstaff, Gregor, and Rivalen were exceptional swordsmiths, but none of them had magical blood. And this is why the king both revered and feared your father."

"A warlock? My father was a warlock?"

"Yes, and you are a *Sha'tar*, my dear," Zarnoc said. "You may be the last of your kind. The type of magic you have is powerful, but it must be developed and controlled. Not only can it restore powers to dormant magical weapons, but it can also strengthen the powers of other magic users who are in your presence. The magic Wren, Jaelle, and I had at birth will grow stronger the longer we are near you. I certainly have grown stronger."

"So, the king knew my father was a warlock and had him murdered," Taliesin said, trying to absorb everything. "But why? I've seen what *Wolf Killer* can do. My father could have made many magical weapons for the king. Why not ask for my father's help instead of killing him?"

"I suspect there was another reason," he replied. "Who can say? To keep you from harm, Osprey agreed to look after you, and he swore never to reveal the truth to you or anyone else. In time, you will become a powerful *Sha'tar*, but you have to believe in magic for that to happen, Taliesin. You have to believe in yourself and your abilities."

"I can read the map."

"Ah, the map. Zoltaire made his specialty item to be used by others of our ilk. It was a way of meeting friends and avoiding royal troops. That's why it's full of trickery, lies, and deceit. Zoltaire was an evil sorcerer; he enjoyed harming people. That map has caused many people, both greedy and innocent, to die. Now you've found me, I can train you to make even a spoon dance."

Taliesin smiled. "How hard can that be?"

With a snap of his fingers, Zarnoc was standing before her, taller than even Roland, and had changed from his gypsy garments into a bright yellow robe and a matching long cap with a white tassel. "Madam, I am a professional," he said. "I could train an idiot to cast a spell on a spoon."

"No need to shout," Taliesin said. She listened to the night and heard only an owl hooting and the rustle in the bushes made by a startled rabbit; nothing dangerous. But she felt uneasy, not only by what he'd told her about her heritage and her father's death, but by all the other questions she hadn't asked; about her mother, the true reason her father had been murdered, Roland's motives, Sertorius' allegiance, and her own future.

"We must find *Ringerike* before anyone else," Zarnoc said as if he'd read her mind. "The Raven Clan once held dominion over the Eagle and Wolf Clans. King Korax kept the Caladonians from crossing the northern border, but that changed at the Battle of Triplet when the three clans gathered under the Raven King's banner to fight Prince Tarquin Draconus and the barbarian horde. They say the sword shined a brilliant blue that day and blinded the enemy. None could stand against Korax. He killed hundreds before Prince Tarquin pierced his eye with a magical arrow. Be warned, child. All magical swords have a fatal flaw. For whatever reason, the eyes are the only spot *Ringerike* cannot protect.

"After Tarquin killed Korax, he took *Ringerike* and crowned himself King of Caladonia. The Raven Clan was reduced to nothing more than looters, yet the Wolf and Eagle Clans prospered, and now each is attempting to gain more power.

"*Ringerike* was made for Korax. It eventually betrayed Tarquin and led him to a horrible death," Zarnoc said. "Korax and *Ringerike* were buried in the cave, by order of Tarquin's heir, and the usurper's body now lies in the royal crypt in Tantalon Castle. But that's not the point. Only someone born of the royal line of King Korax Sanqualus can control *Ring-*

erike, for it will eventually cause the death of anyone not of his ancient royal line."

"That does me no good," Taliesin said. "King Korax has no descendants. The House of Sanqualus died with him."

"The map can tell you if a descendant exists, Taliesin. Have you ever looked?"

"No," she said. "I didn't know it was important."

Taliesin unfastened the knotted leather cord on her pouch, reached inside, and made certain the medallion was there. She felt an egg-shaped pouch that contained medicinal herbs, a necklace with medium-sized blue beads that was broken at the clasp, a case of needles and stitching thread, and a tiny dagger no more than the length of her index finger. Nestled among her treasures, she found the palm-sized folded piece of parchment, its texture coarse to her fingertips. The map reacted to her touch and, as she pulled it out, turned into what felt like homespun cloth. She held it by the two top corners. The night breeze ruffled the material as if it were a small flag, making it flap and twist in her grip.

"Stop that," she said. "I need a map, not a scarf." In an instant, she was holding a solid, square-shaped board that dropped onto her lap.

"That's interesting," Zarnoc said. "Lose your temper and magic comes naturally to you."

The kingdom of Caladonia and the eight dukedoms were displayed in earth tones with black borders. Raven's Nest was a tiny black blur, which she interpreted to mean it had been burned to the ground. She wanted to see her location, and a tiny white dot appeared twenty-five miles west of the Volgate, in the dukedom of Garridan. Red stars for magical weapons appeared on the map, but none showed the location of Korax's heir. It was obvious either an heir didn't exist, or the map was lying.

Taliesin thought about Roland and her friends. A white dot was coming from the south on the very road where she and Zarnoc waited. She thought of Prince Sertorius, and a dot appeared five miles to the east, followed by many smaller dots;

Wolfmen were trailing after the prince, and their numbers were swelling as they moved at an alarming rate.

"What do you see?" Zarnoc asked, puffing on his pipe.

"A map of Caladonia," she said. "Borders are outlined. Every castle, town, village, and ruin are marked, including Raven's Nest. I see a green sea serpent swimming in the Pangian Sea. White dots show our location and those of Roland, Sertorius, and the Wolfmen. There are red stars for magical weapons, but I don't see a mark for Korax's heir. Is the map lying?"

"Perhaps," Zarnoc said, sounding excited. "But look at all the magical weapons shown! There is *Calaburn, Flamberge,* and *Graysteel*—all mighty swords! If only we had the time, we could make a fortune finding and selling magical weapons."

Taliesin put away the map. "That's not why I'm doing this," she said. "I want to find *Ringerike* and try to do some good, Zarnoc. I believe in magic and in my abilities, so I have to believe *Ringerike* will be loyal to and obey me."

"Then let's hope that is precisely what will happen," Zarnoc said.

Riders emerged from the dark and came toward them. Taliesin and Zarnoc stood. Tamal, in the lead, shouted to the others and reined in his horse while Roland charged toward Taliesin and jumped off his horse. His long legs swiftly carried him to Taliesin, and before she had time to blink, he snatched her into his arms and kissed her. Her knees buckled, and she clung to his shoulders, feeling her worries fade away as she gazed into his eyes.

"I was so worried," Roland said in a tender voice. "Thank Heggen you were not harmed. I wanted to look for you, but Zarnoc said he could find you. Are you all right?" He wore a look of concern that touched her heart.

Taliesin wasn't quite sure where to start, or what should be told to the knight. "I'm fine, Roland," she said, wanting to keep it simple.

The Fregian knight set her down. "We have a bit of riding to do before we can stop and rest," he said. "Let's get you onto your horse. I'll help you; I know you're exhausted."

She followed Roland to her black stallion and let him help her into the saddle. Zarnoc hurried to his little mule, stroked her nose, and climbed onto her back. Thalagar gave a snort, and Taliesin patted his neck and watched Roland mount Kordive. Hawk, Wren, Rook, and Jaelle looked relieved they'd found her, and she smiled at them. Tamal had asked the Nova brothers to remain with them. The Ghajar waited quietly behind the Ravens; Taliesin was glad to have them.

"The Wolfmen are not far behind," Tamal said. "The wind has changed direction, and so will we. I know a place outside of Tunberg where we will be safe. Follow me."

Thalagar lifted his hooves in an almost dainty fashion, and, sniffing at the wind, tucked his head and watched the road ahead as the group moved out. Taliesin followed Tamal as he turned off the road and entered the forest at a fast clip.

"Your horse is loyal, as Andorrans are bred to be," Tamal said. "He did not run away when you fell into the pond. He stayed there, waiting for you, but came when I called him." She glanced at Tamal, surprised to hear that. "I have a way with horses," he said. "I train horses, but seldom see any as fine as your own. My Gazel is a mix of Andorran and Brennan, bred for endurance and speed. Andorrans have long legs and short necks, which is why they run faster than any other breed. But loyalty cannot be taught, it must be earned."

"Thank you for taking care of my friends," she said. "Now we're out of the Volgate, I thought the scouts would return to the caravan. I'm pleased they are coming with us."

"For now," Tamal said. "There is safety in numbers."

Two of the Nova brothers were sent ahead to scout the trail. Taliesin gazed over her shoulder. On the far eastern horizon, the first rays of sunlight appeared and cast a pink and orange hue across the sky. The pine trees blocked out the sun itself, casting dark shadows upon the ground. Taliesin let

Tamal move ahead, allowing Hawk to take his place beside her.

"I'm glad to see you're alive," he said. "What happened? One minute you were in the saddle, and the next you vanished into the pool. I thought you'd drowned."

"The marsh gas made me faint," she said, "but I appreciate your concern."

"Without you, there wouldn't be much point in going on. Try not to fall out of the saddle again," he said. "Roland was beside himself with worry, and I'll admit I was worried, too."

He gave a nod and fell into line.

* * * * *

Chapter Eighteen

Day was upon them by the time Tamal led them across a rocky ridge with views of the sprawling city of Tunberg and, located on a hill, Castle Stalker. Duke Volund Fortinbraus lived in Havendor Castle, further east, but one of his sons lived in Castle Stalker. The Fortinbraus family was loyal to the King, she thought, as a long line of heavy cavalry come out of the castle and ride away on the winding road.

Taliesin lost sight of the cavalry as the path led away from the ridge and into the thickness of the pine trees. She wondered if the Aldagarns were headed to Maldavia to join the royal army or if the duke's son was hoping to waylay Prince Sertorius. She wanted to ask Roland, but when she turned, she found Jaelle riding behind her; Roland brought up the rear. The gypsy girl urged her horse closer as they passed under a low branch. The narrow path twisted and opened to reveal a clearing with a rocky escarpment that opened into a cavernous dark cave. Tamal dismounted, drew his sword, and entered the large cavern. At his whistle, the four gypsy brothers rode into the cave, taking Tamal's horse with them.

"What happened to you in the Volgate?" Jaelle asked, drawing her horse to Taliesin as she slid out of the saddle. "Were you injured? One bite from a Wolfman...."

"No, I wasn't bitten," Taliesin said. "I didn't get that close to them."

"There is no cure, you know. Don't fall from your saddle again," the gypsy girl said. "It could mean your life if you fall off your horse in the desert. You *griegos* are not known for your riding abilities. In the desert, those who fall are left behind."

"Well, thankfully, Zarnoc doesn't feel the same way you do."

Taliesin led Thalagar into the cave and went about removing her gear and the saddle. Rook walked over to take Thalagar's reins as well as the reins of the rest of the Ravens' horses, led them to the back of the cave to a pool of water, and fed them. Taliesin dropped her trappings beside the cave wall and noticed the gypsies had gathered at the entrance of the cave and talked softly together. Tamal and Jaelle glanced with disapproval every now and then in her direction. One fall and she was labeled a bad rider. Wren and Hawk joined Taliesin, placed their gear beside hers, and rolled out their blankets. Roland helped Rook with the horses while Zarnoc sat on a rock and quietly smoked his pipe.

"We will be safe here, but no fires," Tamal said. He left two of the four brothers on guard at the entrance. Jaelle walked at his side as they came to Taliesin and her friends. "We're close to Stalker Castle and can't risk cooking food. You saw how many of Lord Valesk's knights were on the road. You'll have to make do with bread and dried meat."

"Are we safe here?" Hawk asked.

"This forest is patrolled by knights," Tamal said. "Duke Fortinbraus' eldest son is a very cautious man and does not care for gypsies."

"You sound worried," Hawk said, lying on his pallet. "I didn't know the Ghajar scare so easily."

Tamal's cheeks flushed bright red. "For years, I have come here to trade, avoiding capture by Duke Fortinbraus and his sons," he said. "Being a prisoner of Lord Valesk is the last thing you want, Master Hawk. I am not afraid of this man or his knights, but I am careful. Smuggling you and your friends across the border will be difficult. The roads will be patrolled and so will the bridges across the Minoc River. You would do well to show me a little respect; I am the only person keeping you from the dungeons of Castle Stalker."

Hawk rolled his eyes. "Don't get your feathers in a ruffle." He glanced at Jaelle as she helped Wren make a pallet. Jaelle had taken the space Taliesin intended to use, so Taliesin moved her gear over to accommodate the girl.

"You are arrogant and foolish, Hawk," Tamal said. "My sister is not impressed with you, nor am I. Duke Fortinbraus and his sons are loyal to the king. They will not ask questions when they slit your throat."

Roland tossed his bedroll beside Taliesin's. He'd changed out of his gypsy garb and wore leather pants, but no shirt. His massive, hairy body was a welcome sight to Taliesin, and she immediately started to make their pallets. Days without shaving had sprouted hair growth on top of his head, and his beard was getting thicker.

"If we have any problem with Lord Valesk, I'll handle it," Roland said. "I know Valesk and his father quite well." He regarded Tamal and Hawk with a stern look. "I expect each of you to take your turn on guard duty. Tamal, keep watch with your men for two hours and then wake Hawk and me. Your other two men will take the last watch."

Tamal bowed. "As you wish, Sir Roland," he said, returning to his men.

"You handled that well," Taliesin said when Roland sat on his blanket. She could smell his body odor, found it pleasing, not repellant, and cuddled close when he laid beside her. He turned toward her, his eyelids already growing heavy, and slid his arm around her.

"Let me handle things from now on," he said. "This is what I was trained to do and why you need me. Tamal and Hawk will be at each other throats if I don't keep them on a short leash. I don't know the names of the Nova brothers, but they take orders, so that's good."

Taliesin rested her head on his shoulder. "You act so tough, but that's why I love you," she said, her voice so soft she wondered if he'd heard her. When Roland didn't say it in return, she grew concerned, fearing he didn't feel the same way and looked at him. His eyes were closed, but he was smiling.

* * *

Taliesin awoke to the sound of Wren screaming. She wiped the sleep from her eyes and sat up. Roland wasn't beside her, and she assumed he was on guard duty. Nor did she see Hawk or Rook. Wren lay three pallets over, beside Jaelle, who was holding onto the girl's hand.

"Wake her up, Jaelle!" Taliesin said in earnest. "She mustn't shout."

"I've tried. I can't wake her."

A dark silhouette appeared and blocked Taliesin's view. Rook set aside his silver spear, knelt beside Wren, and shook her gently by the shoulders, trying to rouse her from the nightmare. Zarnoc hurried over and placed a hand on Rook's shoulder. As Taliesin stood up and prepared to go help, she felt a tap on her shoulder and turned. Roland, fully dressed and holding *Moonbane*, stood behind her, a serious look on his face.

"We've seen riders," he said. "Yellow banners. Valesk's men."

"She'll alert the enemy to our position if she is not silenced," Tamal said, jumping to his feet. Showing no concern for Wren, he drew Jaelle to her feet and led her away. The four Ghajar scouts gathered near their pallets and muttered together, glancing at Wren in concern. Hawk was on guard duty at the entrance.

"Zarnoc, is there anything you can do for her?" Taliesin asked. She sent Roland to stand watch with Hawk. The girl's shouts grew louder.

Zarnoc knelt next to Wren and lifted her head in his hands. He spoke softly to her in a language Taliesin had never heard before. She assumed it was his native language, Lorian, and the words were a magical incantation, for after a few minutes, Wren grew silent, stirred, and opened her eyes. Rook immediately pulled Wren into his arms. Wren flung her arms around the young man's neck and clung to him as if she'd never let go. Jaelle came back and placed her hand on Zarnoc's shoulder. He patted her hand.

"Wren has had a powerful vision," Zarnoc said. "It required a spell to wake her. Jaelle, get Wren some water. Don't look so worried, Rook. Our little Wren will be all right, especially with so many mother hens to look after her. Now move aside, boy, so I may talk to her."

The young man reluctantly released Wren, moved out of the way, and stood beside Taliesin, tears in his eyes. Zarnoc sat cross-legged, took Wren by the hands, and gazed steadily into her eyes, a tender smile on his wrinkled face. In the time it took Wren to calm down, Jaelle returned with a flask of water and handed it to the wizard, who in turn helped the trembling young girl take a few sips. He gave the flask to Jaelle, took Wren by the hands, and gave her a cheery smile.

"Now, my dear, take a few deep breaths. Each time you exhale, you will feel more refreshed and calmer." Zarnoc said something in Lorian and waited while Wren took several large breaths through her nose and exhaled through her mouth. Her chest heaved with each breath, while Zarnoc patted her hands. "There, there, now. You have a pretty glow on your cheeks now, my dear. There's no reason to be afraid. Your family is here."

"But...but I saw our family. I saw Talon and Falcon. I saw them all."

"What about them?" Taliesin asked. "You told us before everyone was dead."

Rook sighed heavily and shook his head at her. Taliesin fell silent. The wizard placed his arm around Wren's shoulders and helped her sit up. "Now try again," Zarnoc said. "Tell us what you saw, little Wren. What has happened to the twins? It's all right, my dear. Simply tell us what happened."

Large tears rolled down Wren's cheeks. With her hair now worn short and colored black, she looked much different from the girl who had left Raven's Nest. Her makeup was smeared by her tears, leaving two black trails on her pale cheeks. Zarnoc released her hands to wipe the tears away with a kerchief that magically appeared, and just as quickly vanished when he took her hands into his own.

"The twins were turned," Wren said. "Chief Lykus bit them."

"Simply ghastly," Zarnoc said. "You poor child. I cannot imagine what you have seen, but you must not fear these visions. Embrace this gift from the gods, for they may prove helpful to our quest. Now tell me, child, what did you see? You spoke of the twins?"

"Yes. Talon and Falcon were turned."

Rook knelt beside Wren. Taliesin knew he'd been fond of the twins, and all the children had loved Rook. The twins had not taken to many people other than Minerva, but Rook had easily won them over.

"Take your time, Wren," the wizard said. "Start at the beginning. What did you see?"

"I...I saw Osprey and Glabbrio being led away by Lykus. The Wolf Chief wanted to know where Taliesin had gone and whom she was traveling with. Osprey explained Taliesin had been sent away, but he didn't know where. When Lykus grew angry, Glabbrio tried to appease him by offering him Duke Hrothgar's armor and sword, but Lykus rejected the bribe, and Osprey refused to tell him anything more."

Taliesin felt rage building inside of her. "Then what happened?" she asked.

"Osprey, Glabbrio, and Minerva were brought before the Wolf Clan," Wren said, her cheeks flushed pink with the hint of a fever. Jaelle gave her the flask of water again, and she drank before continuing. "Lykus asked them to decide whether they wanted to be turned or not, and that's when the twins were brought forward. Those dear, sweet boys were given no choice and were held as Lykus bit them. The same was done to Minerva."

"Monsters," the wizard said. "Despicable monsters."

Wren clutched Rook's hand. "One by one, the Ravens were led before Lykus and killed," she said. "It was horrible to watch. They were ripped apart and devoured while poor Osprey and Glabbrio watched. When it was Glabbrio's turn, Lykus butchered him and fed him to the clan." The pink had left her face, leaving her pale as a sheet. "Osprey was so brave, so very brave. He didn't beg for mercy or show any fear."

"Yes?" Zarnoc said, anxious. "What happened then?"

"The Raven Master looked at me, right at me," Wren said. "He saw me, he must have, for he said, '*Dead things don't stay dead for long.*' I don't know how he knew I was there, or why he said what he did. No one has ever spoken to me during a vision, but after he spoke, Lykus tore off Osprey's head and made the twins eat him."

There was a long silence before anyone spoke.

"Wren, what happened to the Eagle legionnaires? You said nothing about them, only Glabbrio," Taliesin said. Her mind was reeling from the images—she wanted revenge.

"Lykus released them," Wren said, leaning into Rook's arms. Jaelle remained beside her, one hand on the girl's shoulder. "I don't know why. Maybe he wanted the survivors to return to Lord Arundel with the story. I looked for Master Xander, Lord Arundel's son, but I didn't see him at Wolf's Den, and no one mentioned him."

Taliesin cursed under her breath. "I bet Xander was never at Wolf's Den," she said. "Of course, the Eagles weren't harmed. Glabbrio was big enough to keep those monsters fed for days. They didn't have to kill everyone. I will not rest until Lykus and his clan pays for what they have done."

She thought of Minerva and the twins. Though Taliesin never liked the old woman, Minerva didn't deserve being turned into a *Wolfen*, and neither did the two boys. She nodded at Zarnoc, who stood, stretched, and walked with her to the cave entrance.

"It is just as I said, Taliesin," Zarnoc said. "The longer Wren and Jaelle are in your company, the stronger their powers will become. Jaelle may be a palmist and a reader of cards, but her fortunes will become more valid and Wren's visions more accurate. Even I am far stronger than I was before you came to Pelekus. Soon, your powers will emerge, I should think, though I cannot tell you precisely when or what they will be. I've never had a *Sha'tar* as an apprentice."

Roland and Hawk stood at the cave's entrance. Both had heard the fate of the Raven Clan and looked equally troubled.

"I will kill Chief Lykus with my own hands," Hawk swore.

"Taliesin, I am so sorry." Roland stepped forward and slid his arm around her and pulled her close, his gaze traveling to the dense trees. "Osprey was a good man. When the king hears of what happened, I know he will give the order for the destruction of the Wolf Pack, and I'll gladly lead the attack."

"All of our friends are dead," Taliesin said. "If you all hadn't come with me, you'd be dead, too."

"Lord Arundel could have stopped Chief Lykus," Zarnoc said after a moment. "His soldiers were spared, so I suspect there may be a pact between the Wolf Clan and the Eagle Clan. Taliesin mentioned Master Xander is missing. Perhaps the map will reveal his location; then again, perhaps not. We should check later, just to be sure."

Roland held Taliesin tighter. "This is painful news," he said, and brushed his nose against her cheek, wet with tears. "Master Osprey was wise to send you away. I only wish we'd stayed at Raven's Nest and put up a fight. It's what you wanted to do."

"Damn the Wolf Pack," Hawk said. "And damn the Eagle Clan. Arundel and Lykus are probably having a good laugh right about now. They never liked Osprey."

"They'll pay for this," Taliesin replied. "When I find *Ringerike*, I'll lay low their clans. This I swear."

"Their fate is for King Frederick to decide, dearest," replied Roland. "We need to find *Ringerike* and return to Padama so we can help put down this rebellion. The king needs our help and I, for one, intend to do whatever is necessary to see Frederick Draconus remains on the throne."

Taliesin pulled away from him. "I don't care about King Frederick," she said, angrily. "I don't care which prince sits on the throne. If you want to find magical weapons for your stupid king, Roland, then I'll help you, but you can't have *Ringerike*. Quite a few magical weapons are on the way to the Cave of the Snake God. We can collect them, and you can take them back to your king with Tamal and his men. But that's all I'll do for your king."

"*Ringerike* is the only sword I am after. With the Raven Sword, we have a chance to save the king and avenge our clan," Roland said passionately. "The king is still healthy and fit to rule another twenty years or more. Let me use *Ringerike* to defeat Frederick's sons. I swear I'll avenge Osprey and destroy those who caused his death."

Taliesin could tell by the expression on Roland's face he was convinced he was right, but she was determined to keep the sword out of King Frederick's hands, as well as every other prince, nobleman, or eager knight's.

"I am the Raven Mistress," she said. "The Raven Sword will only be used to help avenge our clan. I'm sorry, Roland. I know you are loyal to your king, but the Draconus family killed King Korax and turned our clan into scavengers. That same king has allowed our clan to be exterminated. I will not help him. You must understand. I have lost two fathers because of this king, and I will not lose any more people I love."

For a moment, she found herself looking at Grudge. He looked murderous. She'd never known him to lay violent hands upon a woman, and, though he did not make a move toward her, she moved away until Zarnoc stood between them. Roland began quaking with rage, and Hawk placed his hand on the larger man's shoulder, only to be shoved to the ground.

"You will do what is best for the realm, woman!" Roland shouted. "We cannot allow Prince Almaric to take Padama. His army contains not only Skardanian barbarians, but mercenaries from the east and outlaws. Thousands will die if *Ringerike* is not used to protect King Frederick and the realm from this threat. The King's enemies are our enemies, Taliesin. Make no mistake about that! I said I would avenge the Raven Clan, and I will, but I must have *Ringerike* to accomplish that. It's the most powerful of all weapons."

"Only as powerful as the one who uses it," countered Taliesin, remembering what Zarnoc had told her. How could she believe in herself or her magic abilities if Roland didn't think her decision was the right one? She didn't want to be at odds with him, but her mind was made up.

"You do not trust me," Roland said, at last. His tone was surprisingly cold. "Don't fool yourself into thinking Prince Sertorius will help you. That snake does not support his father. Sertorius will change sides on a whim. I do not know what happened between you two in the Volgate, but I know you were childhood friends. The king was very specific that you two should not be allowed to renew your friendship. I may not know the details as to why the king fears this union but be warned. Side with this snake against me, and you both shall suffer."

The cavern seemed unnaturally still. No one spoke. Even the horses remained quiet and merely flicked at flies with their tails.

Taliesin and Roland glared at one another, their animosity and anger so visible and deeply felt it could have been cut in two with a sharp blade. She'd never seen Roland so furious before, nor had she felt such a deep hatred for another person. All she saw standing before her was the king's own champion. She didn't care he knew she'd encountered Sertorius in the marshes or suspected they'd formed some type of alliance. He felt threatened, and like any threatened beast, he was ready to attack. But a quick glance from Zarnoc made her lower her eyes and her voice.

"Must we draw battle lines this minute?" Taliesin forced her voice to sound light-hearted, trying to appeal to Roland's heart, but she feared it did not belong to her; it belonged to the king. "I do trust you, Roland. I trust you with my life, but on this particular issue, I am resolute. I have no love for Sertorius or any of the princes. We may never find *Ringerike*. We may be able to find other magical weapons if the map is true, and I'll even try to find Master Xander, if you think he's important, but the Raven Sword will never serve a Draconus again."

"That is your final decision?" Roland asked, his voice lowered to a growl.

"Yes," Taliesin said. "That is my answer, Sir Roland. You swore you'd do what I asked, so I'm asking you to help me avenge the Raven Clan. The Raven Sword is not for sale."

With a snort of disgust, Roland stormed off, his knuckles white around the handle of his battle-ax. Hawk gave Taliesin a sad smile and walked to the knight, leaving Zarnoc, who looked stoic as he lit his pipe and watched the two men bicker.

Taliesin knew she risked losing Roland's love by refusing to help his king, but Frederick Draconus was an usurper, not fit to wear the crown. Roland had sworn to follow her; it wasn't her fault if he was now torn between his oath and his honor. If her decision to use the Raven Sword for the Raven Clan meant she couldn't be with Roland, she was willing to make that sacrifice. Heaving a sigh, she turned and walked into the cave.

* * * * *

Chapter Nineteen

Tears in her eyes, Taliesin brushed Thalagar with a soft bristle brush, removing a layer of mud and dust from his thick black coat. The argument with Roland had left her unsettled, her stomach hurt, and she was angry and confused about what she needed to do versus what she wanted to do. She liked to think of herself as a strong woman—one not dependent upon a man—but having Roland upset with her, especially over what was best for King Frederick and the realm, had left her wallowing in self-pity.

Roland wanted to ride to Padama with the Raven Sword and rescue his beloved king from a siege. He didn't care how she felt about it, and, like all men, he assumed a woman would eventually do what he wanted. She'd taken him to bed, but that didn't mean she belonged to him any more than he belonged to her. Loving Roland left her confused and unable to sort out her priorities, and in her frustration, she absent-mindedly brushed Thalagar harder than intended. The horse let out an angry snort and stomped his front leg, nearly crushing her toes under his large hoof.

"Watch it there," Taliesin said. She gave Thalagar a pat on the rump. "I'm sure you heard all that nonsense between Roland and me, old boy. What am I supposed to do? If there were a Raven heir, I'd give him the Raven Sword. But there isn't one, and I won't help Frederick Draconus keep his throne. If Roland can't understand the king is a monster and a murderer, then that's his problem, not mine. I kneel to no man. All that makes Roland is the dumbest turkey in the woods. I hate him, Thalagar. I really do. I hate all men."

The stallion turned his head, caught her gaze, and with a snort, ended her tirade with a smack of his tail against the side of her head. It was a deliberate sneak attack, and Taliesin imagined Thalagar laughing inside of his horse head. Most people didn't think animals had a sense of humor, but they did. A lopsided smile tugged at one corner of her mouth, and she wiped away her tears. The stallion again snorted and tossed his head. Taliesin looked to her left and spotted Tamal walking toward her. The young man carried a flask of wine and a chunk of bread wrapped in colorful cloth.

"You need to keep your strength, Raven Mistress," Tamal said. "Eat. Drink. I'll brush your horse." He handed her the wine and bread, took the brush, and started to brush it across the stallion's neck. "Start at the top and work your way down. Long, soft strokes, that's what horses like."

"Thank you, Tamal," Taliesin said. She tried to smile, but her face muscles felt frozen. She took a bite of the bread and watched him brush her horse. "Thalagar usually doesn't like strangers. I've always believed you should trust the instincts of an animal. If an animal likes a person, then it's a good indication you can as well. Not always, but usually."

Tamal continued brushing the stallion. "I feel I need to tell you what really happened that night," he said, keeping his voice low. "What happened between Roland and me was not quite as either of us led you and my father to believe. Knowing what was at stake, I thought it best to agree with Sir Roland. My men and I were trading in a nearby town and stopped for the night at a farmer's house. There we met a beautiful girl who made it quite clear she wanted me. When the others went to bed, she led me outside and kissed me under the stars. I thought I was doing what she wanted, but when Sir Roland arrived and caught us together, she told him I'd forced myself upon her. I didn't realize the girl was his wife until that moment, and so I took the beating in silence and went my way."

"The girl was Sir Roland's wife?" Taliesin choked on the bread and quickly took a drink of wine. It was well past noon, and she felt distraught, so she drank more. "Roland never told me he was married. Are you sure she was his wife, Tamal?"

"Yes," he said, pausing in his work. "Her reputation was well known in town; she even told me her husband was often away for months at a time. She lived with her father and was lonely; at least that's what she said. Sir Roland must have known her reputation yet blinded himself from the truth. The girl's father pulled him off me and helped me get away, or I think he would have killed me that night."

"What happened to her?" Taliesin asked. "Is she waiting for him to come home?"

Tamal shook his head. "When I returned to the area a year later," he said, "I heard the girl had died, and the farmer had moved away. The townsfolk believed Sir Roland killed her in a jealous rage, but I do not believe that to be true, Taliesin. I believe Sir Roland is an honorable man, and I would not have agreed to come with him if I believed otherwise."

"Who was his wife? What was her name?"

"Does it matter?" Tamal asked with a shrug. "I did cause the man harm, unknowingly, and I hoped to make amends by agreeing to be his squire. I hope he feels the same."

"I don't know what to say, Tamal. That is a horrible story. I dare not ask Roland about it, and now I feel even worse for quarreling with him. No wonder he thinks so little of women."

"That is not my place to say. I believe the knight carries great guilt in his heart. You made me swear I would obey you over Sir Roland, and so I told you what happened, but I also say you should not let an argument split you apart. Kings will come and go; that is the way of things, now and always. My father says true love is hard to find and harder still to keep. If this man means anything to you, Raven Mistress, then you will find a way to set things right. You spared my life for a reason. I want only to make amends. He grieves still, and perhaps you can take that burden away."

Tamal turned away and brushed out Thalagar's tail, leaving Taliesin to consider what he'd told her. Not once had Roland ever mentioned he'd been married; then again, she'd never asked. It made sense now why he'd never told her he loved her; he didn't because he still loved his dead wife. But had he murdered his own wife for sleeping with other men? She didn't want to believe it. She couldn't believe that of him. Yet, Roland stayed with them because he wanted the sword for the king. He didn't stay because he loved her and wanted to be with her; if he did, he'd not have said those painful things to her. If he loved her, he would do as she requested, but that's not what he'd done.

Sometime later, Hawk found her sitting at the back of the cave and offered a blue kerchief from around his neck to dry her tears. The pearl earring dangling from his left earlobe caught her attention and gave her something to look at; a distraction. He was still dressed like a gypsy, with hair dyed dark and his eyes outlined in black. After she dabbed her eyes and blew her nose into the scarf, she handed it back. He seemed disinclined to accept it but stuffed it into the pocket of his baggy black pants.

"In the past," he said, "I enjoyed hearing you and Grudge bicker like two old magpies, but this time it's different. It's your own damn fault for growing attached to an outsider. Roland considers himself a White Stag, not a Black Wing; that much he admitted. We'll never be able to sell that sword, but I had no idea you wanted to keep it. What will you do with it?"

"It's always about money with you," Taliesin said, bristling. "*Ringerike* belongs to our clan, and I'm not about to give a sickly old king a piece of our heritage, so if you've come to ask me to reconsider, you might as well forget it, because I'm not going to."

The young man threw up his hands. "I'm offended you would think so lowly of me," he replied. "My only interest is keeping the Raven Sword with the Raven Clan, and now I know you aren't going to part with it, I won't make any suggestions about lords who might be interested in buying it...it wouldn't be right. This mission isn't about making money, anymore. It's about pride in our clan and preserving our heritage."

"I'm glad you feel that way," Taliesin said. She smiled at Hawk and poked him in the ribs. "It's not like I think all of your ideas are bad. You'd make a decent Raven Master if you were ever inclined to put the clan before your own needs. Who knows? Before this is all over with, you might be just the person to wear Master Osprey's shoes."

"You mean you don't want to lead the clan?"

Taliesin saw the wheels turning inside Hawk's head. He had a look on his face that made it clear the idea had never occurred to him, and now that she'd mentioned it, he was already picturing himself wearing a raven-feather cloak and crown.

"Raven's Nest has to be rebuilt, Hawk, from the ground up, and I can't do that alone," she said, glad he was so easily led. "That's not a marriage proposal, mind you, so don't jump to conclusions. We're Ravens. Putting the clan first is what we're supposed to do. I simply meant you'd make a wonderful Raven Master, with or without me."

"Yeah, I see your point," he said. "I *would* look good in a crown."

Within the hour, Taliesin and her friends had saddled the horses and loaded their gear. Zarnoc meant to ride the mule on a permanent basis, so Tamal decided it was best not to burden the animal with additional weight, and the wizard seemed quite content that his mount had been elevated in status. Any opportunity to make amends with Roland seemed to sidestep Taliesin. Though she wasn't eager to seek him out, she noticed he kept close to Tamal and the gypsies instead of the Ravens. Although they'd heard no wolf howls, nor seen any Aldagar soldiers milling about the area, the knight and the five men readied their weapons as if they anticipated trouble on the road and rode out of the cave without waiting for the others.

When she finished saddling Thalagar, Taliesin put on her black cloak, fastened her sword belt tight about her waist, and climbed into the saddle. Jaelle led a small roan, with white tassels hanging from its bridle and saddle, out of the cave and mounted beside her. The gypsy girl tossed her long, curly, black hair and motioned in the direction taken by her brother.

"Sirocco, Khamsin, Simoom, and Harmattan Nova are staying with us," Jaelle said. "The brothers are all seasoned fighters, but Harmattan is the best. The eldest, Sirocco, is my brother's best friend. It is known when Tamal becomes the next Shan, the Nova brothers will become his personal guards. My father will not be surprised they have chosen to remain with us."

"I'm glad they did," Taliesin said.

"Sirocco desires to marry me, even if I have no intention of marrying," replied Jaelle, sounding more than a little conceited. "If I stay with the tribe, I suppose I must marry one of the Nova brothers one day; if it comes to that, I'll ask Harmattan to fight for the honor of marrying me."

"Both are fine-looking men, Jaelle," Taliesin said. "You could do far worse. Your brother is also a very good scout; he seems to know when trouble is afoot."

A friendly smile appeared on Jaelle's beautiful face.

The Ghajar were beautiful people, overall, thought Taliesin, and the Shan's daughter was without a doubt the loveliest woman she'd ever seen. The expression in the girl's eyes confused her, though. It wasn't Harmattan Jaelle had feelings for. While Taliesin didn't quite understand it, she knew the girl was interested in her in the same way Taliesin was interested in Roland. The revelation wasn't an unpleasant one, but it was strange territory, and Taliesin didn't want to give Jaelle any false hope.

"Many thoughts fill your head, Raven Mistress," Jaelle said in a husky voice. "I heard your argument with your man. Roland is torn between his loyalty to the king and his love for you."

Glancing at the sun through the tree limbs, Taliesin wanted to forget about what had been said between her and Roland. Hawk, Rook, Wren, and Zarnoc were still inside the cave packing the last of the gear, taking more time than was necessary, but the delay gave her time to put an end to Jaelle's curiosity about Roland.

"Roland is a King's Man, not a Raven," Taliesin said. "The king sent Roland to join our clan with orders to bring me to Padama. As soon as we find *Ringerike*, Roland will surely try to get me to return with him, but I have no intention of doing so."

"Tamal believes Roland is a good man. My brother's opinion is of value."

Taliesin hated herself for doubting Roland, especially at this point in their journey, but her trust in him was shaken. It was ironic that while Tamal had tried to kill Roland and Jaelle has attempted to strangle her, she considered them the least problematic. The pair was honest about their feelings, and that counted for something, unlike Roland, who had too many secrets.

"Best keep an eye on Roland," Taliesin said, sounding angrier than she'd intended. "Too many people are interested in finding *Ringerike*, and far too many know we are looking for it; that makes me nervous. I don't want to be caught off guard or surprised, not for any reason. Tamal can think what he likes about Roland, but I can't take that risk, and I'm not thinking clearly, so you'll have to do it for me, Jaelle."

The gypsy girl nodded. "Love makes you blind. I understand. You can count on me, Taliesin. I will watch your man."

Hawk, Wren, Rook, and Zarnoc rode out to the two women, and Jaelle led them west, through the tall pine trees. Rook only nodded as they took the opposite direction from Roland and the gypsies, who had not returned. An argument was going on between Hawk and Wren that clearly had both upset.

"*Varguld* is real," Wren said in a defensive voice. "The Age of the Wolf is upon us. Zarnoc said so."

"The world's population cannot possibly be eaten by giant wolves," Hawk said. "All the talk about Ragnal, the God of War, dropping to all fours and turning into a giant wolf to join his sons, Varg and Cano, is but a legend. Zarnoc also said he's been to Mt. Helos and spent an afternoon in the Hall of Immortals with Stroud the Maker and his wife, Broa. It's a bunch of bird crap. Don't believe everything that old man tells you."

"I'm right here," Zarnoc said, sounding quite offended. "I do not invent stories to mislead young ladies, Eugene, and I did spend an afternoon with the gods. We had roasted boar and spring wine and talked about a great many things!"

The old wizard carried his belongings across his lap. His pipe was put away, and he'd changed the color of his robe into a dark forest green. Something besides Hawk's angry snort abruptly caught his attention, and despite a sudden tug on the reins in the opposite direction, his mule brayed loudly and took off through the trees. The group's laughter ended at the sudden, forlorn howl of a wolf. Hawk drew a silver cutlass, horse dancing as he wheeled, and pointed with his blade toward the north.

"Get the women out of here, Rook!" Hawk shouted. "Don't wait for us. Get across the Minoc River. We'll meet you on the other side."

Spinning his horse around, Hawk took off after the wizard as Jaelle took the lead again, riding hard, with Rook, Wren, and Taliesin following. They heard a chorus of wolf song and the immediate clang of steel behind them. Although Zarnoc's magic grew stronger by the day, and Roland and Hawk fought beside the gypsies, Taliesin had a sinking feeling she may never see any of them again.

* * *

Riding quickly through the trees, Jaelle led the way around a cliff, along a path, and onto a gravel-covered road lined by tall pine trees. They rode hard until they arrived at an intersection; one path led up the hill to Stalker Castle and the other toward the city of Tunberg. Taliesin saw no other roads, and although they'd meant to avoid either place, said nothing about the chosen path, seeing how distraught Jaelle looked.

"I know where I'm going," Jaelle said, sounding angry. "We can ride through town and still reach the river before nightfall. No Wolfman will come into the city. Pull the hood of your cloak over your head, so no one notices you," she told Taliesin.

Taliesin rode alongside her, already able to smell the city on the breeze. It seemed less hazardous when they passed a man chewing on a blade of straw with a cart of vegetables. He nodded as Taliesin glanced in his direction and she settled in the saddle, content, for now, to ride through the town and make their way to the river. Jaelle's mood seemed to be improving, and Rook and Wren looked happy, if that was possible. It dawned on her that she'd been stuck, like some old nanny, with the three teenagers.

"I like Rook. Most men talk too much. Not him." Jaelle glanced over her shoulder then turned forward with a blush on her cheeks. "Wren is fortunate to be so loved. The Erindorian waits on her hand and foot like a castle servant. He asks nothing and gives everything. That is a rare quality in a man. A man like that could make me think differently about their gender."

"Rook can talk but chooses not to. Something happened to him when he was a boy, and he's never talked since," Taliesin said. "Of course, playing the part of a mute would be a wonderful disguise for a spy, but that's the romantic in me." She heard the flapping of wings and saw a flock of wrens fly away from the trees, startling her horse. She patted Thalagar on the neck to calm him, and her hand came away slick with sweat and black horsehair, which she wiped off across her pant leg. She watched the flock pass over the road and sang, "*We hunted the wren for Baldor. In the glade, we hunted his wife. We hunted the wren for Baldor; in the glade, he took her life.*"

"Wrens are birds of fair weather," Jaelle said. "What song do you sing?"

"What? Was I singing?" Taliesin shook her head, unaware she'd spoken aloud. Of all the plays written by Glabber the Glib, she found it odd that particular one came to mind. "It's some stupid song from a stupid play about birds and bird wives. Glabber the Glib wrote it; he's my favorite playwright.

I guess it's a habit; you know, think of old sayings and attach them as omens about whatever type of bird you see."

"It is a tragic play?"

"Rather," Taliesin said. "A wood nymph falls in love with a knight before the eve of battle. She is married to a warlock, who learns of her unfaithfulness, turns her into a wren, and convinces the knight and his comrades the wren is an evil omen. They pursue, determined to kill her, but the warlock arrives first and kills his wife. When the bird-wife cries out, the knight and his companions are discovered by the enemy and slaughtered. So now, soldiers fear seeing wrens before a battle, thinking it's a bad omen. Glabber's plays have that effect on people."

"Superstitious people. Like my people. We have many stories about birds and even more about wolves." Jaelle sat straighter in the saddle as they passed a man and his children walking toward town and carrying baskets of eggs. "The father smiled at me. Not many people smile at the Ghajar. They think we'll kidnap their children and turn them into gypsies. We've never done that, so I don't know why people think that about us."

"The Raven Clan did," Taliesin said. "That's what happened to me."

"Mind your hood—your hair is too red." Lifting a hand, Jaelle wiped the sweat off her brow and glanced to make certain Taliesin did as she requested. "I know it is hot today. It will continue to get hotter during the day and colder at night as we approach Garridan. The desert is an inhospitable place. I have not been, but Tamal and the brothers have. They know the way, and they will find us before dark, I promise."

The city walls loomed before them. A small creek ran under a bridge that led to the open gates, and guards stood in the towers—city guards—not the duke's men. The road was getting crowded. Carts, wagons, and riders were coming and going from the town. No one took much notice of four gypsy riders, but Taliesin sensed Jaelle was uneasy.

"Have you been to Tunberg before?" Taliesin asked. "I haven't been to any big cities, not since I was a child." Taliesin thought of Tantalon Castle, in the royal city of Padama, and how different it looked in comparison to the smaller Stalker Castle, which was more a fortress than a palace. Tunberg was impressive, but not half as beautiful as Padama. "I'm sure you've seen far more interesting places than I have. Most of my life has been spent looting battlefields, leaving me little time to go to market. Women usually stay home and let the men handle trading the goods, although I sometimes went with Osprey and Grudge."

"Grudge?"

"Sir Roland," Taliesin said. "That was his clan name. Hawk's real name is Eugene, but don't tell him I told you. He'll be mad at me; he doesn't like that name."

"It's a nice name." Jaelle leaned forward and made certain her skirt covered her ankles, obviously not wanting to show any skin. "Here you can buy and sell anything you can imagine. I'd like to buy a new pair of riding gloves. I did not bring any, and the sun is unmerciful in the Salayan Desert." She pulled to the side of the road and stopped their progress as a knight in a yellow tunic passed, heading toward the city.

"What's wrong?" Taliesin questioned. "Don't you want to go into town?"

"Duke Volund Fortinbraus is not as bad as they say. He protects these lands from the Djaran tribes; they are not liked by my people." Jaelle looked around, obviously uncertain if going into the city was a good idea. "The Minoc River will take one day to reach. It not only separates this dukedom from Garridan but keeps the Djaran from raiding Tunberg."

"Let's turn around, then," Taliesin said. "We can find a way around the city and reach the river. You seem nervous. I'd rather not take any chances."

A loud trumpet call came from the castle. Taliesin and her friends turned their horses and watched as a line of armored knights rode out of the castle gate. An alarm must have been given, she thought. Lord Valesk was sending more men along the road, away from the city and into the forest. Riding into battle against the Wolfmen, she thought, as the last man disappeared into the dark, gloomy forest; she hoped they were armed with silver weapons.

"There is a small trail, used by the farmers, we can take," Jaelle said. "I know you're worried, Taliesin, but Lord Valesk's men will offer aid if they arrive in time. I know he has no love for Chief Lykus because my brother says the hall of Stalker Castle is filled with wolf pelts. If you skin a Wolfman before he turns into a human, it makes a very fine pelt."

"Lord Valesk is someone I don't want to meet," Taliesin said. "The sooner we are away from this place, the better for all of us. Lead on, Jaelle. I want to cross the Minoc before nightfall."

With a whistle to her friends, Taliesin let Jaelle take the lead and followed her, riding away from the gloomy castle, leaving the town far behind.

* * * * *

Chapter Twenty

Taliesin and her friends, riding along the outskirts of the city, encountered only a few farmers headed to Tunberg with their goods. A patrol of armored soldiers rode by and paid no attention to the travelers dressed as Ghajar gypsies. Taliesin wore her own clothes but was covered by the cloak that belonged to Jaelle. The path was beaten down by use and proved a wise decision. No one stopped them, and no one bothered them. Miles went by as they passed fields of cotton and corn, and as the sun started its descent in the west, they came upon a small village with thatched cottages, a small church, and a tavern. Children played in the road, tossing a ball, and several dogs barked and ran after them, trying to catch the ball. Women wearing aprons sat outside one of the cottages, drinking lemonade and chatting together while their husbands worked behind plows on small patches of land.

"I'm starving," Wren said, glancing toward the tavern. Several horses were tied to posts outside the sagging walls of the old building. "Can't we stop? Please, Taliesin. My legs are so sore. I swear I can't ride another mile; we don't have to stay long."

Taliesin glanced at Jaelle. "What do you think? Is this place safe?"

"No tavern is ever safe," Jaelle said, "but I am hungry as well."

"Then let's go in. I have money." Taliesin shook a small bag, and the coins jingled inside. Jaelle gave a nod and reined in her horse. The first to dismount and tie her horse, she waited for her friends at the tavern entrance. "I'll go first," Taliesin said. "Everyone keep quiet and stay together. I'll do the ordering since my accent sounds similar to what's spoken here."

Taliesin pushed the doors open and walked inside, followed by her three friends. The tavern was dark, and the air smelled musty. Cobwebs hung from the rafters and straw littered the floor. Two men wearing traveling cloaks leaned against the bar and talked over tankards of ale, while a handful of farmers, seated at poorly-made tables, ate their late dinner. Taliesin picked a table in the corner and waited for Jaelle to slide along the bench before taking a seat herself. Wren collapsed on the bench and placed her head on her arms, which she had crossed on the table. She'd removed her scarf, and her short, black hair stuck out like the feathers of a bird. Rook leaned his spear against the wall, looked around to count the heads of the customers, then sat with his back to the table. Arms crossed, and silent as the grave, he kept his attention on the front door and clearly expected trouble to appear at any moment.

"Will you be eating, then?" The tavern keeper called. He was a thin man with a nose that slid from his face as if broken in a fight more than once. "We have fresh fish!"

"Sir, we would eat crumbs if that is all you had," replied Taliesin. "Fish will do."

"Well, I also have a shank of lamb, just off the spit," he said. "It should suit you four; I know not everyone enjoys river fish. How about some ale to wash the dirt from your throats?"

At Taliesin's nod, the man wiped his dirty hands across his apron, filled four tankards with ale, and brought them on a tray to the table. A young girl, about fourteen years of age, came out of the back room with a platter of a leg of lamb, stewed vegetables, bread, cheese, and a carving knife that she placed on the table. She went to fetch plates and forks, returned within seconds, and set them on the table before returning to her duties in the kitchen. Taliesin looked at her dirty hands and wished for a place to clean up, but didn't see any washroom, so she wiped them on her cloak.

"It won't kill you to eat with dirty hands," Jaelle said. She took the knife and cut into the lamb, carving it for them. Rook produced his own dagger and stabbed a potato, lifted it to his mouth, and stuffed it in. He made yummy sounds as he chewed. "Doesn't he ever talk?" Jaelle asked.

"I suppose he will when he's ready," Taliesin said.

Wren lifted her tankard. "Rook comes from the Isle of Valen. He might not talk, but there is nothing wrong with his hearing. He has other ways of communicating; he speaks with his hands. I can translate for you. It's easy to learn, so I can teach you, too, if you'd like."

Rook turned and swung his long legs beneath the table. He studied Jaelle while he stabbed a piece of lamb with his dagger, chewed it thoughtfully, and drank the ale. Setting aside the knife, he gestured with his hands and conveyed to Jaelle that he, along with Wren and Taliesin, were members of Raven Clan. He pointed at himself and went through the story of his capture as a child, how he came to join Raven Clan, and how he felt about Wren. All this was conveyed to Jaelle with such ease she had no trouble following along and understanding Rook and grew a new appreciation for the dark-skinned warrior. Reaching into her jacket, Jaelle drew out a deck of well-used Tareen Cards and spread them out on the table. Rook leaned forward and tapped a card with a long finger. Jaelle turned it over and smiled.

"The card of Love. I am not surprised," Jaelle said. She pushed the card toward Wren. "You have no cause to worry, my friend. Rook loves you deeply."

"I wasn't worried. I know how Rook feels about me."

"You are lucky. Most men lie." Jaelle held her hand out toward the cards. "You pick one, Wren. Let us see what the future holds for you."

Wren shook her head. "I'd rather not. The Tareen Cards frighten me."

"They are but cards." Jaelle took a sip of ale. "There is no reason to fear your future."

"When you have visions such as I do, it is hard not to be fearful. I see so many terrible things, Jaelle. I'd rather not. I don't want to know about my future."

Reaching out impulsively, Taliesin picked a card and flipped it over. The figure of a skeleton riding a flaming skeleton horse was painted on the card. The word below the figure read DEATH. She turned the card over with a shaking hand and reached for her tankard. It was warm but tasted good. Jaelle explained the card represented more the death of old ways and bad habits than of impending doom, but Taliesin could only think of Roland being devoured by Wolfmen. Only Rook still seemed interested in the cards, and at Jaelle's bidding, he selected two more.

"I'll be back," Taliesin said. "Service is poor, and I am thirsty."

Taliesin stood and went to the bar to order another round. The two travelers at the bar looked at her, saying nothing as she paid in coin, but she noticed dark-blue tunics beneath their cloaks. Maldavians, she thought, probably soldiers. Trying not to give them any reason to question her, she turned her head and scratched her neck, trying to see if they wore greaves or carried swords. They had both. The bartender came over and slid a large pitcher of ale toward her. She grabbed it and turned just as a group of more cloaked figures walked into the tavern—blue and black cloaks, and all were armed.

"Greetings, Your Grace! We are relieved you could join us," a man said at the bar. "Sir Duroc and I have scouted ahead. We've seen no sign of Wolfgar or his pack."

His companion added, "Lord Valesk assured us he'll sweep the forest and have every Wolfman skinned by nightfall. Sir Gallus, give him the Duke's ring. A gift. Proof of his father's loyalty. They weren't hard to convince to join us when they heard you were nearby."

A familiar figure stepped forward and pushed the dark-blue hood off his face. Taliesin's eyes widened as she recognized Prince Sertorius, no longer dressed as a Knight of Chaos, but wearing Maldavian blue. She quickly lowered her head and was glad the hood did not fall from her face, for she did not wish to be recognized. She held the pitcher against her chest and veered away from the prince. Her escape seemed clean until his men stormed through the door and briefly surrounded her as they made a hasty charge toward empty tables and benches. Jostled from all sides, Taliesin was spun around, and she heard someone chuckle when she sloshed beer on the front of her leather bodice as she tried to get free.

The men made crude comments about where she'd spilled the ale, but before anyone dared to wipe her dry, Taliesin brushed by the men and returned to her table. Setting the pitcher aside, she sat with her back to the men.

"Do you know those men?" Jaelle asked, refilling her tankard. "I see spurs. They must be knights. What Order do you think they are?"

"Knights of Chaos. They are dangerous," Taliesin whispered. "Do not look at them, Jaelle. I don't want them to question us." Her heart, already pounding, quickened at the sound of approaching footsteps. She now regretted her hair was no longer black; it would have helped. A look of delight appeared on Wren's face, and Rook nodded, equally impressed by whoever stood behind her. Jaelle didn't turn, and Taliesin was grateful for that.

"Pardon me for interrupting. However, I could not help but notice you are Ghajaran," a melodious, seductive voice said. "It's interesting there are so few of you and no wagons. Three women and one man, well, that's practically unheard of. Where is the rest of your tribe? Behind you? Ahead of you? Or are you on your own?"

Only one man possessed such a voice or talked in such an annoyingly arrogant manner. Taliesin knew without looking Prince Sertorius stood directly behind her. She smelled wood smoke and lamb and sweat and wonderful cologne. She caught herself sagging forward, remembering the boy, fearing the man, and shivered when he spoke.

"That's our business," Jaelle said. "Who wants to know?"

"Allow me to introduce myself. I am Prince Sertorius. I'd introduce you to my knights, but we left the squires and servants outside with the horses. To avoid rancor and jealousy among my men, I would prefer you did not tarry long after your meal. Three beautiful women will only invite trouble. My men have not seen their wives and loved ones in a long time. I'm sure you ladies understand my problem."

Taliesin said nothing but thought, 'What a conceited lout. Handsome and horrible. I am quite certain no lady ever told him *no*, and I'm sure his men never stopped to ask before they forced themselves on a woman. His problem was he can't control his men.' She hoped he had said what he wanted and would return to his men; the bartender was bustling about to feed them all. She imagined the prince was hungry and tired, but the royal fool remained at their table. Someone walked over, gave the prince a tankard of ale, and returned to his comrades, leaving the prince to flirt.

"Perhaps you know the whereabouts of a certain young gypsy girl I briefly made the acquaintance of, only yesterday," Sertorius said. "I'm sure I'll never see her again since I have traveled so many miles since meeting her, but when one meets a green-eyed, red-haired Ghajaran girl, it is hard to think of anything else. What is your name?"

"My name is Becca," Wren said with a flash of her teeth.

Taliesin groaned as the prince laughed and kissed the girl's hand. Wren sat, her hand held to her cheek, and it was Jaelle's turn to start to wiggle. Neither girl was fickle, yet that was precisely how they behaved. Prince Sertorius must possess a magical charm that caused women to act like idiots.

"The gypsy girl I met claimed to be the Shan's fifth wife," Sertorius said, gazing at Jaelle. "Her name was Jaelle. Wouldn't it be a coincidence if that were your name? Surely, a girl like you has a lovelier name than Jaelle. Now, wait—let me guess. Is it Shanna, Tywa, Ladeen, Mary, Pasinapa, or Angeline?"

"It's not Pasinapa," Jaelle said. "And there are many green-eyed girls in our tribe. I'll remember to scratch out the eyes of the one pretending to be me. I am Jaelle, the one and only, and my father is the Shan."

Taliesin felt like thumping Jaelle. The less the prince knew about them, the better chance they had of escaping. Any moment, he would question her, and she'd be discovered the moment he saw her eyes.

"Well, I do get around," the prince said, with a hearty chuckle.

Much to Taliesin's horror, Jaelle immediately stood up, twisted to face the prince, leaned forward, and gave him a full view of her abundant cleavage. Sertorius was not the only man who stared or was lock-jawed and silent. A gloved finger touched the tip of Jaelle's chin, turning her head ever so slightly as her knees buckled. She sank onto the bench and batted her long black lashes at the prince. Taliesin wanted to kick her under the table.

"You are quite lovely, Jaelle," Sertorius said in his honey-smooth voice.

"Whoever gave you my name last night was obviously attempting to trick you. I'm sure it was Malaya. She dyes her hair bright yellow or orange and goes to the nearest town in hopes of catching a husband."

"I met this girl in the Volgate. I pulled her out of a pool of water."

"That couldn't have been Malaya, then," Jaelle said.

Taliesin couldn't resist and kicked Jaelle in the leg. The girl let out a hiss but fell silent when Sertorius drew his dagger. He grabbed Jaelle's arm before she realized what was happening and pressed the knife to her throat. Wren pulled Rook to the table, while Taliesin tried to make herself look smaller by hunching over.

"As much as I am enjoying this little game, I have a feeling you know who I am talking about," Sertorius said. "Tell your companion to remove her hood, Jaelle. Call her by name and tell her I wish to see her face."

There was an uncomfortable pause as Jaelle helplessly stared at Taliesin and whimpered as the knife pressed against her throat. Taliesin stood and heard a voice in the back of her head. *'Oh, don't do that. Act as if you're going to vomit and run out of the tavern. No one wants to question a girl puking out her guts.'*

Without hesitation, Taliesin covered her mouth with her hand as if she was gagging, making it sound loud and convincing, and rushed to the door. Emitting horrible noises, she went out the door, aware men were laughing and pounding on the table with their forks and knives. But it was no better outside. A large group of men stood near their lathered horses, drinking from wine flasks, and watched as Taliesin went around the side of the building. Leaning against the building, she breathed slowly and tried to be calm. Minutes slid by with no sign of her friends, and her attention drifted to the squires and servants. No one had raised an alarm, but if her friends hadn't followed, it was clear they were in trouble and needed help; she had to go back for them.

Taliesin lifted her chin and marched around the building, just as the door opened, and without missing a beat, she spun around and headed to Thalagar. Wren, Rook, and Jaelle hurried out of the tavern. Playing it cool, Taliesin busied herself, making sure the cinch to Thalagar's saddle was tight enough, and waited until her friends approached before raising her head. A small figure slid around Thalagar and caught Taliesin's arm.

"That was a close call," Wren said. Despite the concern in her voice, she grinned. "How clever of you to fake you were getting sick. Jaelle told them your name is Agnes. Not a very nice name. The prince didn't believe her at first, but when she told him you're pregnant, he let us go. Jaelle told him we were meeting a larger group of gypsies at the border, where you will be turned over to the Djaran to repay a debt. The prince seemed to believe her because he let her go and gave her a gold coin for scaring her."

"I don't look pregnant!" Taliesin grimaced. She'd spoken too loudly. "Why would the prince buy a stupid story like that? He has to know Jaelle was lying. He knows I'm the one he fished out of the pond last night. Best get on your horse. We need to leave right now."

Rook and Jaelle walked to their horses. The burly Sir Barstow and Sir Morgrave, with his drooping mustache, followed on their heels. Wasting no time, Taliesin removed a bright scarf from Wren's neck, tied it around her head, made certain her red hair was hidden, and went about fussing with her saddle.

"Don't gawk. Get on your horse," Taliesin said. "And do it now." She climbed into the saddle and watched the girl run to the white mare. Rook came to help her, like he always did, but she climbed right into the saddle. He walked to his horse, a wounded expression on his face, mounted, and took hold of the silver spear he'd strapped to the front of the saddle. It was an expensive weapon, and Taliesin noticed a few squires admiring it.

"We must be going, Sir Barstow," Jaelle said. "I'm so sorry about the misunderstanding. Please thank the prince again for being so gracious. We must meet the others before nightfall. Perhaps we'll meet again one day."

"Hold up," Sir Barstow said. "We travel in the same direction. You may need our protection on the road." He stuck his thumbs under an immense leather belt strapped around his tunic and chainmail. "You have but four hours to reach the river before sunset. If you don't cross by then—if delayed for any reason—you will find the night comes with great danger." His nearby companions nodded and grunted in response. "See, even my brothers-at-arms know it is not safe at the border at night. There is safety in numbers. I can't let you ride off on your own. You're such a pretty thing. Stay a while longer."

"Ride with us, Becca," Morgrave said, though he looked right at Taliesin. She made an ugly face. He was far more threatening than Sir Barstow. In his thirties, Morgrave was in his prime. "You have no idea what lurks out there, waiting to devour Agnes' unborn child. Wolfmen have been on our trail for days."

"She has a man," Sir Barstow said. "Leave her be, Morgrave. You have a better chance with the pregnant woman than with a virgin. Come to think of it, Agnes doesn't look pregnant to me. How many months does she have to wait? Riding a horse will certainly jar the baby around, and no one is that stupid to ride when they're that far along."

Taliesin hugged her arms around her middle stuck out her gut, trying to look fat, and kept her head down, not looking directly at the knights. Trying to play her part well, Taliesin said, "Two months," making her voice sound deep. Sir Morgrave and Sir Barstow stared at her, and their hands dropped to the hilts of their swords. She saw in their eyes an unusual blend of malice and fear.

"We must be going, gentle sirs." Wren rode between the two knights and Taliesin and offered a sweet smile. "Don't rush the prince—he's tired. Let him rest a while longer. I'm sure we won't meet any Wolfmen on the road. We'll be fine, I assure you."

"Farewell," Jaelle said, pulling on her reins.

"Remember me, dear Jaelle." Barstow puffed out his chest as she rode by.

With a quick tap of her heels, Taliesin set her horse into a canter. She rode right by her friends, away from the armed men, and onto the road. She heard her friends following and let out a sigh of relief that ended the moment she spotted a black bird flying across the road ahead. She hated omens. A black raven crossing in front of a rider meant danger ahead. To someone in the Raven Clan, it should be a good omen, but Taliesin had heard it said too many times by others not of her clan. When they were half a mile from the tavern, the gypsy girl let out a shout and kicked her horse, hard. Thalagar and Jaelle's horse broke into a gallop. Rook and Wren kept up behind, pushing themselves and their horses. They traveled for several miles until, at last, Taliesin slowed Thalagar to a trot.

"You think they are following us?" Jaelle said. "Why didn't you tell us you'd met Prince Sertorius last night and gave him my name? I hate the prince, and I hate that type of man. In general, I hate men, but that Sir Barstow is a beast. As if I'd consider bedding him."

"The way those two knights looked at me," Taliesin said, "I wouldn't be surprised if they come after us. Thank the gods their horses are worn out. We rested for several hours this morning, but they obviously didn't have that luxury. I hope they'll stay at the tavern for the night. We'll ride on, cross the river, and wait for our friends to arrive."

"We will trust your instincts," Jaelle said.

"It's simple deduction. Put yourself in your enemies' position and then react accordingly." Taliesin felt like a fool for not having left the tavern the moment she'd spotted the two men in blue cloaks. The prince had obviously changed his tunic. He probably had many changes of clothes for the journey; a prince would, and he would make his men carry his gear.

"The bridge Barstow mentioned is out," Jaelle said. "It's been out a long time, but they don't know that. I'm taking another direction to a place we can cross the river. There's a strong current, but the horses should be able to make it without much trouble. The water is highest in summer when underground geysers fill the river until it's overflowing at the bank, but since it's fall, it shouldn't be that bad."

Taliesin glanced over her shoulder and checked to see if Rook and Wren were right behind them; they were, and no one followed. She turned and tapped her heels against Thalagar's flanks. The horse started galloping and put a few more miles between them and the Maldavians. She didn't imagine the third time she met Prince Sertorius she'd get away so easily.

* * * * *

Chapter Twenty-One

Vegetation grew scarce over the next ten miles, and the air became more arid. Dead trees poked out of the dry ground, and sporadic clumps of dark brown grass and thorny weeds grew out of the sand. Granite boulders protruded from the ground like the backs of giant sea turtles, around which grew tall, slender cacti and bushes yielding purple berries and tiny white flowers. The faint roar of the river grew louder, drawing Taliesin's attention long before they reached it. The closer they came, the more small, gnarled trees grew, struggling to survive in the hostile environment.

Reaching the riverbank proved challenging for Taliesin and her friends. To get close to the Minoc River, they were required to ride along the ridge, hemmed in on one side with rocks and thorny bushes, while a forty-foot drop into the river waited on the other side. Taliesin saw the Minoc River for the first time in her life. Green as emeralds under the golden light of the setting sun, the big river wound its way through a deep ravine. The remains of a rope bridge hung across the waterway. On the opposite side lay the remains of a once-great watchtower. A soft bank of red dirt ran along the water's edge, and flat stepping-stones led into the water, used long ago by whoever had lived in the tower. There were some large boulders another twenty feet from the riverbank, forming an obstacle that created a fast-moving cascade and strong eddies where dead logs floated.

Taliesin saw a great waterfall further upstream, and high cliffs created a canyon that seemed to stretch on forever. She looked at the tower. Rocks jutted out of the hard ground on the far right of the ruins which created an entrance to the canyon, measuring more than eighteen feet tall. Ages ago, the tall rocks might have been statues of some long-forgotten gods. Purple flowers grew along the sides of the formation like the long, wild hair of a giant.

The river was swollen and offered little welcome; there was nowhere safe to cross. Taliesin was about to comment when she spotted a large black bird soaring over the canyon toward their direction. She wondered if it was Zarnoc.

"The canyon wall drops to about twenty feet, there, below us, and that's where we will cross," Taliesin said, not waiting to hear Jaelle's idea. Seeing the raven was a good omen. "We'll have to get our horses to jump. The fall won't hurt them, or us, as long as we hang onto the saddle, and they can take us across." She dismounted, holding onto the reins, and gazed over the side of the cliff. "Here," she said, waving her friends over.

"It's still pretty high," Wren said. "I can't tell for sure, but it doesn't appear there are any submerged rocks below us. I don't want to risk breaking any legs. Rook and I can walk a bit further upstream to make sure this is the best place."

Taliesin studied her companions. Rook and Jaelle looked ready and able to attempt crossing a river known to be dangerous, but she had serious doubts about Wren; she was terrified despite her brave words. The rapids were treacherous enough, but there was also the consideration of what lurked in the depths of the water. Taliesin didn't ask Jaelle if there were crocodiles or poisonous water snakes, because she didn't want to know.

Rook dismounted and walked his horse along the side of the bluff a short distance before stopping. He crouched, peered over the edge, and pointed, nodding his head. He was twenty yards away, not far upstream from the tower, and well away from the boulders in the water.

"What was this place called?" Taliesin asked, pointing at the ruins.

"This used to be called the Tower of Uruk," Jaelle said. She slid off her horse, holding the reins tight. "The monks who lived there worshiped the Goddess of the Moon. They lived in peace for centuries, panned gold from the river, and used it to create statues in her likeness until they were overrun by desert marauders. That was a long time ago. Legend says the Djaran murdered the monks in their sleep and sold their servants into slavery after taking their gold and jewels. They lay ruin to the tower as a reminder that the worship of foreign gods would not be tolerated among the Dune Dwellers."

"Is that what the Djaran call themselves?"

"They do not call themselves anything but 'Lords of the Desert,'" Jaelle said. "My people refer to them as such, among other things. They are nomad dogs. Nothing like gypsies. Though your people think we are the same, we are nothing alike. Perhaps once, long ago, but no longer."

"I know Barstow wasn't talking about the rope bridge. If there is a larger bridge nearby, let's check it out. There may be nothing wrong with it," Wren said. "I don't want to swim across the water. It can't be that far away, can it?"

Jaelle snorted. "If the Mayfair Bridge is out, then it's out. I doubt Lord Valesk or his father took the time to replace the bridge, especially if they don't want the Djaran crossing into their lands. They probably destroyed the bridge in the first place."

"Why doesn't Duke Richelieu de Boron repair the bridge? He rules Garridan where we're headed," Wren said, a frantic note in her voice. "Surely there is another bridge we can cross?"

"His castle and towns are on the opposite side of the desert," Jaelle said. "Garridan's western border is open to the sea, and they rely on ships for a living. Forget about the bridge, Wren. There is no other bridge within a hundred miles."

"Think we can get across here?" Taliesin asked, tired of the debate. She wanted to cross, and she was going to do it. The gypsy shrugged. "Okay. We might as well try. I'll go first. I should think if you hold one end of a rope and I tie it off on the other side, it will make it easier for Wren, Rook, and then you to cross. I want my best fighter bringing up the rear, and that's you."

"Thank you," Jaelle said, flattered. "I will not disappoint you."

"Are we really going to cross here?" Wren's voice was filled with apprehension and worry. She climbed out of the saddle and stroked the white mare's neck. "Merryweather is frightened, and I don't want to end up drowning."

Taliesin and Jaelle glanced at one another. Having someone that afraid attempt something so dangerous was bound to lead to disaster. It was Taliesin's plan, though, and she knew she had a bit of convincing to do before Wren would make her horse jump into the river. She handed Thalagar's reins to Jaelle and walked to where Wren stood trembling beside her horse. She put her hand on the girl's shoulder, aware Rook had already got a long rope and was finding a boulder to tie an end around. He, at least, was willing to try to cross.

"When Thalagar and I jump into the river," Taliesin said, "the other horses will see there's no danger, Wren. When we're across, I'll tie off the rope, and we can slide the gear to where I'm standing on the riverbank. The less weight your mare has to carry, the easier it will be for her to swim with you across the river. All you have to do is hold onto her mane; don't let go, and she'll do the work. Horses are strong swimmers—this river won't be any problem for them. It looks scary, but it won't be that bad once Merryweather starts swimming. She's so strong and brave. If you are strong and brave, too, you both will make it across with no problem. I promise. It'll be okay."

Wren turned toward her horse and tried not to cry. She rubbed the mare's nose; pink nostrils flared and sniffed at her. "Merryweather is brave and strong," she said. "I believe she can get us both across safely. All I have to do is hold onto her mane and let her do the work."

"The horse does the work," Taliesin repeated. "All you have to do is hang on. Simple."

Jaelle stepped forward. "You can do this, Wren. I have faith in you. And I have faith in your mare. Stay here while we get everything ready; talk to your horse and reassure her there is nothing to be afraid of. I always talk to Durell. She is a very smart horse. Mares are the bravest, you know. Not stallions; that's why I have always ridden a mare."

"That makes sense," Wren said. "Females are just as strong as males."

"Stronger," Jaelle said, reassuring her. "And smarter."

With a smile, Jaelle walked off with Taliesin, leaving Wren stroking her horse's neck. Together, the two women removed their saddlebags and dumped them on the ground. Rook came over with the end of the rope, lugging his bags. He'd tied the spear to one of his sacks. He set his things aside and went to fetch Wren's gear, pausing only to give her a swift kiss on the cheek before he collected her javelins and tied them securely in a blanket.

"You're doing it all wrong," Jaelle said. "What kind of knot is that, you stupid *greigo!*"

A brief scuffle erupted as Rook and Jaelle fought over tying the knots on the three bundles. The young man swatted at the gypsy girl, who waited until he walked off before she retied his knots.

Taliesin knotted a rope around her waist, tossed the end to Jaelle, and climbed into the saddle. The black stallion stomped his front hoof. Taliesin leaned over to stroke Thalagar's neck and remained hunched over in the saddle. The stallion seemed to know what was expected of him, for the moment she tapped her heels, he bolted forward and jumped off the cliff.

The big horse hit the water, hard, and they briefly submerged before rising to the surface; Taliesin clung to the saddle and swallowed a mouthful of water. She hung onto the saddle horn, her leg muscles tensed about the horse's sides. Water stung her eyes as Thalagar lifted his head high and swam. Her friends shouted encouragement from the bluff above, and she heard the cry of the raven circling above. Thalagar surged forward in a straight path. She could feel the stallion straining as he fought against the current, doing his best to swim to shore.

"You can do it, boy," she said.

Using his massive strength to fight the current, Thalagar reached dry ground. The cinch broke when he trotted out onto land, and Taliesin and the saddle fell into the mud. The horse gave a shake of his head and ran along the bank, kicking his hind legs like a colt, and let out a whinny answered by the other horses.

A sudden yank on the rope pulled Taliesin and her saddle toward the water. She scrambled to her feet, embraced the saddle like a lover, and with all her might dragged the saddle to a section of the old tower wall that lay among the weeds and scraggly bushes. She pulled the saddle and rope around a large stone, removed the rope, and tied it securely with a Fregian sled-knot, which was the type of knot Roland had taught her to make when she first met him. She set the saddle on top of the stone to dry in the sun.

"I'm okay!" Taliesin waved at her friends.

"I'm sending Wren over, then Rook," Jaelle shouted. "The bags will come after Rook makes it across; he may need to help you pull them over since the current is so strong."

Wren was mounted and ready to make a leap of faith into the water. Rook and Jaelle stood beside Wren's horse, Merryweather, their gear stacked at their feet. The petite girl urged her white mare forward with a tap to her flanks. Merryweather jumped off the bluff and landed in the river. By some miracle, Wren remained in the saddle and, as instructed, let the horse do the work. The mare safely made it across the river and struggled out of the water. Wren slid out of the saddle and led her horse to where Thalagar nibbled on blades of grass around the base of a tower stone. She removed the saddle and blanket, set them out to dry, and hurried to Taliesin.

"That wasn't so hard," Wren said. "But I don't want to do it again."

"Me neither." Taliesin waved to Rook. "Come across. We're ready for you."

With another loud splash, Rook and his large bay hit the water, and then popped up like corks. The young man held onto the horse's saddle as the animal swam through the current, and Wren watched nervously. The horse and rider reached the shore, and Wren ran to Rook and threw her arms around him after he dismounted.

Taliesin grabbed the rope as Jaelle pushed their gear off the cliff and into the water. Rook and Wren joined her, each holding the rope with feet planted firmly on the ground, and all three pulled the gear across. As soon as everything was on dry land, Taliesin left Rook and Wren to pack the gear on the horses and stood on the shoreline.

"It's your turn, Jaelle!" Taliesin shouted.

Jaelle was already in the saddle. She turned her horse, rode a short distance, and then spun around. The horse and gypsy girl flew off the side of the cliff at full gallop but separated in mid-fall and landed far apart from one another. The horse seemed unaware her rider was gone and headed straight to the shore, leaving Jaelle to helplessly float down the river.

"What are we going to do?" Wren asked, pacing along the shoreline.

"Swim, damn you!" Taliesin shouted. "Swim for shore, Jaelle! I don't think she can swim! One of us needs to go after her!"

Struggling out of his boots, Rook dove into the river and swam after Jaelle. Each powerful stroke brought the young man closer to the wide-eyed gypsy girl. Her horse reached the riverbank, climbed out, and was greeted by Wren, who grabbed the reins.

Taliesin kept her eyes on the pair floating downstream and saw Rook grab Jaelle and start to swim to shore, barely able to keep both their heads above the white, churning water. A bend in the river took them away from sight.

"Now what do we do?" Wren cried out. She turned toward Taliesin, her fear turned into raw anger. "This is your fault!

You should have asked Jaelle if she could swim. Now she'll drag Rook along with her and both will drown!"

"Pack the horses," Taliesin said. "Rook knows what he's doing."

"Aren't we going to help them?"

The rocks along the riverbank prevented them from running along the side to follow their friends. Taliesin headed toward Thalagar, intending to ride the crest and find them further down the river. Wren let out a frustrated scream and charged. Taliesin stepped aside and watched as Wren tripped and hit the ground face first. Before the girl had time to scramble to her knees, Taliesin placed a foot on her back and pinned her to the ground.

"Calm down," Taliesin barked. "I'll go after them." She removed her foot.

"If Rook dies, I'll never forgive you!" Wren wailed.

"Just stay here and do what I say. Follow me when you are done. I'll find a way to pull them out of the river. It'll be all right, Wren; I'm not going to let either of them drown."

Taliesin fastened her sword belt as quickly as she could. All four horses stood together, but none were saddled. Confused, Taliesin reached for Thalagar's reins, eager to ride after Rook and Jaelle, but stopped when she noticed all four saddles, along with most of their gear, lying off to the side and ripped to shreds. A trail of wolf prints led from the saddles to the brush. Where there was one Wolfman there was more, she thought, knowing they'd been discovered. Taliesin ran to the remains of Rook's saddle, removed the silver spear, and hurried to Thalagar. She'd have to ride bareback, and the spear seemed easier to use than a sword. Wren stood at the side of the river and stared at the destroyed saddles and provisions, fighting a scream.

"Mount up and let's get moving," Taliesin said in a firm voice. "I'll take the lead. Bring Rook and Jaelle's horses. We'll have to make our way along the river. Well? Don't just stand there. Let's go, Wren."

Taliesin stuck the spear point into the soft ground and wound her hand into Thalagar's thick, black mane. She pulled herself onto his back and then yanked the spear out of the ground. Leaving Wren to mount her mare and bring the two other horses, Taliesin headed along a rocky trail to the top of the hill. In less than a minute, Wren, her bottom lip quivering, had caught up. The girl trailed Taliesin as they followed a narrow path that was overgrown with weeds. There was no way to ride beside the river, which they could see from the path, and neither Rook nor Jaelle were in sight.

"The Wolfmen are close," Taliesin said, glancing over her shoulder.

"I'm so scared. What if the Wolfmen found Rook and Jaelle? What are we going to do?"

"Kill them. What else?"

The path descended through the weeds to the shoreline. Tall reeds and cattails at the edge of the water grew high enough that it was difficult to see the river, although Taliesin could hear the roar of it. Rook and Jaelle had floated straight into the rapids, and though she was worried, her attention remained focused on the reeds blocking the view of the river.

"This is a perfect place for the Wolfmen to hide," Taliesin said. "Stay here, Wren. I'll go to the river and see if I can find Rook and Jaelle."

Thalagar walked through the reeds with his ears pricked up, and Taliesin leaned forward and held the silver spear, ready to stab anything that growled. A rustling in the reeds produced a long-legged white crane that took one look at Taliesin and flew off across the river. An old story Osprey had read to her when she was little came to mind, about a girl carried off by a flock of cranes into the sky, never to be seen by her parents again. She shivered, despite the warmth of the day.

"I see something," Wren said. "I think its Rook. Can you see him?"

Taliesin swiveled her head and looked at the muddy ground. The tall, green stalks gave a hard shake, and she tensed. Rook and Jaelle stood up. Both were covered from head to toe with mud and looked frightened. Taliesin heard a deep snarl as they ran toward Wren and their horses, and Thalagar reared as a large shape rushed toward Taliesin from the opposite direction and cut in front of the stallion. She spotted a contorted human face that morphed into a long muzzle with sharp fangs. The Wolfman lunged toward Taliesin, and she thrust the spear with all her might. It pierced the beast's chest and came out its back; the creature let out a roar and jerked away, pulling Taliesin off the horse.

She landed in the reeds, not far from the flailing arms of the wounded Wolfman, and released the spear. He thrashed, his efforts growing weaker, and Taliesin stood up when he stopped struggling. Thalagar had trotted out of the reeds. She spotted the spear sticking out of the body of a naked man, but he looked different from the other Wolfmen. His body was covered with blue tattoos; they were tribal designs that told the story of a boy turned into a wolf. Taliesin drew her sword and made swift work of removing the head from the body before she tugged the silver spear out of the Wolfman's chest. As she turned toward her friends, Rook appeared beside her and reached for the spear.

"There are more," Rook announced quietly.

Rook held up two fingers and pointed to where the Wolfmen were hiding. Two giant wolves slid from the reeds, and, once in the clear, came rushing toward the Ravens. Rook threw his silver spear, which slammed into the first wolf, and it dropped to the ground. Taliesin swung her sword at the second wolf and struck off its head; it fell into the reeds. Returning to Rook's kill, she cut off the head and watched as the body turned into human form. Rook yanked out the spear, a worried look on his handsome face.

"Do you think these are Wolfgar's men?" Rook asked. "It would mean they move faster than we originally thought, and only you and I are armed."

"I can't be sure until I look at the Deceiver's Map," Taliesin said. "I know Wolfmen can run all day without tiring, but that means they would have slipped past Roland and Sertorius in order to reach us, and I don't think that's what happened. It makes more sense that they were stationed here waiting for us, which means more could be hiding in the desert."

"We can't stay here and wait for Roland and Hawk," Rook said as he pulled himself onto the large bay horse. He wore only pants, and Taliesin noticed his tattoos were similar to the Wolfman, though Rook's were nautical in nature. She wondered if the Wolfman had been Erindorian since tattoos were common in the south, but now wasn't the time to inquire.

"I'm sorry," Jaelle said. "If Rook hadn't come after me, I would have drowned."

"You nearly got him killed!" Wren exclaimed. "Don't pretend you can do things, Jaelle, if you can't! Do you even have you any idea where we are going?"

The gypsy girl looked offended and didn't say a word. The last thing Taliesin wanted was an argument in the ranks, so she gave Wren a stern look.

Taliesin rode to Jaelle, looked her over, and saw no bites or scratch marks. Nor had there been any on Rook. The sun began to sink behind a line of purple-tinted clouds, and the breeze had picked up. She smelled the dead Wolfmen on the wind, knew other predators would catch the scent soon enough, and wanted to leave immediately. She tapped her heels to Thalagar and headed west over a grassy hill.

"We need our clothes and gear," Rook said. "Going into the desert without supplies is foolish, Taliesin. Where are you going? We have to return to the river where we crossed. All our weapons and supplies are there, along with our saddles." He spoke with ease as if he'd never pretended to be mute and deaf, and Taliesin felt annoyed to hear him talking so much. She looked over her shoulder and reined in her horse.

"Our saddles were destroyed," Taliesin said. "We can't go back to salvage the rest of our gear; not with Wolfmen hiding in the reeds. If we keep going west, Roland, Hawk, and Zarnoc will eventually find us, and they'll have supplies and weapons. For now, we'll have to find food and water on the way. I have the map, so I'll lead from now on."

"Wren is right about me," Jaelle said as she rode up to Taliesin, a troubled look on her face. "I have never been this far west before. Tamal and the brothers know this place, but I don't. I'm not a tracker, either, or a warrior. Everything I own is at the river, along with my weapons and cards. Without them, I will be useless, Raven Mistress. It would have been better if Rook had not come after me; you would still have your supplies."

"Jaelle, your life is far more valuable than supplies," Taliesin said. "Wren! Rook! We aren't going back for our gear, so forget about it. I don't want to hear another word about who is at fault, who isn't able to swim, or who doesn't carry their own weight. I have the map, the key, *Wolf Killer,* and faith in what we are doing. Navenna has not brought me this far to let me fail. There is no looking back and no regrets. Now let's get moving."

Taliesin rode ahead of her friends and led the way over a small hill. The river and the shade of trees were left behind, and a low valley, covered with rocks, yellow bush weed, and green cacti was revealed. Beyond the valley was miles of white sand. Jaelle came alongside her, and Wren and Rook were right behind.

"Don't look so worried, Jaelle," Taliesin said. "Zarnoc will find us. I've no doubt that raven we saw at the river was the wizard. You'll see your brother again."

"I know of no towns in this area," Jaelle said. "And it will be night soon. We'll be camping in the open. No wood for a fire means no flames to keep the Wolfmen away. I can't help but wonder if we shouldn't have misled Prince Sertorius and his men. I sent them miles down the river to cross a bridge that isn't there. We would be safer with them."

"No, we wouldn't, and you did the right thing. I've been in worse situations than this before. Trust me." Taliesin offered a smile. "We ride until its dark. I'll find someplace where we can make camp."

As they rode, Taliesin removed the magical map and checked positions, locating Wolfmen scattered throughout the area, but no ambushes. The prince was far to the north and stuck at the river, unable to cross, but the map refused to show Roland, Hawk, or Zarnoc, no matter how hard she willed it to obey. Nor did it offer a place to camp, as if it wanted them to fail; it only showed open sand that stretched ahead as wide and expansive as the sea.

They rode for an hour, and the temperature started to drop as the last rays of sunlight offered a splash of purple, orange, and red throughout the sky. The dramatic beauty was not lost on Taliesin, and she felt hope lift her spirits and her gaze.

In the waning light, she spotted a raven winging its way toward them and knew it was Zarnoc. Taliesin lifted her arm, whistled, and the raven landed on the offered perch and gave her a wink.

"I had a feeling it was you, Zarnoc," Taliesin said. "We have no water and no provisions. Lead us to a safe place to camp. We'll follow." She tossed her arm upwards, and Zarnoc flew into the air and took the lead. "No worries, my friends. I told you Zarnoc would find us. Never doubted it for a second."

"Your goddess looks after you, Raven Mistress," Jaelle replied.

Taliesin knew someone was watching after them, and that person was an old wizard, though she didn't discredit the help of her spiritual protector. They were going to need all the help they could get to reach the Cave of the Snake God, and she knew it.

* * * * *

Chapter Twenty-Two

Taliesin felt her mind connect with Zarnoc's, and through the eyes of the raven, she watched four riders cross the sand dunes. The raven flew ahead, and she spotted a lone torch stuck in the sand, a bright flame that glowed in the thick blackness. There was no sign of a camp, only the torch. Zarnoc broke contact, and she was back in the saddle. Taliesin kicked her horse into a gallop and reached the torch ahead of her friends.

Dismounting, she ran to the torch, pulled it out of the sand, and held it high. Before her eyes, a camp appeared, with three large tents and a campfire but no sign of life. Zarnoc returned and landed on her shoulder. At his loud caw, Roland and Hawk came out of the nearest tent, looking refreshed and well-rested. Roland had shaved off his beard. Startled, she couldn't help gasping out loud. There was no doubt he was handsome, but the lower half of his face was pale and in sharp contrast with his sunburned head. The other riders came to a halt, stirring a cloud of sand.

"Couldn't see us, could you?" Hawk asked, laughing. He went over and took the reins to his sister's horse. "Zarnoc has cast an enchantment over the camp, so it can't be seen by anyone else."

"I couldn't find you on the map, either," Taliesin said. "How did you get ahead of us?"

Roland approached her horse and took the reins as she slid out of the saddle. "Zarnoc made us a bridge out of thin air, or we would have lost all of our gear, just like you did. He also told us you had a bit of trouble with the Wolfmen. I'm glad you didn't wait for us since we made it here ahead of you. But you're safe now."

"Barely," Taliesin said. "I wasn't worried though. I knew you'd find me. Why in the world did you shave? I think I liked you better with a beard."

Roland rubbed his jaw as she slid out of the saddle. "I thought I needed a change," he said with a shrug. "You'll get used to it."

Tamal and the Nova brothers came out of a tent. Harmattan led Thalagar into a small tent where Khamsin, slender and long-haired, took the other horses. Sirocco, with his defining scar on his left cheek, joined Tamal in brushing away the hoof prints around the tents with large brooms. Jaelle ran to her brother, who paused in his work, embraced her, and listened as she whispered to him. Taliesin assumed Jaelle told him what had happened and how she nearly drowned. At the first opportunity, she meant to let Tamal know his sister was no coward, and despite what had happened, she was proud of her. Hawk led Rook and Wren inside the nearest tent.

"Zarnoc knew right where you were," Roland said, pulling Taliesin into his arms. He kissed her then pulled away, wrinkling his nose. "You smell like a wet dog."

"Comes with the job," she said, laughing.

The raven hopped to the ground and turned into the familiar form of Zarnoc, dressed in a long, flowing Ghajaran robe and slippers. Zarnoc took the torch from Taliesin, placed it into the sand, and the flame grew dim. The horses' tent vanished, and then the tent where Hawk had led her friends, leaving only one colorful tent still in view. Zarnoc shuffled over, put his arms around Taliesin from behind, and burrowed his head against her back with a contented sigh.

"It's good to have you home, darling," Zarnoc said.

Taliesin laughed as she turned in the wizard's embrace. She leaned over and kissed the top of his rumpled head. He wriggled out of her embrace, walked in the direction everyone else had taken, and simply faded from view. Roland walked her to the one tent in view and held aside the flap.

"Please, come inside, my lady," Roland said.

Taliesin caught Roland before entering the tent and kissed him full on the lips. "Don't ever leave me again without making up," she said. "I've been worried about you. Let's promise to never part after an argument without making up first."

"I can live by that rule."

With a growl, Roland kissed her harder, passionately, and when she sank against him, he suddenly gave her a soft push into the tent. Light-headed and happy from the intensity of the kiss, she turned to study the interior of the tent. It appeared far larger inside than it did outside, and Taliesin had to blink several times to make sure what she saw was real. The floor was covered with beautiful carpets. There was a large bed with drapes. In the corner was what appeared to be a commode hidden behind long curtains that hung from the top of the tent. There were a table and chairs and fancy tasseled pillows to lounge on.

"It's a palace," Taliesin said. Zarnoc's magic made the interior of the tent warm, for the desert night was already cold, and the temperature would continue to drop before the sun rose. "This is a bit extravagant, Roland. A bedroll beside a nice, cozy fire would have been fine. Did you tell Zarnoc to do this, or was this his idea? There's only one bed. Is this for...us?"

"You deserve to be spoiled after the boorish way I acted this morning. I had no right to come down on you like that, Taliesin. I'm sorry. I really am. What about a hot bath? Hmm?" Roland chuckled. "Would that be a waste of magic? I know how much you love a hot bubble bath; I'm sure the old goat would make one for you. And this is his idea. I won't take credit for it, but I was hoping to sleep here beside you."

Her mouth fell open. "A bath? Are you serious?"

"Zarnoc would do whatever you ask, of that I'm certain. All this is for you. He didn't go out of his way inside the other two tents; one looks more like a barracks, and the other is a barn. Since you didn't say no, I assume you want me here."

Roland removed his sword belt and took Taliesin's weapon and belt from her, placing them together on a rug. She sat on a chair, and he pulled off her boots.

"We had a close call, as well," Roland said. "Wolfgar had set a trap outside the cave, but Lord Valesk's troops arrived and put him to flight." He tossed her boots aside, filled two glasses with wine, and handed her one. "We saw no sign of Sertorius. He'll probably end up in Wolfgar's stomach. If we're lucky, we should reach the caves in a few days."

"Let's not talk about that royal pain," Taliesin said. "I've had quite enough of that man and his threats. Ran into him at a tavern. Shouldn't have stopped, I know, and we just barely made it out of there between Wren's blushing and Jaelle's flirting. But I suppose it's really my fault, not theirs. He's the one who fished me out of the pond last night, which I know I should have told you about, and you have every reason to be upset with me. I'm sure Zarnoc told you about it anyway; that little goat knows far too many things about us. I think he may be in league with the gods." She laughed. "Not really. But he does know too much."

Roland put on a broad smile. "Zarnoc knows just enough to be helpful, and we should be grateful he's on our side." His voice was tender, gentler than she'd heard it in some time. "Zarnoc also told me I should make more of an effort on my appearance, so I let him tidy me up. I even dabbed on cologne—Hawk's—but it won't go to waste. I intend to join you in that bed just as soon as you wash up, get some food into your belly, and catch your breath."

"I could get used to this," she said. "Had our own bit of excitement today, but I don't really want to talk about it. I'm here now, and we're alone, and I'm happy you're happy."

"I'll go fetch your dinner; I think it's lamb stew."

"Wait!" Taliesin caught him at the entrance, standing half-inside, half outside of the tent, took his hand, and held it to her chest. "Even if we do fight in the future," she said, in earnest, "you must promise to always come back to me."

Roland laughed, lifted her hand to his lips, and kissed it. "I'm just going to get you a plate," he said. "I am coming back. We both have tempers, Taliesin. I can promise not to fight about politics, and religion, and the weather. And I will always come back to you."

"Promise."

He smiled. "I promise."

The knight left, leaving her with such a feeling of protection and love that she couldn't imagine why they'd ever argued in the first place. When she turned, in the center of the tent was a large tub filled with hot water and bubbles. She hastily stripped off her clothes, sank into the tub, and submerged. The bath was glorious; the soap gave off a lavender scent, her favorite, and she sponged every inch of her body, removing sand, mud, and the stench of Wolfmen.

"May I come in?" Wren entered the tent as Taliesin combed her freshly-washed hair. Wren's gypsy skirts were replaced with baggy pants, her boots with sandals, and she wore a jacket instead of a blouse. Rook came in after her, dropped saddlebags on the floor, and glanced at the tub with envy. It vanished in a twinkle of colorful lights, startling Rook, who backed out of the tent, leaving Wren and Taliesin laughing. Wren turned, admiring the interior of the tent, and offered a shy smile. "I shouldn't have acted the way I did at the river. You knew what you were doing. I was scared; I'm always scared. If I could be more like you or Jaelle, I wouldn't feel so helpless."

"You did fine," Taliesin said. Wren came and sat beside her, and Taliesin started to brush the girl's hair. "We're far from home, constantly on the run, hunted, tired, and yet we persevere. I've been watching you, and despite what you may think, I'm glad you're with us. Bringing Jaelle along was your idea, and it was a good one. Between the two of us, we'll make a warrior out of you, yet."

"I can't swim," Wren said. "I can't use a sword. I'm practically blind when it comes to looking for tracks, and I made a complete fool of myself with the prince. I can't do anything right. I'm useless."

Taliesin put her hands on Wren's shoulders. Her muscles ached with the movement, and she was glad to be wearing a soft, wool gown, not her leathers. "Jaelle can't swim either. Why didn't you both tell me the truth?" she asked. "I'd have figured out another way across the river."

"I was too embarrassed. And Jaelle is too proud."

"You're a seer. You're amazing. We can teach you to swim and swing a sword, but no one else has visions, Wren. And no one knows herbs like you do. You can mix a tonic to soothe a belly ache, and you can tend injuries. I can't do those things."

Wren threw her arms around Taliesin and sniffled ever so slightly. Taliesin reached up and stroked Wren's hair. The tent flap opened, and Roland entered with a tray of food, a curious look on his face. "I just came to say goodnight," Wren said. She got up, blew Taliesin a kiss, and dashed out of the tent.

Roland placed the tray on the table. He had brought a bowl of stew and a loaf of bread. There was also a chunk of cheese, though it looked hard, and a flask of wine. He took a seat on a rug at her feet, and he watched while she spooned in large bites of the hot stew. "Jaelle said you ran into Prince Sertorius at a tavern. If he follows the instructions Jaelle gave him," he said, "he won't be crossing the river until morning. She said he's a very handsome man, not overly nice, but I could have told you that. I know the man. Know him quite well, in fact, and I've never liked him."

"Sertorius wanted to slit Jaelle's throat," Taliesin said, slurping. The stew was delicious and tasted better when she dipped a chunk of bread into the broth and soaked it up. "Maybe all princes are cruel, but this one takes delight in terrifying women. All of his men give me the impression they are brutes. I wouldn't be surprised if they'd been bitten by Wolfgar's men. They act like animals, that's for certain, and Sertorius most of all." She wanted to tell Roland she'd known the prince as a boy, yet couldn't bring herself to tell him, nor understand why the secret stuck in her throat.

"Sertorius wants one thing only," Roland said. "He wants *Ringerike*. Trust me when I say he doesn't have his father's best interest at heart. Nor yours. When I think how close you came to being captured, it convinced me I should never let you out of my sight." He smiled as she sliced off a piece of cheese. "Goat cheese," he said. "It's palatable, but I found a worm in mine, so watch out."

"I'm so famished, I don't care. This is delicious. What else is there to eat?" Taliesin looked around the tray, spotted a fig, and popped it into her mouth, moaning with pleasure as it burst open in her mouth. A dribble of juice slid down her chin. Roland caught a drop on the end of his finger, licked it off, and grinned.

"Is that an invitation?" she asked. "I can stop eating, and we can get undressed and climb into bed. We'll have to be very quiet. No one will know what we're doing as long as you don't groan and moan, Sir Roland."

"I picked up armor on the way," he said, changing the subject. "A traveling salesman gave me a good price. I bought two more hauberks for Hawk and Rook. It's hot wearing armor in the desert, but it will come in handy if — and when — we run into trouble. Did you enjoy your bath? I'm sorry I was gone so long, or I'd have washed your back."

"Absolutely," Taliesin said, feeling slightly guilty at being so comfortable and alone with her lover while everyone else had to share a tent.

The chainmail he'd mentioned lay folded on a pillow; it had silver links and was expensive. She watched him remove his coat and shirt, and his hairy back made her smile. When he sat on the bed to remove his boots, she slid off the mattress, took the Deceiver's Map out of her pouch, spread it on the bed, and lay beside it. The map had rolled out like heavy parchment, which is what she'd wanted, and she traced a path to the Cave of Chu'Alagu. On the way there was a red star; somewhere in the desert was a magical item buried in the sand. She glanced at Roland, checking on his progress, and had a full view of his pale buttocks as he bent over to place his clothes in a neat pile. She turned to the map and memorized what she was looking at, noting both the landmarks etched in black ink on the tan parchment and that it was over two hundred miles to their destination. She also noticed Sertorius' location.

"How many days in the desert will it take us to reach the caves?" Roland turned, completely naked; one hand rested on his hairy chest, and the other held the flask of wine. He took a drink and came to sit next to her. "Zarnoc said four days of riding, at most, so we don't wear out the horses. I'd rather travel at night because of the heat, but with Wolfmen lurking about, it's safer to ride only during the day and rest at night. Zarnoc has enchantments around this camp, and he can always find us water, so I don't think we have to worry about it. Keep him safe and well-fed, and he'll get us there."

Taliesin removed the flask from Roland's hand and sipped the wine. She let him roll the map and return it to her pouch. Capping the flask, she set it aside as he crawled into bed and tossed a blanket over their bodies, his hand already pulling up her gown.

"We need him, that's for certain," Roland said, able to talk and touch her at the same time. She lay still as he managed to pull the gown off, toss it aside, and return to his former position; his face nestled on her shoulder.

"Rook was amazing today. You should have seen him brave the rapids to…" she paused, feeling his lips on her neck and whispered, "…gypsies don't swim. Did you know that?" He shook his head and nibbled on her shoulder. "Something else happened today. No one else knows about this, and you must swear you'll never mention it. Rook talked. I wonder if he's a spy. I mentioned it to Jaelle, but I was kidding; only now, I'm not so sure. It's possible. I mean, Sertorius is after the Raven Sword. The map makes it look like he's following our exact trail, which shouldn't be possible, but he is. Do you think Rook is leaving clues behind?"

Roland looked up, his dark brown eyes smoldering. "Doubtful. Not Rook," he said. "He's the last man who would

SEEKER OF MAGIC | 319

betray the Raven Clan. They took him in when he needed shelter. That boy is loyal. Trust me." Pulling her into his arms, he held her tight as his lips brushed against hers. "Where do you come up with these crazy ideas? Rook? A spy? Is there anything else I should know? Is that what you think of me?"

"No," Taliesin said. "I don't think that about you, and I really don't think that about Rook, either, but I'm concerned the Maldavians are right on our tail. The Wolfmen can follow our scent, I get that, only it doesn't make sense—the prince never seems to falter or get lost."

"I wouldn't say that. He was lost in the Volgate. I agree he must have hired a scout; he'd be a fool not to. The man deserves some credit; he's a good commander, but it will take more than a scout or a spy to reach the Cave of the Snake God. He needs a magic user."

"And I need you," she said.

"Am I interrupting anything?" Jaelle, dressed in her brother's clothes, came into the tent, not waiting for permission, and startled both Taliesin and Roland. Her eyes narrowed, and she caught her breath seeing them in bed together. "May I join you?" She came closer, kneeling at the foot of the bed.

"I've no objection," Roland said, "though it's up to Taliesin."

"Not this time," Taliesin said, wanting to be honest. "In the morning, I wouldn't be able to bear anyone knowing. Though you are very beautiful, and I admit I have thought about it, I think you should return to your own tent, Jaelle. This can't happen."

The gypsy girl's eyes narrowed. For a moment, Taliesin saw what appeared to be hatred within her eyes and a certain coldness in the false warmth of her smiling red lips. A man might have been tricked into thinking it was passion, but it couldn't be that; only hatred bore a black heart. Then it was gone, both the look in Jaelle's eyes and her company, as she spun and ran out of the tent into the night, leaving Taliesin utterly confused. She heard Roland's chuckle, rich and reassuring, and she settled against him, beneath the blanket.

"The girl is in love with you," Roland said, yawning.

"Forget about her," Taliesin said. "What you said...about being in love...are you in love with me? Roland? Is that what you meant?"

No answer came from the knight; he'd fallen asleep beside her, one arm draped over her body. Tiny snores came from his parted lips. She snuggled against him, exhausted herself, and was content with being close to him. But they were not alone. Either Jaelle had stuck around to spy on them, or perhaps Zarnoc watched in the form of a mouse. The feeling someone or something watched caused her to pull the blankets to their chins. She lay still, listening to the night and trembling at every little sound, until at last, her eyelids grew heavy, and she fell asleep, hearing only Roland's snoring.

* * * * *

Chapter Twenty-Three

Tamal led them west across the sand dunes, the sun at their backs; the four Nova brothers brought up the rear, staying in a single line to limit the number of hoof prints left behind. The wind stirred and whipped across the sand; in the distance, Taliesin spotted a dust devil whirling across the dunes. For three days they'd ridden across the desert without seeing another soul, traveling under Sir Roland's Order of the White Stag banner as his entourage — one squire, four guards, three grooms, two servants, and a white-bearded priest riding a mule.

Every day, Taliesin, Wren, and Jaelle bound their breasts, braided their hair, and hid behind the appearance of grooms. The only thing that made the heat bearable was gypsy cloaks transformed to appear white; the cotton material allowed airflow, protected them from the sun, and hid their gender. Roland and Tamal, the knight helmed and the squire in a coif, bore the brunt of the stern sun and broiled in chainmail. The Nova brothers, Sirocco, Simoom, Khamsin, and Harmattan, wore the padded coats of guards, with leather belts, hose, and low-cut shoes. Hawk and Rook were allowed to wear their Raven clothes, altered by magic to appear no more than the plain, drab garments of servants. Zarnoc, dressed in a frock, rode in the middle and carried an outlandish pink parasol. Held open by wooden spokes, the parasol was, in reality, his magical staff. He had kept his pipe and smoked whenever the mood took him.

"We've been lucky so far," Hawk said. He rode behind Taliesin and spoke loud enough for her to hear. "That little toad sticks out like a sore thumb. Anyone who sees us will think your Fregian knight and his companions have a lunatic for a priest."

"That's the idea," Taliesin said, scowling beneath her cap. "You think I like having my breasts tied down? It's painful enough for me, Wren need not bother, but Jaelle suffers the most, and all you can do is grumble about a pink parasol."

"Why are you angry with me?" Hawk asked. "It wasn't my idea to bind your breasts. The point is to make you women look like men. But I'm positive Jaelle hates me," he went on. "I sleep right next to her, yet she keeps her back turned. I don't understand why she finds me so repugnant. I am handsome, clever, always ready to lend a hand, and yet she rebukes me."

Taliesin slowed her horse and allowed Hawk to catch her.

"Jaelle doesn't hate you," she said, keeping her voice low.

"No? I'm pretty sure she does, yet I think she's the most beautiful woman in the world. She doesn't notice me. She barely talks to me; I might as well have two heads and a tail," Hawk continued. "Nothing I say or do can soften her heart. She's colder than you, and Heggen knows, I tried for months to win your affection."

"I'm not that cold. I just don't think of you that way, Hawk. You're family." Taliesin glanced at the ground and watched a green lizard scurry beneath a curious, bleached skull that had belonged to a creature she wasn't familiar with. "Jaelle's lack of interest has nothing to do with your face or your personality. The truth is Jaelle doesn't like men. She likes me."

"Of course, you'd say that. Everyone wants you. It's always about you." Hawk leaned forward, trying to get comfortable in the saddle. "All these days in this saddle have created sores on my backside. I didn't realize I hated riding a horse long distance. Nor did I realize you are such a bore. You could at least try to be amusing."

"You mean humor you?" Taliesin snorted. "Your problem is you don't want to work hard for anything—it's all supposed to fall right into your lap. Roland has us dressed in this fashion to fool the Djarans that we are but pilgrims. Apparently, the desert dwellers allow knights to travel freely through their lands, but not Ghajarans. Instead of complaining about your misfortunes, you could try to be pleasant. Try to be nice to Jaelle, instead of bothering her with your silly compliments. A woman wants a man to be thoughtful, not rutting about like it's mating season, and if you've already forgotten, coming here was all your idea, you dumb poult."

"It was not," Hawk said, offended. "Zarnoc put us up to this, and I'm not a baby turkey being raised for food, so don't start calling me names, or I'll call you a few that you won't like."

Taliesin ignored Hawk and gazed at the horizon. The sky was bluer than a robin's egg, without a cloud to offer shade or the hope of rain, and she knew as soon as the sun reached its zenith, they would start to bake. "We'd best find an oasis today," she said. "I saw one on the map. We should be getting close."

"Eyes watch us," Hawk said. "Felt this way for the last few days. It's not the Wolf Pack or Prince Sertorius who are harrowing us. Did you notice that flock of desert gulls that flew overhead about a mile back? Gulls are beggar birds. I figure we're taking a route used by Djaran caravans. The Djaran are nothing more than marauders, and if they find us out here, they'll strip us, spread us out on stakes, and leave us to the scorpions. Or worse."

"There are others who live in the desert," Taliesin said. "Bandits, thieves, and giant crabs that live under the sand to keep cool, only to reach out with a claw to pluck an unfortunate rider and eat them, slowly, armor and all. Roland says there are Swahini goat herders at the edge of the desert and the Hammada cattle cult who live in villages all year round. But the Garunsi, they're farmers; I can't imagine their crops are that impressive in this climate. Did you know the Garunsi believe the sun and moon are gods, and the stars represent the souls of those who die or who are about to be born? Roland says the Garunsi think knights are servants of the gods. The women folk wash the feet of traveling knights and dry them with their hair."

"Sir Roland might have made me a squire," Hawk grumbled. A fly appeared and buzzed around his head. He swatted it away. "He doesn't know everything. I don't know why you're so in love with him when it's obvious he doesn't intend to marry you. Knights in his order cannot marry, or didn't you know that?"

"Who told you that? It's not true. Tamal said...." Taliesin bit her tongue. She'd almost told Hawk about Roland's wife, but Hawk was staring at her, and she had to finish the sentence, so she lied, "...after he's knighted, he'll marry, so you obviously don't know what you're talking about, as usual."

Hawk's dark brows knit together. He glanced over his shoulder and turned right around. "I thought it was only a wind devil," he said, excited, "but that cloud of sand is growing larger by the second. We are being followed! It has to be marauders!" Cupping his hands to his mouth, he shouted, "Roland! Tamal! We have company!"

Taliesin turned at a shrill cry in the distance and saw a large cloud forming on the horizon that moved in their direction. Roland spun on his big bay stallion, *Moonbane* in hand, and signaled for their procession to halt. Within seconds, a large group of turbaned raiders in white cloaks, riding camels, surrounded them. Taliesin felt close to panic, imagining all sorts of horrible ways to die at the hands of the Djaran, until she heard Zarnoc shout her name.

"Taliesin!"

As the wizard lifted his parasol high, it turned into a staff, and Taliesin stared in amazement as everyone around her froze in place; even the breeze stopped, and the sand cloud hung in the air. Nothing moved. Taliesin felt her heart pounding and watched Zarnoc turn his mule and ride toward her.

"What's going on?" Taliesin asked. The big black horse stomped his foot and nudged the mule in the side. "Are we in danger? These are Djaran marauders, aren't they?"

"Well, yes and no," the wizard said. "We are in considerable danger, Taliesin, but it's not quite as you imagine. True, there are Djaran among these men, but they serve as escort only. Look closer. Many of these riders wear the spurs of knights or the gold cloaks of Eagle legionnaires beneath their Djaran costumes."

"I don't understand," Taliesin said. "You mean there is a third group looking for us? How did they know where to find us, Zarnoc? I'm the only one with a Deceiver's Map. If these men are looking for me, then they knew all along where to find us, and that would mean someone has been leaving signs for them to follow."

The wizard remained mounted as Taliesin slid off her horse. Thalagar gave an angry shake of his head, and she tousled his mane as she ran to the riders who were frozen in place and positioned exactly as they'd been moments before when Zarnoc cast his spell; it was as though Taliesin were looking at a painting. She brushed her hand across a camel, raised the cloak of a rider with his mouth and eyes wide open, and examined his spurs and chainmail armor. In his hand was a Rivalen sword—the design was unmistakable—and most of the others were also outfitted with exceptionally-forged weapons. Gold spurs sparkled beneath white cloaks, and silver longswords, not the customary scimitars used by the Djaran, were held in the hands of the bearded riders, though she did see curved swords among the men with swarthier complexions.

"These are Knights of the White Stag, and Eagle Clan legionnaires," Taliesin said, more disgusted than shocked at the obvious betrayal by the man she loved. She glanced at Roland, stuck in a position with *Moonbane* held above his head, and resisted the urge to push his large body off his horse. Returning to Thalagar, she grabbed the reins and climbed into the saddle. "I'm not sure what you want me to do, Zarnoc," she muttered. "There are more than five hundred riders. This is clearly an expeditionary force, that much I can tell, but what are they doing here?"

"Master Xander Aladorius, son of Lord Arundel, leads these men," Zarnoc replied. "They are here because this is where Sir Roland told them to find you. I had hoped I was wrong about Roland. When he told you he wanted to give *Ringerike* to King Frederick, I had a feeling his Order was working with the Eagle Clan, and that is why I have taken the opportunity to place a hold on time. You and I can go on to the Cave of the Snake God without your friends, or we can simply let things play out."

"Roland lied to me," she said, finding the truth hard to swallow. "He knew all along Master Xander wasn't a prisoner of the Wolf Clan; he's been playing me from the start. Why can't we take my true friends and leave the others here for the Wolf Pack?"

"Is that what you really want to do?"

"No," Taliesin said. "I'm not that type of person. I wish none of these men any harm, even though they want to use me to help their king defeat his sons. I know what you can do with your magic, so I see no reason to fear the unknown. We still have many miles to go, the Wolf Pack is right behind us, and so is Prince Sertorius. Though I appreciate your concern, Zarnoc, let things be. I would not tamper with time or fate, so let things be as they are meant to be."

"So be it."

The old sorcerer snapped his fingers, and with a blink of an eye, Taliesin was surrounded by a maelstrom of white-turbaned riders on camels, who circled their group and stirred sand so thick in her mouth she removed the scarf from her hair and tied it around her face. The noise of the riders and camels was deafening, yet Taliesin remained calm as they surrounded her group. As anticipated, Sir Roland and Tamal, carrying the knight's standard, rode to a cloaked rider on a white camel. The camel was dressed in an ornate blue saddle over a red and gold blanket edged with silver tassels, suggesting its owner was the leader and of noble birth. In the rider's hand was a whip used to push away the hood of the cloak. The face of a twenty-year-old man stared at Roland and Tamal. His complexion was pale, and he had sharp, gold eyes that Taliesin thought looked hard and cruel, even at a distance. A conversation between Roland and the strange young man ensued, and Taliesin hardened her heart as her lover pointed at her, making it clear her identity had been revealed.

"What's Roland thinking?" Hawk asked. "Is he mad? That's Master Xander—I've seen him before. I thought he was a prisoner of the Wolf Pack. We've been conned, that's what this is about, and Roland played us all for fools."

Zarnoc let out a heavy sigh. "I tried to warn Taliesin."

"When?" Hawk asked. "You've been behind Roland since day one, old man. Don't tell us now you had doubts about Roland. He's led us into a trap, and you jolly well let him."

"It's no use arguing or pointing fingers," Taliesin said. "Roland arranged for an escort to make certain we arrived at the Cave of the Snake God. The Eagle legionnaires and Knights of the White Stag are in cahoots, but that doesn't matter. Nor does Roland's deception. We can use them to reach the cave in safety and ditch them at the earliest opportunity. Agreed?"

"Agreed," her friends said.

Roland removed his helmet, placed a fist against his left shoulder, tapped twice, and then swept his arm forward, fingers stretched out. Any resemblance to Grudge had faded, and to Taliesin, he now looked every inch a Knight of the White Stag. The young man returned the salute. A flash of gold on Xander's finger caught Taliesin's trained eye—a ring of pure gold. As he lowered his arm, she saw he wore a gold chain that would have brought a handsome price at market. No one had any business being in the desert wearing such expensive ornamentation.

"Sir Roland Brisbane of Ruthenia, it is good to see you again," the young man called out in a voice loud enough for Taliesin to hear. Banners snapped in the breeze and blocked much of what he said. "...Grand Master, Banik Dzobian, sends his regards, as does my father." He turned his head as a cloud of sand blew past, and his voice faded, but he continued to speak while Roland nodded and pointed toward Taliesin.

"Roland must have a good reason for betraying us," Wren said. "But I don't see why we had to dress as men. These are Djaran. What harm can it be for them to know our gender?"

Rook placed his silver spear across his lap. "Keep your voices low," he said in a deep rumble as the others stared at him, shocked to hear him speak. "We can't be sure what Roland has told Master Xander. Think what you like, but I know Roland well enough to believe he wouldn't have led them here if he had any other choice. He's trying to protect you three women; that's why he had you dress as men, so don't make things worse by revealing your gender."

"Or that you four are anything but what you seem," added Hawk. "Those men are all wearing heavy armor. I say we make a break for it; they'll never be able to catch us. Taliesin has the map. We have everything we need to reach the cave."

"No reason we can't leave a trail," Taliesin said. She pulled the scarf off her neck, wrapped it around her dagger, and then dropped it onto the sand. The sand blew over the scarf, hiding half of it, but she knew any Wolfmen could smell her scent and follow.

With a nod at Master Xander, Roland remained at his side while Tamal rode to Taliesin and her friends. The legionaries and knights fanned out, formed two straight lines, and at a shout from their commander, headed west toward the sun. Tamal looked stoic as he approached Taliesin and her friends. Five legionnaires broke rank and rode to them as if expecting trouble as Taliesin rode forward to meet the squire.

"You can tell Roland we know what's expected of us, Tamal," Taliesin said, speaking before he had a chance to relay any message. "I assume we're to be escorted to the Cave of the Snake God to turn *Ringerike* over to Master Xander."

Hawk let out a snort. "Like that will ever happen," he quipped.

"I apologize for what has happened," Tamal said. "Sirocco, you and your brothers are to make certain no harm comes to Taliesin. I do not have time to explain everything that was said, but this man expects your full cooperation. I am to accompany Sir Roland. As his squire, I must stay at his side at all times."

"And that's it?" Taliesin asked.

"We all have roles to play," Tamal said. "I am certain Sir Roland regrets what has happened, Mistress Taliesin. I could see it on his face." He glanced at his sister. "Do not give away your identity, no matter what happens, Jaelle. These men are not our friends, and we are all in great danger."

Tamal turned and rode toward the head of the procession. A lump formed in Taliesin's chest where her heart used to be, and she couldn't help wondering what might have happened if she'd left with Zarnoc when she had the opportunity. Since she'd decided on remaining and letting fate run its course, she had no other choice but to follow. Sirocco took the lead of their small party and rode to the side of the knights and legionnaires. Zarnoc lifted his parasol over his head and rode along beside the eldest brother. Taliesin fell in behind them with Jaelle. Wren and Rook came next, and then Hawk and Harmattan, the youngest brother, while Simoom and Khamsin trailed behind. The escort of five Eagles remained behind them, lances lowered, making it clear they were prisoners.

"Why did you agree to go with them?" Jaelle asked. "You didn't even act surprised when we were set upon by these men. Did you know what Roland was planning?"

Taliesin nodded. "I found out too late to do anything about it," she said. "But trust me, I do not intend to let Master Xander get his greasy hands on the Raven Sword. His father, Lord Arundel, allowed the Wolf Clan to slaughter my clan, though he could have prevented their deaths. Roland is only doing what he's been told to by his Grand Master. It's my fault for trusting him; I knew his loyalty lay with King Frederick, not with me. I'd be lying if I said I wasn't hurt by his actions, because I am, but so be it."

"You hide it well, Raven Mistress." Jaelle picked up a flask of water and took a drink before handing it to Taliesin. "If you desire revenge, I could slip into Xander's tent tonight and slit his throat. I could do the same to Roland—he has betrayed you."

Taliesin heard Zarnoc singing in a merry voice while the camels grunted and snorted. She didn't respond right away and listened to the noises around her before taking a sip of water and returning the flask to the gypsy girl. The sun beat on their heads. The wind was fading, and she wondered how far the horses could go before requiring rest and water.

"I don't blame Roland for being who he is," Taliesin said, at last. "My father taught me to forgive but never forget an injustice, nor to be surprised when it happens again. I wanted to believe Roland loved me, but this isn't the first time I've been disappointed by someone I love. Prince Sertorius was my childhood friend. He didn't recognize me at the Volgate or at the tavern. But I remember on my eighth birthday he gave me a gold locket. It disappeared later, and I cried for days thinking it was stolen. Afterward, I saw a nobleman's daughter wearing the same necklace and realized Sertorius had taken it and given it to another."

"Then you can't trust either man," Jaelle said.

"I know that," Taliesin said. "I expect nothing but absolute honesty and loyalty from a friend. Anyone who lies or proves dishonest is no friend of mine. I loved Sertorius, and I loved Roland, but both went out of their way to hurt me. It doesn't matter why they did it or how long ago it happened. Neither man was ever my friend."

"I swear I will never betray you, Taliesin. I would do anything for you. *Anything.*"

Jaelle reached out and put her hand on Taliesin's arm. Taliesin could hear Hawk chuckling behind them, but whether it was about the sign of affection or something else, she could only guess. She felt compelled to place her hand over the gypsy girl's hand.

"Then no matter what happens, Jaelle, you must help me keep *Ringerike* safe. It cannot fall into the hands of the enemy. The Raven Sword is mine," Taliesin said, her lips tightening. She wanted to unbind her breasts, let her hair loose, and lay havoc upon the line of armored men that rode escort. Damn them all, she thought. "I know it requires the true Raven heir to call upon the sword's magic powers, but I don't care. We're going to all this trouble to find it, after all this time, and I do not intend to give it to *any* man. I feel like I was born to have that sword, and one day I will avenge the deaths of my clan and the two men I called 'father.'"

* * *

A rush of purple spread across the evening sky with the setting of the sun, and Taliesin sagged in the saddle. Throughout the day, Jaelle had handed her leaves rolled into balls filled with a powder that tasted like mustard seed. But when placed beneath the tongue, the strange powder lowered her body temperature and lessened her thirst. "The powder is made from the ground bark of the Banyok tree, found only in Erindor," Jaelle said to her. "My people trade for it when we travel south each spring. It will keep you alive, Taliesin."

And it did help, along with the short breaks allowed to water the horses, until the water brought by Master Xander and his army ran dry, and riders were sent ahead to find the closest oasis or well. When at last the cavalcade stopped for the night, Taliesin was so tired that all thoughts of escape seemed more burden than a sense of freedom.

The Eagles and knights set up their small tents around a few small campfires. The camels rested beside the tents, while the horses were tied to tether lines. Taliesin and her group were watched but not bothered by the men, and when Zarnoc set his three magical tents, the most interested party was the Eagle legionnaires. But even they had sense enough to be leery of a wizard and avoided coming to the Raven tents, preferring to watch from a distance.

"You did well today," Taliesin said as she removed her saddle from Thalagar. She'd placed more than one of the rolled leaves under the horse's tongue during the day, trying to keep him cool, and had used the last of her own water to quench his thirst.

"The Djaran have come and gone," Rook said. He held the reins to the other Ravens' horses and took Thalagar's reins out of her hand. "We have enough water to last a few more days. I'll brush the horses and feed and water them.

Rook led the horses—Thalagar, Merryweather, Thunder, the mule Bessie, Jaelle's horse Durell, and Rook's horse Slap-Dash—into the tent used as a barn. The Nova brothers brought their mounts into the same tent to groom and feed them. Roland and Tamal's horses were left outside the largest tent, which had been confiscated by Master Xander. Taliesin stood beside her saddle and gear, outside her own tent, and waited for Wren and Jaelle. Both girls carried their saddles and backpacks into Taliesin's tent. The interior was the same as the night before with the exception of additional beds.

"All I want is a hot bath and a pillow," Wren said. She collapsed on the carpet beside a bed and pulled off a boot. "I can't manage the other. I'm too sore. Everything hurts."

"I'll help," Jaelle said, laughing.

No sooner did Jaelle pull off Wren's boot than a tub, large enough for eight people, appeared in the middle of the tent with steam rising from hot water. Both Wren and Jaelle laughed and started taking off their clothes as Taliesin sat at the table and poured a tall glass of water. The crystal was delicate and felt cold when she drank the contents. She heard splashing and kicked off her boots. She watched the two younger women tussling over a sponge and decided to join them. Removing her clothes—stiff with sand which produced a mess on the carpet—she hurried to the tub and sat in the hot water with a contented smile on her face.

"I'm going to stay in this water until it turns cold," Wren said. "Zarnoc thinks of everything."

"The water he is using doesn't appear out of thin air," replied Taliesin. She soaped her hair into a lather. "This is drinking water stolen from our escort. I hope he'll put it back where he found it when we are finished—Xander can drink the scum off our bodies."

"He'd probably enjoy it." Wren ducked beneath the water. The black dye in her hair washed out, leaving it bright yellow and sticking out on end. She appeared boyish and far younger than her years since cutting it. Her breasts were small enough not to be bruised from binding. Taliesin watched Jaelle rub her own breasts, producing a rosy glow as a low moan came from the gypsy girl.

"You're enjoying that too much, Jaelle...knock it off," Taliesin said, content to relax in the hot water without massaging herself. She thought of Roland and his large hands but forced images of their lovemaking from her mind; that wasn't going to happen again.

Afterward, Taliesin and the girls found clean gowns on the bed—blue, pink, and red—arranged in a tidy row. Wren helped brush everyone's hair, and Jaelle braided Taliesin's before her own. It was dark outside when they finished, and Zarnoc, Hawk, and Rook joined them. The wizard wore a bright violet robe and sheepskin boots and smelled fresh as daisies. The other two men wore their Raven gear, glad to be rid of their armor, but were unwashed and smelled like horses. Rook had brought a dice game, and Hawk had news about Tamal and the brothers, who were ordered to attend a dinner with Roland and Master Xander in the large tent. Zarnoc let out a sigh as he created a table and two long benches out of thin air.

"Dinner is served, my friends." Zarnoc waved his hand, and a fine feast of lamb shanks, potatoes and greens, and piping hot bread with butter appeared on the table. A goblet of cold water appeared before each of them, along with a crystal glass filled with red wine as they sat. "Waste not, eat your fill," he said as he set about serving the assembly, though he looked tired. He sat at the end of the table on a large chair and he ate with his hands instead of using the silver utensils. "Lamb is best when you lick the grease off your fingers," he explained.

"How do you have so much magic to use?" Wren asked, buttering a slice of bread. "You have been at it all day, Zarnoc. I'm so tired. I haven't had a vision in three days. It's really quite a blessing; I realize now that the best way to avoid visions is sheer exhaustion."

"Your visions are very helpful, my dear. I'm sorry you've had none about the Eagle Clan," he said, "but even I was surprised when they appeared. I really didn't see them coming. I suspect Master Xander carries a charm that protects him from being seen. That would explain how they made it here without running into any Wolfmen or Prince Sertorius. I don't think he or those soldiers like me; but then, I could always turn them into mice if they get in my way." He sighed. "Poor Ginger. She's not eaten in a few days, but tonight she'll taste this delicious lamb, and she'll be compelled to find something to eat."

Wren, seated closest to Zarnoc, stood, leaned over her plate of food, and kissed him on the cheek. "I don't see how anyone couldn't care for you. You're a darling, Zarnoc," she said in a sweet voice. "None of us would have made it this far without your help. Here you are serving us when we should be washing your feet and drying it with our hair, like the Djaran women do. Tamal told me how their women take care of their men after a long day's ride. Women are never allowed to sit at the table, and they eat last, even after the children and dogs."

"Thank the gods we are not Djaran," Jaelle said. "We are fortunate we haven't run into them. But they know we are here; they are watching us from a safe distance. They are nothing but savages. Women are but possessions to them, to be used and traded like camels and goats. Their men do not have more than one wife as we Ghajaran do but cast them aside when they find a younger or richer one. The days when we traded with them have long since passed. My father won't trade with the Djaran—he considers them thieves and brigands."

"Now, now, let's not get ugly." Zarnoc licked his fingers with a smack. "I have always heard it said the gypsies and nomads are 'king makers and crown breakers.' The common people keep a king, a Shan, or a sheik in power. There has always been competition between your people and the Djaran, but the line between grazing and cultivated lands moves according to the strength or weakness of whatever king sits on the throne. The Kings of Caladonia rule both the desert dwellers and the gypsies."

"And three clans," Hawk said, downing his wine. He refilled his glass and poured more for Rook, who showed signs of being tipsy. Rook didn't like lamb, though he ate everything else, and he grew sleepier by the minute.

"The Djaran may be good fighters, who can melt into the desert," Jaelle said, "but they don't pay taxes, and they disrupt caravans and steal from them whenever they get the opportunity. What few settled communities exist in this horrible place pay a tariff to the Djaran to ensure peace since Duke Richelieu doesn't care what happens this far away from his capital. We Ghajaran always trade for what we want, and we have never terrorized villagers. We migrate as do the nomads, but we return to the same place quite often, and we are always welcome."

"Your people are a very fine and noble race," Hawk said. "Your father is the finest man I have ever met. I wish we were with him right now, sleeping soundly in one of those wagons. Notice there is no music; soldiers don't play the violin and guitar. I prefer a gypsy camp and the gypsy way of life; it is much like our own at Raven's Nest." He sighed and pushed his plate aside. "I'm stuffed. Think I'll stretch my legs. I'll be back."

"I should have very much liked to have seen you dance, Jaelle," Zarnoc said as Hawk walked out of the tent. "You have never danced for me, and I've known you all your life."

"That's because I'm always on my best behavior when you're around."

After the meal was finished, Zarnoc cleared away the table, plates, and chairs with a wave of his hand. Enough rugs and pillows lay on the floor that the group gathered to play the game of dice Rook had brought with him. Leaning on a large pillow, Taliesin wiggled her toes and watched Wren roll the dice. Jaelle curled next to her, resting her head on Taliesin's shoulder, and tickled her feet whenever the dice were handed to the Raven Mistress. More wine was drunk, and from the bottom of Zarnoc's wine glass came the sound of gypsy music. It rose and spread across the room, creating a festive atmosphere.

A cold breeze swept into the tent as Hawk stomped in and tossed an armload of gear and weapons onto the floor.

"Our tent has been taken over by that pompous, little creep Xander and his precious bodyguard. Roland said we're to sleep in here," Hawk said, furious. "The pavilion fell over in the wind, so they wanted a magical tent. We're in for a storm tonight." He pulled off his boots and tossed them aside. "And you should see the meal they're having. Peach pie and port are for dessert. The good stuff. Master Xander has made Tamal and Sirocco serve them wine. Poor Simoom is singing to Harmattan's lute playing. Harmattan never should have told Master Xander he plays; they'll be at it all night, entertaining those bird brains."

"Xander is not fit to be served as a lord," Taliesin said angrily. "Sit. You can roll the dice. Wren is winning. Maybe you'll break her lucky streak." She looked over at Rook. "You can't even keep your eyes open. Go to bed. We'll sleep on the floor. Wren can join you."

The young girl opened her mouth in shock. "Taliesin!"

"Give me those dice!" Hawk plopped next to Jaelle and slapped at her foot when she tried to kick him. "Master Xander wants to see you, Raven Mistress. It didn't sound like a request. Nor did Roland say a thing about it. He's sitting there beside that little worm, laughing at every joke he makes and agreeing with everything he says. I was thrown out of the tent, though I only asked for a piece of pie. If the wind comes, I just bet those soldiers toss out the horses and take possession of the barn tent. If they do, I'm putting my foot down."

"You're such a little girl," Jaelle said, laughing. "Can I braid your hair, Hawk?"

The dice game continued. Taliesin stood up, found her saddlebags, turned her back, and slid on her Raven attire. Stepping into her boots, she reached for her sword, only to find Jaelle at her side. Jaelle took the weapon from her. "Do not take this with you," Jaelle said. "It could be confiscated." She placed a dagger in Taliesin's boot. "Use this instead. My brother and his friends are being treated like servants. I do not like it. Nor would my father approve. The dagger is very sharp...."

"Our commander," Hawk said, "at least did one good thing; he told Xander that Tamal is his squire and that Simoom, Harmattan, and the others come from Erindor. Xander believed him. What an idiot."

"Erindor? This truly is the last straw!" Jaelle grabbed the dice and threw them across the tent. They reappeared in front of her. She threw them again. "Stop it, Zarnoc! I'm angry. I have to throw something." The dice returned, in front of Wren this time. "Do we look like we are from Erindor? I do not paint the soles of my feet with henna or pierce strange parts of my body to dangle jewelry." She caught Rook smiling at her, amused by her outburst. "I mean you no respect, dear Rook, truly, I don't. I'm sure your dukedom is a lovely place. When you are Ghajaran, however, being called anything else is an insult. I am proud of who I am, and I hate this Master Xander for making us have to hide our identity."

"People believe what they want to believe, and sometimes it's best that they do," Zarnoc said, sounding wise and profound. "If Sir Roland exaggerated and told Master Xander you are from Erindor, then we may assume it is because the Eagle Clan is prejudiced against gypsies. I have personally met Duke Dhul Fakar and spent a short time at his court performing the usual card tricks and pulled ferrets out of the most unusual places on his harem girls. A very noble man, much like Shan Octavio; perhaps a bit vainer, yet he sets a fine banquet table. He likes cheese as much as I do."

Taliesin grabbed her black cloak and fastened it at the neck with a silver brooch. "I believe his family owns a magical scimitar called *Tizona*," she said. "It's been passed down for generations and can cut through anything without breaking, but as with all magical weapons, it has a few harmful side effects. Makes you crazy if you use it too often, so they say. Probably crazy enough to eat cheese with maggots."

Wren sighed and took Rook's hand. "I love hearing about where Rook comes from," she said. "Zarnoc, is it a beautiful place? Like the Isle of Valen?"

"There are men on the island who eat fire, swallow swords, and charm snakes with their eyes. Most of Fakar's entertainers come from the islands," Zarnoc said, rising as Taliesin, taking her time, walked to the tent entrance. "Fakar also enjoys camel racing. I believe an ancestor of the duke once visited Garridan and took such a liking to camels that he brought an entire herd home with him."

"Perhaps Roland is onto something," Taliesin said, able to say one nice thing about him. "Eagle's Nest is located in Erindor, so they would not be suspicious of anyone from that area." She gazed at Zarnoc. "I was angry with you earlier. I expected you to know everything, and I wasn't very happy to see Master Xander arrive with his men."

"I know this much," Zarnoc said, the room quieting as he spoke. "Master Xander is a very crafty man. Lying is second nature to him. Whatever you do, do not let him turn you against Roland. You don't support Roland, but I do. I don't think your knight will allow any harm to come to you, Taliesin. Roland cares for you. Try to follow his lead, won't you? He won't lead you astray."

"Why should I trust Roland?" Taliesin asked.

"My dear, Roland didn't know it would be Master Xander coming after you. Nor did he know his Grand Master had sided with the Eagle Clan, so he really didn't lie to you. 'Vermillion,' by the way, is the secret code used by the White Stags to verify the Grand Master has issued an order. And now you know the secret code, too." He patted her on the bottom. "Off you go, dear!"

* * * * *

Chapter Twenty-Four

The obnoxious noises made by the camels, combined with the stench of their ripe manure, overpowered Taliesin's senses as she headed toward Master Xander's tent, and she felt any semblance of a good mood fade.

Everywhere she looked were Eagle legionnaire, with their nomad garb removed, displaying armor and gold cloaks. She remembered how Prince Sertorius' camp had been overrun by Wolfmen at the Volgate. The Eagle Clan's camp was exposed on all sides — the desert offered no protection. She'd even left a trail for the enemy. As long as Zarnoc had neglected using his usual magical charms to ward off evil, she had every reason to expect an attack before morning.

Two Eagle guards stood outside the large tent. Taliesin entered before they had time to announce her to their master. Once inside, she came to a halt, and her mouth dropped as she gawked at the sheer size of the interior and the lavishness of the furnishings; Zarnoc had gone all out to make the Eagle heir quite at home. Tamal, polishing Roland's helmet, stood behind a low dining table where Sir Roland and Master Xander were seated on pillows. A chainmail coif made it hard to see his hair, but it looked like someone had cut it right above his ears; a comical look for any Ghajaran.

"The Raven Mistress is here," Tamal said.

"I can see that for myself," Xander replied. "Wine for our guest. I can't remember your names — one of you fetch wine for the *Sha'tar*. Sit, sit, my dear. No ceremony here. You are with friends."

Khamsin walked over as Taliesin approached the table and motioned at a pillow near Roland, at the end of the table, for her to sit upon. Khamsin was missing his long braid which had apparently been cut off since she'd seen him last. Sirocco, also shorn and with an angry look on his face, poured wine for Master Xander, filled a glass for Taliesin, and refilled Roland's before returning to his corner. Harmattan sat on a pillow in the corner and played the lute, while Simoom sang in a soft voice. Something appeared wrong, for Simoon kept touching his throat, and several notes were too high to sing.

Taliesin noticed fresh bruises on Simoom's neck and felt her temper rise. It was clear Master Xander wanted a hostile atmosphere, and a smug look hung on his sickly, pale face. His thinning blond hair, still wet from his bath, was plastered against his skull. He wore clean robes and his gold jewelry. She found him ugly and couldn't imagine anyone who looked so sickly being able to lead an army. But he was a magic user; she smelled the odor of burnt feathers on Xander, a sign she'd come to recognize meant that dark magic was at work.

"This is Taliesin, the Raven Mistress," Roland stated. "And this is Master...."

She remained standing. "I know who this is. Xander Aladorius."

"That's right," the Eagle heir said. "I never thought I would meet a *Sha'tar* in my lifetime. Sir Roland, this is a momentous occasion. On this very eve, the tide of war has turned in our favor. Alas, she is not quite as beautiful as you said she was. Her hair is too red. She has lips like a cat and far too many wrinkles. As long as she's the genuine article, I suppose it matters not. My father is most anxious to meet her."

Master Xander's voice struck Taliesin as odd, for it was far too old for his body; it was the voice of an elderly man. He slid thin fingers through the strands of his hair. His pale eyebrows wrinkled together, and he regarded her with disapproval.

"She's the real thing," Roland said as he popped a date into his mouth.

Taliesin glared at the Eagle heir and placed her hands on her hips, her feet planted apart. "I was led to believe you were a prisoner of Chief Lykus," she said. "Obviously, that was a lie."

Xander's eyes widened, but he revealed little else; he gave her an annoying, thin smile as he giggled like a child. Roland merely smiled, making her wonder if he was under some type of spell, for he acted differently around the Eagle heir.

"Is that what you were told? That I was a prisoner of the Wolf Pack? Chief Lykus *wishes* he had the ability to capture me. He tries, but I always manage to slip through his claws. Wolf's Den is no place for any human, I assure you. My father should have burned that pitiful place to the ground years ago. One day, he will."

'Not if I beat Arundel to it,' she thought, 'and then I will destroy Eagle's Nest.' Both thoughts brought a smile to her face, but she refrained from sitting. Not until she had said what she wanted to say.

"Secretary Glabbrio wanted Sir Roland to go in search of you, but he decided to come with me instead," Taliesin said. "I'm sure Lykus ate the secretary; Glabbrio was fat. In fact, the Wolf Clan made a meal out of the Raven Clan, and yet you say nothing about it. Just why have you come all this way, Master Xander, if not to apologize for your clan failing to intervene and stop the slaughter? Surely, you have not come all this way to join me on my quest? I assume you know why I'm here."

"Of course. And you know why I am here."

"I'm surprised you made it this far. It's either dumb luck...or magic."

"Have you not told the girl our meeting was prearranged, Sir Roland? A real *Sha'tar* should have sensed we were near, one magic user to another. A true practitioner of magic would have hidden. For all your praise of this *Sha'tar*, all I see is a Raven renegade seeking fame and glory. Many, far better than you, have tried and failed to locate *Ringerike*. You will fail unless you have my help."

"Not needed," Taliesin said, but Xander wasn't listening. He turned to Roland.

"I dare say it's a shabby affair when your squire is one of Fakar's bastards and your servants are Raven tomb raiders. You should have waited for me at Castle Stalker."

Taliesin kept her face expressionless. Roland had indeed lied to Xander about his squire and the Nova brothers. Taliesin thought it well-played by the knight; he was trying to protect the Ghajar. And himself.

"Sertorius was on our tail," Roland said. "I couldn't risk running into him, nor could I suffer Lord Valesk's company more than a minute. I have never liked Valesk. He and his father may yet side with Prince Almaric. Keep a sharp eye on Aldagar, my lord. They are far more dangerous than the Wolf Clan. But Taliesin is right; nothing was done to prevent the massacre."

Xander snarled. "How dare you blame the Eagles for what happened to the Ravens. My father supports King Frederick and does what is necessary to keep that bitter old man on the throne. I need not explain why Chief Lykus spared our legionnaires, nor why he chose to kill everyone else, including the *fat* secretary! Wolves will be wolves!"

The look of contempt thrown in Taliesin's direction set her on edge. 'Like father like son,' she thought, hating Lord Arundel and Master Xander equally.

"Lykus would be a fool to kill Eagle legionnaires," he continued. "Neither of you can understand or appreciate the long association between my father and the Wolf Chief. They have been friends a *very* long time. Now that *Doomsayer* is in Almaric's possession, we must counter with a stronger sword. We need *Ringerike* to win the war!"

Roland helped himself to a leg of mutton. "Don't get your feathers in a ruffle, you two. We are on the same side," he said in a gruff voice. "I know you are upset, Taliesin, that I didn't forewarn you about Master Xander joining our quest, but he *is* here to help. We need his men to prevent Prince Sertorius and the Maldavians from stopping us. Sertorius is working for Almaric. Tell her, my lord?"

"It's true. Sertorius only goes to Garridan to raise an army against King Frederick. If he gets his hands on you, he'll either entice you to find *Ringerike* with promises of gold, marriage, and a crown, or he'll torture your friends until you give him what he wants. That man has no scruples. Are you satisfied, Roland? I have just warned your mistress this prince has far more teeth than Lykus or my father."

The little worm Xander grinned at Taliesin, his teeth small and even, but with gaps that reminded her of tiny, white cobblestones. His inability to pick one emotion and stick with it annoyed her more than the offensive words that came out of his mouth. The idea anyone actually liked Xander for himself was impossible to fathom; a more despicable character she'd never met in her life. She watched Roland chew on the mutton.

"Grudge would never have accepted the help of anyone, especially an Eagle," she said. "You know how I feel about the Eagles, how they twist everything around to get their way and how they use people to get what they want. Arundel and Lykus work together. All this could have been avoided if you'd but told Osprey that Xander was not a prisoner but intended to ambush me. Why the deception? If you'd told the truth, Roland, my clan would have stayed at Raven's Nest and the Black Wings would have beaten off the Wolf Clan, as always, and wouldn't have died. Their deaths are as much your fault as the Eagle Clan's. Perhaps even more so, because you could have prevented it. And don't deny it. You told me you want to give *Ringerike* to the king."

"I had my orders."

Taliesin turned bright pink. "Did your Grand Master tell you to sacrifice Duke Hrothgar and Jasper? All you had to do was tell the duke that Sertorius and Peergynt waited in ambush. You could have told Hrothgar about the Deceiver's Map. It should be Hrothgar and Jasper, not Xander, who joined us on the quest, you stupid magpie!" She looked for something to throw, but Roland caught her by the arm and yanked her to the pillows.

"Don't accuse me of being dishonorable. Fregians died that day. I would have prevented the battle if I could," Roland growled. "Strategy is clearly not your specialty. Hrothgar died so the rest of the High Council would see Sertorius for what he is and join their king. The duke died a martyr of patriotism and its great cost to achieve."

Applause came from the far end of the table. "Oh, this is rich," sang out Xander. "Who would have imagined we'd be having a lover's spat? What a wild stag you are, Sir Roland, rutting with the *Sha'tar*. Seducing a normal woman to get her under your control is one thing, but tampering with this hellcat is another. If she doesn't agree to help us, then she should be chained and dragged to the cave. Convince her to come along willingly, or that's precisely what I'll do. I don't have time for this, though it is quite amusing."

"A moment, please, sir!"

Roland released her arm. She scooted away.

"I swear I did not know the details of my Grand Master's and Lord Arundel's plan; I only knew that I was to meet my Order here. Now that Xander and his men have arrived, since we are being pursued by the Wolf Pack and the Maldavians, we need his protection. He's right. We can't reach the cave without him."

"I've heard all I care to hear. I don't trust you anymore, Roland. I want nothing to do with either of you. If you want *Ringerike*, get it yourself. I won't be chained."

"Out of the river and right into the eagle's claws," Xander said, laughing. "Had you not bedded her, Roland, I would have done so. Such spirit! But I thought your order did not allow its members to fornicate."

"That's the Order of the Blue Star, my lord," Roland said. "They are warrior monks and follow Duke Fakar's every whim. As I told you, my squire, Tamal, was to have joined the Blue Stars, but his father sent him to me instead. Duke Fakar is the cousin of Grand Master Banik Dzobian. Many Erindorians are sent to Fregia to train to be knights."

The urge to tell Xander the big oaf lied was tempting, but she couldn't put the gypsies in harm's way. It *was* a clever cover story. Tamal, a bastard of the Erindorian duke, accompanied by four servants and sent to serve Roland as a squire, had to be the best lie the big lout had yet to invent. She wasn't about to tell Xander otherwise, so she sat on the pillows, downed a glass of wine, and listened to the two idiots.

"It's not that, Roland," Xander said. "Your servant, Rook, is the one who resembles Duke Fakar, not your squire, but I suppose it doesn't matter. Fakar has so many bastards. Most women favor men with dark complexions; not us pale types, Sir Roland. The *Sha'tar* must find something about you attractive in bed, but it certainly isn't good looks."

"It's not his looks, I assure you," Taliesin muttered.

Xander ignored her. "Sir Roland, you were selected for this mission by your Grand Master, who recommended you to my father. I admit I had doubts about you getting this far, but you've done well. Let's have a look at the Deceiver's Map. I trust the *Sha'tar* has it with her at all times."

"Taliesin, show it to him," Roland said.

"I will not."

Taliesin reached for Roland's glass and drank the wine in one gulp. A tall figure appeared beside her as Sirocco provided her with her own filled glass. She drained it as well and pushed both goblets away. They were refilled, and Khamsin appeared and set a plate of food before her. Simoom continued singing while Harmattan strummed his lute.

"You mean Roland arranged for me to find the map? I don't believe you." Taliesin stared at the plate of sliced meat and wished it were the knight's heart. "All any of you had to do was ask me to help, and I would have. Instead, you went to elaborate lengths to mislead everyone, and in so doing, caused the destruction of my clan."

"Osprey's death was unfortunate, but it did motivate you to leave Raven's Nest and search for the Raven Sword. Of course, you will be rewarded...."

Without hesitation, Taliesin pulled the gypsy knife from her boot and charged around the table toward Xander. Tamal and the Nova brothers watched, but none attempted to stop her. Only a few feet from Xander, a pair of large arms caught her around the middle and pulled her away. The knife fell from her grasp. Roland held her as she struggled to get free; she screamed, bit, stomped on his feet, kicked at his knees, and did whatever else she could to get away from him, and yet, he held on.

"He's a murderer! My clan will be avenged!"

Roland spun her around, squeezed tight, and waited until she gasped for air before he deposited her onto the pillows, where she glared at him. Xander had the gall to laugh at the scene and snicker while pointing at the couple.

"There's more at stake here than avenging your clan, Taliesin," Roland said, his tone sympathetic. "Xander had nothing to do with their deaths. He's on our side."

"He is not on my side! No Eagle is on the side of a Raven!"

"Xander is a King's Man, like me. Of course, he's on *our* side. All of us support King Frederick, and that's what's important. Fortunately, Xander reached us before the Wolf Pack or Prince Sertorius, and now we'll have an escort to the Cave of the Snake God. What's important here is finding *Ringerike*. It can ensure King Frederick retains his throne. The king depends on us, Taliesin. What greater honor is there?"

"Yes, what greater glory?" Xander echoed.

Something in the Eagle heir's tone — womanly, yet laced with malice — and in his eyes — pale, like those of a corpse — was a warning sign; Taliesin, in that instant, feared for her own life and the lives of her friends. Taliesin remembered Zarnoc's warning about the Eagle heir being dangerous, and she knew she had to rein in her anger and act compliant before he put her in irons. It was obvious he didn't think highly of women, so she resorted to tears in the hope it would make her appear weak and helpless. As expected, Roland looked horrified and inched away from her. The fool actually thought she was sincere, and if Roland believed her nonsense, then surely Master Xander would also fall for a few tears.

"I don't know why I'm acting this way," Taliesin said, through her tears. "So much has happened since Raven's Nest fell. Everyone is depending on me, and I simply can't handle all this unwanted attention. The pressure is getting to me. Of course, neither of you are at fault for what has happened. You just don't understand. I'm a woman, and everyone thinks I can do this on my own, but I can't, I just can't, it's just too much to ask of me."

"This is why I never allow women to join me on a quest," Roland said. He grabbed his glass of wine, took a large gulp, and set it down. "You sound like a mad woman, Taliesin. I know you are upset, and I don't blame you; however, Master Xander is just as devoted to his own father as you are. Try to understand things from my point of view."

"From a man's point of view?" Taliesin sniffed. "How can you possibly expect me to see things from your point of view when you continually lie to me?"

"What a fine performance, my dear. If only Glabbrio the Glib was alive, he could pen your eloquent words. 'I am a woman, and everyone thinks I can do this on my own, but I can't, I just can't.'" Xander lowered his hands and smiled thinly. "I almost believed your crocodile tears, but there is anger in your eyes, Raven Mistress. I believe you would have gutted me like a fish if Sir Roland hadn't stopped you, but I do appreciate the waterworks. Bravo, my dear. Bravo. Please, allow me to show off my own artistic talent; I do so love good theater."

Roland groaned and buried his face in his hands. Taliesin watched as a wicked gleam appeared in Xander's moon-pale eyes. He stood, one hand over his heart, and snapping his fingers at Harmattan, the Eagle heir started to sing. Harmattan caught on within seconds and played along to Xander's shockingly high-pitched voice.

"We hunted the wren for Baldor.

In the glade, we hunted his wife.
We hunted the wren for Baldor,
In the glade, he took her life.
The wolf pups heard, the ravens wept,
And the eagle raised his head.
Within that fated hour, husband
And lover would soon be dead.
We hunted the woods for Baldor.
With orders to take his life.
We hunted the hills for Sir Calador.
Killing both men with a knife."

Xander finished and picked up his wine glass, his eyes never leaving Taliesin's face as he resumed his seat on the soft pillows. Taliesin was stunned. Of all the songs Xander might have sung, it had to be that one. The same song she'd been singing outside of Tunberg. Coincidence, she thought, possibly, but she had a feeling the Eagle heir had been spying on her, and the image of a flock of wrens flying overhead that day she'd sung entered her mind. It wasn't as if the Eagle Clan didn't have magic users of their own; she'd suspected they did, for they certainly had magical weapons. Somehow, Master Xander had overheard her talking to Jaelle on the road, and she doubted any of the farmers or peddlers they'd seen were guilty.

"The 'Tale of the Wren Wife' is one of my favorites," Taliesin said. "Shall we dispense with the charade, my lord? I think you and I understand one another. Why didn't you simply come to Raven's Nest and ask me to help find *Ringerike*?"

"If I had, everyone would now know you are a *Sha'tar*, so instead, my father and his allies decided to send Sir Roland to infiltrate the Raven Clan, which he did with marvelous ease. Glabbrio was sent to confirm you had the Deceiver's Map, yet remained unaware of our plans. We didn't want him knowing the extent of our involvement in finding *Ringerike* had Lykus captured him. I am sorry about your clan, Taliesin. Had your clan gone into hiding and not gone with Glabbrio, I am quite certain they wouldn't have been found by the Wolf Pack and killed. As it is now, none but the Eagle Clan and the Order of the White Stag are certain you are a *Sha'tar*, and so we still have the advantage."

"Will your father avenge the Raven Clan?" Taliesin asked.

"Doubtful." Xander glanced at Sirocco as the gypsy refilled his wine glass and stepped away. "Try to understand what's at stake here—Prince Almaric has raised an army in the east and will stop at nothing until his father is dead. Almaric sold Galinn to the northern barbarians and holds Konall prisoner in a fortress, which leaves only Dinadan to help their father. As for Sertorius, he seeks only to improve his own position, nothing more. Now that Almaric has *Doomsayer*, it has become a race for each side to collect as many magical weapons as possible."

"We've passed several magical weapons on the way here," Taliesin said. "I offered to find them for Roland, but he is only interested in *Ringerike*."

"Because *Ringerike* is the prize," Xander stated, clasping his hands before him. "It is the most powerful of all magical weapons, but without a *Sha'tar*, its powers cannot be activated. You are equally as important, my dear. Consider yourself fortunate the Eagle Clan and the Order of the White Stag have taken you under their protection, for if you fell into the hands of Chief Lykus, he would either turn you or eat you. Roland is the only reason you are still alive. Now that I am here and reinforcements are on the way, we have a better chance of finding *Ringerike* before Captain Wolfgar or Prince Sertorius."

"I do appreciate what Roland has done for me," Taliesin said, her tone soft. She felt Roland's hand seek hers under the table. She swatted his hand away. "If you knew what I was and wanted my help, all you had to do was ask Master Osprey, and he would have cooperated."

"What fun is that?" Xander asked. "Sir Roland could have warned Duke Hrothgar about the trap set by Prince Sertorius, but instead, he remained with you. Had the Fregian duke come to Padama instead of attacking Prince Sertorius, he would still be alive. Deception is the only way to cull the herd. Hrothgar believed the rumor that Sertorius possessed the Deceiver's Map, and Sertorius was told Hrothgar had the map. The deception was necessary to discover which side the prince would choose, and as it turns out, he seeks only to improve his own lot."

"Your sense of fun has caused many people to die." Taliesin thought the Eagle heir either insane or cruel-natured. He laughed at her comment, convincing her he had to be both in order to feel nothing for the harm he'd caused.

"Jasper was Hrothgar's heir, but he is dead," Roland noted. "The House of Volund was wiped out, my lord, just to verify which side Sertorius is on, and as it turns out, it's neither. Who then has assumed control of Fregia?"

"Grand Master Banik controls Fregia, and for his good service will be made a duke. When you return home, Sir Roland, it is agreed you will become the next grand master of the Order of the White Stag, a promotion well deserved."

"Me?" Roland sounded shocked. "I don't know what to say, my lord."

Taliesin dropped her jaw. His reward for betraying her and her clan was a handsome one. Any knight offered the post of grand master would have done the same, and she didn't believe it was the first time he'd heard about it; nor did he act surprised the Duke of Erindor and the Grand Master, along with the Eagle Clan, were in a marvelous position to assume command of the realm.

"What about the other dukes?" Taliesin wondered aloud. "Have they all agreed to support the king and Erindor? Do they know the extent of your father's plans to become one of the most important men in the entire realm?"

"Taliesin," muttered Roland. "There is no cause to make accusations. Lord Arundel is trying to protect King Frederick. Master Xander is only doing the same."

Xander shrugged. "It's all right, Roland. The girl has questions, and I'm very happy to answer them. Scrydon, Fregia, and Erindor support the King; however, Thule and Bavol have sided with Prince Almaric. The Duke of Aldagar is undecided. The Fortinbraus family will come around to our way of thinking, once they know we have obtained *Ringerike* and cannot be defeated. Maldavia remains our main concern. Duke Peergynt favors Almaric and believes Sertorius is his friend, but that remains to be seen. That leaves the Duke of Garridan as the one nobleman who may yet tip the scales; Duke de Boron is far removed from Maldavia, but he has the largest army and navy. Prince Sertorius is headed to his capital, and that is why I will go to Garridan as well. Duke de Boron must be convinced to help the king. I will ask Sertorius to be arrested and held captive, of course, while you and Sir Roland return to Padama with *Ringerike* and do whatever the king asks of you."

"You think Duke de Boron will agree to give you an army?" Roland asked after taking a drink of wine. Sirocco came over with a bottle, looked inside Taliesin's glass, and filled it with wine. Sirocco also picked up Jaelle's dagger with the skill of a thief and walked away with it, returning to stand beside his brothers.

"Sertorius isn't a politician," Xander replied in a silky voice. "He's a soldier. If I reach Dunatar Castle ahead of him, I am certain I can convince Duke de Boron to take Sertorius into custody. After all, we have the *Sha'tar*, and once we have *Ringerike*, Sertorius, Almaric, and the rebel dukes will be powerless to stop us. Of course, de Boron will side with us; he doesn't want to be on the losing side." His limpid eyes turned upon Taliesin. "Doesn't it make you feel good to know how important you are, my dear?"

"Yes, very. I want only to help the King," Taliesin said, holding back her true feelings. She couldn't help feeling sympathy for Prince Sertorius and his desperate race to beat Master Xander to the capital of Garridan. Even though he cared only about himself, the boy who had given her a tiny purple flower stuck in her mind. Like her, Sertorius was caught in a spider's web, but the difference was he didn't realize the spider was coming to eat him. It didn't seem likely he would want to help her, but he didn't want to help the Eagle Clan, and the Wolf Clan had turned against him. Nor did he support his father. But if he would support her, they could escape the web together. That was something she needed to think upon. She caught Roland staring at her, felt him trying to pry into her private thoughts by searching her eyes for answers, and quickly looked away.

"We will have to push hard tomorrow," Xander said. "Between here and Dunatar Castle, we must kill every Djaran, Ghajaran, Wolfman, and traitorous Maldavian we meet. It's not an easy thing we do for a living, but it must be done." He took a sip from his glass and gazed at Taliesin over the rim. He finished his wine in three gulps. "Oh, don't look at me like I'm a devil. Duke de Boron has been in dispute with the Djaran for years. We need his support, and we will do whatever it takes to get it."

"I'll see guards are posted outside the Raven tent," Roland said, standing up. He held his hand out to Taliesin, but she refused to take it and crossed her arms.

"You go so soon?" Xander half rose and motioned for them to return to the table. He watched her every move, a red tongue, like a snake's, flicking across his thin lips several times before he spoke. "You are very remiss in your duties, Sir Roland. You have not informed the *Sha'tar* that once we have the Raven sword, both of you will join me at Dunatar Castle. From there, we will book passage on a ship, sail around the eastern coastline to Erindor, where the royal army is gathering, and then we'll march east to fight Prince Almaric."

"Well, you've told me now," Taliesin said. "If that is all, I must rest. It's been a long day, and I'm tired, Master Xander. Sir Roland need not escort me; I know the way." Xander's eyes narrowed and never left her face as he fiddled with the collar of his tunic. He apparently wanted something more from her. It dawned on her Xander's intentions revolved around his bed and her spending the night. The man stared so intently at her with his creepy corpse eyes that she stood up, eager to leave. "Goodnight, gentlemen. I'll see you in the morning."

"Right," Xander said, rising to his feet. "Like a wild hawk, you must be kept on a short tether. In the morning, you shall find the sword of King Korax of the Raven Clan. Once you have found *Ringerike*, you will carry the sword, and you will present it to King Frederick Draconus. I've heard stories about the side effects brought on by enchanted weapons in the wrong hands. Some men lose their minds, others the ability to breed, while others grow old before their time or lose overnight what they'd acquired in a lifetime. Whatever side effects come with *Ringerike* is the price the King will have to pay to save his realm from anarchy. Not I. But fear not, you will be guarded at all times."

Master Xander glided around the table with movements that reminded her of a desert snake and reached out to take her by the hand. At that moment, she desperately wished Sirocco would plunge the gypsy knife into Xander's back while Tamal ran his spear through his black heart. The Eagle heir was much shorter than she was, almost the size of a child, which she hadn't noticed until now. The way he scrutinized her as he lifted her hand to lips and placed a cold kiss upon her knuckles made her dinner churn in her stomach.

"It's been a pleasure," Xander said, but he didn't release her hand. "Sir Roland, his squire and servants, and the wizard will go with you to the Cave of the Snake God. To make certain you do as you're told, your companions will remain my guests and travel with me to Garridan. I need insurance you won't try to trick me. I've been dealing with the Raven Clan far longer than you realize, my dear, and I know how your minds work."

"For a boy of fourteen," Taliesin said, unable to resist, "I am impressed."

"Fourteen? Really? Is that how old I look to you?" Xander's laughter filled the tent like the squeals of a little girl. He released her hand. "Did you hear that, Sir Roland? The Raven Mistress believes I am an unshaven, untried boy." He stroked his chin as if he had a long beard, but no whiskers grew on his face. "I take that as a compliment, my dear, for I am well past fifty. I hope you do not judge by appearances alone; if so, you are in for countless disappointments during your lifetime, as short as that may be."

Roland pushed himself away from the table. "Maybe I should walk Taliesin to her tent, my lord," he said, taking her by the elbow. She brushed his hand away.

"Oh, posh!" Xander snorted. "I have never met a female I cannot tame, no matter the species. She knows I'll kill her friends if she disobeys me. She won't run away." He lifted his hand but refrained from touching her again. "I know how to handle wild things, Sir Roland. It's nature's way of testing us, and I assure you both, I am a survivor." His pale eyes slid over her. "Of course, other arrangements could be made to guarantee your friends' safety, my dear. What do you think, Sir Roland? Do you mind if I offer this woman my protection?"

"She is her own woman," Roland said, the expression in his eyes unreadable. "She does what she wants, when she wants."

Taliesin crossed her arms and prepared to flee. Xander's hand fell upon her shoulder. She left it there, like a contemptible pale bug, and trembled when he caressed her cheek with his slender, girlish fingers.

"I was right, Sir Roland. You have not broken her in," Xander said, surprised. "She is still wild. Very wild. If you have no claim, then I'll keep her here for the night. If she pleases me, I may consider letting one of her friends come with you."

Roland sucked in his breath and said nothing. Taliesin wanted to club him.

"He doesn't want you, girl," Xander said, perking right up. "But I do. If you want my protection, you may have it, by all means." He patted her on the shoulder like a good little girl, a lascivious expression on his face. "Go to your tent, then, and return with the two other boys who travel with you. I like boys as much as girls."

"That's certainly an offer I can't refuse," Taliesin said. Her sarcasm was picked up by Roland, but the nitwit didn't seem to care as he placed his hand over his groin and smiled. "This is far more than I hoped for, great lord. Far more than I deserve."

The Eagle heir laughed with delight. "Yes, yes. I know," he said, eager with lust. "You may show me how grateful you are tonight, my little *Sha'tar*. You and your friends."

Spinning on her heel, Taliesin tried not to gag as she walked out of the tent. She didn't bother glancing at Roland, and didn't expect him to follow her, not after he'd let Master Xander lay claim to her. He'd just stood there, saying nothing, and let the pervert take charge of the situation. Forgive, but never forget, she thought, wondering why she couldn't hate Roland. Ignoring every Eagle guard she passed, she returned to her tent and found her friends snoozing on pillows scattered across the floor. Jaelle was first to awaken, sat up, and curiously watched as Taliesin went to her saddlebags, checked to make certain the map and key were inside the pouch, and then belted on her sword. The others woke up, one by one, as Taliesin stuffed her gear into her saddlebags, muttering under her breath.

"Are we leaving?" Hawk asked. "It's about time."

Wren let out a yawn and stretched her arms over her head. "I just had a horrible dream," she said. "I saw you and Roland parting company, permanently. What happened?"

"It's obvious they had a fight, and we're leaving, so get up, get dressed, and let's ride," Jaelle said, quickly rising to her feet. She started packing her gear.

Taliesin merely nodded.

"Oh, dear," Zarnoc said, clicking his tongue against the roof of his mouth. He waved his hand over his chest and turned his sleeping robe and fuzzy slippers into his dirty, old traveling clothes. "You need not tell us what was said, Taliesin, for it's plainly written on your face. Master Xander is not known for his charm. Personally, I'm glad to be rid of him.

It is a pity Roland is at this man's mercy, for I assure you, to have such a master is to be a slave."

"Poor Roland," Rook said. He was dressed and ready to leave, the silver spear strapped to his back. He lifted his saddlebags onto his shoulder. "I will be glad to be free of the Eagle Clan. I'm sure he regrets what has happened, Taliesin. Do not judge him harshly."

The wizard twirled around holding his staff. "Escaping from the Eagle heir's clutches will require a little magic," he said. "The horses and mule are already saddled. That much was easy to do. Reaching them without being seen will be harder; it will require a diversion if we are to make good our escape. I can arrange that, too."

"What about the gypsies?" Hawk asked. He was loaded with gear and stood at the entrance to the tent. "We can't leave without Tamal and the brothers. They are in danger. Are they coming with us, Taliesin?"

"No, they stay with Roland," she said, picking up her saddlebags. "Xander thinks they are from Erindor, and as long as they give him no reason to think otherwise, they will be safe. Roland is not without honor. He is a King's Man, through and through, but he'll protect Tamal and the brothers. Come here, Hawk. We're going under the side of the tent — the entrance is being watched."

"You go first," Hawk said. "I'm last out. I've got your backs."

Feeling like thieves in the night, Taliesin and her friends slipped under the side of the tent, crept to their horses, and found them already saddled, as Zarnoc had promised. The Eagle Legionnaires were encamped away from the horses and slept inside small tents with their camels tied outside. As her group, trying to remain as quiet as possible, tied on their gear and climbed into the saddles, Taliesin spotted several furry bodies moving across the sand and headed straight for her abandoned tent.

"Wolves," Jaelle cried out. "They've found us!"

Dozens of huge wolves rushed in, making no sounds as they tackled the Eagle guards and ripped them to shreds before moving onto the next. If that was Zarnoc's diversion, sending in the Wolfmen, it was all they needed to escape. With Jaelle in the lead, they took off at a gallop and headed west as a bugler blew his horn, alerting the camp of the attack. As Taliesin and her group crested a large dune, she glanced back to see her tent bathed in bright red flames and frightened men and camels scatter as the giant wolves swarmed the camp. She turned away and tried not to think about Roland's fate.

* * * * *

Chapter Twenty-Five

The afternoon sky held no cloud cover, only an endless expanse of blue that stretched across a dry basin and ended with the rise of giant mountains in the west. The map had made it appear the journey was just another day's ride. At the end of the third day, the mountain range appeared twenty miles away, under a hazy sheen that rose from the ground and created the illusion of water. Wearing their cotton cloaks and sucking on leaves to stay cool, they slowly made their way to the Cave of Chu'Alagu, relying on Zarnoc to keep them fed, watered, and protected. But even his magic had limits, for the enchanted water which trickled through their bodies had no real value, and the food lacked real protein, offering flavor, but yielding no calories, and riders and horses suffered for it. Zarnoc promised to find something nutritious to eat and rode to the north on his mule, fearing they'd turn it into steaks. That was the evening last, and he had not yet returned.

Taliesin frequently pulled out the Deceiver's Map, forming it as a board so it would not fly away in the breeze, and kept track of their route, the Wolf Pack, the Eagle legionnaires and Sir Roland, and Prince Sertorius' band of knights. All appeared as tiny dots on the map following after them; though Hawk and Rook did their best to wipe clean their trail, the enemy still gave pursuit. For an hour, they'd been tracking an oasis that moved about on the map, taking them miles out of the way, only to lead them back to the correct path. Taliesin was exhausted, barely hanging on by a thread, and she knew her companions were in no better shape. Her urine had turned dark gold from dehydration. She no longer sweated, and every few seconds a chill set her teeth chattering and made her stomach heave. With no sign or word from Zarnoc since he left, she kept the group moving, promising they'd reach water by the evening. Jaelle's horse was limping, so she'd chosen to walk beside the mare and straggled behind the others. They went on for another few miles as the sun set behind the mountains, until Taliesin, able to hear Jaelle speaking soothingly to the horse, at last signaled the group to stop.

"Where is the oasis?" Hawk asked, sinking to the ground. He caught sight of a green lizard, stabbed it with his knife, and ate it raw. "You promised us water by nightfall. Wren has a fever. If we don't find water soon, Taliesin, it's the end of us."

"I'm not ready to kill our horses, so stop eyeing Jaelle's mount." Taliesin slid out of the saddle, shivering. "It's getting dark. I'll look at the map again, the oasis can't be far." She heard something hard hit the ground, a saddle, and Rook was already making camp. Taliesin stretched out her legs, took the map from her pouch, placed the board in her lap, and found their location. The oasis was no further than a mile away unless the map lied. She thought about Zarnoc, but he didn't appear on the map, nor in person.

Hawk pulled the saddle from his horse and used his cloak to wipe the sweat off the horse's back and flank. "No one is coming to help us," he grumbled. "Zarnoc has abandoned us. It's useless. We'll never find the oasis, and we'll never reach the cave."

"Don't stop," Jaelle said. "We must find water. Get rid of everything you don't need; keep your weapons and take your water flasks. Give the horses a rest and then push on a little further. I can smell the water—can't you? It's right over the next dune." Her horse collapsed as its forelegs suddenly sank into the sand at a rapid rate while Jaelle tugged on the reins. The bridle slipped off as the horse struggled and panicked, screaming as the quicksand pulled it down. "Help me!" Jaelle shouted, watching the horse lift its head, the only part of its body still visible. The horse met her eyes and conveyed its frantic sense of fear. Hawk was instantly at her side with a rope. He made a loop, threw it over the horse's head, and heaved, but succeeded in only strangling the animal. With a final snort, the horse's head vanished from view, taking the rope with it.

Jaelle screamed and turned on Hawk, a knife in her hand. As he scrambled clear, she brought the dagger to her throat, meaning to take her own life. Hawk dove onto her and rolled them both clear of the quicksand, losing the knife in the process. Jaelle's gut-wrenching sobs faded and turned to gasps for air as Hawk pulled her into his arms and cradled her against his chest.

"Durrell," Jaelle sobbed, gazing at the darkening sky through tear-filled eyes. "My father gave me Durrell when I was a child. She was sister to Tamal's stallion, Gazel. Tamal will be angry with me for being so careless." She buried her face against Hawk's shoulder. "I'll never see my brother or father again."

"I can't stand it," Wren said, who had remained mounted on Merryweather. "I'm going over the dune. I'll find the oasis. I know I will."

The small mare trotted forward and then galloped up the dune before anyone could stop her. The horse and rider cast a long shadow as they went over the mound and disappeared from sight. Seconds later, her shouts brought Rook running toward the dune, but he fell several times, unable to summon the strength to go to her aid.

"Taliesin, go after her," Rook said. "Please. Save Wren."

Taliesin slid onto Thalagar's back, drew her sword, and kicked her horse hard in the flanks. The stallion let out an angry snort and charged forward. Wren was waiting on the opposite side of the dune, pointing at a beautiful oasis. Palm trees spread across a wide area filled with abundant plant life that thrived around a large pool. Urging her mare forward, Wren rode to the oasis, right into the pond, laughing and shouting as she dove out of the saddle into the water.

Taliesin sheathed her sword as she rode back over the dune to see Hawk and Rook finish saddling their horses. "Wren found the oasis," she shouted. "Leave your gear and get on the horses. There's water for all." Hawk brought Jaelle, and Rook was already mounted; as they crested the hill, their shouts of joy caused the horses to run toward the pool of water.

Taliesin waded out of the water, soaked to the skin, and left Thalagar to splash about as she threw herself onto the ground beneath a palm. Wren and Rook played in the water while their horses trotted out and stood together to nibble at tall blades of grass. Hawk's riderless horse let out a snort and also waded out in the water, leaving its owner and Jaelle splashing one another, Durrell's death forgotten, at least for the moment.

Taliesin sat up, shrugged out of her cloak and jacket, and went about rounding up the horses. She removed the saddles, replaced the bridles with braided rope halters, and set a tether line. She kicked off her waterlogged boots and walked about in her bare feet to collect wood, piled it in a tall stack, and crouched to use a bowstring and the bark of a palm tree to spark a fire to life. When she had it going, she lay on the ground and listened to her friends laughing and splashing in the water.

Hawk dropped to the ground beside her, holding a coconut. "There's more on the ground," he said. "Something swam by my leg. Might be an eel? Rook is going to fish, and Wren will look after Jaelle. They're hanging their clothes to dry. It's a miracle we found this place, but you did it, Taliesin. You did it."

A coconut dropped from the palm above Taliesin, nearly hitting her on the head. She looked at the moving palm leaves, which shook hard on their own and dropped coconuts beside her and Hawk with such accuracy she knew Zarnoc had arrived. The fire sparked, rising higher as Zarnoc appeared, with the carcass of a slender antelope hung across the mule. Zarnoc jumped to the ground and pulled the antelope off the mule, letting the thirsty animal head to the pool for a long-needed drink. Rook waded out of the water, with an eel on the end of his spear, and approached them. Setting the eel aside, he drew his knife, drug the antelope off a short distance to clean, and returned with a skinned pink carcass. Hawk helped him make a spit, and soon both antelope and eel were cooking over the campfire.

"I came as soon as I could," Zarnoc said. "Caught the deer early today and decided to head to the oasis, hoping you'd reached it. You're minus one horse; Jaelle's mare, I take it, didn't make the journey." He snapped his fingers, and a large three-sided tent appeared with bedrolls laid out and Taliesin's dried boots at the entrance. He held a blanket that materialized from nowhere and placed it around Taliesin's shoulders. "You're shivering. I know what's needed to remedy a fever. Get out of those wet clothes and go lay on a bed. It won't take me long to concoct an antidote for what ails you."

"Your company is what I need," Taliesin said. "You've been missed."

"And I you," Zarnoc replied, touched by her display of affection. He took a deep breath, stepped away from her, rubbed his lower back, and with an arch, popped his spine into place. "Ah, much better." He reached into his cloak, withdrew a black leather pouch, and set about making hot tea. A pot filled with water appeared on the ground. He crumbled something green between his hands and placed it inside the kettle, which was then put over the fire to brew beside the cooking meat.

"Where have you been?" Hawk asked. He'd set his clothes out to dry on a bush and wore only his wet pants. "No matter." He held out his hand, and the wizard grasped it, shaking hard. "It's damn good to see you, old man. We were on our last legs."

"Pleased to see me, are you?" Zarnoc asked, giggling. "I always knew where you were. My eyes see all, but I promised real food, not the magical stuff. We'll put weight on your bones, lad. Cook it well. I've tea to administer to the ladies."

While Zarnoc handed out cups of tea to Taliesin, Jaelle, and Wren, the two young men remained at the fire and turned the meat. Neither seemed aware that their clothes, along with their hair, had magically dried nor that the meat was cooking faster than normal. A table and benches appeared beside the pool, with rugs and pillows next to it; lit torches materialized along the waterline and flickered in the breeze. A sliced coconut lying on a silver platter appeared on the table. Jaelle, wearing her dark green wool gown and sipping her tea, sat on a bench while Zarnoc filled a bowl with dates he had picked by hand.

Jaelle put a date in her mouth and chewed. "The dates are wonderful," she said. "What's in the tea, Zarnoc? I feel better already."

"Best you not know," he replied. "All of you come over now and sit at the table. Hawk, the eel will burn if you don't take it off—and overcooked eel is mushy. Hurry now, Rook, there's a good lad. That antelope is cooked to perfection. Bring it over on the spits, boys, and place our dinner on the big platter."

Hawk and Rook each picked up a spit and brought the eel and antelope to the table. They set the meat on the same platter that already had a knife laid out. Wren, now with a healthy glow to her cheeks, came and sat. Taliesin rose to her feet and felt stronger and more refreshed with each step she took. She let the cloak fall from her shoulders, not surprised to find she wore a blue gown and slippers. Within the open tent, she noticed her traveling garments already dried and neatly folded on a carpet. No more shakes and no more pain, she thought, grateful yet again for the miracle of magic.

"I thought we'd have reached the cave by now," Taliesin said. She used her fingers to stuff the delicious eel and then a slice of coconut into her mouth. She'd never seen a coconut before, and it was better than anything she'd ever eaten. Wren handed her a cup of milky-white liquid, and she sniffed. It smelled like coconut, and she drank it. "This is good. Everything is good."

"Have a date," Zarnoc said, handing her the bowl of brown fruit. He laughed as Taliesin looked amazed; it tasted like honey. "I have a few tricks up my sleeves you haven't seen."

Even Jaelle managed to smile. Finding himself surrounded by three grateful females, Zarnoc was in his element and started to show off. He snapped his fingers and candles appeared on the table, along with pink lilies floating in a bowl of water. Another snap, and a pile of fudge appeared on a plate. "No calories there," Zarnoc said, "but it tastes just like chocolate, so eat as much as you want." Each girl grabbed a piece. A third snap, and a bowl of green apples, round and shiny, appeared. "It's real fruit. I took a bag from Xander. Try giving them to the horses, Rook; you seem full of energy tonight."

Taliesin took the dagger and sliced one up while the Erindor boy dashed to the horses and mule to give each a green apple. She had a sudden hankering for a chunk of yellow cheese, but none appeared; the wizard couldn't create real cheese out of thin air. Zarnoc sighed heavily as if zapped of his last ounce of magic, leaned back in his chair, crossed his legs, and stuck his lit pipe in the corner of his mouth.

"Wolfgar's men, reinforced by tribesman they'd met along the way, caught Xander and Roland by surprise, as you're aware," Zarnoc said. "I had nothing to do with them overwhelming the Eagle legionnaires, though I might have helped by not setting enchantments to protect their camp. Sir Roland and Master Xander fought side by side, rallying the men for a last stand. Both survived and gave chase to the Wolfmen. They may still be chasing them, all the way to the mountains, right where we are headed." He snorted, and smoke blew out his nostrils, creating a dragon that drifted away on the breeze as he continued his story.

"Master Xander, you see, is not human, nor is his father's line. They are creatures so foul they have no name, nor do they age as we do. By appearance, he looks like a strange boy, for that is how he wishes to be seen. The Aladorius family has been in power a very long time, and father, son, and mother alike take on the forms of any human they wish, just to hide how long they've been alive. When Lorians lived in the Salayan Desert, when it was green and wet, we fairy folk feared the Aladorius, for they crept out of the sea on their bellies and took human form to live among men. Korax was a Lorian, did you know? He couldn't very well call his clan the Fairy Clan, now could he? But the raven, ah, that was his favorite bird. He knew Arundel and Lykus, too, and they each have been alive for more than a thousand years. Why Arundel picked the eagle and not a sea serpent is beyond me. Lykus was cursed by Korax for a thing I dare not mention, and the wolf was his chosen clan name. Sadly, my race died out when Korax died, yet those other two creatures, Arundel and Lykus, made certain their clans prospered." He winked at Taliesin, puffing on his pipe. "It's but a story, but there is truth to be found in my words."

"Grudge was not harmed?" Wren spoke, her violet eyes conveying her fondness for the knight while the others, even Taliesin, felt only betrayal. "I do not forget the kindness he's shown me in the past. He kept me from harm when Rook and Hawk were away at the market. Men can be cruel. But not Grudge. Not Roland."

"The man is the same regardless of his name," Zarnoc said. He took a puff on his pipe. "Sir Roland was magnificent in battle. That ax of his, *Moonbane*, took many lives before Captain Wolfgar tucked his tail and ran."

"I wish the Shan had given me a magical weapon," Hawk said, finishing the last of the eel. "How many have we ridden past without picking up, Taliesin? You said there were several stars on that map between here and the cave, and each represents a magic item."

The wizard shivered from head to toe. "Stopping for trinkets is the best way to be captured by the enemy, young Hawk. None of you seem to realize the Eagle heir is a dangerous adversary, perhaps more so than Captain Wolfgar. One little mistake on our part, and Xander will take full advantage. Be thankful Taliesin had the good sense to get you out of the Eagle camp, or you'd each be chained to the foot of Xander's bed each night. Only the gods know what he had in store for you girls and Rook."

Rook whipped his head around, and his long dreadlocks swung forward. "Do I understand you correctly?" he said. "Xander summoned us to his tent to be his sex slaves? I once killed a man who laid hands on me when I was but a boy, something my father pretended did not happen in his own house. I wish nothing but death and sorrow for those of the House of Fakar and the Eagle Clan." He stood up and upset his glass, a temper upon him that none had ever seen. "It was easier when I pretended I heard nothing and said nothing. Some memories are best forgotten—a lesson you should learn, Raven Mistress. Stop seeking the truth about your father's death, for when you get to the bottom, you will only find a pit of vipers." He grabbed his spear off the table and stormed away, heading around the pool to seek solace in his own company.

"I should go to him," Wren said, tears streaming down her face.

"Leave him be, child," Zarnoc said, cautioning her. "Rook has many ghosts that haunt his mind. It's a lonely place, being lost in one's thoughts, but if he's to heal and love you, Wren, as a whole man and not a broken one, then the boy must come to terms with his past. Your coddling him won't help, so let him be."

Taliesin watched the wizard blow smoke rings into the night sky. Wren wiped her cheeks and smiled when the smoke turned into a winged horse that flew off into the night.

"Zarnoc, explain how I restored *Moonbane*'s powers," Taliesin said. "You said your powers are stronger, too. Both Wren and Jaelle have special gifts. Yet, Wren has not had any recent visions, nor is Jaelle able to accurately predict our future with her cards. I mean no offense, Jaelle, to you or to Wren. I'm simply curious how this all works."

"You're a *Sha'tar*," Zarnoc said. "It's not that hard to understand. When you met me, I wasn't able to use my magic to catch a rabbit and relied on Ginger to do that for me. I survived by doing things the old-fashioned way. As a *Sha'tar*, your gift is the ability to attract magic, to shape it, to mold it, and to restore it, if need be, simply by being near it. It's the same for magical items or magic users or those with special gifts like Wren and Jaelle. *Moonbane* was dormant, but you awoke its powers, as you have done for *Wolf Killer*. All of us will benefit if we remain near you."

Taliesin wrinkled her brow. "But *Wolf Killer* is just a silver sword."

"*Wolf Killer* has magic," Zarnoc replied with enthusiasm. "Never doubt that, nor doubt your own natural gifts. You don't have to touch a magical item or magic user to give them a little energy boost, my dear. Because of you, I am more powerful than I have been in centuries; and so, it seems, is Master Xander, for he is a sorcerer, just like his father. Do you think Xander came through the desert with such ease because he and his men ride sturdy horses? Not at all. Xander used magic to help on their journey. No doubt Wren and Jaelle will grow in strength as well. It just takes time."

"Xander is not a knight? I thought he was," Hawk said. "I mean, he wears armor."

"A plow horse can be dressed in armor, but that doesn't make it a knight." Zarnoc emptied his pipe, refilled it out of thin air with a leaf that smelled like pine, lit it with the tip of his finger, and smoked contently. "I've been thinking about what we're doing, and perhaps being less involved is the answer. Why place ourselves in danger when we could go north to Skarda and live among the barbarians? No one ever goes there, and we could have a quiet, happy life herding sheep. Or, maybe, we can all seek passage on a ship to some faraway place like the realm of Shinar, a land where women warriors rule, found far to the west."

"I've always dreamed of being a captain of my own ship," Hawk said. "But I also never run from a fight, and this is one that will follow us no matter where we go. Besides, both you and Taliesin are magic users, and I heard they don't allow magic in Skarda."

"Ever been there?" Zarnoc asked, blowing smoke rings. Hawk, annoyed, waved his hands to turn the cloud in another direction. "No, I didn't think you had. Talas Kull isn't quite as awful as they say he is. I believe he has a nasty reputation for beheading trespassers simply to keep Scrydon and Bavol from encroaching on their lands."

"Well, if the barbarians don't like magic, then we don't need to go there," Hawk said. "I don't like the snow or mountains; Skarda is the last place I would go."

Jaelle rose from the table, a glass of wine in hand, and made herself comfortable on the rugs and pillows next to the table. While continuing to mutter about Skarda, and why it was a wonderful place, Zarnoc drifted toward the gypsy girl and curled between the pillows to quietly smoke his pipe. Taliesin, Wren, and Hawk joined them.

"How is Tamal? Is he safe?" Jaelle asked. Her voice quivered with emotion. "Please tell me he's safe? And Harmattan? He may be the youngest Nova brother, but he's very brave. Simoon is too proud to notice anyone but Simoon, and Khamsin and Sirocco always try to take the credit, when it's Harmattan who works the hardest. I worry about them all."

"I assure you they are all quite fine. Tamal fought like a lion, by the way," Zarnoc said. "Harmattan is fierce, yes, and a good fighter; Simoom, Khamsin, and Sirocco have noticed. The Nova brothers and Tamal have blossomed under Roland's guidance. You don't need to worry about them, Jaelle. Sir Roland will keep them all safe and they, in turn, look after him. A very fine fit, if you ask me, and you did. They'll join us as soon as they can."

Jaelle sighed with relief. "Good. Because we won't get very far now I'm without a horse," she said. "Riding double will wear out the horses in this heat, and your poor little mule is burdened enough without me riding behind you."

A grin wrinkled the white-bearded sorcerer's face. "Have you ever ridden a horse with wings, my dear?" He laughed at their startled expressions. "If any of you carry a feather, I should be able to cast a spell."

"Wings?" Jaelle let out a loud laugh. Her entire demeanor altered, the idea ending her worry about the men-folk and her sorrow over the loss of Durell. She sat straighter and clapped her hands in excitement. "I have always wanted to ride a horse with wings!"

A loud commotion from the direction Rook had taken brought Taliesin to her feet, and she'd drawn her silver sword before her companions realized there was trouble. Rook shouted and ran around the pool, splashing water in his haste to reach the tent. Zarnoc remained on the pillows and smoked his pipe, while the others drew their weapons and stood like a wall in front of the tent. The grunting of camels and the shouts of men preceded the appearance of the riders, who were heading straight for the oasis.

"It's the Djaran!" Jaelle and Hawk shouted in unison. They exchanged a quick glance and drew their weapons, ready to fight the marauders.

"Everyone calm down," Zarnoc said, waving his hands as he rose. "It is not quite the raiding party that you all imagine. We'll see if it's worse or better."

The nomads rode to the water, dismounted, and allowed their mounts to drink, ignoring the small group. The desert men, their faces painted with curious dark designs, wore spiked helmets and black leather breastplates over bright red robes. They rode with Maldavian soldiers—royal guards in dark-blue tunics and gold cloaks—under Prince Sertorius' lion banner, carried by Sir Morgrave—recognizable by his unique mustache with its curled ends.

Sir Barstow sported a bandage tied around his head. More knights, followed by squires and servants that numbered no more than twenty, came riding to the pond and eased out of the saddle as their horses drank. Last to appear was Prince Sertorius, riding between two of his knights. The Djarans parted to allow the prince space to ride to the water. Taliesin and her companions watched from the tent as the dark-haired man dismounted, gave the reins to a squire, and accompanied by four of his knights, rounded the pool without pausing to drink and headed straight for the tent.

"What have we here?" Sertorius called out in a friendly voice. "Why, it's the last of the Raven Clan and the old Pelekus wizard." He walked to where Taliesin stood. "Have no fear. We mean you no harm, Rosamond Mandrake. I feel like such a fool for not recognizing you, but you have grown quite a bit since we last met. Please, forgive an old friend; our reunion is long overdue." He reached for her hand and lifted it to his lips. "Have you nothing to say to the castle-yard bully? Not even about the locket I stole and gave to another girl?

Taliesin caught her breath. "I...I can't believe you remember me."

"Of course, I do," he said.

The prince gave a knowing smile and placed her hand over his heart, and his dark-blue eyes glimmered with unshed tears. Here she'd thought when the prince found her, he would kill her, and now he kissed her hand and called her "friend." Sertorius' knights paid them no attention; they obviously meant to share the oasis for the night and went about their business, showing no interest or hostility, though it hardly eased Taliesin's concern their whereabouts had been discovered.

"You intend to share the oasis with us?" Taliesin asked.

"If you don't mind," he said. "I suppose you're wondering how I recognize you. I must admit the Djaran told me about you and your friends. They are the best when it comes to gathering information, and they made it a point to find out who you are."

"That's strange," she said. "No one knows I am John Mandrake's daughter; I use the name Taliesin now. I've been very careful to hide my identity."

"Strangers don't frequent the caravan trails. The nomads have been following you for some time. So have we, for that matter," Sertorius said. "I know you won't believe me, but I have always wondered what happened to you since the day you vanished from Padama. When I heard a *Sha'tar* was found among the Raven Clan, I never suspected it was you. Of course, your father had to be a warlock. I should have suspected it, for John Mandrake had a rare gift for making excellent blades."

Zarnoc grumbled under his breath. Taliesin glanced over her shoulder and saw Jaelle had resumed her seat and now leaned on the pillows and watched intently, while Hawk frowned and put away his weapon. Wren looked visibly shaken by the arrival of the nomads and Maldavian troops.

"I've also heard you have a talent for finding valuable weapons on the battlefield." Sertorius smiled when Taliesin pulled her hand away. "'Rosamond' suits you far better than 'Taliesin.' You're lovelier than I ever imagined. Again, let me apologize for not recognizing the woman from the girl. I feel like a cad and behaved far worse. Let me make it up to you; I can provide you and your friends with supplies and protection for the night. It's the least I can do for an old friend."

A servant walked over to hand a flask of water to Sertorius. He took Taliesin by the arm and sat with her on the pillows. Hawk cleared his throat, annoyed.

"Allow me to introduce my friends," Taliesin said. "This is Hawk, Wren, Jaelle, and Zarnoc, who I believe you know. Rook is somewhere around here. Everyone, this is Prince Sertorius Draconus." Her friends said not a word; Zarnoc merely waved. "If the nomads have told you everything, my lord, then I suspect you know why we're here."

"I do," Sertorius said. "But I'm on my way to Garridan. We're not the only ones following you, Rosamond. Master Xander of the Eagle Clan is headed this way. If he knows where you are going, you can be sure he means to join your quest. Xander Arundel is as clever as his father. The Eagle Clan pretends to support my father, but I know they cannot be trusted and secretly conspire with my older brother. That is why I am going to Garridan; to raise an army for my father."

"For him or against him?" Hawk asked, butting in.

Sertorius frowned. "I seem to make your friends uncomfortable," he said. "Come with me, Rosamond. I have so much to tell you." He stood and pulled her to her feet. "I don't think that young man likes me very much—he hasn't stopped frowning at me."

"Hawk always frowns," Taliesin said.

As tents were raised and the horses and camels tethered for the night, Taliesin and Sertorius walked through the camp, piquing the interest of the knights as well as the nomads. They came around to the far side of the oasis, where Taliesin leaned against a palm tree and spotted Rook making his way toward their friends. Sertorius paused to look for something he must have dropped, and with a sigh, finally pulled a white flower from a cactus and handed it to her, grinning widely. She held it, took a whiff, found it fragrant, and placed it in her hair, wondering why she reacted like a love-struck girl.

"You can't imagine what I'm feeling right now," Sertorius said, pressing his back against the palm tree. "I gave you another flower, once. Do you remember? I know it has been a long time since we saw one another, Rosamond, but I haven't forgotten anything. When your father died, you vanished in the night, never to be heard from again." He turned toward her, and his fingers softly caressed her face. "Rosamond, is it really you or is this a dream brought on by the heat? I feel like a boy again. I am so happy we are reunited. That I still feel the same way about you surprises me, too. But I do care for you; I always have."

"So dramatic," Taliesin said, amused. "You always were, Your Grace."

"No, please, call me Sertorius."

The prince pulled her into his arms and kissed her on the lips. He was persistent, and she felt his tongue sliding into her mouth as he kissed her with well-practiced skill. She heard a few of his men laughing, and pushed him away, eyes narrowed.

"Ah, you have reservations about my true feelings," he said. "It's natural to be afraid, but I assure you my feelings are sincere, Rosamond. You are so beautiful. Such green eyes, like morning dew on fresh leaves, and hair that reflects the rays of

the sun. I had no idea Mandrake's little daughter, with freckles on her nose and scabs on her knees, would develop into
such a fine-looking woman. I hope I don't disappoint you—
some say I am quite good-looking."

"I'm sure they do," she said. "And they are right."

Memories of their past together and old repressed feelings
returned with an uncanny swiftness, all from his kiss, and
made her wonder if the prince didn't have a little magic of his
own. Sertorius stared at her, not knowing he had just made
her remember every detail of her father's workshop—the
sound of his hammer pounding out steel on the anvil, how
John Mandrake had sweated over the fire, and how at night,
when the city was quiet, he'd sit beside her bed reading books
of ancient legends to her. She knew her father had loved her,
and she had loved him but had no memory of her mother.

"What are you thinking?" Sertorius asked.

"About the past. I remember studying with you and your
private tutors, learning arithmetic and history. Chasing each
other through the castle and turning the armory upside-down
playing soldiers. My father and I sat at a banquet with your
father and brothers a few times, but I don't recall what they
look like. Nor did they ever take notice of me."

"Almaric often took us on long rides at sunset," he said.
"Sometimes my brothers came with us. Galinn was quite fond
of you. Konall was the shy one, and Dinadan only noticed
other boys. Sometimes your father would bring you to worship Sunday evenings, and I would watch you instead of listening to the sermons." He suddenly laughed. "I remember
the first time I ever kissed you was in the royal orchard, the
scent of lavender in the air. Do you remember?"

"Yes," Taliesin said.

All the memories of her childhood were hers once more, as
were the doubts and questions yet unanswered about her parents. Now she was grown, it made no sense a swordsmith and
his daughter had been graced with so much royal attention.
She let Sertorius kiss her again, though she felt none of the
passion she'd felt with Roland and wondered why.

"Rosamond, oh Rosamond, how have I spent half my life without you?" Sertorius asked, pulling her onto the sand beside him. He held her hand and toyed with her fingers. "And to think my happiness involved one lone raven feather that floated from the sky and landed on my lap as I was riding but yesterday. It was so strange, but when I looked up, I saw a black bird flying overhead, in a place where no raven is ever found. When I touched the feather, I suddenly remembered everything about you, about us, about your father, and about those happy days at court." He laughed again and leaned against her shoulder. "I've always suspected my father didn't approve of you, for he feared we might marry; so, when you vanished from the court, I realize it was to keep us apart. I'm sure my father knew you were at Raven's Nest, adopted by Master Osprey, but I wish I'd known sooner."

"A raven feather made you remember all these things?"

"Yes," he said. "It sounds silly, doesn't it?"

Taliesin wondered what Zarnoc was hoping to gain by bringing the prince into her life. If he meant to be helpful, he actually caused more confusion than happiness. Sertorius reached into a pouch on his belt, removed a feather, and handed it to her. Taking it, she slid it across her face, felt no magic, and placed it into her own pouch.

"You don't mind, do you? It reminds me of home," Taliesin said. "Maybe you know the Wolf Pack burned Raven's Nest to the ground, and my clan was taken hostage. I don't know what's happened to them, Sertorius. We've been running ever since. It's not the Eagle Clan that worries me, not as much as the Wolf Clan and what they may do to my people."

"Rosamond, I swear I'll send a messenger to my father and tell him what has happened to the Raven Clan. If you need anything to help you on your quest, then you have but to ask," he said. "I can see in your eyes something troubles you. I'll call you Taliesin if you prefer, but honestly, with that reddish-gold hair, it's too dark a name for you. I much prefer your real name. Let me call you Rosamond and kiss you again."

"We're not children anymore, Sertorius," Taliesin said. "It was a long time ago, and I'm not the girl you remember. So much has happened these last twenty years. Yes, it's been that long since I saw you. Nor are you the boy I remember. You've changed, too."

"Is it not to our advantage to be adults, who can do what they want without having to answer to our fathers?"

Sertorius' voice was melodious and sweeter than honey. Taliesin knew he expected her to melt at his words, so she played along, placed her head on his shoulder, and let him toy with her fingers and kiss the palm of her hand, as he'd done many years ago.

"You've every right to be angry with me, Rosamond. You were angry with me when we last parted. I was a fool for giving your necklace to another. Children do not think about the consequences of their actions. Now, I think I did it to make you jealous."

"One little feather, and now you remember everything?" Taliesin laughed, keeping it light between them. "I'll admit I'd forgotten about you until I got a strong whiff of the marsh gas. I was so dizzy, I fell into the pool, and that's when you found me."

"It's fate," he said. "That's what it is. We were meant to be reunited; I know that now, and I care as much for you now as I did then," he said. "I did love you, Rosamond. More than you realize. Time can't change true love. What we had was real, despite our tender age, and I am happier than I've ever been, now that I've found you again."

"Do you know how my father died? I don't even know where he was buried. I've never returned to Padama. One day, I should like to visit his grave."

His brows knit together. When the prince spoke, his tone was harsh, "I don't know how Mandrake died, but I blame myself for not being there when the Raven Clan came for you," he said. "Almaric told me after the funeral that our father intended to send you away to a convent where noble girls were often sent to study to be ladies. Almaric never approved of our friendship; he thought it wrong for a prince to consort with the working class. I hated him for saying it, and I hated my father for wanting to send you away from me. I suppose that's why most of my life I've rebelled against both of them. But let's not talk about them. You are here now, with me, and the years of absence are fading away as if they never existed. I'd love to hear about Raven's Nest. Was it really built inside an ancient oak tree?"

"It was a beautiful place," she admitted, "far more magical than Tantalon Castle where you grew up. The tree stood over one hundred feet tall, and on the limbs were rooms with balconies, reached by a contraption built by my adopted father that we called the Bird Cage. It went all the way to the top of the tree, to the aviary, and from there you could see for miles."

"I'm sure it was lovely," he said. "You make it sound that way."

"It was. I didn't think so when I lived there, but now that it's gone, it's the one place I wish I could return."

"Let's go to my tent. My armor is filled with sand, and I can change while we talk."

Rising to his feet, Sertorius offered his hand, and together they walked to an elaborate pavilion set among the palm trees, well away from the nomads and camels. A servant waited inside a tent that, unlike Zarnoc's magical tent, was sparsely furnished, with only a bedroll laid out on a rug. Setting aside his sword, the prince held out his arms as his armor and boots were removed. His thin white shirt and loose white slacks were cut from expensive silk, and his bare feet were clean and without calluses; she noticed everything as he sat on the rug beside her. Another servant entered, carrying a flask of water and a plate of food similar to what she'd eaten earlier. His saddle was brought in, covered with his cloak, and he used it as a backrest. Humble furnishings, yet everything was of high quality.

"Rosamond, will you join me for dinner? Have something to eat?"

"I've already dined," she said. "The last few days of riding have worn me out. I really must return to my tent to rest. As long as you and your men remain hospitable, as you have been, I won't have my wizard turn you into eels. Are we clear on this?"

The prince spit out the stone of a date he'd devoured. "You are blunt and to the point," he said, laughing. "I shall be the same. I'm aware you're headed to the Cave of the Snake God, but my path lies behind the mountains. I am going to Dunatar Castle. My interest in you has nothing to do with your magic abilities or a magical sword."

"You're not going to stop me or sell me to the Wolf Pack or the Eagle Clan? They're on our trail, have been from the start, and I thought you had the same intentions. If I am wrong, then please forgive me, but this—your sweet words, the fond memories—it's in the past, Sertorius. But, if I am right, say what you want from me."

"By Stroud, you are relentless when you want the truth out of a man," he said, wiping his hands on a kerchief. "Very well. I'll be just as blunt. My interest in you is purely of the heart, an old friendship renewed. I wondered what happened to you all those years ago, and now I've found you. Exploiting you and blackmail is beneath me. Nor do I seduce a woman merely to get her to do what I want; at least, not from a political standpoint. Whatever I want, I can get for myself, and I always have; no *Sha'tar* is going to change my stars. My father will keep his throne, Almaric will be subdued, and I will be the chosen heir. Simple enough. No magical sword or clan rivalry stands in my way or holds any interest to me. Leave if you feel you must." He returned to his meal. "Or stay and talk to me. Whatever pleases you."

A minute slowly ticked past as they gazed into each other's eyes. Taliesin wanted to believe the prince. His reputation was hardly the solid bricks to build a foundation for friendship, and memories did not make bricks at all. Apart from his handsome face and pretty compliments, he offered her nothing, only his company. Unless this was just another trap; she considered that as she decided whether to talk or to return to her tent for some much-needed rest.

"My father and brother, Dinadan, wait in Tantalon Castle for my return," Sertorius said, slicing into an eel and assuming she intended to stay. "Almaric will soon attack, that I know, and I have little time to raise an army to help them. I'm well aware of an army in the south, raised by the Erindorian faction, but I have no reason to trust Lord Arundel, Duke Fakar, or Grand Master Banik. Erindor may yet side with Almaric, and if Konall and I are unable to raise our own army, it will come to who can pay the most to obtain the southerners' help. What I won't do is leave the fate of the kingdom to the whims of the Eagle Clan, Wolf Clan, or any knightly orders who are interested only in competing with one another for fame and glory. Nor do I trust any of the dukes, and that includes Fortinbraus and de Boron. Is that plain enough for you?"

"Yes," she said.

"*Ringerike* won't win any battles unless it's carried by an heir of Korax, and none exists," he said, wiping grease from his lips. "I'd throw the sword into the sea, along with every other magical weapon, if I had the means to find them all. My father and I share that in common; neither of us has any love for magic. When I am king, I will make certain there is no magic in the realm or any magic users except, perhaps, for one pretty *Sha'tar.*"

"I can't make a spoon dance," Taliesin said. "I tried. I don't have that type of magic."

Sertorius laughed. "But you do have the ability to find magical weapons," he said. "Everyone knows the dukes still own their ancestral weapons; Duke Galatyn of Bavol has the sword *Flamberge*, Duke Dhul Fakar possesses a magical scimitar called *Tizona*, and my cousin, Peergynt, has the *Horn of Bran*. Duke Vortigern of Scrydon gave his ancestral sword, *Trembler*, to Almaric, who has also managed to get his hands on *Traeden*, stolen right out of the royal armory. The Wolf Clan has Duke Hrothgar's sword, *Doomsayer*, and I'm sure the Eagle Clan has quite a few of their own. All those swords had their magic purged, so they say, and it would take a *Sha'tar* to restore them to full power, which puts you in a rather difficult position. Everyone wants you."

Taliesin thought of the Battle of Bernlak. It was impossible not to feel angry for the death of Duke Hrothgar Volgan and his brother Jasper Silverhand.

"Why did you kill the Volgan brothers?" Taliesin asked, helping herself to a date. "They were loyal to your father. If, as you say, you wanted to help your father, then killing two loyal lords seems to me to be the wrong way to go about it. Did Peergynt put you up to it?"

"It's not like that at all. Hrothgar and his bastard brother thought I had the Deceiver's Map and attacked me. Peergynt was obliged to protect me. The battle, however, could have been avoided," Sertorius angrily stated. "We were played against one another, you see, thanks to the Eagle Clan. You can be sure Lord Arundel knows you are a *Sha'tar*; so does Chief Lykus, and that means Almaric knows. You are in great danger. Not from me, of course. The nobles are all trying to get their hands on magical weapons. The laws of Caladonia still support slaying magic users, but I'll convince my father such weapons are needed if we are going to defeat Almaric. I don't approve of magic, but if it can help, then so be it."

Taliesin watched his eyes, his lips, and every inch of him, waiting for Sertorius to give himself away. He had to be lying to her — all men lied. But he did nothing more than drink wine and finish his dinner.

"If you were king, you could change the law," she said. "Magic isn't evil, just evil men who use it for evil deeds. You could change the laws and help people instead of dividing them. You could end the feud between the nomads and the gypsies, the feud between the clans, and restore my clan to its former status. Magic users need not be punished or left to live their lives in hiding but could be sent to schools to be taught to use magic for good, not evil."

"Is that what you want? To restore magic to the realm?"

"Maybe," she said. "I certainly don't think people should be burned at the stake for being born magic users or learning to use magic."

The prince clapped his hands. A servant, standing at the back of the tent, removed the plates and left them alone. Sertorius stretched out on his bedroll, using the saddle as a pillow, and placed one arm across his chest.

"You have told me how you feel," he said, "and now we have no more secrets between us and can talk freely. I do not want the throne, not at all. I am the youngest prince and have four living brothers ahead of me. I am content to play peacekeeper and ambassador. All my brothers have faults, as do I, but Almaric is the worst. The servants often found dead cats in his room; he likes to kill things. I believe he killed Galinn. He will try to kill Konall, Dinadan, and me, if he is able to find me. Another reason I go to Garridan—it's far from home."

"Sir Roland of the White Stag does not think well of you," she said. "He says you want the throne for yourself. His grand master is from Erindor, the cousin of Duke Fakar, and Fakar is Arundel's best friend. Things have been said to the order about you. These men all claim you want the throne for yourself and will kill anyone who gets in your way."

Sertorius reached out and patted her leg. "You just say that because you were at the Battle of Burnlak," he said, "and so were Sir Roland and his order. It's no wonder you are confused. Find your sword and do with it what you want. I care not."

Taliesin wondered how much she could confide in the prince and found she wanted to tell him everything. "Lord Arundel had Xander arranged for Sir Roland to plant the map on the battlefield," she said. "I was meant to find it. They want me to locate *Ringerike*. But I have no intention of letting anyone have *Ringerike* but me. I won't let Arundel or Lykus, the king or your older brother have the sword. Nor will I give it to you."

"But I don't want *Ringerike*, darling," Sertorius said, yawning. She lay next to him, not touching, but close enough to feel the warmth of his lean body. "Both Arundel and Lykus want to control whomever sits on the Ebony Throne. They say Arundel is a merman, you know, and must sit in salt water five hours a day or he'll grow gills and fins. Lykus, too, is supposedly a monster. Those wolves that attacked us at the Volgate are not wolves at all, but what they call *Wolfen*. They are like werewolves, but both breeds are monsters that parade around in the skins of men in daylight. I'd destroy them all if I were king."

"What about me?"

"There's no reason to have any clans when everything could be departmentalized and run by a secretary or nobleman. Nor is there any reason for you find this sword or lead your own clan. Why not just marry and build a life for yourself? Start today."

"Are you proposing to me?" Taliesin laughed. He didn't. "You're being silly, just like when you were a boy, making things up just to get me to believe in you, only to turn right around and laugh in my face. I'm not falling for it this time, Sertorius. I'm not a little girl."

The prince rolled to his side and lifted his hand to her cheek. His manner was tender and gave her the impression he actually cared, so she let him pull her closer. They lay side-by-side and listened to the sound of a breeze whipping through the palm leaves and pulling at the sides of the tent, the grunting of the camels, and the soft talk of the men. He took her hand and placed their hands across his chest.

"Let's talk about us," he said. "Being with you here is something I never expected to happen. Had I known where to find you, what was really going on, Rosamond, I would have come for you and offered my protection, such as it is. I want you to feel you can trust me, but I can't tell you what to do. I can only win your trust by my actions; that's the only way to judge a man. Marrying me is not such a bad idea, though."

"You're still teasing me," she said. "I can't get involved in this civil war, Sertorius. I just want to find *Ringerike* so it can't be used by someone else. It's the most powerful sword ever created, and I can't let it fall into the hands of the enemy."

"If there are enemies, then you have chosen sides," Sertorius said. "You have chosen to protect the Raven Clan, as you should." He released her hand and pointed at the entrance, a yawn escaping before he could cover his mouth. "Now, since you think it best not to marry me, I must not keep you here any longer. You had best return to your tent, Rosamond. You smell good, and I may take advantage, for you seem willing enough."

"You're not angry with me?"

"Not in the least. I love you," he said. "Sweet dreams, my dear friend."

She rose and left his tent, wondering what manner of man he really was. If she were to judge by his actions, his tactics had been neither seductive nor threatening; he'd asked nothing of her, wanted nothing more than to renew their friendship, and had let her go. However, if he really wanted her to give him the sword and help him claim a throne, winning her friendship and trust, by not toying with her heart or mind, might be part of his strategy. Then again, he might actually be a man of his word and mean precisely what he had said.

Taliesin slipped into her tent, removed the raven feather from her pocket, and placed it on Zarnoc's chest as he slumbered. "Here is your feather," she said. "If your powers are great enough, give wings to our horses, little wizard, and in the morning, we'll fly to the Cave of the Snake God."

* * * * *

Chapter Twenty-Six

Birdsong and a gentle breeze rustling the tent flaps awakened Taliesin. She lay between Jaelle and Wren, who were both still asleep. Rook's soft snores mingled with Zarnoc's, which whistled through his nostrils, and Hawk lay on his stomach, his face buried beneath a pillow, twitching every now and then. She lay quiet for a few minutes and listened to the grumbling camels and the Djarans cooking breakfast over small campfires. She became aware that Wren had opened her violet eyes and stared at her.

"I dreamed about you and Sertorius."

"And?" Taliesin grinned. "Do I want to know?"

"Had you stayed with him last night, he would have formally proposed this morning. I had a clear image of a gold crown on his head and one on yours; both of you were standing in front of a throne with every noble, knight, lady, priest, and magic-user kneeling before you. Do you desire to marry the prince?"

Taliesin wiped the sleep from her eyes. "Propose?" Clearly, she hadn't heard right. "That's madness, Wren. I just met him again...marriage is the last thing on my mind," she said. "I'm flattered, but I would have turned him down. I do not want to marry, nor do I want a crown."

"Roland was in my dreams as well."

"Okay, now I am curious," Taliesin said. Curious because she cared.

Wren pushed herself onto her elbow and kept her voice low so the others weren't awakened by their conversation. "The Eagle legionnaires were in a long line, the mountains at their back, and faced an enemy cloaked in shadow. I do not know who they fought, or if Roland lived or died," she replied. "But I saw a bright light and hundreds of corpses lying face down. One moved, then another, and they turned into giant wolves. Roland was among them."

The implications of the girl's dreams, Roland turned into a *Wolfen* and, least of all, Sertorius' unexpected proposal, left her too troubled to comment. Taliesin slid into her boots and left the tent. She crouched at the water's edge, a light breeze on her face, washed her face and hands, and used a small twig to brush her teeth. The Djarans were cooking, saddling their mounts, or standing around smoking pipes and talking to each other in hushed voices. None seemed interested as Taliesin checked on Thalagar. A snort from the black stallion caused Taliesin to slide her arms around his neck.

"Morning, boy," she said. "I hope you feel like flying today. You're going to be turned into a bird, I believe, unless Zarnoc can attach wings to a horse. Would you like that?"

The horse snorted again and gave a shake of his head. The replacement for Zarnoc's missing mule stood on the other side of Thalagar. The sturdy Brennen roan would suit the wizard far better than a mule; though she knew Zarnoc was fond of Jenny, a stubborn mule seemed dangerous in the air.

"You're up bright and early," Jaelle said, appearing beside her. She held two cups of strong coffee and offered Taliesin one. "The one thing I like about Djarans is their coffee. It's hot, so be careful you don't burn your tongue, Taliesin. The others are packing our gear, so there's no need to rush. Enjoy your coffee."

Taking the cup of coffee, Taliesin took a sip and savored the deep, strong flavor. Jaelle reached into the pocket of her cloak and produced a handful of dates. Not quite what Taliesin wanted to eat, but she was too grateful to turn them down and accepted the fruit.

"The Djarans will travel with Sertorius only as far as the sand stretches and no more," Jaelle said. "Are you certain you do not wish to travel with them? We would be safer with an escort."

"We had one, remember," Taliesin said, sucking the juice out of a date. She gazed at clouds drifting across the sky. "It's better if we travel alone."

"I wish it was just *us*."

Taliesin considered Jaelle at that moment not as a mere companion, but as far more. She'd never been with another woman, but Jaelle was beautiful—her skin tanned to bronze, her gold eyes outlined with black kohl, and her lips painted dark red. The young woman smelled of an exotic blend of oils; if Taliesin were to choose a female companion, it would be her. Roland had offered to be with the two women that night in the gypsy wagon, and it seemed Jaelle still offered an exotic adventure.

Taliesin tapped her cup against the gypsy girl's cup. "You and me, off on adventures together, not worrying about men or their capricious natures," she said. "Only our horses, the wind, the sun, and the sand. I grant you, we have become good friends, Jaelle. More than that?" She shrugged. "Right now, all I want is the Raven Sword. But who knows what the future will bring?"

"At least you take me seriously," Jaelle said.

A loud noise preceded Hawk out of the tent. He was dressed in a ruffled shirt and pants, and he stretched before pulling on his boots and sliding into a leather tunic. He sniffed the air, got a whiff of coffee, and hurried to a small group of nomads to ask for a cup. Taliesin and Jaelle nudged each other, cups held before them, as Zarnoc walked out of the tent, followed by a floating tray with a pot of hot coffee, cream, sugar, several cups, and a pile of magical, warm scones. His complimentary breakfast brought Rook and Wren, still in their sleepwear, stumbling out of the tent to get a cup of coffee. Jaelle grabbed two scones, gave one to Taliesin, a smile on her face, and took a big bite out of the second as if she were starving. The dates had been plentiful and real, not magic-made, but the scone tasted delicious.

"Your friends are more like a family," a deep, resonant voice said from behind Taliesin. She turned as Sertorius approached, dressed in his silver chainmail and the black tunic of the Knights of Chaos. "Good morning, Ravens. Good weather today." He thanked Wren when she offered him a cup of coffee with cream and sugar. "This smells sweet — I like sugar in mine. I've provided a horse for you."

"My mule," Zarnoc said, sounding disgusted. "You traded the prince my mule for a horse for Jaelle. I should have stopped the fat knight with the red hair when I saw him lead my poor Jenny away; I've grown to love that mule. But Jenny would be too afraid to fly, and I don't need her when I can turn into a bird. I still wish I'd been asked so I could have said goodbye; she'll think I don't care, and that's not the case."

"We'll treat her well," replied Sertorius. He smiled over his cup of coffee. "You make a fine cup, Sir Wizard. I've provided supplies for your journey; food and water, enough for five days, at least. I might suggest you join me at Dunatar Castle when you've finished your quest for *Ringerike*. Duke de Boron will welcome you, I'll see to that, as I intend to arrive well ahead of Master Xander. If and when you show up, I hope to have the lizard in a cage."

Rook's eyes widened. "Really? Put that one in a cage, Your Grace, and you shall have my gratitude. I do not like Erindorians, especially not that man, nor the Duke."

"Aren't you from the south?" Sertorius asked, amused. "I could swear you look just like Duke Fakar — same eyes, same nose, same color. Your name is Rook if I remember?"

"It is, but I am from the Isle of Valen, and Islanders do not consider themselves mainlanders. We are under the yoke of the Erindor dukes, but we are not like them. It would be the same as saying Djarans are Ghajarans; nomads and gypsies are similar, but not the same."

"I stand corrected, sir." Sertorius finished his coffee and placed the cup on the floating tray, giving it a quick glance as he waved his hand under it. "Curious, magic. I'll never understand how it works, nor do I want to be near it. The coffee will not turn to mud in my stomach, wizard? It is *real* coffee? It tasted real enough." He winked at Taliesin.

"Magic is real," Zarnoc said. "Real enough to turn you into a lizard, young prince."

"Don't do that!" Laughing, the prince bowed to the wizard. He straightened, glanced upwards, and nodded at the sky. Storm clouds gathered on the western horizon, and the scent of rain was on the breeze. "We're riding into foul weather. Unexpected for this time of year. Be sure to avoid dry riverbeds, which will flood when it starts to rain. See me off, Rosamond?"

"It's Taliesin," Jaelle said, muttering under her breath.

The prince again bowed, and with his hand on Taliesin's arm, he led her from the others. He drew his dagger, and without asking permission, cut a long, red curl from her head, lifted it to his lips, and then placed it carefully within a small black leather bag fastened to his belt. "A memento," he said. "I don't want to forget you again. Duty calls, but I will say goodbye when you are ready to depart...Taliesin." He strode off, his long legs carrying him across the sand, to engage in conversation with his knights.

While packing their gear and saddling the horses, Taliesin noted how eager her friends seemed to be that morning to reach the cave. Jaelle made a fuss over the feisty little roan mare the prince had gifted them. The gypsy girl slid a fancy saddle with tassels onto the mare's back, stroked her soft nose, and whispered into the mare's perked ears. She ignored everyone, made sure the saddle blanket was thick enough and fit comfortably on the horse, and took extra care packing their provisions. "I'm naming her 'Cloud Dancer,'" Jaelle said, "for that's what we'll do when Zarnoc gives her wings and we fly through the sky." Rook and Wren saddled their horses and cast such longing looks at one another that Taliesin knew without a doubt they had consummated their love during the night. They'd been so quiet about it, Taliesin didn't imagine it had been exciting, but it had bonded the pair. When Thalagar was ready, Taliesin walked to Hawk, who stood away from the others, holding the reins of his horse. He had a hand on the hilt of his cutlass, and he gazed at the storm clouds, lost in thought.

"So, what do you think of our chances?" Taliesin asked, shouldering into her friend.

"Reaching the cave before it rains? Or finding the sword before the enemy?" Hawk shrugged. "Depends on how fast winged horses fly, I guess. I'm a little nervous about the idea of flying horses." Taliesin pointed at the wide-open flap of his pants. Horrified, Hawk quickly laced his pants, blushing from ear-to-ear. "Don't want that flapping in the breeze," he said. "I'm rather surprised Prince Sertorius is letting us go. I thought he was after the sword, as well as you. He's not who I thought he was; Roland, and even Zarnoc, painted a rather different picture of the prince."

"I'm surprised, too," she said. "Pleasantly so. He asked us to join him at Dunatar Castle. I'm considering it, but Xander and Roland may be there as well. What do you think?"

"If we live through the day, then ask me again."

Zarnoc shuffled over, still pouting over the loss of his mule. "I have my feather," he said, holding the raven feather. "Won't take but a second to cast a spell on the horses, and don't worry, Hawk, the wings won't disappear once we are aloft. We'll reach the cave around lunchtime, then it's in, out, and on our way to Dunatar Castle for dinner. How's that for a slice of royal, gold pie?"

"It makes me nervous," Hawk said. "You make it sound too easy, and I never said I agreed to go to Dunatar Castle, old man. I thought you said there is a big anaconda that lives inside the cave. I don't like snakes."

"We can manage," Taliesin said.

"Why not take the Maldavians and Djarans with us? We might need help," Hawk said. "Zarnoc, tell her what you told me. Tell her that bit about your magic, how it won't be effective if there are lots of curses and hexes guarding *Ringerike*. Also, what was that last bit, about '*no one has ever returned alive from the Cave of the Snake God.*' My scone is still stuck in my throat. There are only six of us; we may need an army."

Taliesin frowned and shook her head. "I'm not asking him to come with us," she said. "I don't want to involve the prince. Besides, he said he's not interested, so let him get on with his own mission. This was your idea from the very start, Hawk. Don't turn chicken now."

Zarnoc stepped forward, waving his arms in the air while taking large steps on his thin, short legs as he made a wide circle around them. "Bring the horses to me," he said, "but not too close—I don't want to be trampled." He kept walking, although now in a tiny circle, and muttered a spell as the five horses were led forward. A bony finger lifted, and he pointed at each of the animals. A burst of sparkling colors shot from his index finger and struck each horse; in succession, each sported enormous black raven wings, and the saddles changed shape to fit their new forms. Taliesin gazed in awe at Thalagar as the black stallion stepped forward, batted his wings to test them for strength, and lifted off the ground several feet before settling. The rest of the horses also tried out their wings, acting as if it was perfectly natural, stretched them to their full fifteen feet width, and exposed tapering feathers.

With a soft cooing sound, Zarnoc calmed the horses, walking to each one to pat it on the nose. "They'll take to the air just fine," he said. "Nothing to it really."

"If I get killed, I'm going to be upset, Zarnoc," Hawk said as he climbed into the saddle. He placed his legs under the roots of the wings, the tips of his boots pointing at the stirrups, and he fastened a belt across his legs to secure him to the saddle.

"I'm sure your horse will not throw you, Eugene," replied the wizard.

"They call me *Hawk* because I was born to fly!"

Jaelle mounted her winged horse, wearing an expression of great pride and eagerness to be in the sky. A more reserved Rook helped Wren into the saddle, secured her with the safety belt, handed her the bow and quiver of arrows, and went to his horse. He slid his spear into a specially-made sheath on the side of the saddle where it wouldn't stab the wing when in flight and climbed onto his horse. Zarnoc snapped his fingers, turned into a large raven, flew to Jaelle, and landed on her shoulder. The gypsy girl wore a pleased expression at having been chosen to provide a perch for the wizard.

"Nicely done," Sertorius said. "We'd reach Dunatar Castle a great deal sooner if our horses had wings."

"I'd need a basketful of feathers to do that," Zarnoc said, letting out a squawk. He flew into the air and circled around the camp, waiting for the group to follow.

Taliesin walked to Thalagar as Sertorius followed, and slid her hands over a giant wing. The horse tossed his head and snorted when the prince took the reins. When she reached for them, her hand brushed across his, and his eyes filled with emotion. Taliesin saw regret, longing, desire, and concern in the cobalt depths. She was able to scrutinize his face in broad daylight; almost too handsome, a woman's beauty. Not a blemish or even a mole marred his skin.

"I feel I should accompany you," the prince said as his manicured fingers slid along her arm. "Leaving such a diffi- cult quest to a woman...."

"Leave my gender out of this, Your Grace. I can do what- ever a man can do."

"Well, it's not a man I want to kiss," Sertorius replied. "May I?"

Offering her cheek, the prince leaned in and stole a kiss from her lips. Taliesin heard Hawk snicker and put her hand up to keep Sertorius away. In the distance, thunder rumbled, and a patch of lightning zigzagged across the sky. She tied the reins together and tossed them over Thalagar's head, then bumped into the prince, grinned, and slid into the unusual saddle. The stallion stomped his hoof and snorted as she lifted the reins.

The prince nodded toward the west. "The storm is moving in fast," he said. "Be careful, Rosamond. None have ever re- turned from the Cave of the Snake God, and I would see you again."

"*We* will," Taliesin said. "Don't worry."

Sir Morgrave approached. "I hate to interrupt, Your Grace, but if we are to stay ahead of the storm, we must leave now."

"Yes, yes, of course. I'll be there directly." Sertorius gazed at Taliesin and flashed his white teeth. "The invitation to join me at Dunatar Castle still stands, my lady. I hope you will not disappoint me. I will be waiting." He moved out of the way.

Taliesin cast one final look at the handsome prince as she fastened the belt across her legs and shouted, "*Taveachi!*"

Thalagar launched himself into the sky as if he'd been flying since he was a colt, and with the other horses joining him, they flew over the oasis. Flapping his wings, the black stallion soared upwards, gaining altitude and creating an air current that whipped Taliesin's hair about and made her grip the saddle horn, even though she was securely braced in the saddle. Her heart raced as the figures below turned into ants scurrying on the sand. Zarnoc, in his guise of a large raven, appeared beside her and had no problem flying through the air as fast as the winged horses. Talking was impossible when flying, and shouting was no better. Taliesin tried but gave up after Hawk ignored her as he flew by them all. As she veered to the northeast, trailed by Jaelle, Rook, Wren, and Zarnoc, she glanced over her shoulder and saw Hawk turning in their direction, leaning low as his horse chased after the flock.

Flying in a V formation, they kept ahead and below the lead storm clouds that crept across the horizon. Thalagar excelled at flying, and Taliesin felt at peace with the entire world while she flew through the sky. They covered miles in a short time and watched as tiny villages and wild herds of camels appeared and disappeared below, while the sand dunes resembled a large sea that stretched on forever. Taliesin kept count of the oases as they passed; the last one seen on the map was but a few miles from the cave, and she noticed unmoving figures lying along the water's edge, fifty feet below. Buzzards tore into the dead flesh and gorged on what had once been a patrol of knights. More than that she could not tell, and she urged her horse higher into the sky and resumed her leadership position.

As the late afternoon came upon them, they saw giant red stones poking out of the sand. Large plates of rocks, piled on top of one another like sheets of icing on a layered cake, were parted in the middle as if sliced open and created a narrow gorge with rock walls eroded by time. Five large, winged shadows and one tiny shadow fell upon the stones below and glided along to the left side of the gorge as the horses and bird descended. Taliesin, ahead of the others, found a good spot to land and dismounted as soon as she could. The rest of the riders landed, climbed from their saddles, and placed the reins under the rocks so the horses wouldn't fly off.

Taliesin left Thalagar to roam, knowing he wouldn't fly away, and fruitlessly searched the sky for Zarnoc. She went to the side of the gorge and looked over the steep side at a drop of some one hundred feet. The river that created the ravine had long since dried out; the only remaining sign of it was some sedimentary rocks that stood like stalagmites from the river bed. On closer inspection, she realized some type of curious fungus spread from out of the wall beneath her and in either direction.

"Careful," Zarnoc shouted, overhead. Rocks crumbled beneath Taliesin's feet, and she quickly stepped away from the edge, grateful the sheet of rock had not broken off with her on it. Zarnoc landed beside her and morphed into a small man dressed in Djaran garb, complete with a short sword at his side. "It's obvious you don't listen well," he said. "You need to be careful; one slip, and you're dead."

Taliesin glanced over the edge of the cliff. "Did you find the cave?"

"No, but it is close," Zarnoc said. "There is powerful magic being used here. If I get too near, my powers will be rendered useless, and I'd plummet to my death; I dare not risk flight into the ravine. Get the map and see what it says."

Reaching into the side of her jerkin, Taliesin pulled out the rolled map, squatted on her haunches, and spread it out over the ground. Zarnoc's shadow blocked her view, but when he stepped away, she saw not a map but a schematic of the cave. Within the cave were twists and turns that led to cut-offs and dead ends. One route went through several large chambers until it opened into a large vault where the sword was kept.

"I didn't expect the map to show us the interior," Taliesin said. "This is very helpful."

"That's why they call it a Deceiver's Map," Zarnoc said. "Give up and stop looking, and you miss the good stuff. The cave is but a half-mile on your left and one hundred feet below. There's a good-sized temple inside." He pointed at the diagram. "Big pillars. Many secret rooms. A giant statue of a snake wrapped around a sword. Looks like an altar of some kind beneath the sword. Interesting...."

"It reminds me of the Royal Temple," Taliesin said. "Same type of entrance, with stairs coming into a large chamber. These smaller figures are statues. Only one way in or out." She rolled the map. "If there are enchantments like you said, we'd better not fly down there. We can leave the horses here and climb down." She placed her hand on his shoulder. "I know you want to help, Zarnoc, but you won't do us any good inside the cave. Without your magic, you will require protection, and it would be better if you guarded the horses."

"Never mind about my feelings," Zarnoc said. His voice dripped with sarcasm. "I'm only an old man without my powers, and good only to tend to the horses."

Taliesin leaned over and kissed the top of his head. "That's not how I mean it, dear friend. I need you to guard our backs. But you won't be alone." She watched the group wander toward them. "I've decided to leave Wren with you."

The petite girl looked worn out as she pulled her hood over her head and sought shade behind a large boulder. She spread out a blanket and laid on it, an arm over her eyes, and Zarnoc drifted toward her. Hawk, Rook, and Jaelle removed their cloaks, set them aside, and started unloading weapons and gear. A large coil of rope was dropped at Taliesin's feet.

"We have enough rope to reach the bottom," Hawk said. "But there won't be any light inside the cave, so we'll need torches. Rook and I will look around for branches. The cloaks can be torn into strips, and we can use some of Jaelle's perfume to douse them, so they'll ignite."

"Sounds good," Taliesin said.

The two young men went to find wood, and Jaelle joined Wren and Zarnoc. Though exhausted and fighting off a headache, Wren helped cut the cloaks into strips. Taliesin pulled Jaelle's backpack off her horse, brought it to the group, and knelt beside them in the shade.

"King Korax is said to be buried inside," Zarnoc said. "I should like to see him again—we were very good friends. Korax loved to go hawking. We'd hike through the hills for hours, watching our hawks fly. Those were the days."

"You never mentioned you actually knew him," Taliesin said. "What about the snake god? Is the creature real or not?"

Zarnoc cleared his throat when he caught her glaring at him. "Did I not tell you I knew the Raven King? Oh dear. That's a long story for another time. As for the snake god, he was real enough. Alas, I can't say which of the Lorians placed spells over this place, but I can tell you the Snake Cult thrived here for a long time before the Royal Army killed them and sealed the cave. The Snake Cult was feared by all. Their dark magic attracted dark creatures, of that I am certain."

The failure of Zarnoc to mention he'd personally known Korax, Lykus, and Arundel in their youth, and that they were all very old, troubled Taliesin, but not as much as his inability to tell her what type of dark magic had been used to protect both the Raven King and the Raven Sword. Taliesin withheld her retort as Hawk and Rook returned, carrying a stack of old spears with rusted heads. While the two cut the spears into manageable lengths, Wren surrendered to exhaustion and lay down. Taliesin helped tie the bits of cloth around the spearheads. Jaelle poured her perfume over the cloth, making the air reek, and Hawk gathered the torches together.

"We might as well climb down here," Jaelle said. "Rappelling over a cliff is harder than it looks. Someone strong will have to stay behind and make sure the rope is secured. Zarnoc might be able to handle it, but the logical choice is Rook; he's the biggest and strongest. If there are no objections, I'll go first, then Taliesin and Hawk."

Taliesin looked for Rook, but he had vanished.

Frowning deeper than usual, Hawk glanced toward the ravine. "It will be difficult for just three of us to move aside rocks at the entrance to get inside that tomb," he said. "We're going to need Rook with us in case we run into trouble. I can't be expected to protect everyone. Zarnoc can manage the rope; he's stronger than he looks."

"I really am," the wizard said. "Have no fear."

Rook reappeared at that moment and threw something that looked like a large jawbone onto the ground. "Wolfmen," he said, pointing at the sharp teeth. "I found more than skeletons; there are quite a few fresh corpses here. Maybe you should all take a look before you go."

"This is odd. Why didn't the Wolfman change into a man? This is the jaw of a giant wolf," Hawk said.

"Maybe it's not a Wolfman," Taliesin said.

Taliesin, Hawk, and Jaelle followed Rook along the cliff's edge to a colossal pile of bones of all types, from many ages past, left to bleach in the sun. Most were so old they crumbled to dust when Taliesin stepped on them, but just beyond the mound was a collection of rotting animal and human corpses that looked recently gnawed on. Rook dug through the bodies with his spear and found a tattered Fregian banner. He handed the flag to Taliesin, who examined the material.

"This has been lying here for several weeks. I wonder why Duke Hrothgar's men came here," Taliesin said. "They certainly didn't need the Deceiver's Map to reach the cave. Nor did any of these other men; they knew right where to go. I'm impressed."

"The Eagle Clan has been here as well," Hawk said, holding the tatters of a dark gold cloak. He looked unhappier than he had been a few moments before. "Zarnoc said there were three Deceiver's Maps still in existence. Any sorcerer could have used the map to make copies of the trail to the cave. Roland said he'd learned magic from a Fregian knight, so I assume his order knows a bit about magic. Little good it did any of these men."

"There're more bodies in the ravine." Jaelle knelt on one knee and gazed over the side of the cliff. "Lots of them, too. They're fresh. How long do you think they'd been here, Taliesin? A few days? A few weeks?"

Taliesin joined her and looked over the edge, now able to see hundreds of bodies littering the ravine. Knights and soldiers in tunics from all over the realm lay beside nomads and the carcasses of horses and camels alike. Ancient bones lay scattered around them. Men had apparently been coming to the ravine for ages, and they had made it no further than where the group now stood.

"Something caught those men by surprise," Taliesin said. "I don't think it was Wolfmen; they have no reason to guard this place. The way the bodies are stacked looks like these men were fighting in small groups before they were pushed over the cliff. They died when they hit the ground, that's why their bodies are so twisted and stacked that way. Any predator or scavenger could have been eating the dead. The jawbone Rook found is probably one of them."

The wind picked up, and the sky turned grayer. The smell of rain hung heavy in the air. "We could come back tomorrow," Hawk said. "If we're stuck over there once it starts raining, we'll be washed away in a flash flood."

Jaelle placed her hands over her nose. "The stench is overpowering," she said, gagging. "I don't know how your clan makes a living scavenging."

"I could go in Hawk's place," Rook said. "I am not afraid. Hawk can stay and make sure the rope is held firm."

"I didn't say I was afraid, brother," Hawk countered. "But I know a suicide mission when I see one. Forget I ever said anything about wanting to be a rich man before I die. I didn't mean it. Let's go to Dunatar Castle and book passage on a ship. I don't care where we go, as long as it's far away from this cursed place."

Taliesin walked to their gear. She picked up the end of the rope and looked for a place to tie it off; aware her friends were standing idly by watching her. Light droplets of rain fell from the sky, and the crackle of thunder in the far-off distance rumbled through the ravine. As she started toward a boulder, lightning struck on the far side of the ravine, making her hair stand on end; it nearly deafened her with its thunderclap.

"Can we go now?" Hawk asked.

"Yes," Taliesin said. "Load everything, and let's find somewhere else to make camp. We'll return after the storm passes."

At Wren's cry, Rook and Jaelle ran to her. Zarnoc was trying to rouse the girl but was having little luck.

"You must pick her up, Rook, and carry her on your horse," Zarnoc said.

Rook lifted Wren into his arms and walked to his horse. Jaelle assisted as he climbed into the saddle, and she adjusted the belt to fasten both Wren and Rook securely in place before they took off. Another streak of lightning zigzagged across the sky as Jaelle mounted her own horse and joined the couple in flight. With a flap of his arms, Zarnoc turned into a raven and circled overhead. Hawk climbed into his saddle and wasted no time flying into the air and joining the group.

Raindrops hit Taliesin's cheeks. She went around Thalagar and climbed into the saddle as he held his wings out. As she fiddled with the safety buckle, trying to secure the latch, the horse let out a warning snort as a large, furry body slammed against her. Thalagar flew upwards, but Taliesin tumbled out of the saddle, her arms locked around a huge body as they rolled and twisted across the ground, halting at the edge of the cliff. A giant wolf stood on top of her and snarled, its frothing jaws wide open. With a savage cry, Taliesin placed her hands against its chest and sent it flying over the side of the cliff. She quickly stood and drew *Wolf Killer*, hoping her friends would return, but either they hadn't noticed she wasn't on her horse, or they were too frightened to come back.

A crackle of thunder brought a downpour and the arrival of the rest of the Wolf Pack. Wolfmen in partial states of transformation rose from behind the red rocks. Big, hairy, fanged creatures oozing drool appeared around Taliesin as she felt a strange electrical current in the air. She glanced at her sword as a bright blue light struck the tip. The bolt of lightning knocked the weapon from her grip and sent her spiraling through the air into the onrushing creatures.

The silver sword flew upwards, then fell point downwards and sank deep into a boulder. A spray of electrical discharge shot out of the weapon and struck the creatures as Taliesin threw her hands over her head. The Wolfmen, yelping loudly and with singed and smoking fur, ran for cover. Taliesin gazed at the sword sticking out of the rock, unaware something approached from behind, until she felt sharp fangs sink into her shoulder. Poison spread through her veins, and with a loud scream, she toppled, writhing in pain, and lost consciousness.

* * * * *

Chapter Twenty-Seven

Taliesin felt a throbbing pain in her skull as she awakened. Her shoulder ached where she'd been bitten, as did many other places where fangs had sunk into her skin. A quick examination alerted her to the gravity of the situation. Bite marks covered her arms and legs, and the wounds burned as if laced with salt. The monsters had *turned* her instead of eating her; which, she realized, called for an ounce of gratitude, but she felt only hatred for her enemy.

She lay at the far end of a large cave. Around her slept giant wolves that growled in their sleep, twitched, turned, and raised hind legs to scratch at fleas. The males curled around one another as littermates, or lay sprawled on their backs, legs in the air, and whimpering in their dreams.

She winced at the intense pain as she struggled to lift her head and gaze toward the entrance. It was raining with such violence a sheet of water covered the cave entrance with the force of a waterfall. A lone man in a black fur cape stood at the entrance and looked out. Behind him, the flames of a campfire snapped and sputtered from the touch of the rain. The man sensed she'd awakened and turned. Slanted eyes changed from yellow to a vibrant green, and even in the dark, she recognized the captain of the Wolf Pack.

"They will not bite," Wolfgar said, his voice carrying to her. "You are one of us now."

Pushing herself off the ground, Taliesin held her hand over her wounded shoulder; through the torn material she could feel the gash was nearly healed. A toothy smile appeared on Wolfgar's face as she limped toward him, walking over the sleeping wolves that filled the cave, and tried to count them. At least two hundred forms slept on the ground. She stopped counting and wondered where they came from or if their ranks had grown along the way. The smile remained on Wolfgar's face as he watched her stretch out her hands to cup water from the waterfall and splash it on her face and neck. It was cold and refreshing. She stuck her head into the heavy flow, gazed at a raging river one hundred feet below, and considered jumping and letting the water take her away. A hand grabbed her arm, as if the captain had read her thoughts, and he pulled her away from the edge and to the fire.

"A good sleep is what you need. When you rise again, you will be fully *Wolfen*."

"Did your pack kill those men I found on the ridge and in the ravine?" It was the first question that came to her mind. She'd already been cursed — what was the use of asking about the details of her new, hellish life? Hawk had been right to get her friends to leave when they had, or they would have been slaughtered.

"Only the Fregians," Wolfgar said. "I sent scouts ahead. They arrived to find the Fregians looking for the Cave of the Snake God. My men were killed as well. Something else killed them, something that lives in the ravine. Pity your friend Sir Roland and the Eagle legionnaires were not discouraged by our attack and continue to ride this way. There are fewer of them now. This time, when they arrive, I will kill them."

"And my friends? They got away?"

Wolfgar nodded. "Yes," he said. "I had no need to kill the last of the Raven Clan." A full blond beard grew on his angular jaw. He was naked beneath the cloak, smooth-muscled, and hard as a rock. "Are you afraid of me?" he asked, his voice rough and deep.

"I am," Taliesin admitted. "What prisoner is not afraid of her captor? You and your kind are frightening; I would rather kill myself than be one of your pack."

Wolfgar turned away from her and sniffed the air. His green eyes were shadowed under thick black eyebrows, and his long blond hair hung in tangles. His skin and cloak were covered with mud and dried blood that was not his own. Despite the journey through Maldavia, Aldagar, and the Garridan desert, the captain had a healthy glow, suggesting he was well-fed. He feeds on humans, she told herself, gazing at the crackling flames. Rumbling laughter that ended with a snarl rose from his throat. Taliesin reached for her sword, only to remember it had flown out of her hand and lodged into a large boulder. She turned toward Wolfgar and shuddered as she found him changing; his ears grew long and furry, and a muzzle emerged and lengthened, contorting his features. Wolfgar touched his muzzle, and his features returned to human.

"Everyone is afraid of our kind," Wolfgar said, kicking at the logs with a barefoot. "The Ghajaran has made it their life's mission to kill my people, and so we hunt them when we have the time. I do not blame you for being afraid, Taliesin. A wolf is a savage beast. It is an animal, and it kills without remorse or guilt. Being *Wolfen* is different—we retain our human intelligence even when changing or in full wolf form. Legends say our kind turn only at a full moon, one night a month; on that night, we hunt and kill humans. It's not true. We kill whenever we want, day or night; we change whenever we want, day or night, but we feel regret or guilt like any normal human. You are blessed by Ragnal, truly, Taliesin. I have lived a very long time, and now you will outlive your friends, their children, and their grandchildren. We pray to Ragnal, the god of war, for a reason. Ragnal is protected by two giant wolves, Cano and his son Varg, whose mother was a woman. We *Wolfen* are from the lineage of Varg, able to turn into half-things and wolves, just as he does."

Taliesin didn't need a reminder; she knew of the bloodthirsty god and his two evil wolves. Osprey had often talked about *Varguld*, the Age of the Wolf, the end of the world when evil would reign unchecked. She thought of Lykus, the first of the Wolf Clan, and wondered if he'd been Varg's son, or if it were only legend, and the gods didn't even exist. Navenna certainly hadn't protected her, despite her prayers.

"But you...you are a *Sha'tar*," Wolfgar said. "You can be as powerful as the new gods if you so choose, and now that you are *Wolfen*, it is only a matter of time before Varg will come out of his cave at the center of the world to welcome you to our clan."

"That doesn't sound pleasant. I'd rather not meet him."

"No?" he said, laughing. "But how could he resist coming from Mt. Helos to meet the one and only living *Sha'tar*? Perhaps he will choose to breed with you; such a child would have godly powers. Can you imagine? You'd be treated like a queen in our clan, and your child might even be given a clan of his own to lead. Now come. You must eat and regain your strength. There is much yet to do before we head east to join Prince Almaric and Master Phelon."

The mention of Chief Lykus's son, Phelon, made her wonder if he'd object to such a child being born. If Lykus *was* a thousand years old and had yet to turn over the leadership of the Wolf Pack to Phelon, then she doubted any rival would be tolerated or even allowed to live. A large paw of a hand closed around her elbow and guided Taliesin through the sleeping wolves to a section of the cavern where a rabbit was roasting on a spit over another fire, previously unnoticed. One end of the spit lay in the dirt, the rabbit was uncooked on that side, while the other part had burned black and crispy. Wolfgar held the raw section of rabbit and removed the carcass from the spit. He motioned for Taliesin to sit. She obeyed, and he unceremoniously dropped the rabbit at her feet. While she picked at the blackened end, he retrieved a flask lying on the ground and brought it to her. The burnt meat stuck in her throat. "Awful," Taliesin gagged, spitting out the rabbit. "Tastes just awful." She opened the flask and took a drink. Red, heavy wine, so thick it was almost syrup, poured into her mouth. Wolfgar chuckled as Taliesin kept drinking, the sound more animal than human. His eyes kept turning from gold to green, wolf to human, and the sight greatly disturbed her. Taliesin drained the flask, dropped it to the ground, and grabbed the rabbit again. She sank her teeth into the raw section; it was tender, delicious, and melted in her mouth, and, when she'd eaten it all, she belched.

"The change is already upon you," Wolfgar said. "It is a pity you lost your silver sword. You must leave it, and the silver you carry, behind, Taliesin. The pain of silver touching your body is worse than the scorching from a fire." He caressed her face. "And I would spare you that pain. Together, we will find *Ringerike* and..."

Taliesin thrust his hand aside. "I won't help you find the sword," she said, a fierce temper upon her. She still wore her sword belt, and the pouch containing the map and the key was still in her possession. The Wolfmen apparently hadn't searched her, and they felt confident, now that she was infected, that she'd help them retrieve *Ringerike*. She'd rather die than help them or Prince Almaric. "I no more want to be a wolf than I want to help your leader gain a throne," she said, feeling sick to her stomach. Waving Wolfgar off, she turned her head and retched. The raw meat she'd hardly chewed came from her roiling guts and splattered onto the ground.

"How do you feel?" Wolfgar asked, placing a hand on her arm to steady her.

"Awful."

Wolfgar knelt beside her and watched her face. "It's obvious you know little of the legend of our clan, or would you feel honored to have been chosen to join us," he said. "Varg was a halfling, never able to turn into a wolf or a human; his form was always stuck between the two. Like his father, he mated with a woman, and their son, Caninus, the first *Wolfen*, was able to turn human or wolf at will. The Wolf Clan did not come to power until led by Lykus, a decedent of Caninus. Once Almaric is crowned king, he has promised to make Lykus a duke and give us lands of our own. You will make this possible, Taliesin, by bringing *Ringerike* to the true king."

"Are you sure Almaric can be trusted?" Taliesin asked, thinking the captain mad.

"Chief Lykus has promised Almaric to turn him into one of us," he said, "once he has the throne. What man does not lust for immortality?" He lifted his arms and slowly pivoted. "I was turned two hundred years ago but look the same as I did on that day near the town of Riordan when I stumbled upon a black wolf hunting a white stag. One bite was all it took. Phelon, son of Chief Lykus, turned me, and when asked to join his clan, I was happy to do so. I left a wife and three children behind, long since dead, and now you will outlive your own friends and never age. You'll always look just as you do now."

"What I am, is cursed!"

Wolfgar was standing so close it was impossible not to smell his strong body odor—the same wet-dog scent shared by every Wolfman in the cave. He took a step from her and flung open his cloak, the transformation already upon him, and hair sprouted over every inch of skin. His legs grew long and bent oddly at the knees as his torso lengthened, his shoulders hunched over, and claws hung from the ends of his fingers. Terrified and unsure of what he meant to do, she backed against the cave wall as the creature loomed above her. His jaw was open, exposing long rows of fangs. She turned aside and trembled as his head lowered and a rough, long, red tongue slid across her forehead. Her reaction was involuntary; she kicked him between his furry legs, slid under his outstretched arms, and ran toward the exit of the cave.

A cry of rage woke the other Wolfmen, and they pursued as she scrambled over wet rocks and slipped and slid over the escarpment. The roar from the waterfall and the rushing river below drowned out the echoing howls inside the cave. She worked her way to an ancient stairway cut into the rock and reached the top of the cliff no more than ten feet from the dead Fregian knights and soldiers. Unsure where to go or where to hide, she dove into the midst of the rotting bodies and held her breath as the Wolfmen scrambled over and around the dead, searching for her among the rocks. The loud howls and snarls sounded further away, but she remained among the bodies, the ripe stench filling her nostrils as maggots wriggled across her face and closed mouth.

"Where is she, Udolf?" Wolfgar's voice carried to her. He was twenty yards away, yet she clearly heard him. "One bite should have been enough to turn her. Yet, despite having been bitten numerous times, the Raven Mistress remains human. Master Phelon will not be pleased if she's escaped us yet again—I dare not fail him."

"Perhaps she doubled back," the lieutenant said, in a gruff voice. He stood next to the pile of bodies where Taliesin lay, close enough she could see his bare, dirty legs; he'd not yet turned. "The rain washes away her scent, making it difficult to detect her. Yet, I see no footprints, nor hear the sound of her running."

She heard Wolfgar sniffing the air. Every muscle stiffened as she prayed to Navenna he'd not notice her, that he'd move on to search for her elsewhere, and she'd be able to escape. A scream caught in her throat as she spotted Wolfgar's glowing, amber eyes right above her.

"I see you, little raven," he said with a snarl.

Hands started removing the bodies. The moment she was spotted, Taliesin scrambled over the bodies, choking on the stench as she felt soft innards squishing beneath her hands and feet. Wolfgar and Udolf, in human form, reached out and tried to grab her. Breathing hard, her heart racing, she scrambled over the pile of corpses. Her fingers curled around a broken spear that lay on the body of a Fregian knight, and she spun and stabbed a dark form behind her. Udolf let out a grunt of pain and toppled to his side, holding the spear that protruded from his stomach. Wolfgar leaped onto the bodies, his hand raised, and a hard blow knocked her off her feet. She tumbled to the ground and screamed as he jumped on her and grabbed at her with clawed hands. She fought and tried to break free.

"You killed my family!" Taliesin shouted. "Your father and your clan ate Osprey and turned the twins into monsters. I'll never help you! Never!"

Wolfgar's mouth pressed against her ear. "Yes, you will, or I'll hunt down your friends and let my men roast them over a fire until they are burned to a crisp. Then we will hunt Sir Roland and Prince Sertorius and eat them while they beg for mercy."

"Zarnoc will stop you! He is a powerful wizard and can turn you into worms!"

"I fear no wizard," Wolfgar said. He pinned her arms to the ground as rain pelted his back. He leaned over her, blocking the raindrops from hitting her face. Large, dark forms crept around them and moved closer. The snarls and growls died out. "There is no escape, Taliesin. You will return to the cave and show me on the map where we can find *Ringerike*. As soon as the rain lets up, we will go to the Cave of the Snake God and retrieve the sword; then you will come with us to meet Prince Almaric."

Taliesin was dragged into the cave and thrown to the ground, close to a fire. The Wolfmen entered the cave, and, wrapped in cloaks, watched as Udolf took her by the arms and held her still. Wolfgar knelt, slid his hands along her back and across her breasts, unfastened her belt, and took her pouch. Udolf released her with a snarl and gave her a hard slap to the side of her head, before moving to the opposite side of the fire. He threw wood onto the blaze and sparked it to life, while outside the rain slowed to a drizzle.

Wolfgar sat beside Taliesin and handed her the pouch. Feeling like she had no choice, she opened the bag, removed the Deceiver's Map, and willed it to turn into a board. The map opened on her lap and showed their position in the cave, showed the ravine, and then revealed the dukedom of Thule where Prince Almaric was encamped with a massive army.

"What do you see?" Wolfgar asked. He sat cross-legged beside her and peered at the map. "I see nothing, but I am not a warlord or wizard. What does the map show you?"

"Prince Almaric and his army," she said.

"Try again," he insisted. "Tell the map to show you the cave."

Taliesin spread her hand across the map. Colors swirled about, formed landscapes and bodies of water, revealed her location to be not more than one hundred feet from where she'd been taken captive, and showed the route to the Cave of the Snake God. As she stared at the map, the interior of the cave appeared as it had before and outlined the temple built within. Steps led to a large chamber with a statue of a six-headed snake that stood over forty feet tall; in one of its jaws was *Ringerike*.

"The cave isn't far from here," she said. "The sword is in a chamber at the back of the cave." She also saw a number of clearly-marked traps and flags warning of the chambers to avoid; that information she withheld. "The door to the cave is sealed by a rock slide. It will take all of your men to clear away the stones, but we still need a key to get inside."

"You have this key?" Wolfgar questioned. "What else is in your pouch?" He grabbed it from her and dumped the contents onto the ground. A gold medallion, a necklace of blue beads with a broken clasp, a small knife, several jade stones she'd collected on the way, a comb, a leather string, twelve gold coins, and a large sapphire were all examined by the captain. He held the medallion, and his finger glided over the image of a snake. "This is the key, isn't it? Don't lie to me, or I may decide to cut off a finger or two. They will regrow, but it will be painful. I will do far worse if you think you can outwit me, Raven Mistress. Far worse."

"Yes, it's the key," Taliesin said. "But you shouldn't touch it. It's magical and could hurt you." He instantly dropped the medallion. She placed everything, except the map, into the pouch. "I think I see something else of importance." She slid her finger across the map and thought of her friends. They were camped a mile from the ravine. She thought of Sertorius and saw a tiny Maldavian flag with a caravan headed west to Dunatar Castle on the eastern coastline. But the person she really wanted to find was Roland. Her heart leaped in her chest as a tiny white stag and a gold eagle appeared, headed toward the ravine; Roland and Xander were no more than ten miles to the east.

"What else do you see?" Wolfgar demanded.

"It's a very strange map. It shows me many things." Her mouth felt dry. Taliesin licked her lips and looked for a flask of water or wine. Wolfgar sensed what she wanted and turned toward Udolf, who fetched a flask and brought it to her. "Thanks," she said, taking off the cap and grimacing as she swallowed the thick, syrupy wine. It tasted horrible but quenched her thirst. "We'll need ropes to descend into the ravine and to reach the top of the statue. Do you have ropes?"

"We have backpacks we wear when in wolf form," Wolfgar said. "There is enough rope at our disposal. What about the Eagle legionnaires? Do you see them?"

She nodded and lied. "Twenty miles to the east. The desert has flooded, and they must cross a river to reach us. It will take them a day, maybe more, to do so."

Wolfgar growled. "Very well," he said. "But you had better be telling the truth." He reached out and placed his large hand on her thigh as she folded the map and stuffed it into the pouch. He allowed her to fasten the belt around her waist. "It will be dawn soon, and the rain is letting up. Udolf, see if the river in the ravine has abated. As soon as it's dry enough, get the ropes so we can rappel down the canyon wall."

The lieutenant went to the entrance and looked out. The Wolfmen went to the far side of the cave and retrieved their backpacks, which were fastened onto a harness designed to fit the body of a large wolf. Ropes and small bags of food were taken out of the packs, and the men sat and ate, talking in soft whispers. One brought Wolfgar his cloak, and he put it around his shoulders. He wasn't cold, none of them were, but at least he had the decency to cover his hairy genitals and block his musky odor. He lay beside the fire, rested his head on his arm, and closed his eyes.

Taliesin was tempted to ask him why she hadn't changed yet, what was keeping her from turning *Wolfen*. Perhaps it was her magic. Her senses had sharpened; she could see every hair on Wolfgar's chest and the rippling of his skin when the breeze blew across his body, and she could smell the meatiness of his breath. She could see everything in the cave and was even able to discern quartz and lines of gold running through the wall. Her nose picked up the odor of decaying flesh, but this information she also withheld, not wanting to tell the captain anything more than he needed to know.

With a predator's yawn, Wolfgar shifted his position, tossed a side of his robe out, and motioned her to lie beside him. "I suggest you stay close to me," he said, without opening his eyes. "If you need to relieve yourself, wake me, and I will take you out. Udolf's injury has healed, but you should not do anything to give him reason to hurt you."

Taliesin lay beside the captain, aware of the heat radiating from his body; the Wolfmen seemed to be hot-blooded. She pressed against him, miserable in her wet clothes, but was not willing to remove them so they could dry. He snuggled behind her, spooning, and she caught a whiff of his primal body odor. She allowed herself to shut her eyes and, wishing it were Roland she was lying next to, soon fell asleep.

* * * * *

Chapter Twenty-Eight

Once it was daylight, the Wolf Pack began removing the boulders and other rocks that blocked the entrance to the Cave of the Snake God. The monstrous creatures, transformed into the juxtaposition between man and wolf, proved incredibly strong and, stranger yet, able to communicate. Their rugged voices echoed through the ravine, though many growled and snapped at one another as the day grew hotter. Wolfgar, the only *Wolfen* in human form and dressed in armor, ordered the largest stones used to build a dam on either side of the entrance, so if it rained again, the floodwaters would be kept from flowing into the temple. The rock wall grew larger and higher. His lieutenant, Udolf, flanked him, a massive gray beast on hind legs that barked every order given by Wolfgar in a voice twice as loud and threatening.

Within the hour, an entryway with six giant pillars, cracked and chipped but still standing, was revealed, and Wolfgar shouted for Taliesin to join him at the entrance. The large door was engraved with images of giant snakes and Lorian priests of the Snake Cult standing and kneeling; some being devoured and some mating with the snakes in a profane, twisted ritual. She sensed a strange, pulsating evil in the air; dark magic protected the door. She removed the medallion from the leather pouch, searched for a lock, and after a few moments, found a circular indentation on the right side of the door. The medallion fit snugly and, seen only by her, the enchantments on the door shimmered as it opened inwards with a groan.

"Keep close to me, Taliesin," Wolfgar said. "Get the map and warn of us any traps. I smell death inside this cave; we must be careful."

Taliesin took the medallion out of the door and followed the men inside. She placed the key inside her pouch, removed the Deceiver's Map, opened it wide, and found the blueprints of the temple. A brightly-glowing path led all the way to *Ringerike*.

Wolfgar waited beside her. He held a lit torch and a longsword but seemed reluctant to enter. His eyes glowed bright amber, and his ears had turned long and covered with fur. The others remained in *Wolfen* form.

"Do you want me to lead the way?" Taliesin asked. She glanced at the map. "The hallway narrows in thirty feet, so we'll have to walk in single file. It'll be cramped, too. How many are coming with us? If we run into trouble, I want to be able to get out the door."

"Udolf and ten of my best fighters, but I'll lead. This way, lads." Wolfgar held the torch in front of him and entered the tunnel. He walked ahead of Taliesin, who was followed by Udolf and his men. "Don't fall behind, and don't touch *anything* unless the Raven Mistress says it's safe."

"In here, nothing is safe," replied Taliesin.

Within the tunnel, the torches cast swaying shadows upon the walls as a draft blew on the flames, producing a cloud of black smoke that seemed to go from torch to torch. Ghostly voices drifted to them, coming from the interior. Taliesin kept close to the broad-shouldered captain and carried only the map; no torch or weapon. They walked through a large circular chamber carved out of the red limestone. The room had a high ceiling and eight mysterious doors, but the map only showed one.

The artisans who built the temple had created a network of smaller rooms and niches that led away from the main corridor and deeper into the rock. Although sealed for centuries and untouched by living creatures, the cave still retained a feeling of profound sacredness; the torches illuminated paintings depicting the carnal worship of the Snake God. The ceiling was over fifty feet above them and painted with colorful scenes of nude Lorian fairy-folk, both men and women, swimming with snakes in a large river.

"The Snake Cult of Chu'Alagu was killed and buried inside this cave by King Titus Draconus, son of Tarquin Draconus," Taliesin said, hoping one of the Wolfmen knew more than she and would volunteer information. "Do you know much about history, Wolfgar? Did you know King Korax was Lorian, too? The Raven Clan is descendent from the Lorians, which is why the Raven Sword is so important to my clan and why I wanted to find it in the first place."

Wolfgar glanced over his armored shoulder. "Just read your map and tell me if there is a trap, or if I'm making a wrong turn," he replied. "I care not about history or past events. Dead memories mean nothing to me, nor does the return of the Raven Clan."

"I just thought it interesting this place was built by fairy-folk. When I was a little girl, I always thought fairies were little, winged creatures that lived in flowers."

Taliesin thought about Zarnoc and his failure to mention that the Lorians had once worshiped the snake god. Whether it was out of embarrassment, shame, or even anger, she could only guess. Zarnoc, Korax, Lykus, and Arundel had all known each other 1,000 years ago when the Lorians had flourished and ruled Caladonia, and the ancient Raven Clan had been practitioners of dark magic and strange religious rites. It was the heritage of her people, darkness and dabbling in magic, which had led to the Draconus family destroying them, and eventually, every magic user and enchanted weapon.

The carved images showed Lorian women with infants nursing at their breasts, women feeding their children to the snakes in dark sacrifices, and men standing before giant serpents allowing themselves to be swallowed whole. The further they walked, the grimmer and more disturbing the images became, and Taliesin found herself holding Wolfgar's arm for comfort. He glanced at her hand.

"How do you know this about your clan?" Wolfgar asked. His voice echoed along the corridor. "I didn't know King Korax was a Lorian. Nor did I know the fairy-folk were dark beings or that your clan had anything to do with the Snake Cult."

Taliesin wanted to ask why he was interested, but hearing his voice was soothing, and she didn't want to anger him, so she answered truthfully. "Zarnoc, a wizard, told me a little about the Lorians, and the rest I can read for myself in the images they left behind. King Korax chose a raven as his clan insignia, instead of a snake. Perhaps he didn't approve of what his kinsmen were doing here, but I really don't know why, or if there is another reason. Do you?"

"I am not interested in Korax," Wolfgar said, gruffly, "but I am interested in the treasure within this cave. Prince Almaric needs gold to pay the mercenaries, and now we have found it. If you can tell me where to find the treasure, then I am very much interested in what you have to say about this place." She merely shrugged, and they walked on.

The corridor widened significantly, growing to fifty feet across. Ten-foot-high statues of Lorians stood on each side of the hall, dressed in ornate armor with their hair pulled to one side to reveal pointed ears. The fairy-folk had a dark, frightening look about them. Many of the marble statues showed couples or trios, unclothed and fornicating with their snake god. Though the Lorians had been consumed with carnal lust and fanatical faith in Chu'Alagu, Taliesin found the elaborate carvings and illustrations on the walls beautiful, as well as horrific.

The cave floor was covered by skeletons so brittle with age they shattered underfoot and crumbled to white dust. Despite the age of the temple, Taliesin could still detect the scent of the exotic incense the worshipers had burned in large golden bowls held in the hands of some of the statues.

At the end of the chamber were gilded double doors, carved with intricate designs of mating snakes. Several of the Wolfmen pushed at the gates, trying their brute strength to break through, but they held firm. Udolf pushed the men aside and pointed with a clawed finger at an indented circle, the same shape and size as at the main door, in the center of one door. An image of a hydra was engraved in that door.

"Use your key," Udolf snarled.

Taliesin stepped forward and placed the medallion in the circular lock, the lieutenant's hot breath on her neck. This time she turned it clockwise until she heard a latch click. The doors didn't move, and she glanced at Wolfgar, feeling rather helpless. "This calls for brute strength," Taliesin said. "Do you mind?"

"Get to it, men," Wolfgar ordered.

Udolf and three brawny Wolfmen placed their shoulders to the doors and pushed. With a loud groan, the doors swung inward to reveal an enormous chamber with a domed ceiling cut out of the rock. The dome was covered in blue tiles to give the impression of an immense sky, under which stood a colossal golden statue of a six-headed hydra so large and wide it nearly filled the entire chamber. Four stout legs with emerald-covered talons held the preposterous pot-bellied monstrosity, covered with golden scales and standing in a room filled with treasure. Each head, so large it must have weighed over a ton, faced a different direction; the eyes in one were rubies, emeralds in another, and then diamonds, sapphires, jade, and onyx. The enormous mouths, large enough to swallow five horses, were opened and revealed two-foot long golden fangs. A scaled tail wrapped around the room.

One head stared at the ceiling, where, in the center of the dome, there was an opening large enough for a human to climb through. Waning sunlight shined through the hole, and a light sprinkle of rain dripped upon the statue; despite centuries of exposure to the elements, not a speck of moss or mold grew on the statue or floor. Clenched between that head's fangs was a beautiful longsword made of gold with a jeweled hilt that glittered as tendrils of sunlight caressed it. The blade was uncommonly wide and the hilt so long four hands placed side-by-side could have held it. Longer than an average-sized human's height, it was suspended fifty feet in the air, kept from falling by the curl of a forked tongue and fangs.

"*Ringerike*," Taliesin said. "The Raven Sword."

Ringing in her ears followed the sound of a swordsmith hammering on an anvil, the twang vibrating inside of her head. It was a response from the sword; it knew her and knew why she was there. How she was able to sense the sword had intelligence or that it was communicating with her was baffling.

"We're rich," cried one of the Wolfmen. "Bloody rich!"

Taliesin walked toward the hydra, her gaze on a marble coffin under its massive gold chest. The name *KING KORAX SANQUALUS* was engraved on the lid. She slid her hand along the lid; not a speck of dust, no bird droppings, not even a bug. Nothing lived inside the tomb, and nothing had disturbed the Raven King's grave in centuries. The Lorians had built an incredible shrine for a legendary hero, yet it made little sense to her. The king was surrounded by dead snake-men and guarded by a six-headed hydra statue, instead of being encased in raven feathers and buried in a forest, surrounded by ancient oak trees and nestled safely in the bosom of the earth. Another mystery that surrounded Korax—King of the Raven Clan, yet protected by a Snake God and a deceased snake cult that had fallen into the realm of myth.

"Over here, Captain Wolfgar! We've found corpses," Udolf shouted.

The lieutenant spoke too loudly, and his voice echoed in the chamber, which stirred the dark magic, angered the sword, and disturbed the rest of the dead king. Taliesin joined the Wolfmen as they morphed into naked men, their dirty skin and strong odor a vulgar imprint within the chamber.

"They must have come from the hole in the ceiling." Udolf pointed behind a horde of treasure and weapons collected over the ages that lay behind the fifty-foot-high gold statue. Mummified knights and snake-men lay comingled. The snake-men had human lower-halves, crocodile-like upper bodies, and faces more snake-like than human. The stiff creatures, long since dead, were pale of skin, scaled, seven feet tall, and long-tailed; in life, they would have been over five hundred pounds of muscle, scales, wicked claws, and sharp teeth. A battle had been fought between the Caladonian knights, who had defeated the Snake Cult, and Chu'Alagu's acolytes. They'd been sealed inside the temple, forgotten.

"I thought you said the worshipers of the Snake God were fairy-folk," Wolfgar said, staring at the bodies. "What manner of creatures are these?"

"You said Varg mated with a woman and created the *Wolfen* race. Perhaps the Lorians mated with snakes to create a breed of snake-men," Taliesin said, disgusted to think fairies were that depraved. The creatures' decay was somehow suspended, maybe by the same process, possibly dark magic, that kept the statue and the floor clear of debris and moss. "I know no more than you, Captain, and can only make assumptions...assumptions that would best be left unsaid."

Udolf gestured at the dead knights. "Maldavian," he said. Five corpses in ancient armor wore faded, frayed dark-blue tunics, and the material turned to dust in his hands when he touched one. "There is flesh on the bones," he said. "After all these centuries, there should be nothing left but brittle bones, but these, they are still decomposing." He reached out, pulled a gold ring from a rotten hand, and slid it on one of his fingers. The body's arm came off at the shoulder and fell to the ground, and Udolf sneezed in a cloud of dust.

"Legends tell that King Tarquin's son, Talas, had *Ringerike* sealed in the temple once he was crowned king. King Talas had dared not keep the Raven Sword, fearing it would destroy him, so he took it and the Raven King's body into the desert to bury. When they arrived here, they found the Snake Cult already occupying the cave, so King Talas killed them and used their temple for King Korax's tomb."

Wolfgar snorted. "And King Talas buried a treasure with the Raven King. Why?"

"Perhaps dark magic requires a gift," Taliesin said. "I don't know why. I only know the Raven King and Raven Sword were buried here by King Talas, and the cave was sealed off. King Talas' sorcerers placed dark enchantments on the temple, and then were killed, they say, but you can feel the darkness of this place. There's an ancient evil here. I don't think you should steal from the dead. It would be considered sacrilege."

"You're a scavenger," Udolf said. "No better than us. We'll take what we want, and there is nothing you can do about it." He kept the ring but didn't disturb the bodies of the knights, leaving them where they lay.

Wolfgar walked to the front of the statue of the hydra. "Enough talk," he growled, showing no more interest in the treasure. "Taliesin, climb the statue and retrieve the sword." When she didn't move fast enough, he grabbed her arm. "Perhaps I have not made myself clear. You will do what I tell you, or I'll make good on my threats. Now bring me that sword, or by Ragnal, I will cut a finger or two from your hand."

"I'll get right to it, Captain Wolfgar, just as soon as you tell me how to do it. The statue is gold, the scales are smooth, and there are no footholds. Cut a finger or two, and I won't be able to climb at all."

"Udolf, get a rope and lasso that snakehead," ordered Wolfgar. "Our little *Sha'tar* doesn't know how to climb a statue. Unlike her horse, she apparently cannot sprout wings and fly."

The large hairy creatures spread out as Udolf waded through the gold coins, jewelry, and weapons lying on the floor and made his way to the base of the statue. His body shuddered as he turned into a naked man, removed a slender rope from a bag, and made a large noose. Taliesin was compelled to look away when she saw his naked body. He was just as hairy a man as a *Wolfen*, and one of the ugliest she'd ever seen. Looking up, Udolf threw the rope into the air and looped it over the giant hydra head. He pulled on the rope to make sure it held tight and would not slip. "Good enough,"

Udolf said and scratched at his flabby belly. "Climb, Raven Mistress, or I'll toss you up there."

Taliesin slid a tendril of reddish-gold hair behind her ear, grabbed the rope, and pulled herself upwards, inch by inch, as the Wolfmen paced beneath the colossal statue. Dark magic radiated from the statue, causing her skin to tingle, and she again felt like she was being watched. She climbed upwards, one foot wrapped around the rope, and moved hand over hand, slowly making her way until she was able to stand on one of the heads. The Raven Sword's hilt was within reach. Holding the rope with one hand, she took the jeweled hilt with the other and pulled hard, but the sword seemed unwilling to budge.

Her captors below were busying themselves by packing treasure into large bags, and a few had put on golden armor and helmets. Udolf picked up a chest filled with gold coins and carried it out of the chamber, followed by several men dragging bags filled with coins, jewels, scepters, and crowns. She heard a loud grating sound beneath her. Unable to see what was making the noise, she gave another yank on the sword.

"What's the delay," Wolfgar snarled.

"I'm trying," Taliesin said, continuing to jerk on the sword. Something heavy crashed to the floor, but the Wolfmen were so busy gathering treasure they hadn't heard the sound. A feeling of dread came over her, and she gazed over the snake-head, to see the lid to the coffin on the floor. "I think your men should leave the treasure alone. It's an offering to Chu'Alagu and was left here for a reason." A green, rotting hand appeared and gripped the side of the coffin—Korax had been awoken! She looked away and pulled harder on the sword, wanting to escape with it before the rest of the undead woke and joined Korax. No one else seemed to notice what was going on beneath the statue. She'd tried to warn them, but they wouldn't listen; again, she tugged on the sword. "I think it's moving," she shouted.

"Get the job done, Raven Mistress," Wolfgar said, walking to the door as his men hauled out treasure. "If you climb to the top of the snakehead, you can straddle it and reach to pull out the sword. Hurry. I like this place not."

Taliesin wrapped her arms around the hydra head and swung her body around so she could straddle the neck. A bent scale gave her a foothold and, balancing her weight, she reached out with one hand to grab the hilt and pull. She kept wiggling the sword, tugging hard, as she inched up the large head. Lying on top of the head, with her legs dangling, she tried to slide the sword from the snake's golden fangs. Something fell onto her head. She gave a shake and saw a large raven feather flutter and spin as it dropped to the feet of King Korax, who was now standing. She used both hands to slide the sword through the snake's jaws, aware of a horrible *chittering* sound at the feet of the hydra. Another feather fluttered in front of her face. Zarnoc, she thought; had to be. She glanced at the hole, expecting to see her friends, and saw a third feather floating down. Looking down, she saw Wolfgar so engrossed in looting he didn't notice the feathers, nor realize King Korax was slowly walking toward him, leathery arms raised and making an insect-like sound.

"*You must hurry, child. Korax is awake.*" Zarnoc's voice sounded so close, Taliesin knew he was on top of the roof whispering to her. The Wolfmen hadn't heard. She closed her eyes to shut out the distractions, cleared her mind of thoughts, and counted: *One, two, three.* The sword vibrated in her hands. She drew a deep breath and flicked her right hand, gripping the hilt, and the sword slid from between the fangs. She sat on the snakehead, sighing audibly, and held *Ringerike* in the air. Below, she heard the Wolfmen's shouts turn to cries of fear as Wolfgar spun around and saw Korax's gnarled hand reaching for his throat.

The undead knights and snake-men rose to their feet and joined the Raven King, their groans mixing with the terrified howls and snarls of the Wolfmen. Wolfgar turned into a towering monster and grappled with Korax. The undead shambled toward Udolf and the twelve Wolfmen, who turned into giant wolves to fight against the mob. Taliesin felt the sword throbbing in her grip. She could climb down and help or flee. The end of a rope appeared in Taliesin's face, dangling from the hole in the ceiling. Taliesin looked up and saw Hawk and Rook holding the other end.

"*Grab the rope,*" Zarnoc said, his voice louder than before.

Taliesin heard a snarl behind her; a snake-man had managed to climb the statue, and his pale-green eyes stared at her as it reached for her legs. Grabbing the rope in her left hand and holding *Ringerike* in her right, she gazed at her friends as they plucked her off the statue.

"It's alive," Udolf shouted. "The hydra! It's moving!"

A hideous roar was repeated five times as each of the hydra's heads started moving, and the large body lurched forward. The statue had turned into a living creature; bright red and green scales covered its body, and each head snapped at the Wolfmen, eating them along with the undead guards. The roaring of the hydra and the groaning of the undead mixed with the snarls and howls of the Wolf Pack, ringing in Taliesin's ears as she was lifted toward the temple roof. Rook and Hawk hauled her to the hole, grabbed her, and dragged her onto the roof as the battle raged below.

"You will pay for this, *Sha'tar,*" Wolfgar howled.

Hawk pulled Taliesin into his arms, dragging her to her feet as he hugged her. "I thought we'd lost you," Hawk said. "We've got your horse. Everyone is here. Come on!"

Taliesin followed Hawk and Rook across the orb-shaped roof. The evening sky was oddly bright, and she held the over six-feet-long sword over her shoulder as she ran beside the two young men toward Wren and Jaelle. Both girls were mounted on their winged horses, and Wren held the reins of Thalagar and the two other horses. The horses nervously pawed at the roof as the roars of the hydra grew louder. Zarnoc, in raven form, sat on Jaelle's shoulder. The roof started to shake, and entire sections collapsed behind Taliesin and her friends as Wren and Jaelle screamed. A hole opened in front of

Taliesin; Rook and Hawk separated and ran around it as two enormous snakeheads burst through the roof and blocked her path.

"Hurry up," Hawk shouted. He drew his sword as a shadowy form jumped from the cliff above and landed on the roof in front of him. As the giant wolf jumped toward him, a head spun around, snatched the beast in its jaws, and swallowed it whole. Hawk slashed at the snake's neck and shouted as a third head came through the roof. More wolves jumped onto the roof and attacked Rook and Taliesin, who were busy dodging snakeheads that poked through the roof and gobbled Wolfmen as soon as they landed.

Wren lifted her crossbow as her horse flew into the air. Two arrows whistled by Taliesin's head, silver glinting in the fading sunlight, and pierced a wolf behind her. Jaelle now held the reins of the three horses as the raven flew into the air. Hawk reached his horse and climbed into the saddle, but Taliesin and Rook were cut off, unable to get around the now-eight hydra heads; the Wolfmen must have decapitated two heads, and a new pair had sprouted from each neck. Wolves and *Wolfen* dropped off the cliff and continued a mad attack against the enormous hydra to get to Taliesin and *Ringerike*. Zarnoc flew higher, and Hawk and Jaelle joined him, taking Rook and Taliesin's horses with them. They flew low over the heads of the wolves, carefully hovered out of reach of the hydra's eight snapping heads, and Wren and Jaelle shot arrows. Rook held off one hydra head with his silver spear, too busy to worry about the wolves around him being picked off and gobbled. He reached Taliesin and grabbed her arm, but her feet were firmly planted on the roof as if nailed.

"Come on, Taliesin," Rook said. "We have to get out of here!"

"I can't. *Ringerike* won't let me. I must fight. I must do as the sword commands."

Rook tried again to pull Taliesin along as the horses landed, then he turned, ran to his horse, climbed into the saddle, and stabbed a Wolfman that rushed toward him. Taliesin felt her body released by the sword's magic, and she ran to Thalagar. She jumped into the saddle, and her horse beat his wings and rose into the air. As her friends flew away, Taliesin turned and swooped into the fray. Holding *Ringerike* in a tight grip, she leaned far to the right, swung the sword, and severed one of the hydra's necks. The head fell onto the roof and broke through, while the neck danced around and sprayed green blood. Apparently, the magic in *Ringerike* prevented the heads from regenerating, much as silver killed *Wolfen*. Taliesin turned Thalagar, made another flyby, and cut off a second head; she felt unable to leave until she cut off all eight. The sword was light in her hand and easily cut through the thick-scaled hides of each neck until no heads were left. The snake-men and undead knights, now joined by undead wolves, climbed the hydra's corpse and poured out of the gaping holes in the roof.

Taliesin flew over the ravine and glanced down as furry bodies raced along the riverbed, chased by the undead creatures. Under the rising pale moonlight stood a long line of two hundred horse-mounted Eagle legionnaires, one thousand Djaran light cavalry with spears and bows, and eight white-clad knights in silver chainmail carrying lances. Roland had to be among them, she thought, flying lower for a better view. There, at the front of the army, she found Roland, mounted on Kordive holding a silver-tipped lance. He looked up at her as he placed a silver kettle-shaped helm over his head and took his shield from Tamal. A white stag was painted on the front of his shield. The other knights rode beside Roland and formed a small line in front of the army as the surviving Wolf Pack came running out of the ravine, pursued by a larger pack of slathering undead wolves and hissing snake-men.

At Roland's signal, the mounted knights and combined cavalry charged forward. The sight of the horses and camels and riders racing toward the army of the undead as the sunlight faded was spectacular to behold. Lances pierced bodies, horses reared, camels toppled under the weight of undead wolves, and the snake-men screeched as they were trampled under the charging cavalry. As swords flashed and lances cracked, she suddenly felt *Ringerike's* presence, and became aware it was driving Thalagar away from the battle; away from Roland, and toward the west.

"Farewell, Roland," she whispered, the wind drying her tears as she flew from the battle and the sounds of combat, away from her love. She refused to look back as Thalagar soared upwards into the dark clouds, a cool breeze moist on her face. With a roll of her shoulders, she straightened in the saddle with *Ringerike* resting across her lap. A faint whisper made her glance at the sword as Thalagar headed toward the sea and Dunatar Castle, where her friends had gone. Why hadn't they waited? They seemed thoughtless and cruel, and she looked for them in the sky but saw only a flock of desert gulls heading in the same direction. It was cold; the air was thin where they soared among the clouds, the stars winking above, yet there was no chill in her bones.

Again, she heard a whispering female voice. *'I am Ringerike. I make all things possible.'* That the sword could speak was enough to frighten her to death, and she involuntarily placed her right hand around the jeweled hilt. The sword had waited until she'd left the temple before speaking, and she considered the dark magic that had kept it locked away for centuries; now the sword was free, it finally had its voice.

Thalagar snorted and shook his head, sensing magic at play, and she knew he was worried. In her mind appeared an image of Prince Sertorius, seated beside her on a matching throne, his gaze for her alone, a smile of love on his face, and the sword of the ancient king, Korax Sanqualus of Raven Clan, on his lap. She removed her hand from the sword and the image faded. She would not give the sword to Sertorius. She would not be his queen.

The moon gleamed upon puffy clouds; beneath them, she knew it was raining, but it was dry above. She concentrated on the horizon and was able to see the Pangian Sea beyond the edge of the clouds. Her horse flew fast, crossed into the clear sky, and dove. Within an hour, she spotted her friends flying beneath her, dropped down and joined them. Hawk waved at her, Rook and Wren glanced in her direction, and Jaelle smiled wide. The black raven dipped in front of Thalagar and headed lower. Below she spotted a green valley, a town, and hills. Finally, they reached the ocean and followed the rugged coastline south as the lights of the city of Dunatar twinkled in the distance like fallen stars.

'The Sha'tar touched me and brought me to life. The Sha'tar fed me hydra blood, the blood of a god, and I am now awake,' the soft and alluring female voice said.

Taliesin tensed. The voice was only in her head; the sword had spoken to her, but it shouldn't have been talking at all. She glared at the weapon. Magical swords didn't talk or think. Something was terribly wrong. "I am the Raven Mistress. You belong to me," she replied. The stallion snorted at hearing her voice.

'I am yours to command, Mistress. As long as you want me, I serve only you, and I shall obey at all times. I serve only the rightful heir of King Korax. For you, Raven Mistress, are Lorian, and thus, you are his heir. You are a fairy. You are the Sha'tar.'

'Who are you?' Taliesin mentally asked, hoping she wouldn't hear a reply.

'I am Ysemay the Beguiling. For my sins, the Raven King bound my soul to this sword; for Korax was my lover, and I betrayed him, as Roland betrayed you.'

A cold finger slid along her back and made her tremble. She leaned over the sword and pressed one hand against Thalagar's neck. His skin was warm and solid; his heartbeat right under her palm. She placed her hand on *Ringerike* and felt the metal vibrate at her touch. For a second, she imagined herself throwing the sword in the air and letting it fall where it may. She knew she was in danger if it was possessed by a witch's dark soul. Yet, she had to ask, had to know the truth of her lineage, and asked aloud, "Am I of Korax's bloodline?"

'Yes, Sha'tar, you are. You are the daughter of John Mandrake: warlock, swordsmith, and descendant of King Korax of the Raven Clan. Murdered. Murdered. Because of his blood. Your blood. You

*are the heir. Ringerike belongs to you. I belong to you. But beware
Zarnoc. He betrayed the Lorians, betrayed our people, and betrayed
me...with his kiss.'*

Taliesin tried to clear her thoughts; she didn't want to listen to the witch, not until she'd spoken with Zarnoc. She saw the raven flying in front of her; Zarnoc must know the sword was possessed. Taliesin tried not to think about the past, but it was impossible not to. The witch wanted her to ask questions. Ysemay wanted her to know. If she'd been the king's lover and betrayed Korax by sleeping with Zarnoc, why hadn't the wizard saved Ysemay from such a fate? Why should she believe an imprisoned witch that she was of Lorian blood, dark-fairy blood, and the true heir of Korax Sanqualus? But it *felt* right. When she'd looked at the Deceiver's Map to see the Raven heir, she saw only a dot representing herself. She'd assumed no heir existed, and yet now realized the map had shown the truth; the dot had been her, she was the heir, and *Ringerike* was hers. But not the witch. The witch kept *Ringerike* from being its own sword; she possessed the sword, and somehow Ysemay had to be freed.

* * * * *

Chapter Twenty-Nine

The Pangian Sea rolled in upon a long stretch of beach, white ripples stretching along the coast. Thalagar flew ahead of the other riders, keeping up with the raven, and dipped low, snorting as he touched the tops of the waves with his hooves. Taliesin laughed at Thalagar's whinny, not worrying about witches and warlords or princes and war as they glided above the water. They passed fishermen's boats in neat rows along the beach as the lights of Dunatar grew brighter. A large spray of water hit Taliesin; the cold splatter revived her and cleared her thoughts.

She spotted a harbor further along the coast, where thirty warships lay at anchor, overlooked by Dunatar Castle, which was built on a cliff. The imposing citadel had eight towers with blue domes, a large wall that circled the castle, and a second wall that protected the city. Torches on the battlements cast the castle in a yellow glow.

The odor from the city was intoxicating; a mixture of fish, smoke, fire, perfume, and other scents, captured in nostrils sharpened by the *Wolfen* curse. The city was beautiful, made rich from its sea trade. Compared to the royal city of Padama and its Tantalon Castle, the seaside city of Dunatar was something out of a dream. As they flew over the city, Taliesin gazed at magnificent marble estates with tall pillars, streets lined with shops, taverns, markets, and lush gardens where temples lay, and a midtown arena for jousting tournaments. There were bright colors everywhere she looked, from carpets sold at shops to the curtains in the windows of houses—built side-by-side and painted white. The streets were lined with white seashells. Even Dunatar Castle was painted white.

Still asleep in their beds, the citizens of Dunatar took little notice of the six shadows flying over their city. Taliesin searched among the flags and banners flown at each castle tower for Prince Sertorius' standard but saw only Duke du Boron's flag, a blue sea serpent on a field of green. *Ringerike* stirred and adjusted itself across her thigh and the flank of the horse.

'The castle is cloaked with magic. There is a sorcerer here.'

Taliesin had no time to think of a response. As the horses swooped lower, the guards on the battlements spotted them and set off an alarm. When no arrows were shot at her, she allowed Thalagar to land. The soldiers remained at a safe distance and eyed her warily as she slid off the side of her horse while the large animal pulled in his wings. A small contingent of well-dressed men came out of the main tower. She remembered what Ysemay had told her about a sorcerer and searched the group of nobles and courtesans for anyone who even remotely looked like a magic user. She held *Ringerike* in her right hand, aware the red scabbard on her left side was missing a valuable silver sword she'd never see again. As she walked around Thalagar, his wings vanished, as did the wings on the other horses, and a murmur was heard from the nobles and the guards. Jaelle ran to her with a cloak, fastened it around Taliesin's neck, and placed the side of the robe around *Ringerike*, making it less visible to the crowd. Rook took Thalagar's reins, while Hawk and Wren held the reins of the other horses.

Taliesin stepped forward and thought of Master Osprey, how he'd always addressed nobles; he'd speak up and treat them with respect but show no sign of inferiority. "I am the Raven Mistress," she said, expecting the title to have meaning. "We were asked by Prince Sertorius to join him here, and I believe Duke de Boron is expecting us. Will one of you inform the Duke that the Raven Clan has arrived? We are weary and ask for his hospitality, as we would show him at Raven's Nest."

"Greeting, Raven Mistress!" a voice said in a lilting, western accent. A tall, impressive-looking man wearing a dark-green long coat trimmed with gold stepped forward. His black hair, graying at the sides, fell to his shoulders like a velvet curtain, and his immaculately-groomed black beard was speckled with gray. Everything about him was polished; the only thing spoiling his noble appearance was a jagged scar that crossed the left side of his face, across his eye and cheek, leaving him blind in that eye. His good eye, a shade of sea green, conveyed a kindness she hadn't expected to find in the Garridan lord. "I am Duke Richelieu de Boron," he said, a hand held over his heart. Each finger bore a jeweled ring. "Welcome. Welcome! We have been waiting for your arrival. Prince Sertorius arrived only a few hours ago, bringing word of the troubles in the realm. You've come a long way to seek sanctuary, and it is yours, of course."

"Thank you, Duke de Boron. My companions and I are grateful for your hospitality," Taliesin said, wondering what Sertorius had actually told the duke upon his arrival. She was not a noblewoman, nor did she want to use her birth name, but the prince seemed to have his own opinion in that regard. The duke's good eye lowered to the sword outlined in her cloak. To avoid questions, she held out her hand and was grateful for the distraction when he took and kissed it.

"The prince went to bed a short time ago," Duke de Boron said, "but my lords and ladies couldn't possibly think of closing our eyes after hearing about the Raven Mistress and her journey across the Salayan Desert."

The sword wrapped in Jaelle's cloak shuddered. Taliesin held it against her chest and was glad the witch possessing *Ringerike* remained silent, though she had a feeling Ysemay knew Richelieu. A flutter of wings brought Zarnoc, his beady eyes focused on the protuberance in her cloak, alighting upon her shoulder.

Grooms came forward to take their horses but found Rook and Hawk unwilling to hand over the reins. Likewise, servants coming to assist Jaelle and Wren as they unpacked their equipment were also waved off. The girls, moving quickly, removed the gear from each horse and tossed it on the ground in a pile, leaving only the saddles in place. Two male servants came over, picked up the gear, and remained close to both women, who eyed them suspiciously.

"This is Shan Octavio's eldest daughter, Jaelle, and Wren of the Raven Clan," Taliesin said, turning toward the two young women. She nodded at Rook and Hawk. "Our mounts have carried us here from Raven's Nest, and now it is in ruins, the horses have naturally become part of our family. If your servant would show Rook and Hawk to your stables, they will tend to our horses' needs and will join us when they have finished."

"Yes, yes," replied Richelieu, motioning for a servant to show the two Ravens to the stables. As the horses were led off, he held his hand out and led the way to the main keep with Taliesin, Jaelle, and Wren; his entourage followed behind at a respectful distance. "I have never seen such a fine-looking Andorran stallion," he said. "I own many Andorrans, but yours is exceptional. The wings...a wizard travels with you?"

Taliesin nodded. "Yes," she said. "Without Zarnoc's assistance, we'd never have reached Dunatar Castle, my lord. I hope you do not mind a wizard being here."

"Not at all," the duke said. "So much is happening, so many difficulties." He slowed his pace and glanced at Jaelle and Wren. "Ladies, please. You are guests in my home. Follow me," he said. "Whatever you require will be provided. A servant has already been sent to Prince Sertorius' chamber to inform him you have arrived safely. I knew Master Osprey by reputation only; I never had the pleasure of meeting him. A man revered by his clan and respected by those who called him friend. "

Dawn filled the sky with brilliant pinks and purples on the eastern horizon as they approached a large blue door alongside a garden filled with blooming flowers to the side of the keep. Taliesin was able to smell each flower separately—roses, lilacs, periwinkles, and yellow daisies. She could also smell fear from Duke de Boron, the scent like spoiled milk. Her shoulder throbbed where Wolfgar had bitten her—the other, smaller bites were not nearly as troublesome—and heard Ysemay say in her head, '*The change is upon you; it is slower than most, but you will turn, eventually, and eat the duke and prince and all of your friends. Unless you free me. Only I can help you.*'

At once, Zarnoc, riding on her shoulder, gave a loud squawk, arched his neck, and snapped at the sword, though it was still covered with Jaelle's cloak. She sensed hatred between the two magic users, a rivalry that hadn't lessened with the passage of time, and the nature of which would soon become known.

Taliesin, Wren, and Jaelle followed Duke de Boron toward another blue door, this one oval-shaped with silver studs and adorned with a mermaid brass knocker, and they paused as the morning sun appeared. A golden glow spread across the white stones of Dunatar Castle, as well as the slender towers, the ramparts, and the high walls. The pounding surf was a steady background presence, so tranquil and serene after being pursued, thirsty and hungry, for a week in the harsh desert. Six guards in sea green tunics and breastplates and helmets of silver stood at attention along the path. More guards stood sentry duty on the battlements, and teams of three walked through the courtyard. As the Duke approached the door, it was opened from the inside by a male servant in a bright yellow coat and turquoise shoes.

"We'll take wine on the veranda," Duke de Boron said. The servant rushed off and two more appeared. A young woman in coral pink and a young man in lavender opened two large doors tiled in cobalt, yellow, red, and orange, and they led the way into an L-shaped room that served as the dining hall and throne room. Heavy white beams supported the roof, adorned with the flags and banners of ten generations of the de Boron family and the royal Draconian flags of King Frederick. If Taliesin had any question as to the House of de Boron's loyalty, it seemed to favor King Frederick.

Five long wooden tables, covered in gold tablecloths and decorated with bouquets of fresh-cut flowers, filled the length of the room. Twenty high-backed wooden chairs with blue and red embroidered cushions were placed in perfect alignment on each side of the tables. At the end of the dining hall, facing the main doors, was a massive stained-glass window, over thirty feet tall and twenty feet wide, that showed the story of a de Boron nobleman with a trident fighting a sea serpent, taming it, and then chaining the creature to the cliffs beneath the castle, facing the sea. Two white ash chairs with blue cushions of different sizes were placed upon a dais on the left side of the room, beneath an oval stained-glass window of a green sea serpent with jaws wide open. The base was surrounded with beautiful seashells, the smallest the size of a sea turtle, that was filled with red and yellow flowering plants.

"Dunatar is not quite as fine as the throne room of Tantalon Castle," Duke de Boron said, turning to smile at Taliesin and her two companions as they walked past the throne. "When this castle was built, it was intended for a Draconian prince but was bestowed upon my family instead. Our sea trade has made Garridan one of the richest dukedoms, and we have open trade with seven dukedoms and the royal city, keeping them supplied with rare silks, spices, mined gold and gems, as well as foreign products."

"At one time," Jaelle said, breaking in, "my father, Shan Octavio, and the Ghajarans shared trading rights with the Djaran, but in recent years those trading lanes have been cut off by the nomads and desert raiders."

"Something I mean to discuss with Duke Fortinbraus; I need his help to maintain law and order at the Minoc River," de Boron said as his servants opened a side door that led to a beautiful veranda that overlooked the garden. Several large white wicker chairs with patterned cushions sat about the area, along with a bench covered in leopard skin, fringed pillows set on rugs, and a low round table where small plates of fruit and a slender pitcher of wine had been set.

Zarnoc jumped off Taliesin's shoulder, landed on the table, and waddled over to take a grape from a bowl with his black, slender beak. As she took a seat in one of the wicker chairs, Taliesin placed the sword, still covered by the cloak, on the ground next to her and accepted a glass of wine from the woman in pink, who shyly avoided her gaze. The duke sat beside her and glanced now and then at the draped sword. Jaelle took the bench, and Wren lay on the cushions, her forehead creased from an oncoming headache. While they were served wine, Taliesin studied de Boron; he was sweating, a sign he was nervous, though his fears had lessened with the presence of the other two girls. But it was obvious, at least to Taliesin, he was uncomfortable sitting next to her, and she waited for him to ask about *Ringerike*, wanting to see what he'd been told by the prince and court gossipers.

"This was my wife's favorite room in the castle," the Duke said. "This is far more charming than taking refreshments in the hall." He raised his glass. "Let us drink to the health of Shan Octavio and hope we will soon reopen the trading routes to your tribe." Everyone lifted their glasses and took a sip of the red, fruity wine. "How fortunate the Shan sent you, his eldest daughter, here so we might have the opportunity to talk and sort out this matter. And to you, of course, Raven Mistress, and your late father, Master Osprey. You honor me by coming so far to seek sanctuary in this time of civil unrest."

"Please, call me 'Taliesin.' We should be thanking you, my lord. There was no place else for us to go. If Prince Sertorius hadn't suggested we meet him here, I really don't know where we would have gone; I only know we couldn't go home." The Duke took another drink. He wore a smile, pleasant enough on his long face, yet she wanted their conversation kept short, and she hoped for the opportunity to clean up before she saw Prince Sertorius. Her boots were splattered with mud and dried green blood from the hydra. Self-consciously, she lifted a hand to her hair—it would take hours to comb out the snags.

"You are a natural beauty, Mistress Taliesin. Please, do not worry about appearances. You and your friends have been through a terrible ordeal. Have something to eat to tide you over until the banquet this evening," Duke de Boron said, pushing a plate of food closer to her. "Prince Sertorius told me the Raven Clan had been wiped out by the Wolf Clan. I am saddened to hear about the fate of your father, Master Osprey. I am quite certain Prince Sertorius will personally handle this matter on your father's behalf. There will be an inquiry, of course, and if Chief Lykus is found guilty, he will most likely be banished."

"Chief Lykus has sided with Prince Almaric," Taliesin said. "The only way to handle this matter is to destroy Wolf's Den and the Wolf Clan."

A servant came to the Duke and stood with her head bowed until motioned forward to whisper into Richelieu's ear. An annoyed look appeared on the Duke's disfigured face, and he waved the servant away, cleared his throat, and held out his long-fingered hand to Taliesin. "It seems the prince has requested he be allowed to join us in an hour. He was quite exhausted when he and his men arrived last night," he said. "Not to worry. We now have a little more time to get to know one another. I'll have my servants escort you to your rooms when they are prepared. The view of the ocean isn't available in Maldavia; this will be a treat for you all."

"Thank you," Taliesin said. "Your kindness is greatly appreciated."

"My father has often spoken of you, my lord," Jaelle said, selecting a pear out of a bowl of fruit. "The Shan says you are a just and fair man. What will you do when the Wolf Pack arrives? They have been hunting the Raven Mistress and our party for weeks."

"Prince Sertorius warned me of the Wolf Pack's approach," the Duke said. "I have doubled the guard, but most of my army has boarded the Eagle ships in the harbor, which will leave as soon as Master Xander arrives. He and Prince Sertorius will be going south, to Erindor, to join the main royal army gathering there. The Wolf Pack will be turned away without seeing the inside of Dunatar Castle. You are quite safe here, I promise."

"Where is your wife?" Wren asked, feeding Zarnoc grapes. For whatever reason, he had not shown himself to the Duke, nor had the Duke asked about the wizard traveling in their company. "Will she be joining us at the banquet tonight?"

"My wife is dead," Duke de Boron replied, fielding the question without showing any emotions. "We have a daughter who you will meet tonight. Lenora is about your age and will be filled with questions about the Raven Clan and the Ghajar. I warn you, you will not get in a word edgewise once she gets started. She wants to ask everything and to listen to nothing, especially not to her father. Lenora looks just like her mother. My wife, Denira, was a beautiful woman. Her death has been hard on my daughter as well. One never really gets over the loss, but as long as we remember the dead as alive, they remain with us."

"I look forward to meeting her," Wren said, sweetly, as she sat on the pillows with her knees pulled to her chin. She was attentive and sincerely impressed with the Duke and his hospitality. Zarnoc, meanwhile, had hopped onto a chair and watched everything with sharp, beady eyes.

"It is my understanding the clans allow their members to choose their own names when they join," Duke de Boron said. "A very lovely custom. The name 'Wren' suits your delicate features. I always wondered what name I'd choose. When I was about your age, I had a particularly annoying cousin who called me 'Stork,' on account of my long legs; it is a name I never liked, but among the Raven Clan, it would have suited me, yes?"

"I think it's a nice name," Wren said, laughing. "My brother is called Hawk, my sweetheart is Rook, and we had a Quail, a Leech, a Talon, a Plume, and a Grudge at Raven's Nest. Any name would do, though it was common to pick the name of a bird, if and when it was available."

'Richelieu is not interested in your clan, only in Ringerike,' Ysemay warned. Zarnoc seemed to be able to hear the witch's voice. He jumped onto the table again, walked to stand in front of Taliesin, and glared at the sword. The duke made no comment about the raven, or about the whereabouts of their wizard, which Taliesin found more troubling than her possessed sword. Surely, the Duke suspected the raven was more than a bird. He was being careless; any decent magic user could read people's thoughts, which was one of the reasons the Draconus kings had them rounded up and killed during the Magic Wars. If the Duke was lying or bending the truth to suit his purpose, he had to know she'd be informed. She wasn't prepared for his next question, for if minds were being read, she felt like hers was an open book.

"I take it you found the Cave of the Snake God and found the Raven King's sword?" Duke de Boron sipped his glass of wine. "I should very much like to see this sword. Many people have sought it throughout the ages, but none have found it or even returned to tell their tale. Although the cave is on my lands, I assure you I have no claim on the sword. The jewels in the hilt, they say, are worth a king's ransom. May I see it?"

'Be careful,' Ysemay said. *'Richelieu wants to know who you support, the King, Almaric, or Sertorius. The youngest prince has not made his intentions yet known. No magic user can foretell the future; we only know what has happened in the past and what is happening now. If Zarnoc has told you otherwise, then you cannot trust him either.'*

'And you should keep quiet, you old witch,' Zarnoc replied. *'I'll deal with you soon enough. Taliesin, if the prince is in the castle, I am unable to read his thoughts, but I'll keep trying.'*

Rubbing her temples and unhappy *two* people were now inside her head, Taliesin sidestepped the Duke's request. "I'll be glad to show you once Prince Sertorius joins us," she said, setting aside her glass. "I'm simply exhausted, my lord. My friends would like to freshen up and rest for a while. It's been a hard journey. We haven't felt a real pillow beneath our heads in weeks."

"Of course. This can wait." The Duke stood and straight-ened his robe, and the male and female servants came over. "The Ravens need to rest," he said. "Show the two ladies to their rooms, and I'll take Taliesin to the west tower, where I think she will enjoy the view from Denira's room. It's quieter there, and she'll hear if anyone approaches."

"Should I be worried?" Taliesin asked. She picked up the sword and carried it at her side as she came around the chair, avoiding a potted plant with a red flower that spilled out and grew across the floor. She didn't hear a reply as the Duke fol-lowed Jaelle and Wren, who were close behind his two serv-ants. Zarnoc flew over and landed on Taliesin's shoulder as they filed off the veranda, walked through a short hallway, and ascended three flights of stairs to the next level. The two servants led Jaelle and Wren along a hallway that stretched to an enclosed room with six doors. Taliesin walked behind Duke de Boron, aware he was sweating heavier than before; he was more nervous than when they'd started. Her instincts were right, for when the foursome was out of sight, the Duke caught Taliesin by the arm, drew her back along the short hall, opened a door in the wall she'd missed—a secret door—and led her up a narrow flight of stairs.

"I would speak to you in private, Mistress Taliesin. This stairway leads to my late wife's chambers. No one uses this staircase but me. We can talk here and not be overheard by servants." Richelieu closed the door and led the way up the winding staircase. Zarnoc flew ahead, not revealing himself as a wizard. The staircase forced both the Duke and Taliesin to duck their heads. "Your coming here places me in a difficult position. I never believed you'd actually find the Raven Sword. My father kept sending men into the desert to find the blade; men who never returned. I learned from his mistakes and have never ordered my knights to find the cave. I never believed anyone would go to the lengths you have to find it."

"Let me speak bluntly," Taliesin said, hearing a door open at the top of the stairs. She had an impression of Zarnoc, standing as a man, peering out the door and letting sunshine and fresh air fill the stairwell. Ysemay remained silent, listening, and the sword lay still in her arms. "Prince Sertorius isn't here, is he? The prince calls me by my real name, but you've not done so, so I assume you don't know who I really am."

The duke paused on the steps and turned to her. "I know you are the *Sha'tar*, and your arrival has endangered not only my daughter and me, but my entire dukedom. At this very moment, Lord Arundel's aides, Orell and Ethon, are waiting for Sertorius and Xander to arrive, but they do not know you are here. Those are their ships in the harbor, and they are filled with my soldiers, ready to embark on a voyage."

"Lord Arundel wants *Ringerike* and me," Taliesin said. "I have no intention of waiting for Xander or boarding one of those ships or letting anyone take the sword from me. This is one civil war I plan to avoid. With your help, I'd like to book passage on a small ship with a trustworthy captain and find someplace very quiet to hide. Can you arrange that?"

They continued to ascend the stairs. She again heard a door open at the top of the stairs, and the sound of the surf mixed with the shrill calls of seagulls. She knew Zarnoc had turned human to open it and was impatiently waiting for them. He sent no more messages, so she assumed the wizard was satisfied the Duke was being forthcoming.

"Master Phelon arrived last night with five hundred Wolfmen. I have managed to keep the Wolfmen separate from the Eagles, so far, but I do not know for how long I can continue the deception. If Master Xander and Prince Sertorius don't arrive, I fear Phelon will attempt to seize control of the castle, and I am concerned for my daughter's safety. This predicament requires me to petition you and your tiny clan for assistance."

"What can we do?" Taliesin asked. "Have your soldiers disembark and reinforce your guards. Arrest Phelon and his pack and toss them into the dungeon. When I left the cave, I saw Master Xander, Sir Roland of the White Stag, and the Eagle legionnaires facing an army of undead; whether they were victorious or not, I don't know. You can't rely on them, my lord. Take matters into your own hands; arrest Phelon, and I'll do whatever I can to help you."

"Lenora is in the castle," the Duke said, pausing at the top stair. The wind came through the door and ruffled his hair. "I've not had the chance to sneak her out. If I can find a ship, I'd like you to take her with you. She is my only heir and must not be harmed. Master Phelon does not know you have arrived either. Nor have I sent word to the Eagle envoys. I need time to get my daughter out of the castle." He walked through the door onto a walkway that led to a slender white tower facing the ocean. The Duke glanced over the railing, crossed the walkway, opened the door to the tower, and, in a conspiratorial fashion, motioned for her to follow. "Hurry. I don't want anyone to see us. You will be safe in this tower. Come."

Taliesin hurried across the walkway as Zarnoc flew into the room, followed by the Duke and Taliesin, who caught her breath as she entered the circular room. It was a large chamber with a vaulted ceiling supported by heavy wooden beams, large windows with stained glass and gold drapes, and a four-poster bed with ornate carving. A wooden tub shaped like the skull of a dragon sat near a window. The tub was lined with gold to hold water, and the sides were engraved with aquatic creatures. The bed was free of dust and covered with green velvet drapes. A vanity with a round mirror held a vase of fresh flowers, an open box of jewelry, and a hairbrush that had strands of dark brown hair.

"No one has used this room since my wife died," Richelieu de Boron said, moving to stand in front of the mirror. "The west tower was her favorite. Denira was the daughter of Duke Hrothgar of Fregia. I know he and his brother were killed by Prince Sertorius. Now you know why I am in such a difficult position; I must do the right thing by her."

Taliesin placed *Ringerike* upon the bed. Zarnoc flew over, landed on the coverlet, and picked at the cloak wrapped around the sword. Taliesin could hear the wizard and witch yelling at each other in the back of her mind, but she refused to be party to the argument. She turned, sat on the bed, marveling at how soft it felt, and watched the Duke gently grasp the hairbrush.

"Denira was a beautiful and wise woman," Richelieu said, his voice finally reflecting his heavy grief. "It has been difficult to rule these last five years without her at my side. My wife had an uncanny ability to tell if someone was telling the truth simply by looking at them. Her insight was invaluable to me."

"She had the gift then?"

"Yes, my wife was a witch. But she used her arts for healing only, and she, along with her coven, took care of the rich and poor alike. It wasn't until she died that the problems started with the Djarans. They revered my wife for her powers and blamed me for her death. Being in this room reminds me of how much I loved her; I feel like she is still here with me. Some say they've seen her haunting this tower. Perhaps she does, for even now I can hear her tell me that I must protect you."

Taliesin frowned, aware Ysemay and Zarnoc had grown quiet, the argument undecided, and the Duke was scrutinizing her too closely. "The tower is haunted?" She asked the first thing she could think of, not expecting the Duke to nod, but he did. "If you brought me to your wife's room, you must have decided to help us. Don't shame her memory by speaking any lies. If you have troubles here, my lord, then tell me, and perhaps I can help you."

"Denira, Denira," the Duke cried, wringing his hands, turning, and gazing toward the mirror. "If you would but come to me, tell me what to do, then I could know peace." He lifted his hands to his face. "I had hoped that by bringing you here, Denira might appear. The servants often see her here, under the pale moonlight, brushing her hair at the window the way she always used to. I thought you would be able to see her with your magic powers. I thought your wizard might see her, too. The raven is your wizard; I know this, but I don't think even Zarnoc is powerful enough to deliver me from the Wolf Pack." The brush was placed aside. "That is why I sent two knights to find Prince Sertorius and Master Xander and bring them here in haste. I control the castle, for now, and have placed Master Phelon and his men in the north tower to rest. I'm sure they know Lord Arundel's aides, Orell and Ethon, are waiting on board their ships for the arrival of the prince and Xander, and that I have few guards to defend my home. Master Phelon expects me to turn the Eagle aides, the ships, and my army over to them. What can I do? The Wolf Pack was over the walls before I had time to send word for my troops to disembark. As soon as Master Phelon rises, I must go to him and sign the Eagle envoy's death warrant. I have no other choice."

"Then you must gather your lords and ladies and lock them in one of the towers. I can send Zarnoc to the Eagles to ask for their help. All we have to do is hold out until Sertorius and Xander arrive. I said I would help you. Let me." Taliesin saw tears streaming down the Duke's gaunt cheeks. Moved by his plight, she went over and placed her hand on his shoulder. The moment she touched him, Taliesin felt a strong current of energy running through her hand into his body. Richelieu threw his hands over his face, groaned in pain, and turned from her. "What's wrong, my lord? Have I hurt you?" She couldn't imagine what she'd done to cause such a reaction, but when at last he lowered his hands and looked at her, his blind eye no longer looked white. The iris was green, like his other eye, and appeared healthy—alive. He stared at her and openly wept, overwhelmed by the unexpected restoration of his vision, while she could only marvel at the miracle that had occurred.

"You are indeed the blessed *Sha'tar*," Duke de Boron said. A thin smile spread across his scarred face. "I did this to myself. Out of grief. I vowed I would never see another sunrise or sunset without my Denira. My knights stopped me before I was able to blind my other eye. Here I have placed you in the gravest danger, yet you have restored my sight. I am in your debt, my lady."

"Not in the least. I said I would help. I'll send Zarnoc to the Eagle envoys. Do what I said and lock up your lords and ladies. Bring your daughter and my friends to me. I can defend this tower until help arrives."

"Yes, yes," he said. "That's what I'll do. Stay here for now, and I will send everyone to you. Leave the arrangements to me." Richelieu walked to the door. "Bless you for coming, Raven Mistress." He walked out and shut the door behind him without bolting it and locking her in.

Zarnoc immediately turned into his human form and lounged on the bed beside the sword. He waved his hand and the tub filled with hot water. A pot of hot coffee appeared on the table, along with a stack of scones and a bowl of butter. "It's from the kitchen," he said. "Eat, take a bath, and relax. Phelon still slumbers. Ysemay has promised not to trouble you until everything has brewed over."

Taliesin kicked off her boots. "I can't handle the secrets, Zarnoc," she said, angrily. "Like the Lorians. Why didn't you tell me you knew Korax or that the Snake Cult was fairy-folk? Didn't you know what was waiting for us inside the temple? You see some things, but not everything; you tell some facts, and withhold others."

"You might not believe me if I told you everything, and I need you to believe me," he said, flippantly. "I'll get right over to the ships and bring reinforcements, and then I'll find Sir Roland; by now, he should have caught Sertorius. Whatever you do, Taliesin, don't leave this room. Bathe off the scent of the wolves before Phelon starts sniffing around. I'll return as soon as I can, and we'll sort everything out. I promise."

The wizard turned into a raven and flew out the window.

Taliesin went to the door, slid the bolt to lock it from the inside, and went to the bed. Her red scabbard had grown longer, and *Ringerike* could now be tucked away inside; Zarnoc had been most helpful. She opened the pouch, removed the Deceiver's Map, spread it out on the bed, and thought of Master Phelon and the Wolfmen. A diagram of the interior of Dunatar Castle appeared, showing Phelon and his men in the north tower, the rooms where Jaelle, Wren, Hawk, and Rook were now in, the Duke's daughter on the level above them, and the Eagle envoys on the flagship. She thought of the Duke and saw his tiny effigy appear in the grand hall. Her next thought was of Roland. He was still thirty miles away, accompanied by Prince Sertorius and the Maldavians, Master Xander, and an army of one thousand Eagles. She folded the map and put it away.

'It's been nearly a day since Captain Wolfgar bit you,' Ysemay said, not keeping her word to remain silent. *'The only reason you haven't turned is because your magic is strong. If you free me from the sword, I will remove the curse. I don't need Zarnoc's help to make you human again. My own powers were very strong until I was locked away in this sword.'*

Ignoring the witch, Taliesin stripped out of her dirty clothes, wrapped everything in the coverlet, and placed it under the bed. She could still detect a faint scent, but it wouldn't be enough to draw the attention of the Wolf Pack. The water inside the tub was warm, and she sank to her chin, and then went under. When she popped up, she saw a nasty film floated on the water. Wolf scum. Hydra blood. She washed her hair with scented soap, scrubbed the filth off her skin with a hard brush, and remained in the water, thinking about the last few weeks of her life, until it turned cold.

When she climbed out of the tub, she realized she had nothing to wear. Her filthy clothes were bundled and stuffed under the bed, and the rest of her belongings were in her saddlebags, which had been taken to Jaelle's and Wren's room. The girls weren't at her door yet, which she found troubling, but she couldn't do anything about that now. She wrapped a towel around her body, another around her hair, and went to the table to eat a scone. It didn't taste as good as the raw rabbit, but she didn't throw it up, much to her relief, and was able to eat five before she felt full. The coffee was Djaran, hot and strong and her new favorite drink. She sat on a chest pressed against the footboard of the bed, put aside the cup, towel-dried her hair, and thought of the one person able to set things right.

"Hurry, Roland," Taliesin whispered. "I need you. Please hurry."

* * * * *

Chapter Thirty

With nothing but time on her hands, Taliesin sat at the vanity and brushed her hair out with the duchess's brush, mingling her reddish-gold hair with the dark brown ones. She thought about Denira, what she'd looked like, and how she'd died. The wardrobe doors behind her opened with a loud creak. In the mirror, Taliesin watched the sleeve of a blue dress rise and fall. The vague outline of a slender woman stood in front of the wardrobe and watched her as the blue dress fell off its hanger to the ground. The ghostly form smiled.

"Denira?"

The Duchess nodded, glided to the vanity, and gazed at her brush with longing. With a wave of her hand, the blue dress lifted from the ground, floated through the air, and landed upon Taliesin's lap. She set aside the brush and slid her hand across the soft material.

"I'm sorry about your father, Duke Hrothgar, and your Uncle Jasper," Taliesin said. "I didn't see them die, but I saw their bodies. I spoke with Jasper, but I suppose you know that already. They aren't ghosts haunting the battlefield, are they?"

Denira shook her head. She pointed at the ceiling and then at the wardrobe. Taliesin was annoyed Denira seemed unable to speak; this was her first ghost, and the rules of interaction were unclear.

"I guess you mean they have crossed to the other side. I'm glad for that, my lady. Neither should have died, and not a day goes by that I don't think about your father and uncle."

The ghost watched patiently as Taliesin set aside the dress and searched for clean undergarments at the bottom of the wardrobe. She located a stack of neatly-folded drawers and a soft chemise, slipped them on with the ghostly Duchess watching, and then put on the blue dress. Taliesin had lost weight during the last few weeks, and the dress fit, though it was a little short in length and the sleeves, lengthy and tapering, seemed far too long. She found a pair of brand-new slippers that fit her feet. She tied a sash around her waist and turned in the mirror. Not the type of outfit to wear to escape from the castle with her friends, but it suited her red hair and made her green eyes appear blue.

"Not bad," Taliesin said.

The Duchess looked into the mirror, and for a moment, Taliesin was able to see Denira de Boron as she had been in life. Her long brown hair, blue eyes, and smile could have melted the heart of Captain Wolfgar. The magical sword thumped the mattress.

'Sha'tars used to walk the land freely,' Ysemay said. 'They could heal the crippled and mute with a single thought, cure insanity and blindness with mere prayer, and even make magical swords sing on occasion. It is a shame you have not developed your full powers, or you could possibly restore the duchess's life. What you see in the mirror is how she looked and could look again if you would but release me from Ringerike; then I could help you recite the spell to bring her to life.'

"Duchess Denira, this is Ysemay the Beguiling. Like you, she was a witch, though you used white magic, and she was a dark witch. As for me, I'm a Sha'tar, though I really can't say what that involves or what I'm supposed to do with that type of magic."

The ghostly Duchess sat on the bed beside the sword. But it was Ysemay who answered.

'Sha'tars were born to every fifth generation in a line of warlocks and could live more than a hundred years. They were able to shape magic, to give it life, and to restore it where it was needed so it could flourish again. They could bless a sword to give it powers or take those powers away with a single wish. I am but a witch, but there's nothing I wouldn't give to be a Sha'tar. It is a blessing. All you need do is pray for me, Taliesin, and I can be free.'

"First, tell me about your relationship with King Korax and Zarnoc. What happened to you? Why did they place your soul inside *Ringerike*?" Taliesin said. "No woman should ever suffer such a cruel fate. I do want to pray for you, Ysemay. I'll pray to Navenna for you to be free, and in return, ask that you both help me restore Denira's life. It's the least I can do to repay the duke for his kindness."

The ghost had a troubled look on her face—Duchess Denira apparently didn't like Ysemay's energy, which radiated from the sword. Perhaps she knew about the witch's past, and why she'd been condemned to an eternity of imprisonment inside a sword. Denira gazed at Taliesin and gave a shake of her head.

"What's wrong?" Taliesin asked. "Am I wrong? Do you prefer death to life? I just thought you might want to be reunited with your husband."

A ghostly gasp came from Denira as *Ringerike* started shaking violently on the bed. The sword, shining a bright blue, half-pulled out of the scabbard, and a look of concern appeared on the apparition's lovely face. A shadowy form like a black cloud oozed out of the exposed part of the sword, and the dark silhouette of a woman appeared, hovering over the bed.

Ysemay radiated pure evil—a mane of ratted hair covered her head, and crazy eyes turned toward Taliesin as the dark witch's mouth opened, and a scream of rage came out and shook the timbers overhead. A dark-purple bolt of energy shot out of the witch's transparent fingertips and struck the Duchess, sending her flying across the room. The Duchess recovered quickly and attacked with swift revenge, grabbing Ysemay by the throat with ghostly hands. Denira squeezed with all her might, showing she still possessed the aggressive nature of the Fregians, and the witch fell to her knees, half-sinking through the floor.

A pink light appeared like a circular band around Ysemay's throat, and dark-purple light radiated from Ysemay's entire body, filling the tower with sparkling, dancing lights of pinks and purples. The two ghostly women set upon each other, tooth and nail, upsetting objects in the room. Taliesin ducked her head, ran to the bed, grabbed *Ringerike*, and pulled the sword out of the scabbard as the ghosts continued to fly around the room. They created such a ruckus with their frightful screams and destruction that Taliesin knew the guards had to have heard and were coming to find out what was going on.

"I didn't release you, Ysemay the Beguiling," Taliesin shouted. "Stop fighting with the Duchess and return to the sword!"

"But you did pray for me," Ysemay said, speaking aloud. "And Navenna answered."

The witch took solid form, as real as Taliesin, and pointed a finger at herself. The ragged garments vanished, replaced by a long black robe, and her wild gray hair changed into long black ringlets that fell to her hips. The Duchess, however, lay on the floor; she was unharmed and still a ghost, but she needed time to recover from the fight.

"Korax commanded Zarnoc to bind me to the sword in punishment for our love; for Zarnoc and I betrayed the king, but I was the one punished. When Korax went to war against Tarquin, I betrayed him again, refused to strike Tarquin, and so the king was slain. But I did not stop there, for Tarquin refused to free me as well, so I let another strike him down. That is why his son, Talas, imprisoned *Ringerike* in the temple. Your powers are strong, Taliesin, but you have no idea how to use them. I'm in corporeal form now, and I have no intention of returning to that sword or of restoring this bitch's life." Her crazed eyes turned on the Duchess, and she sneered, revealing dirty, yellowed teeth. "Had you killed me while I was a ghost, Denira de Boron, you would have done a great service to your husband and the *Sha'tar*, but you have failed. I am flesh and bone, and you are but a shadowy memory that needs to go back to your grave. Bye-bye."

Ysemay clapped her hands, and the Duchess vanished with a soft cry. Taliesin heard angry shouts and swordplay outside the tower door. A fierce battle was being fought on the landing that led to the tower, but Taliesin kept her attention on the witch and pointed the sword at the old hag as she walked to the window and placed a foot on the windowsill.

"For the last thousand years," Ysemay said, "I have summoned men to the Cave of the Snake God in search of *Ringerike*. All those lost souls who died were claimed by Chu'Alagu. He was once a god and sat among his fellow immortals, Stroud, Navenna, and Ragnal, but like Korax, he fell from Stroud's favor. Both were locked in the temple together; one in the shape of a hydra and the other a corpse. But you killed Chu'Alagu, and Korax's centuries of suffering ended when Wolfgar took his unnatural life. Now both of my keepers are dead."

"How did you get out of the sword?" Taliesin demanded to know.

"You said '*I do want to pray for you, Ysemay. I'll pray to Navenna for you to be free.*' That is prayer. And now I am free." The witch climbed onto the windowsill and laughed madly as she turned into a black seagull and flew out the window.

Heavy bodies slammed against the door, making it tremble and shake on its iron hinges, causing the wood in the center to splinter. A hairy fist punched through the door, extended its fingers, revealing long, tapered claws, and reached for the lock. Taliesin held *Ringerike* in both hands, ran forward, and sliced through the arm. The clawed hand fell to the floor, turned into a human hand, and crawled away as angry voices shouted behind the door. She stepped back and raised the sword over her head, prepared to kill whatever came through. The door broke apart with a crash, and soldiers in black, armed with swords and axes, stormed into the room. Wolfmen. Slain Garridan soldiers lay on the platform, trampled as the Wolfmen rushed toward Taliesin. She lifted *Ringerike* and sliced into the nearest enemy, cutting him in half. She spun and killed another before she was overpowered and dragged to the floor. Hands tore at her dress, tore the sword out of her grasp, and pulled her to her feet. Two Wolfmen grabbed her arms and held her fast, while another attempted to pick up *Ringerike*. The sword refused to budge and remained stuck to the floor despite every attempt. A Wolfman came in with an ax, hacked at the floor to cut the sword free, and suddenly flew backward and crashed into the wall.

"Stand back," a loud, angry voice said.

The Wolfmen moved aside as a lanky, red-haired man in black armor stepped forward, his face elongated into a wolf's visage. He carried a round, hairy object in his hands and tossed it at Taliesin's feet. The thing rolled over several times before it stopped at the edge of Taliesin's gown and oozed blood across the floor. She looked at the eyeless head of Duke Richelieu de Boron. The Wolfmen behind her started to panic and snarl, and Taliesin glanced over her shoulder. Two glowing, golden forms appeared at the window, the Duchess and the Duke, who exchanged a tender kiss before they looked at Taliesin, smiled sadly, and faded away into the sunlight.

"How touching," the red-haired man said. He looked beyond Taliesin, and his slanted yellow eyes filled with rage as he shouted at the Wolfmen behind her. "Can't you pick *Ringerike* off the floor, you idiots? Cut it out if you must. Don't stop. You act as if you have never seen a ghost before. There are ghosts at every battlefield we've visited. Stay here and get the job done. Don't stop until you have the sword."

"It burns to touch it," a soldier said. "It's made of silver and gold."

"Do I care?" The red-haired man lifted his bloody hand, and a claw grew out of his index finger. He stepped forward, slid the claw across Taliesin's chest, and hooked it between her breasts. His wolfish face turned human, for a second, revealing a sharp-faced man, and then turned into a beast. "Who am I?" he asked. "Have you guessed?"

"You must be Master Phelon," Taliesin said.

Phelon nodded. "I know who you are, Raven Mistress," he said in a snide voice. "Pity you made such a commotion and alerted us to your whereabouts; Duke de Boron almost got away with his little plan. Almost. Instead of asking a bunch of silly questions, I simply tore off his head and set fire to the docks. The ships are leaving without one Garridan knight having stepped foot on dry land. The captains know I'll burn their ships if they try to come any closer. When Prince Sertorius and Master Xander arrive, I'll do the same thing to them I did to Duke de Boron. But I have other plans for you...."

Taliesin was dragged kicking and screaming out of the chamber. Phelon whistled and walked beside her as they crossed the bloody walkway. She glanced at the courtyard below. Garridan knights, soldiers, and servants lay dead on the cobblestones. Blood covered the courtyard and filled the fountain where bodies lay over the sides; everywhere she looked, giant wolves ran about and searched for survivors. Fearing for the lives of her friends more than what was going to happen to her, Taliesin fell silent and allowed the monsters to descend the narrow stairs. They went through a corridor and reached a larger, wider staircase that led into the grand hall. The once-beautiful chamber looked like a slaughterhouse. The noblemen and courtiers she'd seen earlier had been gutted, and Wolfmen sat at the tables and feasted on their flesh. The stained-glass windows had been broken, and the two ash thrones had been reduced to splinters. Phelon kept walking and whistling, never slowing, and led them through a maze of corridors and descended another flight of stairs into the lower levels of the castle.

"I have a surprise for you," Phelon said in a cheery voice. "I think you're going to like it, Raven girl. I've gone to a lot of trouble arranging things for this evening's entertainment, so I hope you're in the mood." He spun and walked three steps backward, showing off his agility. "You know, boys, I really don't think she needs to be in that dress. Tear it off so it won't get wet." Phelon turned to the sound of ripping material and jumped down to the next level.

Taliesin, her arms and chest scratched from the Wolfmen's claws, was left wearing only her undergarments—a thin shirt and panties. "It doesn't matter what you do to me," she said, hearing a quiver in her own voice. "*Ringerike* will never be

yours. Fifty men can try to pick it up and will fail. Only someone born with magic can lift the sword," she said, "and only a
Sha'tar is able to call forth its full powers. Kill me, and *Ringerike* is useless to you."

A dead jailor lay on the ground at the dungeon door with a
heavy ring of keys forced down his throat. The heavy iron
door lay open. Phelon led the way into a large chamber with
an arched ceiling and four corridors that led in each direction.
Voices could be heard calling in the dark. Only one corridor,
lined with stones covered by a thick, green mold was lit, and
torches cast shadows upon the closed cell doors they walked
past. The dank odor of unwashed bodies and filth was ripe in
the air. Taliesin was dragged past iron doors coated with
green slime, each containing an occupant who cried out and
begged for mercy. She heard the sound of the sea as waves
crashed hard against a thick sea wall. They were below sea
level, and through the brine and grime, she was able to distinguish between the odors of rotting fish and dead Garridan
soldiers left twisted and mangled on the floor. The rocks grew
slippery under their feet and seawater pooled in crevices;
soon they were walking in an inch of dingy, dark water.

Phelon lifted his hand, halting the procession, and came to
Taliesin. His wolf head morphed, and he appeared human,
looking no more than twenty years old with a scruff of red
hair along his narrow jaw. "I lay in bed this morning,
imagining what to do with you," he said, his grin cruel.
"Winged horses. Nice touch. One of my men saw you arrive
before dawn. When we went to the stables, we didn't find any
horses with wings, so we killed the stable boys and had breakfast. But you see, I couldn't quite understand why the last of
the Raven Clan would come to this place. You could have
gone anywhere, yet you came to the one place you knew everyone was going to meet. I'm a thinking man. I just bet you
thought Prince Sertorius and the Knights of Chaos arrived
first." His eyes lowered to her breasts as he slid his tongue
along his lower lip. "What a happy reunion that would have
been; two childhood friends together after so many years

apart. Only problem is Sertorius didn't arrive first. That slug of a Duke should have sent you away the moment you arrived, but of course, that's not what happened, is it? I wouldn't count on Sir Roland Brisbane arriving in time, either."

"One day I will kill you," Taliesin said, "for what you did to my clan."

"That was my father, not me. I also seriously doubt you'll get a chance to kill me, for my little surprise has everything to do with another kind of happy reunion." Phelon's eyes opened wide, and he stepped away and placed his hand over his heart. "What? You look surprised. Don't you think I know you're one of us? I ordered Wolfgar to turn you. Normally, it's my father who does the turning. I do, on rarer occasions, though I would have loved to sink my fangs into your flesh, Raven girl." He spun around. "We're almost there. Bring her along, boys."

Turning another corner, Taliesin saw sunlight high above from a barred window, and beneath it was a slimy staircase that led five steps down and ended on an iron grate that covered a large drain. The grate was covered with seaweed, and several starfish clung to the dungeon wall at water level. A swell of water rolled from the drain and poured into the small space, covered the staircase and the grate, and then rushed out. The smell from the drain was foul, and Taliesin turned her head. The corridor below was short, with just two cells built along the sea wall; only one door was open. Phelon came to a halt at the open door and scratched behind his ear, like a dog after a flea.

"We're here," he said. "I can't wait for you to see who is inside waiting to say hello."

The two Wolfmen shoved Taliesin inside, and she slipped on the wet stones and fell to her hands and knees. Looking up, she found herself in a large prison cell with a narrow window high above that let in sunlight and a submerged grate below. Chained to the sea wall were Hawk, Wren, Jaelle, and Rook, all shouting her name and talking over one another as Taliesin ran to them. Phelon laughed as she jerked on the manacles that connected Hawk's wrists and ankles to the wall, but she wasn't strong enough to break them. Jaelle and Wren had also been stripped of their clothes and were clad in only their undergarments, which were wet and clung to their bodies. Hawk and Rook were both bare-chested. Lash marks covered their chests and arms, and blood dripped from the wounds into the pool of water at their feet.

"The Duke's daughter?" Taliesin asked, glancing at Hawk.

"I don't know where she is," Hawk said. "They killed nearly everyone."

Water surged in and rose to their ankles. A tiny eel washed in. One of the Wolfmen walked over and stomped it flat with the heel of his boot.

"What do you think of your surprise, Taliesin?" Phelon asked.

"I think you're a monster," Taliesin said.

Laughing, Phelon approached Wren and slid his hand across her breasts. The girl sobbed and turned her head aside. "Good, solid, Raven stock," he said. "The Raven Master certainly knew how to pick his clan members. He liked them young and shapely and without prejudice. We even have a gypsy here. By Ragnal, I'd have liked to have spent an hour alone with her, but the tide is coming in, and the rest of us should be getting topside to await our guests of honor."

"Phelon...please. Surely, we can make a deal," Taliesin said, desperate to prevent what was about to happen. The red-haired man turned with a swift jerk of his shoulders, walked through the water with resolute strides, and caught her jaw as Hawk shouted curses.

"Deals? We're way beyond making deals, Raven girl," Phelon replied. "You might have beguiled the Duke, but I'm not going to let you bewitch me. I know a little about *Sha'tars*, having been around for the last three hundred years, and I can assure you a witch can't cast a spell if she doesn't have a tongue. But wait, even if I rip it out of your head, it will just grow back now, won't it? At least I hope it will since that's the whole point of this reunion."

The other two Wolfmen laughed and walked to wait at the door, drawing their swords and keeping their eyes on Taliesin. Taliesin heard the door to the adjacent cell open and heard men cry out in panic and fear. More Wolfmen could be heard, laughing outside the cell, slapping about other prisoners.

Hawk pulled at his chains. "I'll kill you," he shouted. "Every last one of you!"

"Oh, dear. Someone talked," Phelon said, releasing Taliesin. He walked to Hawk and punched him in the stomach. "I really don't enjoy having to explain myself, but I will this one time since we've only just met. In three hours, the tide will come in, and all of you will drown." He smiled when Jaelle gasped. "She doesn't like the idea of drowning. I thought not."

"Rot," Taliesin said, under her breath.

Phelon ignored her. "Bring in the two Eagle Clan envoys," he said, clapping his hands. "I want to try a little experiment." The guards left and returned with two pale-skinned men in rich robes of gold and silver, herded before them with spears. The two Eagle Clan envoys had been beaten severely; one could barely walk, and his friend had to hold him up. "I told you idiots not to rough them up. Poor Ethon can hardly walk, and Orell looks terrified. Put them over there," he said, pointing at the far wall.

The one called 'Ethon' had a triangular beard, tattoos covering his neck as well as the left side of his face and was taller than his companion. He couldn't keep his eyes off Rook and whispered to Orell, who was bald, short, had one arm longer than the other, and wore gold earrings from his earlobes. Orell glanced at Rook, and his eyes widened in recognition, drawing Phelon's attention to the young Raven. The Wolf heir whipped out his knife, pointed it at Rook, laughed coldly, and proceeded to clean beneath his fingernails.

"It's them," Wren cried out. "The two men I told you about!"

"Shut up," Hawk said, angrily.

"But it's them!"

"I told you to shut up, sister."

Phelon looked up and appeared undecided if he wanted to discipline Hawk or Wren for talking or wanted to find out why the Eagle envoys had a special interest in Rook. Taliesin wondered who Rook had been to solicit so much attention from the envoys. Rook had lived in a palace, and his father had been high-ranking, but he allowed another man to harm Rook when he was a child. But who was his father? She said nothing; it wasn't the time and place and felt her heart race when Phelon selected Wren to torment. He walked to the chained girl, pressed his face against her breasts, and laughed when she screamed. Rook cursed and fought against the iron manacles.

The two Eagle envoys were thrown against the wall and slid into the water. Both kept their attention on Rook and whispered together, but Phelon was too occupied groping a hysterical Wren to care what they did. At a nod from Phelon, one of the Wolfmen who had brought in the Eagle envoys drew his sword, walked over, and stabbed the crippled man's stomach. Ethon slumped against the wall, supported by Orell, who immediately started to beg for mercy.

"Who is the boy?" Phelon asked, pulling aside the undergarment to reveal Wren's breast. "This one is pregnant. Did anyone know? Hasn't been that long, but a Wolfman can always tell. The girl is pregnant with the mystery boy's child. Someone answer me, I am growing impatient. You recognized the boy, Orell. Since Ethon is injured and can't speak, you tell me, and I won't have my men cut open your belly."

"We have a truce," Orell said in a desperate plea. "Lord Arundel and Chief Lykus pledged neither side will harm the other. You broke that truce when you stabbed Ethon. He's dying, you fool. What does it matter who the boy is? He's a Raven. He's no one."

"Well, if that's the case, then I *have* been bad." Phelon walked to stand next to Taliesin and took her arm but smiled wide at the Eagle envoy. "Had de Boron accepted my offer and just given me the *Sha'tar* and *Ringerike*, then none of you would be where you're at. None of this is my fault. I don't like hurting people. I really don't. Had you and your brother stayed on your ship, instead of sneaking ashore with Garridan troops, I wouldn't have had to hurt anyone. You could have sailed away, Orell, and gone off to rescue your besieged King, but that's not what you did. No, you came ashore with the intention of killing me. Now, just answer the question. Who is the boy and what does he mean to you? And tell me quickly before I take this dagger and pluck out your eye."

"You're evil and cruel," Jaelle said. "My father will hunt you if you kill us."

Phelon sighed. "I'm surrounded by people who claim to be important when really all of you are expendable, except Taliesin. And of course, maybe the boy. Tell me who his father is, and I may let him go."

"Don't," Rook shouted. "Don't tell him a thing, Master Orell."

Phelon waved his dagger in the air. "Somebody better talk." He squeezed Taliesin's arm and placed the knife against her throat, drawing blood. The little bit of pain caused her to panic, and she pulled at her arm, trying to break free; knowing it was futile, but desperate to try anything. Phelon held the dagger aside, and with a pull, slammed her against his body, showing just how strong he really was. His grip tightened until she started to whimper. "Well?" he shouted. "Out with it Orell, or I'll blind this poor Raven girl!"

"Duke Fakar," Orell said in a rush. "He's Anwar, the eldest son of Duke Fakar." Orell hushed his brother, Ethon, who grumbled in protest, but the truth was out. Orell cringed when Phelon dragged Taliesin over and glared at him. "I'm telling the truth, Master Phelon. There was an incident at the palace; no one is sure what happened, but the boy ran away and was never seen or heard from again. The Duke searched for him, so did our clan, but we didn't know Anwar was still alive until now. Surely, you must realize Duke Fakar will pay any ransom you ask if you return his son to him. Let me broker the deal, and we can put this behind us."

"You mustn't bargain with him," Ethon said in a raspy voice. "Orell, stop it. You are shaming both of us and our people."

"Please, Phelon," Orell shouted. "Release the Duke's son and me, and I'll make certain you are well paid in gold or jewels or whatever you want."

"Whatever I want?" Phelon asked. He smelled of unwashed dog as he pressed his face against Taliesin's, and she desperately wanted to bite him. Her temper was boiling — she wanted to sink her teeth into his neck, rip out his jugular, and then kill his men. He sensed her aroused state, chuckled, and licked the side of her face. "Welcome to the dark side, sister."

Taliesin closed her eyes. "I won't turn," she whispered. "I won't do it."

Rook shouted. "Release me, Phelon, and I'll make certain you are paid. I'll do whatever you ask," he said, in a panic, "but don't harm anyone else."

"But Taliesin is going to turn *Wolfen*, and that's the whole point." Phelon dragged Taliesin to her friends and kicked Rook in the stomach, knocking the wind out of him. He hung his head, sputtering and gasping, and tried to catch his breath. When Hawk opened his mouth to speak, Phelon released Taliesin and grabbed a fistful of Hawk's hair. Taliesin wrapped her arms around Phelon and tried to pull him away as he slammed Hawk's head against the stone wall. "I really don't like being interrupted. Nor do I like to be bribed. I don't care about the Duke's runaway son any more than I care about the Shan's gypsy daughter. I only care about watching Taliesin turn into a wolf and her eating you. That's what I want! Is that so much to ask?"

"Leave him alone," Taliesin growled. She felt her fingernails digging into Phelon's chest, scraping against his armor, and felt a consuming desire to rip him apart. One push from Phelon sent her tumbling to the floor. The Wolf heir lifted his dagger, went to Ethon, and with a vicious blow, slit open his throat. Blood sprayed across the room and struck Taliesin's face, getting into her eyes and mouth. She spat out the blood and wiped it from her face, but the blood was already absorbed on her tongue, and she felt a wildness consume her. With a snarl, she rushed toward Phelon, jumped onto his back, and sank her teeth into his ear. She yanked on the lobe and ripped it from his head, and as he screamed, she tried to push him to the ground.

Phelon easily knocked her aside and sprang on top of her, his human head vanishing and turning into a beast's; it was monstrous to look at, with a long muzzle and large fangs. As Taliesin struck his face and shoulders and pounded him with all her might, he let out a snarl and sank his fangs into her shoulder. A scream burst from her lips. He silenced her by shoving his wolf tongue into her mouth and wiggled it about until she bit off the tip, and he jerked it out.

Laughing and spitting blood, Phelon motioned his men forward. Taliesin lunged at the closest and scratched his cheek open, but five men managed to drag her to the wall and placed manacles around her wrists and ankles. Orell was right beside her, covered in blood and cringing beside his dead brother, too frightened to move. Phelon and his men left the cell once she was shackled, closing and locking the door behind them. Phelon peered through the barred window, his face again human and dribbling blood from the side of his lips. Taliesin screamed and shouted, trying to break free, but it was impossible. She stopped struggling and stared at the door, catching Phelon's gaze.

"A little warning about our curse," Phelon said with a lisp. "Any transfer of our bodily fluids, say saliva, blood, urine, or whatever, can infect humans, and turn them into *Wolfen*. It's hard for a *Wolfen* not to devour their lover after copulating with a human. But don't get me wrong, that's not what this is about. We dine on humans because we love the taste of blood—it's in our nature. You already saw what happens when you get a little taste, Taliesin. My ear and tongue will regrow; that's the benefit of being cursed, at least for us." His eyes gleamed as he quivered with excitement. "When the tide comes in, it floods this particular room, because the drain in your cell and right outside your door allows the sea to enter the dungeon. Before morning, you'll drown, unless you turn and free yourself from your chains. But if you turn, you'll eat Orell and then you'll eat your friends and then, if you're lucky, you'll be able to break through this door and free yourself."

"I won't turn," Taliesin said. "I won't do it!"

"Oh, yes, I forgot to mention I have Lenora locked in one of the towers. I'm going to eat her as a snack at midnight. You have until then to get out." Phelon licked his lips as he stepped away from the door and whistled a tune that faded along with the Wolfmen's footsteps.

"You're *Wolfen*," Hawk said once he thought it safe to speak. "You've been bitten, and they made you drink human blood. Why aren't you turning?"

"I was bitten yesterday," Taliesin stated. "I haven't turned yet."

Rook turned toward Wren. "The tide comes in at early evening," he said. "We won't have long to wait. I'm so sorry, Wren. I should have told you who I was the first day we met; I should have told you then how much I love you, and every day after."

"It doesn't matter," Wren said, in a tiny voice. "I love you, too."

"You can't let us drown, Taliesin," Rook said. "Orell, get up and try to unlock the manacles. There has to be something sharp you can find to use." The envoy got up, his robes drenched and heavy, and began searching the cell. Rook continued. "Taliesin, listen to me. You may be cursed, but you are still the *Sha'tar*, and that's why you haven't turned. Use that same power to break your chains and then free us. All you have to do is believe in yourself. If you believe you can do this, we can be out of the cell before the water is over our heads. Use your magic, not your anger. Just concentrate and use your will power to set us free. It can work. I know it can. I've seen it with my own eyes. I know what a *Sha'tar* can do, but you have to believe in yourself."

"I knew it!" Hawk swore and cast his eyes to the ceiling. "Why didn't you tell us this long ago, Rook? Instead of being silent, you should have been training Taliesin. Now my sister is pregnant with your child, and we're going to die. Where is Zarnoc when you need him? If he were here, he could free us."

"He went after Roland," Taliesin said.

"I intend to marry your sister," Rook said, his voice strong and steady. He gazed at Wren and tried to lean over far enough to be a little bit closer. "If you will have me as your husband, my dear Wren. Will you be my wife?"

"Yes. Of course," Wren sobbed. "It's not meant to end here. It can't. I saw Jaelle holding our child in a royal court beside a throne. Our child must be born, for my visions never lie, Rook. They always come true. You know that they do."

Jaelle gave Wren a reassuring smile. "Then it's up to Taliesin to free us." She looked at Taliesin. Orell had returned, unable to find anything useful, and gave them a frantic look, ran to the door, pressed his face against the bars, and shouted for help.

The water steadily flowed into the prison cell over the next hour and crept up their legs to their waists. The water came in cold and fast as the sun started to set, and the moon began to rise. Taliesin watched the silver light stream through the window high above as the water washed in, rising fast. Her anger had faded. She tried to will herself to use her magic, but didn't know how; nothing happened, and when her friends' desperate looks turned to resentment, she'd stopped looking at them. She'd watched Orell scream himself hoarse, remaining at the door, never turning back to talk to anyone. There was nothing to say. Taliesin knew Wren would drown first; she was the shortest, and when she finally looked at her friends, the water had already reached the girl's shoulders. Wren stared at Taliesin with tears in her eyes, trembling from the cold and fear.

"I dreamed of this," Wren said. "I knew I would drown here."

"You also said you saw yourself holding Rook's baby," snapped Hawk. He glared at Rook. "I swear, if you do not marry my sister when we get out of here, I am going to kill you. Somehow, this is your entire fault; you shouldn't keep secrets from people."

"I hate my father," Rook said. "He's a cruel man. I thought it best if none of you knew who I was since I never intend to go home. My father has other sons to pick as his heir."

"You never lived on the Isle of Valen," Wren said. She lifted her chin, trying to keep it above water and stood on her tiptoes. "I'd have liked to have lived there. You never said you came from Valen; we just assumed you did, because of your tattoos."

Jaelle splashed about. "How long does it take the *Wolfen* to gain super-human strength? If we're going to survive, Taliesin, you must turn and free us. I don't believe you'll eat us once you turn. You saw how strong Phelon is. You are that strong, too."

"I don't know," Taliesin said. "I've been trying hard not to turn. I feel a tingle in my arms and legs. It might be because I'm cold. It might be because for the last hour I have thought of nothing but using my magic to release our chains. I want Rook to be right about me, but it feels otherwise. If I could lose my temper, if I could feel anger, then I think I may be able to break free. Maybe."

"Say something to anger her," Wren said, gulping. "Hurry!"

"I've never liked you, Taliesin. You're ugly and stupid and shallow," Hawk said, using his nastiest voice. "You found *Ringerike*, but you were too weak and girlish to put up a fight, and you let them capture you. Roland never loved you. He was using you from the start, just like we were, hoping we could make a profit selling magical swords. But you can't even do that. You let Osprey die. You let our clan die. Now you're going to let us die. You led us into this trap, and you're the one responsible."

Taliesin shook her head. She knew it was acting.

"And to think I loved you." Jaelle glared at Taliesin, giving her the same murderous look she had at the gypsy camp, reminding Taliesin that she held her cards close and acted upon principles that were all her own. She was far more convincing than Hawk when she spoke in an accusatory tone. "I trusted you! We all did! I thought you were going to be our savior, but I couldn't be more wrong. You are no *Sha'tar*. You are not *Wolfen*. You are useless!"

"Yes. Useless," Taliesin said, a growl rising in her throat. "Killing a snake god counts for nothing. *Ringerike* is surely at the bottom of the sea now. Our quest is a failure. Raven Clan is no more. Tell me how much you hate me. Say it and mean it!"

"I hate you," Rook said. "You've killed us all. I curse the day you were ever born."

"As do I," Hawk said, in a savage voice. "You're nothing but a coward. Too afraid to turn *Wolfen*. Afraid since you were a little girl. Afraid because the king ordered your father murdered. That's what Grudge told me—the man you chose instead of me. He said the king sent knights to your home that night, and they slit your father's throat and bled him dry. Grudge knows because he was there and saw it happen. He's the one who slit your father's...."

Taliesin felt rage wash over her. Mandrake murdered. The king had ordered it, and Grudge had slit his throat. She started to jerk at her chains. Grudge had done it. Not Roland, not the man she'd loved, but the man who had infiltrated their clan, lied to her, tricked her into being his friend, and all the while, he had blood on his hands. Mandrake's blood. Blood, blood, blood. Her head throbbed, and her heart pounded. She closed her eyes and summoned whatever power she possessed, willing herself to turn. She tasted human blood again and suddenly wanted to taste far more. She could see Wren going under the water, see it rising over her head. With a scream of rage, Taliesin pushed forward, pulling at the chains, wanting to kill everyone who had ever kept a secret from her.

A giant spasm went through her body, and with a final tug, Taliesin yanked one arm free and then the other. The chains on her legs came off easier. She dove under the water and swam to Wren. The girl had sunk to the floor, eyes closed with little bubbles rising from her mouth. Taliesin ripped the chains out of the wall, kicked off the floor, and swam to the surface with the limp girl. "Breathe! Breathe!" Taliesin gave Wren a squeeze. A burst of water shot from the girl's mouth as her eyelids flickered open. One look at Taliesin and she let out a hideous scream and nearly sank beneath the water again.

Taliesin pushed Wren to the wall where she grasped a pro-truding rock to hold her head above water. Taliesin saw the water cover Jaelle's head and went to help her. The ease with which she yanked the chains out of the wall filled her with a feeling of invincibility. Taliesin pushed the gypsy girl to the surface where she also found a rock in the wall to hold on to. The next person she freed was Hawk; it was a decision she consciously made, not caring if an Erindor Duke's son died or not, but she did care about Hawk. Whatever Hawk saw frightened him, and he pushed away from Taliesin and swam toward the door. She found Rook submerged as the water surged in. She braced a foot against the wall, yanked off two chains at a time, and thrust Rook upwards, seeing him break the surface as she followed him. Once on the surface, she saw Orell swimming beside her friends, while his dead brother lay face down on the surface of the water, drifting toward the wall and away again.

"Stay away from us," Hawk shouted.

Ignoring the urge to tear his head off, Taliesin dove un-derwater and swam to the door. She braced herself and kicked the door, buckling it in the middle. Pulling it inward, she en-tered the corridor and swam to the surface. Two feet of air space was left. Diving, she grabbed the large iron grate. It had to weigh over five hundred pounds, yet with a slight tug, she tore it off the opening and dropped it to the floor. Seeing clearly through the seawater, she spotted eight kicking legs; the swimmers had helped the non-swimmers through the cell door, but one person hadn't made it out. Orell. She saw his drowned body slowly drifting to the floor. Able to discern the people above her by their footwear, Taliesin chose the weakest to take out the underwater tunnel. One clawed hand closed around Wren's ankle, and the kicking that ensued resulted in a fierce tug that submerged the girl completely. Taliesin wrapped her furry arms around the smaller girl's body and swam through the drain with the speed of a shark, passing under the wall through a large opening and surfacing in seconds.

Taliesin towed Wren until her feet touched the bottom, released her, swam a few feet away, and pointed at the shoreline with a long finger that sported a yellow claw. The girl mouthed the words 'thank you' and started to wade to shore. Two heads breached the surface, gasped for air, and headed toward dry land as Rook again assisted Jaelle. Hawk was nowhere to be seen.

Taliesin knew he hadn't followed. She dove and headed back to the dark tunnel, the bright blue water turning murky as she entered the moss-lined opening. She looked through the tunnel and into the water-filled corridor and saw a body was pressed against the ceiling with its head in a rapidly-shrinking air bubble. It was Hawk, and he didn't have much air left. She grabbed him around the middle with a hairy arm and yanked his body against her own. Clawed fingers pinched his nose, and a monstrous palm covered his mouth. With a hard push off against the wall, she swam through the tunnel.

Surfacing from the passageway, Taliesin held Hawk's head above the water as she swam through the waves and glided onto the warm, dry sand. Her friends hurried over and pulled

Hawk away from Taliesin as she crouched on all fours, stretched her spine, and gave a loud growl.

"Hawk's not breathing!" Wren cried.

The girl pounded on her brother's chest, only to be pushed aside by Taliesin, now returned to human form. Rook, Jaelle, and Wren watched as she placed her hands on Hawk's chest, pushed three times, paused, and breathed into his mouth. She repeated the maneuver several times and breathed life into his body. Energy flowed from her body and entered Hawk's through her hands pressed against his chest — the magic of the *Sha'tar* — and a white glimmer appeared around his form. Hawk responded in an instant. Seawater gurgled out of his mouth, and he coughed hard, his eyes catching hold of Taliesin's gaze.

"You saved me," Hawk whispered.

Taliesin gave a nod and stood as a strange feeling grew in the pit of her stomach, something akin to being ravenous. Her attention turned to the castle as a trumpet blared, and she was vaguely aware of troops landing on the beach. Countless boats pulled onto the sand, and armored men shouted as they ran along a paved road toward the castle doors. As she stared at the banners rippling in the breeze, a hand touched her bare shoulder.

"Are you all right?" Jaelle asked.

Taliesin let out a soft growl and pushed Jaelle aside. A strong urge to sink her teeth into Jaelle's throat fought to take control of her senses. "Don't touch me," she groaned. "For the love of Navenna, don't touch me, Jaelle. I'm dangerous. You saw me turn. I'm a monster. I can't be around any of you. Not anymore. I'm sorry, but I must go."

Somewhere along the shoreline, as she ran along the sand on bare feet, she morphed into a giant red wolf, the sea spray on her furry back and the scent of fish and ocean strong in her nostrils. *Ringerike* no longer seemed important, no more than Thalagar, her friends, or Roland. Taliesin had to keep going, to find a safe place to hide; she didn't care if it was a forest, a mountain, or anywhere else, as long as it was far away from Caladonia.

* * * * *

Epilogue

Unaware of the distance traveled, Taliesin stopped running when she spotted the white-capped mountains that bordered the kingdoms of Caladonia and Gorum. A winding road seen in the pale moonlight led to a small ruin of a shack that lay at the base of a rocky cliff. The shack was in poor condition, and a single yellow light appeared in the window, a flickering flame from a slender candle, as a face peered through the dirty panes. She loped toward the shack on all fours, but as the door opened, she morphed into a human. Still on all fours, she lifted her head as a familiar figure appeared in the threshold. The person had long hair was gray, her eyes pale, her face that of a crone.

Ysemay the Beguiling laughed as Taliesin stood and walked toward her.

"Now that you have found me, Raven Mistress, we will begin your training in earnest," the witch said. "I shall either make a *Sha'tar* out of you, my dear, or find a collar and chain strong enough to hold you."

"Why do you help me?" Taliesin asked. She heard her voice, human, but still, it seemed strange to her ears. She lifted her hands to her face. Human hands, at least for now.

"Two women alone cannot fare well in a man's world," Ysemay replied. "But the two of us together could make a difference. I would take revenge on those men who brought me harm in the past, and I think you are like me, and you want to do the same. Your clan must be avenged, Raven Mistress. Are we not of the same mind? Shall we help one another, for the night is cold and dark, and only one light offers you welcome; mine."

"Yes," Taliesin said. "I accept your offer, Ysemay."

Weariness settled in her muscles and bones as Taliesin spread out on the floor beside a barren fireplace that sparked to life, warm and golden, and closed her eyes. A blanket was thrown over her slender, nude form, and she wondered what morning would bring. But her sleep was harrowed by images of the past; a clan devoured by wolves, a tall knight fighting zombie lizard men, a dark-haired prince with an infectious smile, and an old wizard, holding an orange cat, who laughed when he caught her gaze.

"Fear not," Zarnoc said, "for we will meet again—very soon."

# # # # #

About the Author

Susanne L. Lambdin is the author of the *Dead Hearts* series of novels. A *Trekkie* at heart, she received a 'based in part' screen credit for writing a portion *of Star Trek: The Next Generation: Season 4, Episode 76*, titled *'Family.'* She is passionate about all things science fiction, horror, and high fantasy. Susanne is an expert on the subject of zombies and is affectionately known by many of her fans as 'The Zombie Lady.' She lives in Kansas with her family and two dogs.

To contact Susanne and to learn more about her current and upcoming projects, visit www.SusanneLambdin.com.

The following is an
Excerpt from Book 5 of the Dead Hearts series:

Immortal Hearts

Susanne L. Lambdin

Spring, 2017

eBook, Paperback, and Audio Book

Excerpt from "Immortal Hearts:"

Captain Black and Lachlan stood beside Cadence, watching as the Royal Fortune sailed toward a gray horizon bordered by a rainbow of bright, sparkling lights. A young crewman flanking the captain peered through a curious brass telescope with a number of gadgets that looked more decorative than useful. The ship sailed into a wall of fog, and the crewman looked around nervously, but her confidence was restored when Black nodded.

"We're entering the first level, Othrys, which is a fly-infected bog," Black said. "Cathrys is next with its fierce, hot jungle, and then comes Minethys, a frozen desert. Colothys has hot mountain winds that will tear the flesh from your bones. Porphatys is dark, with black snow and frigid temperatures, and the sixth level, Agathys, is even worse. But be of good cheer. Caceri is our destination. You may find it similar to Colorado."

"I seriously doubt it," Cadence said, gazing upward at the blimp. "You're sure this ship can pass through each level? Don't get me wrong, Captain. I'm impressed with your airship, but you're asking quite a lot of both your ship and your crew.

"Through fair weather and foul, the Royal Fortune never lets me down," the captain replied. "There's a bit of magic that keeps us in the air. Here, step aside, Commander, and let me take the wheel. It'll take a trained hand from here on."

* * * * *

Also By Susanne L. Lambdin

A Dead Hearts Novel Series:

Morbid Hearts
Forsaken Hearts
Vengeful Hearts
Defiant Hearts
Immortal Hearts

Dead Hearts: Bloodlines

Exordium
Medius
Ultimum

The Realm of Magic Trilogy

Seeker of Magic
Mistress of Magic
Queen of Magic

* * * * *

Made in the USA
Monee, IL
31 October 2020